D1458550

ISAAC ASIMOV'S

ADVENTURES OF SCIENCE FICTION

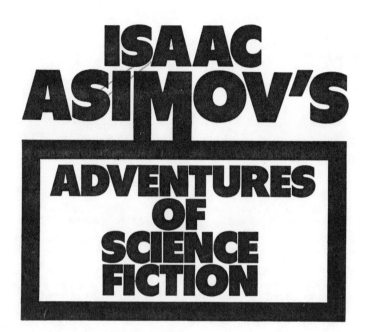

ISAAC ASIMOV'S
ADVENTURES OF SCIENCE FICTION

Edited by
George Scithers

THE DIAL PRESS

DAVIS PUBLICATIONS, INC.
380 LEXINGTON AVENUE, NEW YORK, N.Y. 10017

PS
648
S3
I8
1980

FIRST PRINTING

6.97

10/62

COPYRIGHT NOTICES AND ACKNOWLEDGMENTS

88190

CONTENTS

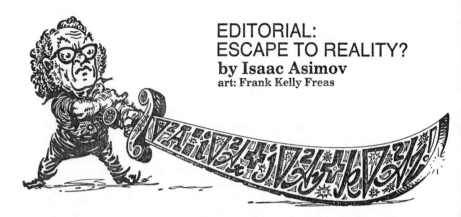

EDITORIAL:
ESCAPE TO REALITY?
by Isaac Asimov
art: Frank Kelly Freas

For some twenty years I've liked to say that science fiction is an "escape to reality." I have done this, for one thing, because in my younger days science fiction was labeled "escape literature" and, in this way, dismissed in contempt.

This has offended one fellow who read the quote in *Time* and who wrote me a very angry letter in consequence. In essence, he complained that if science fiction were an escape to reality, why is it called science *fiction*? What, he demanded, is there in science fiction that is real?

Was I trying to say that sword-and-sorcery is reality; that somewhere out there in the future are mighty-thewed barbarians fighting evil, dark-hued magicians? What else, then? Faster-than-light travel? Multi-dimensions? Intelligent beings on every planet? Galactic Empires? Time travel?

In short, he demanded that I explain to him where and how science fiction represents an escape to reality.

The reader is a perfectly sensible person, but he has revved himself up into indignation and flame-breathing fury over a phrase taken out of context. Had he read the statement as part of an essay he would have had no trouble with it. So let me explain again.

I have always maintained that the prophetic element in science fiction, while present, is small and not very significant. To be sure, we talked about flights to the Moon, for instance, and atomic power and television and robots and overpopulation and artificial brains and a great many other things that have come true in general.

We have even made specific remarks that have been successfully predictive. For instance, I described popular resistance to space exploration back in 1939, long before there was any space exploration

9

to arouse the resistance.

I described pocket computers in 1950 some 15 years before they existed. I described space-walks in 1952, several years before the first one was taken, and apparently I had described the sensations accurately.

If we look elsewhere, we find that Robert Heinlein described the nuclear stalemate in 1941 before there were any nuclear bombs over which to be stalemated; and Arthur Clarke described communications satellites (not in an actual fiction piece, however) in 1945, long before they came to pass.

None of that is important, however. If we weigh these predictions against the vast mass of science fictional incidents and events and societies and discoveries and theories—none of which are likely ever to come true and many of which couldn't possibly come true—then we see that the kind of predictions I have described do not suffice to make science fiction an escape to reality.

In particular, what are we to say of the kind of science fiction we feature in this anthology, where the accent is on action and adventure and where science is de-emphasized so that anything goes provided it isn't actually *bad* science? Perhaps science fiction would appear to be an escape to reality least of all in a collection such as this, as far as my letter-writer was concerned.

Yet even so, science fiction *is* an escape to reality; even in here.

Consider—

All the important social and economic changes in the history of humanity have been the result of advances in science and technology. If you doubt this and wish to mention other change-causing events, just remember you're going to have to match the changes introduced by such things as fire, the wheel, agriculture, metallurgy, the magnetic compass, printing and paper, the steam engine, the internal-combustion engine, television, and the computer.

Advances in science and technology, and the changes they produced, were incredibly slow at first; but they were cumulative. The more science and technology advanced, the more likely it became that further advances would be made. The result is that the rate of change in science and technology has been increasing steadily over human history.

With those factors in mind, you can see that through most of history the rate of advance of science and technology has been too slow to be apparent in a period of time as short as a single lifetime. That meant that the social and economic situation seemed static to a given individual.

That, in turn, meant that through most of history, people have taken it for granted that "there is nothing new under the sun" and that nothing changes. In fact, if anything did happen to change noticeably, people tended to be offended and horrified and considered it a degeneration and would speak wistfully of "the good old days."

But as one passes along the course of the centuries, the rate of change increased steadily; and eventually there had to come a time when change became apparent and unmistakable even in the course of a single lifetime.

To my way of thinking, the turning point came with the Industrial Revolution. After a few decades in which the steam engine came to be used as a way of mechanizing the textile industry and then as a way of powering ships, it became obvious to people living in societies that were undergoing such industrialization (notably in Great Britain and in the United States) that things *were* changing.

Indeed, science fiction came into being in the early 19th century as a direct consequence of this new realization. After all, the coming of visible change produced a brand-new curiosity: "What will things be like after I die?"

Science fiction tried to answer that question, but not necessarily prophetically. It was sufficient to excite, to astonish, to amuse, and that could be done even without true prophecy.

But very few people read science fiction. Even fewer read it with sufficient intention and thought to see what it is saying. The result is that despite the evidence of change everywhere, and the evidence of faster and faster change at that, most people insist on clinging to the age-old belief that things do not change and that any sign of change that forces itself on them is an offensive and horrible sign of degeneration.

By now, though, the rate of change has become whirlwind. In one generation there have been television, jetplanes, microcomputers, the disappearance of colonies, the rise of terrorism, the rise of the United States to world domination *and* its fall to near-impotence, and the shift of the world to oil as its major energy source *and* the dwindling of that energy source.

Under such conditions, imperviousness to change is virtual suicide.

For instance, in ten short years, the United States has gone from energy self-sufficiency to dangerous energy-dependency.

Can the United States take wise measures to prevent disaster? Not as long as most Americans insist on believing that no change has taken place, that the oil isn't really running out, that the United

States isn't really energy-dependent.

And the whole world pursues "national security" and "war-readiness" as though it were still 1938 and there were no nuclear weapons anywhere.

What is the greatest and most important reality in the world today? —The fact of change and the inevitability of further change!

What is the greatest and most important danger in the world today? —The refusal of most people to admit the existence of change.

What is the only activity in the world today that has always been predicated on the existence of change and on the inevitability of change? —Science fiction.

It doesn't matter whether the details of a science fiction story can ever come true. It doesn't matter if the science fiction world of 2080 in a particular story features time-travel, faster-than-light travel, and intelligent monsters from an interstellar gas cloud.

The point is that it tells us that 2080 will be completely different from 1980, and that is *true*. That is the great reality that people will not accept!

It is for this reason that people who leave the everyday humdrum world in order to read science fiction, leave the world of dangerous ignorance and falsehood that tells them everything will always be the same, and enter a world that tells them the reality that everything will inevitably change.

It is that which makes science fiction an escape to reality; and I hope that my letter-writer, having snatched the phrase from *Time,* does a little serious reading now and then, and that he picks up this anthology and reads this essay. He may then even agree with me.

HELLHOLE
by David Gerrold
art: Stephen E. Fabian

When the phenomenon reached the crest of the third hill, Ari Bh Arobi began to be annoyed. Whatever it was, it was keeping her from her ship—and she, an Imperial *Griff*-Princess!

The island was only six kilometers long. If the phenomenon continued to move before the wind at this rate, within an hour it would sweep the entire island—and Ari Bh Arobi with it. She chafed at the thought; it was unfitting for a Daughter of the Matriarchy to be in such a situation. Idly, she wondered how much heat her chillsuit could take before its refrigeration units broke down. Not much. Probably the phenomenon could overload it in a few seconds.

She stood atop a sandy ridge, holding her white helmet with its crimson Imperial crest in one gauntleted claw. A hot G-type star burned yellow-white in an ever-blue sky. It reflected brightly off a sea like wrinkled cellophane. It was an ugly alien panorama; the sight of so much ice in its liquid form bothered her—the psychological suggestion of so much heat made her sweat despite the fact that her chillsuit registered a comfortable –4°C.

Only stray wisps of cloud marred the blueness of that incredible dome of sky—and that was another thing, there was no roof to this world! Ari was used to a comforting close cover of grey. From cubhood, the familiar and ever-present snow clouds had been constant companions and she missed them. The emptiness of this planet's hot sky was disturbing.

Also there was the appalling plume of black smoke rising from the roaring yellow phenomenon below.

It was some kind of a heat-producing phenomenon, that much she was sure of. It flickered in many yellow-orange tongues. From her vantage point above, Ari could still see her scout ship; its hull was blackened, its proud Imperial colors were almost totally obscured, but it seemed otherwise undamaged. (Well, it *should* be able to resist extremes of heat.) She could see it, but she couldn't reach it—that was prevented by the creeping phenomenon that bisected the island.

She wasn't ready to panic though. A Daughter of the Matriarchy *doesn't* panic. Instead, she tried to analyze the problem. She was alone on a small island, a narrow crescent of land in the middle of a molten ocean of an alien planet. Some kind of ravaging and heat-

13

HELLHOLE

producing phenomenon was keeping her from her only means of escape; it moved before the wind and was reducing the land area left to her with every passing moment. The nearest other ship was more than a thousand kilometers out in space.

A brown rodent-like creature came hopping past her, followed by two others. One seemed to be badly "blackened"—a reaction to the phenomenon? Had it been touched? Probably. The plant life had curled and blackened under the influence of the orange flickerings.

The creature stumbled into her and fell to the ground twitching. Guilt twanged at Ari, as if somehow she were responsible for the animal's condition. Reflexively, she said a prayer for its soul. She turned her attention back to the growing tower of smoke, trying to figure out how she could prevent her own death. Undoubtedly, the phenomenon was not going to cease of its own accord—it *would* sweep the island.

Right now, it appeared to be consuming the island's vegetation. It glowed its brightest where the vegetation was the thickest. Obviously, the condition was dependent upon the existence of these brittle brown plants. Could it be a function of the plants somehow? Virulent spores perhaps? No, it didn't seem likely. It had to be something else.

Had the island any kind of a bare area, it would have been a simple matter for her to walk down to it and outflank the crackling phenomenon; but this yellow scrub grass and these black scraggly bushes which the condition consumed so fiercely grew right down to the water's edge, and even a little beyond that.

Patches of oily vegetation could be seen floating on the ocean's surface, apparently anchored by long rootlike tendrils. She wondered how anything could grow in water that hot—why it must be at least 20°C!

She flicked her radio on again, held the helmet close to her hooded muzzle, "Mother Bear, Mother Bear, this is She-Cub One. The phenomenon has topped hill three. Now what?"

A pause. Static crackled out of the speaker. Idly, she swung it back and forth in her hand—*World-Mother! These things are heavy!*

"She-Cub One," crackled the radio. The voice was deep and feminine. "We are aware of your difficulties. We'll have a ship down to you as soon as possible."

"How soon can they get here?"

"Uh—estimated time of arrival is one hour, thirty-three minutes."

Ari made an impatient frown. "That's not going to help."

"Why not?"

"I'm going to run out of island in about forty-five minutes. Maybe less."

"Are you sure?"

Ari growled an obscenity. "You question me?!!"

"Sorry—" breathed the speaker. "Just routine double-checking."

"Oh, that's right," Ari said acidly. "I forgot—'even on an Imperial ship, we have to do things by the rules.'"

There was silence from the communicator.

Ari exhaled loudly and said, "The phenomenon seems to be moving before the wind. When I landed, the wind was blowing about fifteen kilometers per hour, east by northeast."

"That's no wind—that's hardly a sneeze."

"It's enough," snapped Ari. "That *thing* is moving in my direction and getting closer all the time."

"You can't get to your ship?"

"I can't even see it anymore—the smoke's too thick. I'm being driven farther and farther away from it."

"Smoke?" asked the radio abruptly. "Is there smoke there?"

"From the phenomenon."

"Why didn't you tell us this before?"

"I did—"

"You didn't—"

"I distinctly remember—!!"

"I'll play back the tape—!!"

Ari was silent. *Damn these scientific castes anyway! Always trying to refute a Daughter with facts! On Urs, they wouldn't be so presumptuous—not to a member of the Imperial family! That's what we get for creating a new class of upstart cubs!* She growled deep in her throat. *Next they'll be asking for equal breeding rights. We should never have allowed space travel out of the hands of the Imperial classes!*

She hefted her helmet thoughtfully; that ill-begotten daughter was still waiting patiently for Ari's reply. And nothing short of a "proper scientific answer" would suit her. Ari allowed herself a growl, then said quietly, "The phenomenon is producing smoke. Black smoke. The phenomenon itself is a nervous yellow and orange flickering, but its general progress seems slow—about a walking pace. It seems to be consuming the vegetation. It leaves the ground hot and black and covered with ash. The smoke is black at the base, but it turns brown as it spreads out in the air; there's a huge pillar of it—it covers half the sky now. I'd guess that the thing is some kind of combustion, but the scale of it is ridiculous, so it has to be something else. It completely divides the island." She added dryly, "End of report."

"Is that all?" The voice was cold.

"Yes—" She bit off the rest of her reply before the words escaped. Later perhaps.

"Well, look," rumbled the voice of the radio operator; her sudden change of tone startled Ari. "Don't worry. There must be some way to—" A pause. When the other's voice returned, she said, "What about the water? Does the phenomenon cover that too?"

"No. It only exists where there's plant life for it to feed upon."

"Listen, would it be possible for you to swim in that water?"

Ari decided to ignore the familiarity implied in the other's tone; there would be time enough to rebuke her later. If there was a later. She looked at the still blue plane of the ocean. "I doubt it. I'd short out my chillsuit." She pulled at the white hood that covered most of her cone-shaped skull. She felt as if she were peering into an endless oven.

"We were thinking of that," said the speaker. "You'd have to take off the suit. It'd be too heavy anyway."

"Oh, no," Ari protested. "Do you know how hot that water is?"

"Twenty-one degrees," answered the radio.

"That's what I mean. It's way too hot."

"You could stand it if you had to. It'd only be for a short period of time."

"And after that? It takes twenty minutes to get in or out of a chillsuit. It takes another fifteen to charge up the ship's refrigeration units. By that time, I'd be dead from overexposure to this planet's heat. The air temperature here is almost forty degrees. I know some science too!"

Abruptly, she was aware of a new smell in the air, like over-heated—no, *burned*—flesh. Her nostrils quivered wetly. Some of the animals must have gotten trapped by the phenomenon, one more indication that it was a combustion of some kind.

But a combustion—? Of this size?

Was an uncontrolled conflagration of such scope possible? She didn't know—and neither did those damnable scientists in the ship! The only other combustions Ari could remember had been laboratory demonstrations. She knew they used combustions in manufacturing and industrial plants, but she had never seen those; it would not have been seemly for a Daughter to visit *those* kinds of places.

Reflexively she touched the muzzle that cooled the air she inhaled. Her chillsuit was white and coated with a layer of microscopic beads to reflect back most of the glare of the sun; it was lined with conduits that led to the life-support cluster on her back and surrounded her with an envelope of cooler air. She wore dark goggles to protect her eyes and a breathing mask over her nose and mouth. Between the inconvenience, and all the heat and weight, she would probably sweat away five kilos of her carefully fattened bulk. *Mam*-Captain would begrudge the extra rations she would need to gain it back.

Swinging her helmet through the strange dry grass before her, Ari moved down the slope away from the phenomenon. The vegetation crunched under her wide-booted paws. She was not used to seeing plants dead and dry from lack of moisture.

Nor was she used to seeing so many plants so close together. On her home world, if there were fifty bushes like this to an acre, it would be a forest. Indeed, a jungle. She snorted in her mask—this planet would not be valuable to Urs until this Water Age came to an end and the ice-packs could reclaim the seas.

"Ari?" asked her helmet. The tone was respectful.

"Yes?"

"Are you going to go in the water?"

"I'm going to take a look," Ari said, still not admitting anything. "The vegetation grows out over it for at least six to eight meters. I'd have to do more swimming than you think."

She stood on the shore, considering the soupy mass distastefully. The land just seemed to fade away, becoming more and more swampy, until finally the yellow grass petered out in a soggy fringe.

One of the rodent-like creatures, half its fur burned away, and maddened with fear and pain, came bounding past her. It was headed straight for the sea and moved with quick, jerky leaps. Abruptly, it realized where it was heading and tried to halt, tried to turn around—but something in the water went *snap!*

—and the creature was gone. Only an uneasy bubbling of the surface marked where it had been. Involuntarily, Ari took a step back. Then another. "Uh, Semm?"

"Yes?" Semm seemed surprised at Ari's use of her name.

"I don't think the water is such a good idea. Remember those things we found in the northern hemisphere?"

"Yes?"

"Well, they're here in the southern hemisphere too."

Semm was silent. Above, the sun burned impassively, a hole of brightness in the empty blue roof of the world.

"Ari?" asked Semm after a bit.

"Yes?"

"Did you say that the phenomenon is consuming the vegetation?"

"It looks like it. After it moves on, it leaves only blackened ground and what looks from here like ash."

"Then that pretty well settles it."

"Settles what?"

"The nature of the beast. Uva says it's an uncontrolled combustion."

"Huh? On this scale? I thought of that already—it can't be."

"It's got to be, Ari! Think about it—it consumes fuel, the plants; and it releases energy, the heat. What else could it be?"

"I don't know—but still . . . combustion?!! This phenomenon is uncontrolled! It can't be a combustion—who could have started it?!!"

"Look, let's assume that that's what it is and fight it on those terms. It has the same physical properties."

"And what if you're wrong? You're playing with the life of an Heir to the Matriarch!"

"Don't you think we're aware of it—the way you keep reminding us! Our lives are just as important to us as yours—" Semm relaxed her tone. "You're not making it very easy for us."

Ari said, "Do you have an idea?"

"We might. Uva says to break the combustion cycle."

"The *what?*"

"The combustion cycle—it's a laboratory term—"

Ari made a sound of annoyance. "Science again!"

Semm ignored it. She said patiently, "The three elements of the combustion cycle are heat, fuel, and oxygen. If you deprive a combustion of one of these three elements, it can't continue."

"Hm." Ari surveyed the island for a moment, then spoke again. "All right. How? The air temperature in this oven is forty degrees. And there's plenty of free oxygen in the air. And the island is covered with grass."

"You're right," replied the radio. "You can't do anything about the heat or the oxygen. But you can do something about the fuel. Clear an area wide enough that the combustion can't cross."

"You mean dig up the plants? Like a common laborer? *Like a male?*"

"Yes, that's exactly what we mean."

"Do you know who I am? I am the eldest daughter of the Clan of Urs. I do not dig up plants with my hands. Males dig up plants—not Daughters of Urs."

Semm said slowly, "Scientists dig up plants too."

"Then let *them* come here and dig! Daughters of Urs do not!"

Still controlled, Semm said, "You are here on this expedition as a scientist."

"I am a Daughter of Urs!" growled Ari through clenched teeth. "I do not dig!"

"You will if you want to live."

"I will not—I would sooner die than disgrace my heritage."

"You just may have to!"

"Then I will do it with honor!"

"Just a minute," said Semm. The radio went silent.

Ari stood silently on the slope and stared at the phenomenon—she still couldn't bring herself to think of it as a combustion. And yet, the heat from it was oppressive.

She moved down the island, away from the yellow-red beast and its mane of black smoke.

"Ari!" snapped the radio. It was the *Mam*-Captain.

"Yes, *Mam?*"

"Now you listen to me—and listen good! You're going to get down on your hands and knees and clear away some of that vegetation—enough so that the combustion can't cross."

"No," snapped Ari. "I—I will not disgrace my Mother."

"You will if you know what's good for you!" The *Mam*-Captain was angry.

"The Heir to Urs will not!"

"The Heir to Urs *will!* You attached yourself to this expedition thinking it would be a lark. Well, it isn't! It's a lot of hard work and danger!"

"How would I know that? You've been keeping me cooped up on the ship!"

"Exactly because you didn't know—and you refused to learn! Dammit! You foolish young bitches of the aristocracy think that space travel is just a toy! When are you going to learn that it's for the scientific advancement of the whole race! Every time one of you bitches buys her way aboard a ship, you're taking the place of a woman of honor who isn't afraid to get her hands dirty if need be, because the knowledge is more important than dying with honor!"

Ari felt the heat-rage coming over her. "*Mam*-Captain! When I return to Urs, I will have you broken for that!"

"You'll have to get back to Urs first."

"I will die with honor then. Your suggestion is unacceptable. I am not a male."

"You might as well be when I get through with you."

"What do you mean by that?"

"I mean that if you refuse to save yourself—and that very expensive scoutship—I will enter into the log that you committed the *Nin-Gresor*."

Ari was aghast. "You wouldn't. They wouldn't believe you! The Heirs to Urs do not commit the coward's death."

"They will believe what I tell them—and we will tell them that you killed yourself. That is what your refusal to dig amounts to. We will tell them that your presence aboard the ship endangered the lives of all of us and eventually your stupidity killed you—it will not be so far from the truth. Perhaps it will keep the aristocracy away from spaceships in the future.

"They will kill you for that!"

"They will kill me anyway for returning without you. Our lives are bound together, Ari. If you refuse to save yourself, I'll disgrace your name."

"You couldn't do such a thing—" Ari could not conceive of anyone being so—evil.

"You'd better believe I would," the *Mam*-Captain rumbled back. "You'd better start saving youself, noble Daughter of Urs. There is no one else there to do it for you."

Ari grumbled at the helmet, she hissed at it. She circled it angrily. Finally, she said, "All right. What do I do?"

Semm's voice answered, "Dig, Ari, dig. Clear an area as wide as you can as long as you can. Don't leave any plants at all growing."

"It is harder work than an Heir to Urs should have to do."

"Do it anyway. It won't kill you."

"So you say," she grumbled. She picked up her helmet and began striding eastward again, ahead of the combustion phenomenon, looking for a more suitable area to clear a break. Finally, she found a wide area, covered only with the dry, waist-high grass.

She bent to the ground and began pulling at the grass, but the stalks crumbled in her hands. And the gloves she wore didn't aid her dexterity any; she couldn't get a grip.

In a few moments she realized it wouldn't work. The roots of the plants were too firmly anchored and the stalks were too dry. *How does anything grow in this hellhole anyway?* If all the grass was like this, the whole island would be a natural combustion chamber. She said a word.

"Something the matter?" the radio asked.

"I'll say. I can't pull any of these damn plants up."

"All you need is maybe ten or fifteen yards of clear area."

"I don't know about that—I think it could leap the gap." Holding her breath, she pulled her mask off her muzzle and wiped the sweat off her nose. It didn't help.

"Try digging them up."

"With what?" She tried scooping at the ground with the edge of her helmet—

"What in the name of *World-Mother* is that?" cried Semm.

"Just my helmet. I was trying to see if I could dig with it. I can't."

"You aren't wearing it?"

"No."

"Why the hell not?"

"Because it's heavy—and it hurts my ears."

"Ari!" The other was exasperated. "You were given specific orders—"

"Hang the orders! It hurts. And I'm not in any danger. We've been here two months. This is my first time on the ground and I want to breathe some real air."

"Ari," despaired the other. "You're going to be disciplined for that."

"How?" taunted Ari. "You've got to save me first."

"You've got to save yourself!" growled a different voice, the *Mam*-Captain again. Apparently, she had been listening at the radio. "We have no way of getting to you, Ari—at least not before the combustion sweeps the island."

"Fine—then I'll save myself my way! And if that means leaving my helmet off, then that's the way I'll do it. You should have known about this combustion phenomenon."

"There are a lot of things I should have known about," sighed the other. "Unfortunately, I am not as wise as an Heir to Urs. That's why we have rules on how to explore unknown planets. I will only be able to tell the Matriarch the truth—that you refused to follow her rules."

Enraged and swearing, Ari flung the helmet away. Then, realizing that she couldn't answer the *Mam* without it, she retrieved it. "This is all a waste of time," she announced. "There's no point in standing here arguing."

"I agree," said the *Mam*-Captain. "Have you tried shoveling into the earth with your hands?"

Ari dropped the helmet in disgust and kicked it away.

But she got down on her knees and began working. It was true—she didn't want to die. At least they couldn't *see* her working like this. Her great shovel-shaped claws scooped at the dirt. If she grabbed the plant low enough, just where the root system began, she could pull it up enough to dig under it and weaken it and then perhaps she could pull it up some more and. . . .

Shortly, she was able to clear a small area in front of herself, perhaps two or three feet square. She paused, looked up, wiped at her muzzle again, and suddenly realized how close the flames were. She grabbed her helmet and jumped to her feet. "Perdition!"

"What's the matter?" asked the helmet.

"It's no good. The brush is too thick. The island is too wide. I could never clear a big enough area in time."

Semm didn't answer.

Ari could feel the frustration welling up inside of her, "Dammit, Semm—the *Mam*-Captain ordered—no, threatened me. I tried your stupid idea—I disgraced myself. If I get out of this, I'll never live it down—but it didn't work. I can't dig them up fast enough."

Semm remained respectfully silent. Ari was almost in tears; frustration and anger were choking her. She kept backing away from the combustion. Then, for no reason, she broke into a run, loping eastward for several hundred meters. She had to weave her course around the craggly bushes. This incredible heat-world!

She stopped, panting easily, and glanced backward. It should take the phenomenon awhile to close this distance.

"Ari, the rescue ship is in the atmosphere now."

"Fine. They'll arrive just in time to consecrate my body."

"Don't talk like that. You sound like a *Nin-Gresee*. Besides, you've still got more than half an hour to go."

Ari checked her chronometer. "Not much more than that." She sat down on a rocky outcrop, watched as the crackling orange *thing* lapped at the base of the fourth (or was it the fifth?) hillock. Was that where her abortive attempt at clearing the grass had been?

No matter. She tossed the thought away. She tried to brush the dirt from her gloves. Pah! Digging!

"How are you fixed on oxygen?"

"Why?"

"Nivie's got an idea. There's another way to break the combustion cycle."

"Huh? How?"

"Oxygen."

"What? I already told you there's no way to cut off its oxy supply—"

"No, you don't cut it off. You overload it. You feed it oxygen. Pure oxygen."

"You're out of your—"

"The computer says it'll work. If you feed enough pure oxygen into the combustion, you'll create a superheated area. It'll need more and more oxygen to survive and will start sucking it in from the surrounding area. It'll be like a storm—a combustion storm!"

"That's all I need—*more* combustion phenomenon."

"No, no! Listen—after it's used up all the oxygen in its immediate vicinity, it'll have to pull in more and more from the surrounding area in order to keep burning—that'll change the local wind pattern. The combustion on the edges of the phenomenon will cease from lack of oxygen and you could get around it and back to your ship. Now, listen—feed your oxygen to the *base* of the phenomenon—"

"Semm," Ari interrupted. "It sounds awfully risky. And it's pretty hot here already."

"Ari, it may be your only chance."

"You said that about digging up the plants."

"All right, we were wrong."

"I can still think of two reasons why I can't do it." Ari felt her eyes watering from the smoke despite her goggles and chillsuit. "First, I don't think this island is big enough for that storm effect you talk about."

"We don't know until you try."

"I'm here on the scene, Semm—it doesn't *feel* practical. Besides . . ." she hesitated, embarrassed, ". . . all my extra oxy tanks are still in the ship."

A pause. Then, "Why the hell aren't you wearing them?"

"Because I don't need them—and they're heavy, dammit! Gravity here is eleven percent higher than home!" She stopped, forced herself to be calm. "Besides, I don't think I could get close enough to the phenomenon anyway." She wiped the sweat from her muzzle again. "That thing is awfully hot." She peered at a dial on her belt pack. "From here it reads several hundred degrees at its core—this thing must be broken."

Another pause from the radio, a crackle of static.

"If only you could change the wind or something. . . ."

She didn't answer. Semm was right, though. The *wind* was the whole problem. If only it had been blowing in some other direction. If only, if only . . .

"Ari? You still there?"

"Where would I go?" she muttered.

"Nowhere. Just checking," the radio said.

"What do you want?"

"Nothing. Uh, just keep talking, will you?"

"Why?"

"Just keep talking, huh? So we know everything is all right. Tell us how the phenomenon started."

"I did that already."

"Tell us again. You might have left something out."

Ari stared out over the ocean for a long moment, wondering whether or not it was worth the trouble to be obstinate.

"If you don't start talking, *Mam*-Captain says you'll scrub decks for a month."

"She'll have to come and get me." But despite herself, Ari smiled.

"Better talk, Ari. You might survive."

"All right . . . I brought the ship down on a little spit of land on the western edge of the island—I should have made a pontoon landing. That's what I should have done. But I wanted to show off my piloting skill and put down on the land instead. Before I'd gotten fifteen meters away from the ship, I heard a noise. Or maybe not. Anyway, something made me turn around. At first, I thought the ship was exploding. Then I realized it was the vegetation—Semm!" she said suddenly. "That's how it started!"

"Huh?"

"The combustion! It started from the heat of the scoutship! The skin of it was still hot from my landing! Isn't it obvious? The vegetation is the fuel and there's plenty of free oxygen in the air—all that was needed to start the combustion was heat and I supplied that when I touched down!"

"Um," said Semm. "You're probably right. We'll have to add a note to all future landing procedures."

"World-Mother!" said Ari. "What an unstable ecology this must be!"

"Oh, there must be some kind of adaptive mechanisms, for re-seeding and such."

"Semm, you should see this! Nothing could survive!"

The helmet said, "Ari?"

In a quieter voice: "I'm still here."

"The wind? Is there any chance it might let up? Or maybe shift direction?"

Ari sniffed the air thoughtfully. "I can't tell with this muzzle on—and I'm not going to risk taking it off. Anyway, I doubt it. It seems pretty steady."

"Oh. All right. It was only a thought."

"If anything, it seems to be picking up."

"Mm."

"That ship can't get here any faster?"

"Sorry."

"It's all right," Ari said. She grinned wryly. "Just don't let it happen again."

"We'll try not to."

"Semm?" Ari said.

"Yes?"

"Put the *Mam*-Captain on, will you?"

"Huh? What for?"

"Just do it. I want to make out my will."

"All right." There was a pause from the helmet. After a moment, a new voice rumbled out of the speaker, the *Mam*-Captain's. "All right, Ari," she said. "I'm recording. Go on."

Ari cleared her throat, a deep raspy growl. "I, Ari Bh Arobi, Heir to Urs, being of sound mind and healthy body and so on, hereby leave, bequeath and so on, all my worldly belongings to. . ." She paused.

"Go on," the radio urged.

Ari cleared her throat and began again: "I leave all my worldly goods, to be divided equally among all other Heirs to Urs. I hereby grant freedom to all twenty of my personal male slaves, including my brood-husbands. I return all of my titles and nobilities to the body of the *World-Mother*. Uh, and any personal possessions on the ship that any of my shipmates want, well—the *Mam*-Captain has my authority to dispose of them as she sees fit." She trailed off. "Oh, one more thing—I hereby absolve all other members of this expedition, including the *Mam*-Captain, of any responsibility for any actions which may have directly or indirectly resulted in my death. They may not be held liable to any claims made either in my name or against my name; at all times, their actions and their concern have been for the welfare of the aristocracy. As an Heir to Urs, I accept full weight of the burden myself and respectfully petition the Matriarchy not to take any reprisals of any kind against any of the members of this expedition. As an Heir to Urs, I claim the right of responsibility; the fault is my own, let the death be my own as well. That's all. I'm through."

The *Mam*-Captain rumbled, "It's a fine will, child." Her voice sounded strange.

"Did you get it all?"

A pause. Then, Semm's voice: "Yes, we got it." Another pause. "Uva wants to know if she can have your melt-cup."

"Tell her go ahead. And the frozen incense too."

"She says thanks."

"Tell her she's welcome. I'll let her do the same for me someday."

"Sure," said Semm. Another pause. "Keep talking, huh?"

"Uh uh," said Ari. "Throat's getting dry. *World-Mother*, this thing is heavy!"

"What is?"

"This helmet." She found herself looking at it, at the shrinking spit of land left to her, at the helmet again. "What the hell am I dragging it around for?"

She dropped it to the ground.

"Ari!" cried the speaker. *"Mam*-Captain says you keep that helmet with you!" But it was too late. Ari was already walking away from it.

She had maybe fifteen minutes left, and couldn't decide. The flames or the water?

Of course, she knew what was going to happen. Like the rodent-creatures, she would keep retreating from the ever-advancing flames until she was backed into the water. And then, she'd keep swimming for as long as she could, until she could either swim to safety; or more likely, until—

She preferred not to think about the other possibility. Idly she tugged at a bush. The branch was dry and snapped off in her hand. Still holding it, she started walking along the flame front, as close to it as she dared.

On impulse, she held the branch into a tendril of curling flame. The wood smouldered, charred, then puffed afire.

Stepping back with it, she watched as the flame curled up along the dry limb. It was hard to believe that *this* was the same phenomenon as that roaring holocaust. She turned the branch upside down. The fire continued to move from burnt to unburnt. "Won't change direction, will you?" she said to it. "Once you've burned something, you're through with it. Never satisfied though. Always looking for something else . . . I used to have a pup like that; she didn't stop eating till the last dish was empty and she didn't believe it was empty till she'd checked it herself."

Ari started to throw the branch away, then hesitated. She turned and looked at the fire again, frowning—

When the rescue team arrived, Ari Bh Arobi, the Heir to Urs, was sitting on a rocky outcrop next to her ship. She stood as they approached. Her grin could be seen even through the breathing mask of her chillsuit. "What took you so long?"

"Huh?" They scrambled across the black-crusted ground. "You're supposed to be dead!"

Ari was still grinning. "Sorry to disappoint you."

"What did you—Oh, it must have been the water. You swam around, didn't you."

Ari shook her head. "Uh uh. I told you, there's *things* in that ocean."

"Then, how—"

Ari was enjoying their frustration. "Well, it's like this. I'm an Heir to Urs, so I simply applied my superior intellectual abilities and—"

"Wait a minute." One of the two she-bears was fiddling with her radio. *"Mam!* She's alive!—Yes! Yes! *Unhurt!*—No, *Mam!* Not a burn, not a scratch—I don't know. We're finding out now." She looked at Ari. "Go on."

Ari shrugged. "It was simple. The combustion phenomenon was sweeping across the island at a steady rate, right? I had to keep moving downwind to avoid it. The problem wouldn't have existed if I was behind the thing. It could sweep all the way down to the end of the island and it wouldn't bother me at all."

"Well, that was the whole idea, to get you through the combustion. Or around it."

"No, stupid—the problem was not to get me *through* the combustion. The problem was to get it *downwind.*"

"Same thing, isn't it?"

"Not at all," said Ari. "Not at all."

"All right—how *did* you get the combustion downwind?"

"Simple. I put it there."

"Huh?"

"I took a stick. I held it in the flame until it caught. Then I walked downwind and started a second combustion. The wind blew this one toward the east too, right up to the end of the island—and I was safely *behind it.* Although those things in the water sure caught a lot of rodents there for a while."

"Wait a minute—" The pilot was frowning. "That would have put you between two flame-walls."

"Only for a short time. Both were moving eastward at the same rate. It was easy enough to keep between them. When the first combustion reached the ground where the second one had been started, it went out. Lack of fuel. Simple. After the ground cooled enough, I walked back to my ship."

"Well, I'll be damned—"

"Probably," agreed Ari. "See, everybody on the ship was worrying about the combustion cycle and things like that. It took an on-the-scene observer to interpret the behavior of the phenomenon and to use its own characteristics against itself—"

"Oh, Mother—" breathed the pilot. "She's going to be impossible."

"Hey," called the other. "Uva wants to know, does this mean you're taking back your melt-cup?"

"Absolutely." Ari grinned. "And the incense too."

"Wait a minute, Ari. *Mam*-Captain wants to talk to you."

"Uh huh," Ari said, reaching for the radio. "Probably wants to congratulate me—"

"Uh uh—she's madder'n hell," whispered the other. "Something about discipline and a burned space helmet—"

Ari suddenly remembered she had absolved the *Mam*-Captain of all responsibility. She couldn't pull rank on her anymore—

Ari Bh Arobi, Heir to Urs, was about to get her first spanking.

THE LAST DEFENDER OF CAMELOT
by Roger Zelazny
art: Frank Borth

The three muggers who stopped him that October night in San Francisco did not anticipate much resistance from the old man, despite his size. He was well-dressed, and that was sufficient.

The first approached him with his hand extended. The other two hung back a few paces.

"Just give me your wallet and your watch," the mugger said. "You'll save yourself a lot of trouble."

The old man's grip shifted on his walking stick. His shoulders straightened. His shock of white hair tossed as he turned his head to regard the other.

"Why don't you come and take them?"

The mugger began another step but he never completed it. The stick was almost invisible in the speed of its swinging. It struck him on the left temple and he fell.

Without pausing, the old man caught the stick by its middle with his left hand, advanced and drove it into the belly of the next nearest man. Then, with an upward hook as the man doubled, he caught him in the softness beneath the jaw, behind the chin, with its point. As the man fell, he clubbed him with its butt on the back of the neck.

The third man had reached out and caught the old man's upper arm by then. Dropping the stick, the old man seized the mugger's shirtfront with his left hand, his belt with his right, raised him from the ground until he held him at arm's length above his head, and slammed him against the side of the building to his right, releasing him as he did so.

He adjusted his apparel, ran a hand through his hair, and retrieved his walking stick. For a moment he regarded the three fallen forms, then shrugged and continued on his way.

There were sounds of traffic from somewhere off to his left. He turned right at the next corner. The moon appeared above tall buildings as he walked. The smell of the ocean was on the air. It had rained earlier, and the pavement still shone beneath streetlamps. He moved slowly, pausing occasionally to examine the contents of darkened shop windows.

After perhaps ten minutes, he came upon a side street showing more activity than any of the others he had passed. There was a drugstore, still open, on the corner, a diner farther up the block, and several well-lighted storefronts. A number of people were walking along the far side of the street. A boy coasted by on a bicycle. He turned there, his pale eyes regarding everything he passed.

Halfway up the block, he came to a dirty window on which was painted the word READINGS. Beneath it were displayed the outline of a hand and a scattering of playing cards. As he passed the open door, he glanced inside. A brightly garbed woman, her hair bound back in a green kerchief, sat smoking at the rear of the room. She smiled as their eyes met and crooked an index finger toward herself. He smiled back and turned away, but . . .

He looked at her again. What was it? He glanced at his watch.

Turning, he entered the shop and moved to stand before her. She rose. She was small, barely over five feet in height.

"Your eyes," he remarked, "are green. Most gypsies I know have dark eyes."

She shrugged.

"You take what you get in life. Have you a problem?"

"Give me a moment and I'll think of one," he said. "I just came in here because you remind me of someone and it bothers me—I can't think who."

"Come into the back," she said, "and sit down. We'll talk."

He nodded and followed her into a small room to the rear. A threadbare oriental rug covered the floor near the small table at which they seated themselves. Zodiacal prints and faded psychedelic posters of a semi-religious nature covered the walls. A crystal ball stood on a small stand in the far corner beside a vase of cut flowers. A dark, long-haired cat slept on a sofa to the right of it. A door to another room stood slightly ajar beyond the sofa. The only illumination came from a cheap lamp on the table before him and from a small candle in a plaster base atop the shawl-covered coffee table.

He leaned forward and studied her face, then shook his head and leaned back.

She flicked an ash onto the floor.

"Your problem?" she suggested.

He sighed.

"Oh, I don't really have a problem anyone can help me with. Look, I think I made a mistake coming in here. I'll pay you for your trouble, though, just as if you'd given me a reading. How much is it?"

He began to reach for his wallet, but she raised her hand.

"Is it that you do not believe in such things?" she asked, her eyes scrutinizing his face.

"No, quite the contrary," he replied. "I am willing to believe in magic, divination, and all manner of spells and sendings, angelic and demonic. But—"

"But not from someone in a dump like this?"

He smiled.

"No offense," he said.

A whistling sound filled the air. It seemed to come from the next room back.

"That's all right," she said, "but my water is boiling. I'd forgotten it was on. Have some tea with me? I do wash the cups. No charge. Things are slow."

"All right."

She rose and departed.

He glanced at the door to the front but eased himself back into his chair, resting his large, blue-veined hands on its padded arms. He sniffed then, nostrils flaring, and cocked his head as at some half-familiar aroma.

After a time, she returned with a tray, set it on the coffee table. The cat stirred, raised her head, blinked at it, stretched, closed her eyes again.

"Cream and sugar?"

"Please. One lump."

She placed two cups on the table before him.

"Take either one," she said.

He smiled and drew the one on his left toward him. She placed an ashtray in the middle of the table and returned to her own seat, moving the other cup to her place.

"That wasn't necessary," he said, placing his hands on the table.

She shrugged.

"You don't know me. Why should you trust me? Probably got a lot of money on you."

He looked at her face again. She had apparently removed some of the heavier makeup while in the back room. The jawline, the brow . . . He looked away. He took a sip of tea.

"Good tea. Not instant," he said. "Thanks."

"So you believe in all sorts of magic," she asked, sipping her own.

"Some," he said.

"Any special reason why?"

"Some of it works."

"For example?"

He gestured aimlessly with his left hand.

"I've traveled a lot. I've seen some strange things."

"And you have no problems?"

He chuckled.

"Still determined to give me a reading? All right. I'll tell you a little about myself and what I want right now, and you can tell me whether I'll get it. Okay?"

"I'm listening."

"I am a buyer for a large gallery in the East. I am something of an authority on ancient work in precious metals. I am in town to attend an auction of such items from the estate of a private collector. I will go to inspect the pieces tomorrow. Naturally, I hope to find something good. What do you think my chances are?"

"Give me your hands."

He extended them, palms upward. She leaned forward and regarded them. She looked back up at him immediately.

"Your wrists have more rascettes than I can count!"

"Yours seem to have quite a few, also."

She met his eyes for only a moment and returned her attention to his hands. He noted that she had paled beneath what remained of her makeup, and her breathing was now irregular.

"No," she finally said, drawing back, "you are not going to find here what you are looking for."

Her hand trembled slightly as she raised her teacup. He frowned.

"I asked only in jest," he said. "Nothing to get upset about. I doubted I would find what I am really looking for, anyway."

She shook her head.

"Tell me your name."

"I've lost my accent," he said, "but I'm French. The name is DuLac."

She stared into his eyes and began to blink rapidly.

"No . . ." she said. "No."

"I'm afraid so. What's yours?"

"Madam LeFay," she said. "I just repainted that sign. It's still drying."

He began to laugh, but it froze in his throat.

"Now—I know—who—you remind me of. . . ."

"You reminded me of someone, also. Now I, too, know."

Her eyes brimmed, her mascara ran.

"It couldn't be," he said. "Not here. . . . Not in a place like this. . . ."

"You dear man," she said softly, and she raised his right hand to her lips. She seemed to choke for a moment, then said, "I had thought that I was the last, and yourself buried at Joyous Gard. I never dreamed . . ." Then, "This?" gesturing about the room. "Only because it amuses me, helps to pass the time. The waiting—"

She stopped. She lowered his hand.

"Tell me about it," she said.

"The waiting?" he said. "For what do you wait?"

"Peace," she said. "I am here by the power of my arts, through all the long years. But you— How did you manage it?"

"I—" He took another drink of tea. He looked about the room. "I do not know how to begin," he said. "I survived the final battles, saw the kingdom sundered, could do nothing—and at last departed England. I wandered, taking service at many courts, and after a time under many names, as I saw that I was not aging—or aging very, very slowly. I was in India, China—I fought in the Crusades, I've been everywhere. I've spoken with magicians and mystics—most of them charlatans, a few with the power, none so great as Merlin—and what had come to be my own belief was confirmed by one of them, a man more than half charlatan, yet. . . ." He paused and finished his tea. "Are you certain you want to hear all this?" he asked.

"I want to hear it. Let me bring more tea first, though."

She returned with the tea. She lit a cigarette and leaned back. "Go on."

"I decided that it was—my sin," he said, "with . . . the Queen."

"I don't understand."

"I betrayed my Liege, who was also my friend, in the one thing which must have hurt him most. The love I felt was stronger than loyalty or friendship—and even today, to this day, it still is. I cannot repent, and so I cannot be forgiven. Those were strange and magical times. We lived in a land destined to become myth. Powers walked the realm in those days, forces which are now gone from the earth. How or why, I cannot say. But you know that it is true. I am somehow of a piece with those gone things, and the laws that rule my existence are not normal laws of the natural world. I believe that I cannot die; that it has fallen my lot, as punishment, to wander the world till I have completed the Quest. I believe I will only know rest the day I find the Holy Grail. Giuseppe Balsamo, before he became known as Cagliostro, somehow saw this and said it to me just as I had thought it, though I never said a word of it to him. And so I have traveled the world, searching. I go no more as knight, or soldier, but as an appraiser. I have been in nearly every museum on Earth, viewed all the great private collections. So far, it has eluded me."

"You *are* getting a little old for battle."

He snorted.

"I have never lost," he stated flatly. "Down ten centuries, I have never lost a personal contest. It is true that I have aged, yet whenever I am threatened all of my former strength returns to me. But, look where I may, fight where I may, it has never served me to discover that which I must find. I feel I am unforgiven and must wander like the Eternal Jew until the end of the world."

She lowered her head.

". . . And you say I will not find it tomorrow?"

"You will never find it," she said softly.

"You saw that in my hand?"

She shook her head.

"Your story is fascinating and your theory novel," she began, "but Cagliostro was a total charlatan. Something must have betrayed your thoughts, and he made a shrewd guess. But he was wrong. I say that you will never find it, not because you are unworthy or unforgiven. No, never that. A more loyal subject than yourself never drew breath. Don't you know that Arthur forgave you? It was an arranged marriage. The same thing happened constantly elsewhere, as you must know. You gave her something he could not. There was only tenderness there. He understood. The only forgiveness you require is that which has been withheld all these long years—your own. No, it is not a doom that has been laid upon you. It is your own feelings which led you to assume an impossible quest, something tantamount to total unforgiveness. But you have suffered all these centuries upon the wrong trail."

When she raised her eyes, she saw that his were hard, like ice or gemstones. But she met his gaze and continued: "There is not now, was not then, and probably never was, a Holy Grail."

"I saw it," he said, "that day it passed through the Hall of the Table. We all saw it."

"You thought you saw it," she corrected him. "I hate to shatter an illusion that has withstood all the other tests of time, but I fear I must. The kingdom, as you recall, was at that time in turmoil. The knights were growing restless and falling away from the fellowship. A year—six months, even—and all would have collapsed, all Arthur had striven so hard to put together. He knew that the longer Camelot stood, the longer its name would endure, the stronger its ideals would become. So he made a decision, a purely political one. Something was needed to hold things together. He called upon Merlin, already half-mad, yet still shrewd enough to see what was needed and able to provide it. The Quest was born. Merlin's powers created the illusion you saw that day. It was a lie, yes. A glorious lie, though. And it served for years after to bind you all in brotherhood, in the name of justice and love. It entered literature, it promoted nobility and the higher ends of culture. It served its purpose. But it was—never—really—there. You have been chasing a ghost. I am sorry, Launcelot, but I have absolutely no reason to lie to you. I know magic when I see it. I saw it then. That is how it happened."

For a long while he was silent. Then he laughed.

"You have an answer for everything," he said. "I could almost believe you, if you could but answer me one thing more— Why am I here? For what reason? By what power? How is it I have been preserved for half the Christian era while other men grow old and die in a handful of years? Can you tell me now what Cagliostro could not?"

"Yes," she said, "I believe that I can."

He rose to his feet and began to pace. The cat, alarmed, sprang from the sofa and ran into the back room. He stooped and snatched up his walking stick. He started for the door.

"I suppose it was worth waiting a thousand years to see you afraid," she said.

He halted.

"That is unfair," he replied.

"I know. But now you will come back and sit down," she said.

He was smiling once more as he turned and returned.

"Tell me," he said. "How do you see it?"

"Yours was the last enchantment of Merlin, that is how I see it."

"Merlin? Me? Why?"

"Gossip had it the old goat took Nimue into the woods and she had to use one of his own spells on him in self-defense—a spell which caused him to sleep forever in some lost place. If it was the spell that I believe it was, then at least part of the rumor was incorrect. There was no known counterspell, but the effects of the enchantment would have caused him to sleep not forever but for a millennium, and then to awaken. My guess now is that his last conscious act before he dropped off was to lay this enchantment upon you, so that you would be on hand when he returned."

"I suppose it might be possible, but why would he want me or need me?"

"If I were journeying into a strange time, I would want an ally once I reached it. And if I had a choice, I would want it to be the greatest champion of the day."

"Merlin . . ." he mused. "I suppose that it could be as you say. Excuse me, but a long life has just been shaken up, from beginning to end. If this is true . . ."

"I am sure that it is."

"If this is true . . . a millennium, you say?"

"Just so."

"Well, it is almost exactly a thousand years now."

"I know. I do not believe that our meeting tonight was a matter of chance. You are destined to meet him upon his awakening, which should be soon. Something has ordained that you meet me first, however, to be warned."

"Warned? Warned of what?"

"He is mad, Launcelot. Many of us felt a great relief at his passing. If the realm had not been sundered finally by strife it would probably have been broken by his hand, anyway."

"That I find difficult to believe. He was always a strange man—for who can fully understand a sorcerer?—and in his later years he did seem at least partly daft. But he never struck me as evil."

"Nor was he. His was the most dangerous morality of all. He was a misguided idealist. In a more primitive time and place and with a willing tool like Arthur, he was able to create a legend. Today, in an age of monstrous weapons, with the right leader as his catspaw, he could unleash something totally devastating. He would see a wrong and force his man to try righting it. He would do it in the name of the same high ideals he always served, but he would not appreciate the results until it was too late. How could he—even if he were sane? He has no conception of modern international relations."

"What is to be done? What is my part in all of this?"

"I believe you should go back, to England, to be present at his awakening, to find out exactly what he wants, to try to reason with him."

"I don't know. . . . How would I find him?"

"You found me. When the time is right, you will be in the proper place. I am certain of that. It was meant to be, probably even a part of his spell. Seek him. But do not trust him."

"I don't know, Morgana." He looked at the wall, unseeing. "I don't know."

"You have waited this long and you draw back now from finally finding out?"

"You are right—in that much, at least." He folded his hands, raised them and rested his chin upon them. "What I would do if he really returned, I do not know. Try to reason with him, yes—Have you any other advice?"

"Just that you be there."

"You've looked at my hand. You have the power. What did you see?"

She turned away.

"It is uncertain," she said.

That night he dreamed, as he sometimes did, of times long gone. They sat about the great Table, as they had on that day. Gawaine was there, and Percival. Galahad . . . He winced. This day was different from other days. There was a certain tension in the air, a before-the-storm feeling, an electrical thing. . . . Merlin stood at the far end of the room, hands in the sleeves of his long robe, hair and beard snowy and unkempt, pale eyes staring—at what, none could be certain. . . .

After some timeless time, a reddish glow appeared near the door. All eyes moved toward it. It grew brighter and advanced slowly into the room—a formless apparition of light. There were sweet odors and some few soft strains of music. Gradually, a form began to take shape at its center, resolving itself into the likeness of a chalice. . . .

He felt himself rising, moving slowly, following it in its course through the great chamber, advancing upon it, soundlessly and deliberately, as if moving underwater. . . .

. . . Reaching for it.

THE LAST DEFENDER OF CAMELOT   41

His hand entered the circle of light, moved toward its center, neared the now blazing cup and passed through. . . .

Immediately, the light faded. The outline of the chalice wavered, and it collapsed in upon itself, fading, fading, gone. . . .

There came a sound, rolling, echoing about the hall. Laughter.

He turned and regarded the others. They sat about the table, watching him, laughing. Even Merlin managed a dry chuckle.

Suddenly, his great blade was in his hand, and he raised it as he strode toward the Table. The knights nearest him drew back as he brought the weapon crashing down.

The Table split in half and fell. The room shook.

The quaking continued. Stones were dislodged from the walls. A roof beam fell. He raised his arm.

The entire castle began to come apart, falling about him, and still the laughter continued.

He awoke damp with perspiration and lay still for a long while. In the morning, he bought a ticket for London.

Two of the three elemental sounds of the world were suddenly with him as he walked that evening, stick in hand. For a dozen days, he had hiked about Cornwall, finding no clues to that which he sought. He had allowed himself two more before giving up and departing.

Now the wind and the rain were upon him, and he increased his pace. The fresh-lit stars were smothered by a mass of cloud and wisps of fog grew like ghostly fungi on either hand. He moved among trees, paused, continued on.

"Shouldn't have stayed out this late," he muttered, and after several more pauses, *"Nel mezzo del cammin di nostra vita mi ritrovai per una selva oscura, che la diritta via era smarrita,"* then he chuckled, halting beneath a tree.

The rain was not heavy. It was more a fine mist now. A bright patch in the lower heavens showed where the moon hung veiled.

He wiped his face, turned up his collar. He studied the position of the moon. After a time, he struck off to his right. There was a faint rumble of thunder in the distance.

The fog continued to grow about him as he went. Soggy leaves made squishing noises beneath his boots. An animal of indeterminate size bolted from a clump of shrubbery beside a cluster of rocks and tore off through the darkness.

Five minutes . . . ten . . . He cursed softly. The rainfall had increased in intensity. Was that the same rock?

He turned in a complete circle. All directions were equally un-inviting. Selecting one at random, he commenced walking once again.

Then, in the distance, he discerned a spark, a glow, a wavering light. It vanished and reappeared periodically, as though partly blocked, the line of sight a function of his movements. He headed toward it. After perhaps half a minute, it was gone again from sight, but he continued on in what he thought to be its direction. There came another roll of thunder, louder this time.

When it seemed that it might have been illusion or some short-lived natural phenomenon, something else occurred in that same direction. There was a movement, a shadow-within-shadow shuf-fling at the foot of a great tree. He slowed his pace, approaching the spot cautiously.

There!

A figure detached itself from a pool of darkness ahead and to the left. Manlike, it moved with a slow and heavy tread, creaking sounds emerging from the forest floor beneath it. A vagrant moonbeam touched it for a moment, and it appeared yellow and metallically slick beneath moisture.

He halted. It seemed that he had just regarded a knight in full armor in his path. How long since he had beheld such a sight? He shook his head and stared.

The figure had also halted. It raised its right arm in a beckoning gesture, then turned and began to walk away. He hesitated for only a moment, then followed.

It turned off to the left and pursued a treacherous path, rocky, slippery, heading slightly downward. He actually used his stick now, to assure his footing, as he tracked its deliberate progress. He gained on it, to the point where he could clearly hear the metallic scraping sounds of its passage.

Then it was gone, swallowed by a greater darkness.

He advanced to the place where he had last beheld it. He stood in the lee of a great mass of stone. He reached out and probed it with his stick.

He tapped steadily along its nearest surface, and then the stick moved past it. He followed.

There was an opening, a crevice. He had to turn sidewise to pass within it, but as he did the full glow of the light he had seen came into sight for several seconds.

The passage curved and widened, leading him back and down. Several times, he paused and listened, but there were no sounds other than his own breathing.

He withdrew his handkerchief and dried his face and hands carefully. He brushed moisture from his coat, turned down his collar. He scuffed the mud and leaves from his boots. He adjusted his apparel. Then he strode forward, rounding a final corner, into a chamber lit by a small oil lamp suspended by three delicate chains from some point in the darkness overhead. The yellow knight stood unmoving beside the far wall. On a fiber mat atop a stony pedestal directly beneath the lamp lay an old man in tattered garments. His bearded face was half-masked by shadows.

He moved to the old man's side. He saw then that those ancient dark eyes were open.

"Merlin . . . ?" he whispered.

There came a faint hissing sound, a soft croak. Realizing the source, he leaned nearer.

"Elixir . . . in earthen crock . . . on ledge . . . in back," came the gravelly whisper.

He turned and sought the ledge, the container.

"Do you know where it is?" he asked the yellow figure.

It neither stirred nor replied, but stood like a display piece. He turned away from it then and sought further. After a time, he located it. It was more a niche than a ledge, blending in with the wall, cloaked with shadow. He ran his fingertips over the container's contours, raised it gently. Something liquid stirred within it. He wiped its lip on his sleeve after he had returned to the lighted area. The wind whistled past the entranceway and he thought he felt the faint vibration of thunder.

Sliding one hand beneath his shoulders, he raised the ancient form. Merlin's eyes still seemed unfocussed. He moistened Merlin's lips with the liquid. The old man licked them, and after several moments opened his mouth. He administered a sip, then another, and another . . .

Merlin signalled for him to lower him, and he did. He glanced again at the yellow armor, but it had remained motionless the entire while. He looked back at the sorcerer and saw that a new light had come into his eyes and he was studying him, smiling faintly.

"Feel better?"

Merlin nodded. A minute passed, and a touch of color appeared upon his cheeks. He elbowed himself into a sitting position and took the container into his hands. He raised it and drank deeply.

He sat still for several minutes after that. His thin hands, which had appeared waxy in the flamelight, grew darker, fuller. His shoul-

ders straightened. He placed the crock on the bed beside him and stretched his arms. His joints creaked the first time he did it, but not the second. He swung his legs over the edge of the bed and rose slowly to his feet. He was a full head shorter than Launcelot.

"It is done," he said, staring back into the shadows. "Much has happened, of course . . . ?"

"Much has happened," Launcelot replied.

"You have lived through it all. Tell me, is the world a better place or is it worse than it was in those days?"

"Better in some ways, worse in others. It is different."

"How is it better?"

"There are many ways of making life easier, and the sum total of human knowledge has increased vastly."

"How has it worsened?"

"There are many more people in the world. Consequently, there are many more people suffering from poverty, disease, ignorance. The world itself has suffered great depredation, in the way of pollution and other assaults on the integrity of nature."

"Wars?"

"There is always someone fighting, somewhere."

"They need help."

"Maybe. Maybe not."

Merlin turned and looked into his eyes.

"What do you mean?"

"People haven't changed. They are as rational—and irrational—as they were in the old days. They are as moral and law-abiding—and not—as ever. Many new things have been learned, many new situations evolved, but I do not believe that the nature of man has altered significantly in the time you've slept. Nothing you do is going to change that. You may be able to alter a few features of the times, but would it really be proper to meddle? Everything is so interdependent today that even you would not be able to predict all the consequences of any actions you take. You might do more harm than good; and whatever you do, man's nature will remain the same."

"This isn't like you, Lance. You were never much given to philosophizing in the old days."

"I've had a long time to think about it."

"And I've had a long time to dream about it. War is your craft, Lance. Stay with that."

"I gave it up a long time ago."

"Then what are you now?"

"An appraiser."

Merlin turned away, took another drink. He seemed to radiate a fierce energy when he turned again.

"And your oath? To right wrongs, to punish the wicked . . . ?"

"The longer I lived the more difficult it became to determine what was a wrong and who was wicked. Make it clear to me again and I may go back into business."

"Galahad would never have addressed me so."

"Galahad was young, naïve, trusting. Speak not to me of my son."

"Launcelot! Launcelot!" He placed a hand on his arm. "Why all this bitterness for an old friend who has done nothing for a thousand years?"

"I wished to make my position clear immediately. I feared you might contemplate some irreversible action which could alter the world balance of power fatally. I want you to know that I will not be party to it."

"Admit that you do not know what I might do, what I can do."

"Freely. That is why I fear you. What *do* you intend to do?"

"Nothing, at first. I wish merely to look about me, to see for myself some of these changes of which you have spoken. Then I will consider which wrongs need righting, who needs punishment, and who to choose as my champions. I will show you these things, and then you can go back into business, as you say."

Launcelot sighed.

"The burden of proof is on the moralist. Your judgment is no longer sufficient for me."

"Dear me," the other replied, "it is sad to have waited this long for an encounter of this sort, to find you have lost your faith in me. My powers are beginning to return already, Lance. Do you not feel magic in the air?"

"I feel something I have not felt in a long while."

"The sleep of ages was a restorative—an aid, actually. In a while, Lance, I am going to be stronger than I ever was before. And you doubt that I will be able to turn back the clock?"

"I doubt you can do it in a fashion to benefit anybody. Look, Merlin, I'm sorry. I do not like it that things have come to this either. But I have lived too long, seen too much, know too much of how the world works now to trust any one man's opinion concerning its salvation. Let it go. You are a mysterious, revered legend. I do not know what you really are. But forgo exercising your powers in any sort of crusade. Do something else this time around. Become a physician and fight pain. Take up painting. Be a professor of history, an antiquarian. Hell, be a social critic and point out what evils you see for people to correct themselves."

"Do you really believe I could be satisfied with any of those things?"

"Men find satisfaction in many things. It depends on the man, not on the things. I'm just saying that you should avoid using your powers in any attempt to effect social changes as we once did, by violence."

"Whatever changes have been wrought, time's greatest irony lies in its having transformed you into a pacifist."

"You are wrong."

"Admit it! You have finally come to fear the clash of arms! An appraiser! What kind of knight are you?"

"One who finds himself in the wrong time and the wrong place, Merlin."

The sorcerer shrugged and turned away.

"Let it be, then. It is good that you have chosen to tell me all these things immediately. Thank you for that, anyway. A moment."

Merlin walked to the rear of the cave, returned in moments attired in fresh garments. The effect was startling. His entire appearance was more kempt and cleanly. His hair and beard now appeared gray rather than white. His step was sure and steady. He held a staff in his right hand but did not lean upon it.

"Come walk with me," he said.

"It is a bad night."

"It is not the same night you left without. It is not even the same place."

As he passed the suit of yellow armor, he snapped his fingers near its visor. With a single creak, the figure moved and turned to follow him.

"Who is that?"

Merlin smiled.

"No one," he replied, and he reached back and raised the visor. The helmet was empty. "It is enchanted, animated by a spirit," he said. "A trifle clumsy, though, which is why I did not trust it to administer my draught. A perfect servant, however, unlike some. Incredibly strong and swift. Even in your prime you could not have beaten it. I fear nothing when it walks with me. Come, there is something I would have you see."

"Very well."

Launcelot followed Merlin and the hollow knight from the cave. The rain had stopped, and it was very still. They stood on an incredibly moonlit plain where mists drifted and grasses sparkled. Shadowy shapes stood in the distance.

"Excuse me," Launcelot said. "I left my walking stick inside."

He turned and re-entered the cave.

"Yes, fetch it, old man," Merlin replied. "Your strength is already on the wane."

When Launcelot returned, he leaned upon the stick and squinted across the plain.

"This way," Merlin said, "to where your questions will be answered. I will try not to move too quickly and tire you."

"Tire me?"

The sorcerer chuckled and began walking across the plain. Launcelot followed.

"Do you not feel a trifle weary?" he asked.

"Yes, as a matter of fact, I do. Do you know what is the matter with me?"

"Of course. I have withdrawn the enchantment which has protected you all these years. What you feel now are the first tentative touches of your true age. It will take some time to catch up with you, against your body's natural resistance, but it is beginning its advance."

"Why are you doing this to me?"

"Because I believed you when you said you were not a pacifist. And you spoke with sufficient vehemence for me to realize that you might even oppose me. I could not permit that, for I knew that your old strength was still there for you to call upon. Even a sorcerer might fear that, so I did what had to be done. By my power was it maintained; without it, it now drains away. It would have been good for us to work together once again, but I saw that that could not be."

Launcelot stumbled, caught himself, limped on. The hollow knight walked at Merlin's right hand.

"You say that your ends are noble," Launcelot said, "but I do not believe you. Perhaps in the old days they were. But more than the times have changed. You are different. Do you not feel it yourself?"

Merlin drew a deep breath and exhaled vapor.

"Perhaps it is my heritage," he said. Then, "I jest. Of course, I have changed. Everyone does. You yourself are a perfect example. What you consider a turn for the worse in me is but the tip of an irreducible conflict which has grown up between us in the course of our changes. I still hold with the true ideals of Camelot."

Launcelot's shoulders were bent foward now and his breathing had deepened. The shapes loomed larger before them.

"Why, I know this place," he gasped. "Yet, I do not know it. Stonehenge does not stand so today. Even in Arthur's time it lacked this perfection. How did we get here? What has happened?"

He paused to rest, and Merlin halted to accommodate him.

"This night we have walked between the worlds," the sorceror said. "This is a piece of the land of Faërie and that is the true Stonehenge, a holy place. I have stretched the bounds of the worlds to bring it here. Were I unkind I could send you back with it and strand you there forever. But it is better that you know a sort of peace. Come!"

Launcelot staggered along behind him, heading for the great circle of stones. The faintest of breezes came out of the west, stirring the mists.

"What do you mean—know a sort of peace?"

"The complete restoration of my powers and their increase will require a sacrifice in this place."

"Then you planned this for me all along!"

"No. It was not to have been you, Lance. Anyone would have served, though you will serve superbly well. It need not have been so, had you elected to assist me. You could still change your mind."

"Would you want someone who did that at your side?"

"You have a point there."

"Then why ask—save as a petty cruelty?"

"It is just that, for you have annoyed me."

Launcelot halted again when they came to the circle's periphery. He regarded the massive stands of stone.

"If you will not enter willingly," Merlin stated, "my servant will be happy to assist you."

Launcelot spat, straightened a little and glared.

"Think you I fear an empty suit of armor, juggled by some Hell-born wight? Even now, Merlin, without the benefit of wizardly succor, I could take that thing apart."

The sorcerer laughed.

"It is good that you at least recall the boasts of knighthood when all else has left you. I've half a mind to give you the opportunity, for the manner of your passing here is not important. Only the preliminaries are essential."

"But you're afraid to risk your servant?"

"Think you so, old man? I doubt you could even bear the weight of a suit of armor, let alone lift a lance. But if you are willing to try, so be it!"

He rapped the butt of his staff three times upon the ground.

"Enter," he said then. "You will find all that you need within. And I am glad you have made this choice. You were insufferable, you know. Just once, I longed to see you beaten, knocked down to the level of lesser mortals. I only wish the Queen could be here, to witness her champion's final engagement."

"So do I," said Launcelot, and he walked past the monolith and entered the circle.

A black stallion waited, its reins held down beneath a rock. Pieces of armor, a lance, a blade and a shield leaned against the side of the dolmen. Across the circle's diameter, a white stallion awaited the advance of the hollow knight.

"I am sorry I could not arrange for a page or a squire to assist you," Merlin said, coming around the other side of the monolith. "I'll be glad to help you myself, though."

"I can manage," Launcelot replied.

"My champion is accoutered in exactly the same fashion," Merlin said, "and I have not given him any edge over you in weapons."

"I never liked your puns either."

Launcelot made friends with the horse, then removed a small strand of red from his wallet and tied it about the butt of the lance. He leaned his stick against the dolmen stone and began to don the armor. Merlin, whose hair and beard were now almost black, moved off several paces and began drawing a diagram in the dirt with the end of his staff.

"You used to favor a white charger," he commented, "but I thought it appropriate to equip you with one of another color, since you have abandoned the ideals of the Table Round, betraying the memory of Camelot."

"On the contrary," Launcelot replied, glancing overhead at the passage of a sudden roll of thunder. "Any horse in a storm, and I am Camelot's last defender."

Merlin continued to elaborate upon the pattern he was drawing as Launcelot slowly equipped himself. The small wind continued to blow, stirring the mists. There came a flash of lightning, startling the horse. Launcelot calmed it.

Merlin stared at him for a moment and rubbed his eyes. Launcelot donned his helmet.

"For a moment," Merlin said, "you looked somehow different. . . ."

"Really? Magical withdrawal, do you think?" he asked, and he kicked the stone from the reins and mounted the stallion.

Merlin stepped back from the now completed diagram, shaking his head, as the mounted man leaned over and grasped the lance.

"You still seem to move with some strength," he said.

"Really?" Launcelot raised the lance and couched it. Before taking up the shield he had hung at the saddle's side, he opened his visor and turned and regarded Merlin.

"Your champion appears to be ready," he said. "So am I."

Seen in another flash of light, it was an unlined face that looked down at Merlin, clear-eyed, wisps of pale gold hair fringing the forehead.

"What magic have the years taught you?" Merlin asked.

"Not magic," Launcelot replied. "Caution. I anticipated you. So, when I returned to the cave for my stick, I drank the rest of your elixir."

He lowered the visor and turned away.

"You walked like an old man. . . ."

"I'd a lot of practice. Signal your champion!"

Merlin laughed.

"Good! It is better this way," he decided, "to see you go down in full strength! You still cannot hope to win against a spirit!"

Launcelot raised the shield and leaned forward.

"Then what are you waiting for?"

"Nothing!" Merlin said. Then he shouted, "Kill him, Raxas!"

A light rain began as they pounded across the field; and, staring ahead, Launcelot realized that flames were flickering behind his opponent's visor. At the last possible moment, he shifted the point of his lance into line with the hollow knight's blazing helm. There came more lightning and thunder.

His shield deflected the other's lance while his weapon went on to strike the approaching head. It flew from the hollow knight's shoulders and bounced, smouldering, on the ground.

He continued on to the other end of the field and turned. When he had, he saw that the hollow knight, now headless, was doing the same. And beyond him, he saw two standing figures, where moments before there had been but one.

Morgana le Fay, clad in a white robe, red hair unbound and blowing in the wind, faced Merlin from across his pattern. It seemed they were speaking, but he could not hear the words. Then she began to raise her hands, and they glowed like cold fire. Merlin's staff was also gleaming, and he shifted it before him. Then he saw no more, for the hollow knight was ready for the second charge.

He couched his lance, raised the shield, leaned forward and gave his mount the signal. His arm felt like a bar of iron, his strength like an endless current of electricity as he raced down the field. The rain was falling more heavily now and the lightning began a constant flickering. A steady rolling of thunder smothered the sound of the hoofbeats, and the wind whistled past his helm as he approached the other warrior, his lance centered on his shield.

They came together with an enormous crash. Both knights reeled and the hollow one fell, his shield and breastplate pierced by a broken lance. His left arm came away as he struck the earth; the lancepoint snapped and the shield fell beside him. But he began to

rise almost immediately, his right hand drawing his long sword.

Launcelot dismounted, discarding his shield, drawing his own great blade. He moved to meet his headless foe. The other struck first and he parried it, a mighty shock running down his arms. He swung a blow of his own. It was parried.

They swaggered swords across the field, till finally Launcelot saw his opening and landed his heaviest blow. The hollow knight toppled into the mud, his breastplate cloven almost to the point where the spear's shaft protruded. At that moment, Morgana le Fay screamed.

Launcelot turned and saw that she had fallen across the pattern

Merlin had drawn. The sorcerer, now bathed in a bluish light, raised his staff and moved forward. Launcelot took a step toward them and felt a great pain in his left side.

Even as he turned toward the half-risen hollow knight who was drawing his blade back for another blow, Launcelot reversed his double-handed grip upon his own weapon and raised it high, point downward.

He hurled himself upon the other, and his blade pierced the cuirass entirely as he bore him back down, nailing him to the earth. A shriek arose from beneath him, echoing within the armor, and a gout of fire emerged from the neck hole, sped upward and away, dwindled in the rain, flickered out moments later.

Launcelot pushed himself into a kneeling position. Slowly then, he rose to his feet and turned toward the two figures who again faced one another. Both were now standing within the muddied geometries of power, both were now bathed in the bluish light. Launcelot took a step toward them, then another.

"Merlin!" he called out, continuing to advance upon them. "I've done what I said I would! Now I'm coming to kill you!"

Morgana le Fay turned toward him, eyes wide.

"No!" she cried. "Depart the circle! Hurry! I am holding him here! His power wanes! In moments, this place will be no more! Go!"

Launcelot hesitated but a moment, then turned and walked as rapidly as he was able toward the circle's perimeter. The sky seemed to boil as he passed among the monoliths.

He advanced another dozen paces, then had to pause to rest. He looked back to the place of battle, to the place where the two figures still stood locked in sorcerous embrace. Then the scene was imprinted upon his brain as the skies opened and a sheet of fire fell upon the far end of the circle.

Dazzled, he raised his hand to shield his eyes. When he lowered it, he saw the stones falling, soundless, many of them fading from sight. The rain began to slow immediately. Sorcerer and sorceress had vanished along with much of the structure of the still-fading place. The horses were nowhere to be seen. He looked about him and saw a good-sized stone. He headed for it and seated himself. He unfastened his breastplate and removed it, dropping it to the ground. His side throbbed and he held it tightly. He doubled forward and rested his face on his left hand.

The rains continued to slow and finally ceased. The wind died. The mists returned.

He breathed deeply and thought back upon the conflict. This, this

THE LAST DEFENDER OF CAMELOT 55

was the thing for which he had remained after all the others, the thing for which he had waited, for so long. It was over now, and he could rest.

There was a gap in his consciousness. He was brought to awareness again by a light. A steady glow passed between his fingers, pierced his eyelids. He dropped his hand and raised his head, opening his eyes.

It passed slowly before him in a halo of white light. He removed his sticky fingers from his side and rose to his feet to follow it. Solid, glowing, glorious and pure, not at all like the image in the chamber, it led him on out across the moonlit plain, from dimness to brightness to dimness, until the mists enfolded him as he reached at last to embrace it.

HERE ENDETH THE BOOK OF LAUNCELOT,
LAST OF THE NOBLE KNIGHTS OF THE
ROUND TABLE, AND HIS ADVENTURES
WITH RAXAS, THE HOLLOW KNIGHT,
AND MERLIN AND MORGANA LE FAY,
LAST OF THE WISE FOLK OF CAMELOT,
IN HIS QUEST FOR THE SANGREAL.

QUO FAS ET GLORIA DUCUNT.

BYSTANDER
by Alan Dean Foster
art: Freff

*Chapman was on board the rescue ship
on its three-year-long interstellar trip
just in case something unexpected happened
along the way. Of course, something did.*

Sleepy . . . he was so sleepy. . . .

Existence was proven by the depth of his dreaming, dreams of endless green plains across which he ran in slow motion. The dream faded. He clutched at it as it faded. Then it was gone.

He awoke.

Chapman sighed, waited motionless and logy until his vision had cleared. Revitalizing liquids stirred in his veins. There was the expected swabby-cotton taste in his mouth, as if he hadn't swallowed in a thousand years.

The clear domed lid of his suspension lounge slid back smoothly. He unlatched one side. Moving deliberately, with muscles groggy from several years' suspension, he eased himself into a sitting position on the lounge edge and stared around the empty pilot's pocket.

All the other seats were empty. He was the sole occupant of the gigantic bulb ship. Must be in orbit around Abraxis now, he mused. In an hour or so the endangered colony there could begin shuttling its members aboard. Then he could turn over responsibility to the colony leaders.

That was the second dream to be shattered.

"Position?"

"We are slightly more than five standard days out from Abraxis," replied the even voice of the ship's computer, as though it had last spoken to him only yesterday and not three years ago. Chapman considered this unexpected news, forced his so long unused tongue and palate to work.

"Then why have I been awakened now?" Not that a few days wakefulness would hurt him, but there was no reason for early revivification. No programmed reason, he reminded himself.

"We are presently being paralleled by a Dhabian," the ship explained, "and there . . ."

"Scope first." Chapman curtly interrupted the computer. He drew a globe of energized water from the lounge dispenser, squeezed it down his throat.

Obediently, the ship complied with the order. A small viewscreen set into the emergency pilot's console flickered alight. Displayed on the screen was a massive cluster of red-orange blocks. The blocks were connected according to some elegantly inhuman design to form a ship. A Dhabian ship.

Earthmen had encountered the Dhabians over two decades ago. Since that time the relationship between the two races had been an uncertain one. Mankind's curiosity about the Dhabians was met with what was best described as cordial indifference on the aliens' part. Since the Dhabian vessels, for all their ungainly appearance, were faster than those of men, the aliens' privacy had thus far remained inviolate.

Whenever one of the infrequent encounters between human and Dhabian ships did occur, the Dhabians would sometimes communicate and sometimes not. They were never hostile, only uninterested. It was hinted that they had much of value to offer mankind. But neither pleading, threatening, nor a matching indifference had managed to inspire them to talk.

No one had ever seen an individual Dhabian. Chapman couldn't repress a slight thrill of excitement. Maybe he would be the first.

Yet the silent Dhabian was a known factor. The presence of one did not constitute a sufficient reason for revivification. He told his ship as much.

The ship proceeded to tell him about the new flare.

Flares were the reason for his hastily programmed mission. Astronomers had predicted several years ago that the Abraxis colony would have to be evacuated from its world at least temporarily because its sun was about to go through a period of brief but intense activity. That activity would produce enough high-energy radiation to kill any human on Abraxis's surface, or even slightly beneath it.

For the four to six months of dangerous stellar activity, the population would have to live aboard a rescue ship. This information being communicated to the proper authorities, a properly prepared and provisioned vessel was dispatched with barely enough time to arrive and take on the population before the onset of threatening activity.

What was the problem, then? Were the astronomers wrong? No, the ship informed him, the figures given were correct. The cycle of stellar outbursts was not beginning dangerously early. This new flare was an anomaly, a freak not accounted for in the earlier predictions. It would not endanger the colony, safe beneath its amorphous atmospheric shielding.

However, it would be severe enough to critically damage certain vital components and instruments. The bulb ship would be crippled beyond hope of performing its mission. Incidentally, Chapman would die.

"When?" the dazed pilot muttered.

"Twenty-four to forty-eight hours from now." The reply was quiet. The ship was sophisticated enough to take its pilot's emotional state into consideration and generate appropriate vocoder impulses in response.

Chapman requested more information. In the time remaining to him, the bulb ship could not flee far enough to escape the crippling burst of energy from the star. Nor could he reach the sheltering darkside of the colony world.

"Check computations." The ship did so, repeated what was already known to be inevitable. "Check again."

It was no good. Wishing had no effect on the realities of physics. Hoping failed to reduce either the critical distance to Abraxis or the number of energetic particles the star would generate. Chapman considered thoughtfully, analytically. The mission, then, would fail. The two thousand settlers, scientists, and technicians on the colony world would not be rescued in time. They would die. He would die a little sooner. And he was at once frightened and ashamed, because the last item of the two was the more important to him.

A light winked on on his console: an incoming call for position from the still distant world. An automatic relay would reply to personal curiosity.

"The Dhabian ship," he inquired. "Will it be able to escape the effects of the flare, based on what we know of their abilities?"

A pause, then, "Barring as yet undemonstrated speed, predictions are that it cannot."

He might have company, then. "Offer them the standard 'exchange of information request', ship." It would be interesting to learn if they were doomed, too. They seemed to be if his ship was right and they didn't possess some extraordinary particle shielding. Maybe they'd come to the Abraxis system to study the activity of its star prior to eruption and had been shocked and trapped by the same coming, unexpected burst of radiation which would finish him.

Anyway, it was something to do. The idea of returning to suspension, to await the end in ignorance, appalled him.

He did not really expect the alien to reply. He was surprised when a voice of oddly modulated tone whispered at him from the speaker. *"We will exchange with you, man."*

"This star will soon generate a burst of highly charged plasma which will be fatal to me." After a moment's thought, he added, "My ship will also be severely damaged."

"Information." The response was Dhabian-brief. *"No query?"*

"What will happen to you?"

"Will with us be the same as with you, man."

The first intimation of Dhabian mortality, Chapman mused. He felt no elation at the discovery. No one else would learn what he might discover here.

"There's no way you can survive? I thought your ships were fast."

"Not enough. But there may be a way." What seemed an uncertain pause before the Dhabian spoke again. *"You have not detected it?"*

"Detected what?" Chapman was more confused than excited.

"The onu."

"What the hell's an . . . ?" Chapman calmed himself. "Can you give me position?"

"Your figurings correspond not well, but from what we have learned," and the Dhabian shot some figures at him.

"Ship? What do they mean?"

"A moment, Chapman." He imagined he could hear the machine thinking . . . too long in suspension, he thought. "Using maximum amplification focused on region given by alien vessel, it is determined that a large though faint object is indeed located in the position suggested. Alien mass sensors must be more efficient/powerful than our own. Present position precludes visual identification of comet from this angle of observation."

"Comet? Question, ship. Is it big enough to provide adequate protection from the anticipated flare?"

"Yes, Chapman."

"Second question: is it big enough to provide shielding for *both* vessels?"

"Some delicate close-range maneuvering by each ship to prevent damage from the other's exhaust particles will be required. It can be done. But there is a difficulty."

Chapman's hopes scattered like children at playtime. "What difficulty?"

"Drive time to cometary umbra estimated at thirty-nine hours."

"We are going, man," the Dhabian informed him. *"Shall we prepare to adjust position to accommodate your own ship?"*

Chapman considered very quickly. Thirty-nine hours was stretching the upper limits of the time allotted before the expected stellar flare. In thirty-nine hours he could be a good deal further out than the comet's position. Yet his computer informed him he would still be well inside the fatal radius of the flare radiation.

It was an easy gamble to take.

"Yes, I'm trying for it too." The Dhabian apparently accepted this without replying.

"Ship, adjust position to place us behind the cometary nucleus. Keep heading of the Dhabian in mind."

"I will be careful, Chapman," the ship replied confidently.

The ensuing hours passed busily. Studying and recording the

Dhabian vessel as it moved past and ahead of him at close range would provide a great deal that xenologists would find of value. It also kept his mind pretty much off his slim chances. After the twenty-four-hour limit passed and he knew the flare could occur at any time he found himself working ever more intensely.

It was a large comet, all right. At least fifteen kilometers across the head. At thirty-two hours he had his closest glimpse of the Dhabian ship. It was eight hundred meters long, a hundred less than his own craft, but far more massive. It passed ahead of him, racing at its greater speed for the sheltering safety of the cometary bulk.

At thirty-five hours he permitted himself to hope a little. At thirty-six he was planning a full report to the Commission on his narrow escape.

At thirty-seven hours the ship told him he would be too late.

"Surface stellar activity is already showing signs of impending eruption, Chapman. If local conditions do not change, we will arrive behind the cometary nucleus one hour twenty-two minutes ten seconds too late."

"What's the maximum we can take flare radiation for without sustaining irreparable damage to the ship?" Somewhat to his surprise he did not ask about himself.

"Ten and a half minutes."

That was it, then. Drowning, he'd been tossed a rope, and it had fallen short. He turned, let himself collapse in the chair opposite the main viewscreen. His head slumped forward, cradled in the crook of his right arm, to rest close by the cool metal.

He knew the fire would singe his wings, but it was so beautiful, so clean. Just a little closer, that was all, just a little closer. Through the quiet roar of the flames he thought he could hear the computer babbling precisely at him. Which was absurd. Computers did not talk to moths. Computers did not babble. He ignored the meaningless noises, dipped closer to the beckoning succubus. Fiery fingers touched his wings.

He woke up sweating.

And that was wrong. Very wrong. He couldn't have fallen asleep for more than a few hours, he felt. Even so, he had no business being awake and alive. He ought to be dead, snuffed out in a single incendiary *poof*, like a moth in a furnace. He blinked, looked around wildly.

"Ship! The flare, what . . . ?"

"Commencing countdown to arrival of first energetic particles," the computer said calmly. "Twenty, nineteen, eighteen. . . ."

Chapman stared dully at the viewscreen, tried to comprehend what he saw. To one side drifted an object that seemed assembled from the remnants of some ancient construct: the Dhabian ship, its quiescent drive glowing blue-white. Ahead was a dim green mass that as he watched concluded eclipsing the sun of Abraxis: the backside of the comet. In the reflected light from his own bulb ship it shone icy green and sharp. One moment it appeared solid, the next shifting and unstable.

"Four, three, two, one. . . ." The computer concluded. Chapman sucked in a startled breath.

The coma, the thick gaseous envelope which surrounded the cometary head, was shining so brilliantly it almost hurt him to look at it. The tenuous ribbons of gases and particles streaming back all around both ships took on a vibrant, purplish-red hue. In the storm raging off the surface of the star ahead, the streamers assumed a near-solid look, like the silken veil of a Spanish dancer.

While the view from several million miles away would have been even more impressive, there was something in the knowledge that he was *inside* the comet's tail which made him feel very small.

For five and a half hours the two ships rode the lee of the comet. Fiery colors danced around them. Devastating energy sheeted against the head of the comet, producing beauty instead of death.

Then the computer announced that the level of stellar radiation was dropping rapidly. Soon it fell to an acceptable level. At the same time the Dhabian ship began to move. It passed beyond and through the subdued but still dramatic cometary flow before Chapman thought to consider what had happened to him.

His ship could not have reached the safe position behind the comet by itself. Therefore the Dhabians had somehow helped him. Why?

"Initiate request for information, ship!"

After a moment, "They do not respond, Chapman." The alien vessel continued to move away.

"Try again!"

The computer did so, several times more before Chapman spoke directly into the pocket's pickup. "Dhabians! Why? Why save me? I owe you. Two thousand and one owe you." Silence, as the great blocky ship continued to recede from him on the screen. "Why don't you respond? Answer!"

A lilting, stilted voice. *"Multiple query inappropriate. Query elsewhere. Nothing here, man."*

Try as he would, Chapman was unable to elicit further commu-

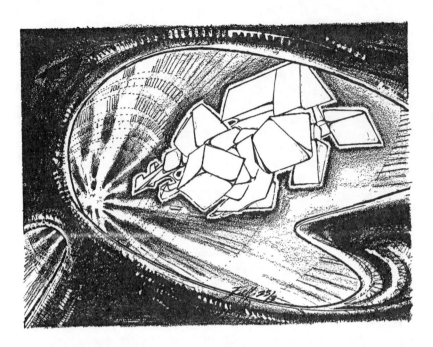

nication from the alien.

Several weeks later, when the colony had been transferred easily and safely on board the ship and they were well out of the Abraxis system, it occurred to Chapman to ask hesitantly of his computer, "Ship, the Dhabians saved us and I don't know why. Do *you* know *how* they accelerated us in time to get us safely behind the comet?"

"Question inappropriate, Chapman." He frowned.

"Why?"

"No evidence to show Dhabian vessel affected our motion in any way."

He felt a little dizzy. Relief, he decided, and too many days on stimulants to stay awake. "What do you mean? If the Dhabians didn't adjust our velocity, then how did we get behind the nucleus?"

"Dhabians occupied fully with own maneuvers," came the reply. "Evidence indicates that comet shifted position to place us within its umbra. Dhabians had to slow, not accelerate, to match altered cometary position."

"You mean the Dhabians moved the *comet*?"

"Negative, Chapman. No evidence to support such hypothesis."

"But the comet changed position."

"Correct."

"That's impossible," he said with finality.

"Event occurred." The computer sounded slightly diffident.

Chapman considered. His eyes grew very wide. Then he raced through the ship until he located its present commander, colony-leader Otasu. The colony-leader was chatting with several other colony officials in the cramped confines of the pilot's pocket. He looked up uncertainly at Chapman's anxious entrance.

Chapman went immediately to the viewscreen. It showed only a view of star-speckled space and the slightly brighter distant spot of Abraxis' sun.

"We've got to go back, sir."

"Go back? We can't go back, Chapman, you know that." Poor fellow, he thought. Suspension does funny things to men. "Our sun's entered its eruption cycle. We'd all be fried."

Query elsewhere, the Dhabian had said before going finally silent. *Elsewhere, elsewhere* . . . where else had there been to query? The comet had changed position. . . .

"Fifteen hours," he mumbled, staring at the screen. "Fifteen hours."

"Fifteen hours for what?" prompted the colony-leader kindly, humoring the hyper emergency pilot. Chapman's face did not look up from the screen.

"I had fifteen hours during flare-time and I used it to make observations and notes about the Dhabian." He sounded numb.

"And very valuable observations, I'm told," acknowledged Otasu, trying his best to sound calming and approving.

"But you don't understand!" Chapman stared harder at the screen. The comet was back there, somewhere, moving about in the way of comets; and what did they know about comets, after all? Very little, very little.

"I spent fifteen hours studying the wrong alien. . . ."

CAPTIVE OF THE CENTAURIANESS
by Poul Anderson
art: Alex Schomburg

The hero is the child of his times, in that his milieu gives him his motives and means. Yet he seizes the world as he finds it and reshapes it as he will; and he remains eternally an enigma to his contemporaries and to the future.

Nowhere is this better illustrated than in the famous but ever strange story of the three whose discoveries and achievements, late in the twenty-third century, set entire races of beings upon wholly new courses. The driving idealism and military genius of Dyann Korlas; the wisdom, mighty, profound, and benign, of Urushkidan; above all, perhaps, the inspired leadership of Tallantyre—these molded history, but we will never truly understand them. The persons who embodied them are still further beyond us. The essential selves of the glorious three will always be mysterious.

—Vallabhai Rasmussen,
Origins of the Galactic Era

I.

Floodlit, the tender loomed against night, above the swarm of humanity, like a great golden bullet. Ray Tallantyre quickened his steps. By George and dragon both, he'd made it! The flight from San Francisco to Quito, the nail-gnawing wait for an airbus, the ride to the spaceport, the walk through a terminal building that seemed to stretch on forever—all were outlived and there she was, there the darling stood, ready to carry him up to the *Jovian Queen* and safety.

He kissed his fingers at the craft and shoved rudely through the crowd. He'd already missed the first trip up to the liner, and the thought of standing around till the third was beyond endurance.

"Hey, you."

As the voice fell on his ears, a hand did on his arm. Ray could have sworn he felt his heart slam against his teeth and his spine fall out of his trousers. Somehow he turned around. A large man was comparing his thin features with a photograph held in the unoccupied paw. "Yes, it's you, all right," this person said. "Come along, Tallantyre."

"*¡Me llama Garcia!*" the fugitive gibbered. "*No hablo inglés.*"

"I said come along," the detective answered. "We figured you'd try to leave Earth. This way."

Sometimes desperation breeds inspiration. Ray's own free hand crammed the fellow's hat down over his eyes. Wrenching loose, he bolted for the gangramp. En route, he upset a corpulent lady. A volley of Latin imprecations pursued him. Shoving aside another

CAPTIVE OF THE CENTAURIANESS

passenger, he sped up the incline—and bounced off the wall which was a Jovian officer.

"Your ticket and passport, please," said that man. He was a tall, muscular blond, crisply white-uniformed, who regarded the new arrival with the thinly veiled contempt of a true Confed for the lesser breeds of life.

Ray shoved the documents at him, meanwhile staring backward. The detective had gotten entangled with the lady, who was beating him around the head with her purse and volubly cursing him. Agonizingly deliberate, the Jovian scanned the engineer's papers, checked them against a list, and waved him on.

The detective won free, followed, and struck the same immovable barrier. "Your ticket and passport, please," said the ship's representative.

"That man's under arrest," panted the detective. "Let me by."

"Your ticket and passport, please."

"I tell you I'm an officer of the law and I have a warrant for that man. Let me by!"

"Proper authorization may be obtained at the security center," said the immovable barrier. The detective tried to rush, encountered a bit of expert judo, and tumbled back into a line of passengers who also grew indignant with him. Every able-bodied Jovian was a military reservist.

"Proper authority may be obtained at the security center," the gatekeeper repeated. To the next person: "Your ticket and passport, please."

In the airlock chamber, Ray Tallantyre dashed the sweat off his brow and permitted himself a laugh. By the time his pursuer had gone through all the red tape, he himself would be on the space liner. Before one of his own country's secret police, the ship's officer would have quailed. However, this was Earth; and the Confeds loved to bait agents of the Terrestrial government; and there was no better way than by putting the victims through channels. Where it came to devising these, the bureaucracy of the Confederated Satellites of Jupiter was beyond compare.

Being in orbit, the vessel counted as Jovian territory; and Ray's alleged offense did not rate extradition.

He went on inside, was shown to a seat, and secured the harness. He was clear! No matter how long, the arm of the Vanbrugh family did not reach as far as he was bound. He could stay till the whole business had blown over. To be sure, he might have difficulty getting a job meanwhile, but he'd worry about that when the time came.

Always did want to see the Jovian System anyway, he rationalized.

Sighing, he tried to relax: a medium-sized, wiry young man with close-cropped yellow hair and a countenance a little too sharp to be handsome. Likewise, his scarf was overly colorful, his jacket a trifle extravagantly flared.

The last passenger boarded. The lock valves closed. A stewardess went down the aisle handing out cookies which, Ray knew, contained medication to prevent space sickness. She had the full-bodied Caucasoid good looks of the ideal Jovian together with the faintly repellent air of total efficiency. "No, thanks," he said. "I've been out before. Acceleration and free fall don't bother me."

"The cookies are compulsory," she told him, and watched while he ate his. A throbbing went through the vessel as the engine came to life; outside the hull, a warning siren hooted.

He turned to the passenger beside him, obsessed with the idiotic desire for conversation found in most recent escapers from the law or the dentist. "Going home, I see," he remarked.

That person sat tall in the gray Jovian army uniform, colonel's planets on his shoulders and a haberdashery of ribbons across his chest. He looked about forty-five years old, Terrestrial, though his shaven pate made it hard to estimate; Ray gauged by the deep facial creases running down to the craggy jaw. Fixing the Earthling with a glacier-pale eye, he responded: "And you, I see, are leaving home. Two scintillating deductions." Though English was his mother tongue also—the one on which his polyglot ancestors had agreed even before the Symmetrist Revolution laid a single ideology on them—he made it sound as if it had been issued him.

"Um-m-m, uh, well," said Ray and looked elsewhere, his ears ablaze. The Jovian clutched tighter to his side the large briefcase he bore.

Announcements and orders resounded. The spacecraft shivered, howled, and sprang into the sky. Ray let acceleration pressure push him back into the cushions; the seat flattened itself into a couch; he gazed upward through a viewport and saw splendor unfold, stars and stars and stars, blackness well-nigh crowded out of sight by brilliance. His companion declined to recline.

The boost did not take long, then they were on trajectory and the *Jovian Queen* appeared. At first the liner was a mere needle to see, shimmery-blue by the light of the Earth she was orbiting. Soon she was close by, and the sun struck her as she swung clear of the planet's shadow cone, and she became huge and radiant. Despite her weight-giving spin, the tender made smooth contact. Whatever you could say against the Jovians—and some people said quite a bit—they did maintain the best transport in the Solar System. Every national fleet on Earth and most private companies were finding it nearly impossible to compete.

The stewardess directed the passengers through joined airlocks and toward their quarters. She promised that luggage would be delivered "in due course." That reminded Ray that he'd checked in a single tiny suitcase containing little but a few changes of clothing. And his third-class ticket meant that he'd have to share a cabin, which it would be ludicrous to call a stateroom, with two others. The decline and fall of the Tallantyre credit account was so depressing a subject that the pseudo-gravity, low though it was, bowed his shoulders; and, forgetting to allow for Coriolis force, he bruised a toe as he rounded a corner in the passage. Well and good to have gotten away from Earth free, he thought; but he'd hit Ganymede damn near broke, and he hadn't really considered as yet how he was going to survive there. This had simply been the sole destination in space for which he could get a ticket at exceedingly short notice. . . .

A number identified the door assigned him. He opened it.

"Put—me—down!"

Ray gaped at the spectacle of a Martian struggling in the clutch of a woman two meters tall.

"Put—me—down!" the Martian spluttered again. He had coiled his limbs snakelike around her arms and torso, and the four thick walking tentacles were formidably strong. She didn't seem to notice, but laughed and shook him a bit.

"I beg your pardon," Ray gasped and backed away.

"You are forgiven," the woman replied in a husky contralto with a lilting accent. She shot out one Martian-encumbered hand, grabbed him by the jacket, and hauled him inside. "You be the yudge, my friend. Is it not yustice that I have the lo'er berth?"

"It is noting of te sort!" screamed the Martian. He fixed the newcomer with round, bulging, indignant yellow eyes. "My position, my eminence, clearly entitle me to ebery consideration, and ten tis hulking monster—"

The Earthling's gaze traveled up and down the woman's form before he said softly, "I think you'd better accept the lady's generous offer. But, uh, I seem to have the wrong cabin."

"Is your name Ray Tallantyre?" she asked.

He pleaded guilty.

"Then you belon vith us. I have asked about the passenyer list. You may have the sofa for sleepin."

"Th-thanks." Ray sat down on it. His knees felt loose.

The Martian gave up the struggle and allowed the woman to place him on the upper bunk. "To tink of it," he squeaked. "Tat I, Urushkidan of Ummunashektaru, should be manhandled by a sabage who does not know a logaritm from an elliptic integral!"

Astounded, Ray stared as if this were the first of the race that he had met in his life. Urushkidan's gray-skinned cupola of a body balanced 120 centimeters tall on the walking tentacles; above them, two slim, three-fingered arms writhed bonelessly on either side of a wide, lipless mouth. Elephantine ears and flat nose supported a pair of horn-rimmed spectacles, his only garb except for a poisonously green vest full of pockets with all kinds of things in them.

"Not *the* Urushkidan?" Ray breathed—the mathematician acclaimed throughout the Solar System as a latter-day Gauss or Einstein.

"Tere is only *one* Urushkidan," the Martian informed him.

For a moment of total irrelevance, Ray's rocking mind wondered how different history might have been if the first probes to Mars hadn't happened to land in two of the Great Barrens—if civilizations upon that world had gone in for agriculture or architecture identifiable by instruments in orbit—if, even, the weird biochemistry of the natives had been unable to endure Terrestrial conditions—

A Homeric shout of laughter brought him back to what he must suppose was reality. The woman uttered it where she loomed over him. "Velcome, male Tallantyre," she cried. "You are cute. I think I vill like you. I am Dyann Korlas of Kathantuma." She took his hand in a friendly grip.

He yelped and got it back not quite crushed. "You're one of the Centaurians, then," he said feebly.

"Yes, so you call us."

He found himself regarding her with some pleasure, overwhelming though her presence was. Hitherto he had only see her kind on television.

Except for the pointed ears, which her braids concealed, she looked human enough externally, albeit not of any stock which had ever evolved on Earth. The similarities extended to all the most interesting areas, he knew. Memories came back to him of scientific arguments he had read as to whether this was mere coincidence or whether form had to follow function that closely on every globe of a given type. There were plenty of internal differences, of course, among them being bone and flesh which were considerably harder and denser than his. Alpha Centauri A III—or Varann, as its most advanced nation had decided to name it after learning from the first Solar expedition that it was a planet—had, among other striking non-resemblances to his world, half again the surface gravity.

Her size reminded him of alienness which went deeper than appearance. Men of her race were smaller and weaker than women. In every known culture, they stayed home and did the housework while their wives conducted public business. In warlike Kathantuma and its neighbor lands, public business usually meant raids on somebody else with the objective of stealing everything that wasn't bolted down.

Nevertheless, this . . . Dyann Korlas . . . was well worth staring at. She was built like a statuesque tigress. Her skin was smooth and golden-hued. Bronze hair coiled heavy around a face which would have inspired an ancient Hellenic sculptor; but exotic touches, such as a slight tilt to the big, storm-gray eyes, made it look not only Classical but sexy. Her outfit consisted of a knee-length tunic, sandals, a form-fitting steel cuirass with twin demonic visages sculptured on the bust, a round helmet decorated with bat-like bronze wings, a belt upholding purse and sheath knife, and a sword which Lancelot might have reckoned just a trifle too heavy.

Ray found his voice: "Are you sure I belong in this cabin? Hasn't somebody made a mistake?"

She grinned. "Oh, you are safe."

He recalled that the titles of aristocrats in her home country translated into expressions like "chief," "district ruler," "warrior," and the like. A few males had accompanied the Centaurian ladies to the Solar System. Arrogantly indifferent to details of ethnology, the Jovians must have assumed from her honorific, whatever it was—doubtless written down on her behalf by some Extraterrestrial Secretariat underling told off to assist these visitors—that she was among those males.

Well, why should Ray Tallantyre disabuse the ship's officers? The overworked third-class steward wasn't likely to care, or perhaps even notice. Not that the Earthling expected any action with his cabin mate, especially in Urushkidan's presence. Indeed, the idea was somewhat terrifying. However, from time to time the view in here ought to get quite nice. They had no nudity taboo in Kathantuma.

Reminded of the Martian and his manners, Ray glanced toward the upper berth. Urushkidan was morosely stuffing a big-bowled pipe. Tobacco-smoking was a vice on which his race had eagerly seized; they didn't exactly breathe, but by the bellows-and-membrane organ which they also used to form human speech, they could keep the fire going. They usually described the sensation as "tinglesome."

"Uh, sir, I'd like to say I know of your work," the human ventured. "In fact, since I am—was—a nucleonic engineer, I can appreciate what it means."

The Martian inflated his body, his way of smiling or preening. "Doubtless you habe grasped it quite well," he replied graciously. "As well as any Eartling could, which is, of course, saying bery little."

"But if I may ask, uh, what are you doing here?"

"Oh, I habe a lecture series arranged at te Jobian Academy of Sciences. Tey are quite commendably aware of my importance. I will be glad to get off Eart. Te air pressure, te grabity, pfui!"

"But a . . . a person . . . of your distinction, traveling third class—"

"Naturally, tey gabe me a first-class ticket. I turned it in, bought a tird-class, and banked te difference." He glowered at Dyann Korlas. "To' if I am treated like tis—" He shrugged. A Martian shrugging is quite a sight. "No real matter. We of Uttu—Mars, as you insist on calling it—are so incomparably far adbanced in te philosophic birtues of serenity, generosity, and modesty tat I can accept barbaric mistreatment wit te scorn tat it deserbes."

"Oh," said Ray. To the Centaurianess: "And may I ask why you are bound for Jupiter, Ms.—Ms.?—Korlas?"

"You may," she allowed. "And let us use first names, no? That is sveet. . . . Vell, I vish to see Yupiter, though I do not think it vill be as glamorous as Earth." She sighed. "You live in a fable! Your beastless carriages, your flyin machines, your auto—auto-*matic* kitchens, your clocks, your colorful clothes, your qvaint customs—*haa*, it vas vorth the long travel yust to see such things."

Long, for certain; fantastically powerful though they were, the exploratory ships needed ten years to cross the interstellar gulf, and there had only been three expeditions to date. Dyann had arrived with the latest, part of a delegation and inquiry group dispatched by her queen. Ray had heard that the crew had quite a time with that turbulent score until everybody settled down in suspended animation. The visitors had now spent about a year on Earth and Luna, endlessly curious, especially as to what their hosts did to pass the time since the World Union had arisen to terminate the practice of war. By and large, they'd caused remarkably little trouble. A couple of times tempers had flared and Terrestrial bones gotten broken, but the Varannians were always apologetic afterward. To be sure, once one of them had been scheduled to address a women's club. . . .

"Tell me this I am not clear about," Dyann requested. "The Yovians, they did begin on your planet?"

Ray nodded. "Yes. They colonized the moons partly for economic reasons, partly because they didn't like the way Europe was becoming homogenized, Asian and African immigrants were getting numerous, and so on. About sixty years ago, they declared their independence. After a lot of debate, the leaders of Earth decided the issue wasn't worth fighting about. That may have been a mistake."

"Vy?"

"M-m-m . . . well, it's true they had certain economic grievances, after the heroic work their pioneers had done—and they themselves are still doing, I must admit. Nevertheless, they live under a dictatorship that keeps telling them they're the destined masters of the Solar System. Last year they occupied and claimed the Saturnian moon colonies. Their pretext was almighty thin, but the Union was too chicken-livered to do more than squawk. Not that it has much of a navy compared to theirs."

Dyann beamed. "Ha, you might really have a var vile I am here to see? Lovely, lovely!" She clapped her hands.

A knock on the door interrupted, and the steward bore in the luggage marked "Wanted on Voyage." When he was gone, the cabin occupants got busy unpacking and stowing. Dyann changed into a fur-trimmed robe, confirming Ray's guess that the scenery was gorgeous. Urushkidan slithered to the deck, extracted from his trunk several books, papers, penstyls, and a humidor, and appropriated the dresser top for these.

Unease touched Ray. "You know, sir," he said, "apart from the honor of meeting you, I wish you weren't aboard."

"Why not?" demanded the Martian huffily.

"U-u-uh-h . . . it was your formulation of general relativity that showed it's possible to travel faster than light."

"Among many oter tings, yes," said Urushkidan through malodorous clouds.

"I can't believe the Jovians are interested in your work for its own sake. I suspect they hope to get your guidance in developing that kind of ship. Then we'd all better beware."

"Not I. A Martian is not concerned wit te squabbles of te lower animals. Noting personal, you understand."

Dyann took forth a small wooden image and placed it on the shelf above her bunk. It was gaudily painted and fiercely tusked; each of its arms held a weapon, one being a Terrestrial tommy gun. "Qviet, please," she said, raising an arm. "I am about to pray to Ormun the Terrible."

"An appropriate god for the likes of you," sneered Urushkidan.

She stuffed a pillow from the bunk into his mouth. "Qviet, please, I said," she reproached him with a gentle smile, and prostrated herself before the idol.

After a while, during which she had chanted a prayer full of snarling noises, she got up. Urushkidan was still speechless, with rage. Dyann turned to Ray. "Do you know if this ship has any live animals for sale?" she asked. "I vould like to make a sacrifice too."

II.

After the *Jovian Queen* got under way, her captain announced that, given the present planetary configuration, she would complete her passage, at a steady one Terrestrial gee of positive and negative acceleration, in six standard days, 43 minutes, and 12 ± 10 seconds. That might be braggadocio, though Ray Tallantyre would not have been surprised to learn it was sober truth. He soon started wishing the time would prove overestimated. His roommates wore on his nerves. Urushkidan filled the place with smoke, sat up till all hours covering paper with mathematical symbols, and screamed if anybody spoke above a whisper. Dyann meant well, but limited vocabulary soon caused her conversation to pall; besides, she was mostly off in the gymnasium, working out. When she wasn't, her forcefulness often reminded him of Katrina Vanbrugh, occasioning shudders.

On the second day out, he slouched moodily into the bar and ordered a martini he could ill afford. The ship's food was so wholesome that he wasn't sure he could choke any more down otherwise. The chamber was quiet except for Wagnerian music in the background, discreetly enough lit that the murals of pioneers and soldiers weren't too conspicuous, and not very full. At one table sat the colonel who had accompanied Ray aloft, still clutching his briefcase but talking with quite human animation to a red-headed female tourist from Earth. Her shape, in a skin-tight StarGlo gown, left small doubt as to his objective. The purity of the Jovian race, "hardened in the fire and ice of the outer deeps, tempered by adversity to form the new and dominant mankind," had been set aside for a while in favor of international relations.

She didn't look as fascinated as she might have. *If I had some money,* sighed within Ray, *I bet I could pry her loose from him.*

For lack of that possibility, he fell into conversation with the bartender. The latter informed him, in awed tones, that yonder he beheld Colonel Ivan Hosea Domenico Roshevsky-Feldkamp, late military attaché of the Confederation's Terrestrial embassy, an officer who had served with distinction in suppressing the Ionian revolt and in asserting his nation's rightful claims to Saturn.

Things got livelier when a couple of fellows entered from second class. North Americans like Ray, they were quick to make his acquaintance and ready to stand him drinks. After an hour or two, they suggested a friendly game of poker.

Oh, ho! thought the engineer, who was less naïve than he often appeared. "Sure," he agreed. "How about right after dinner?"

Joined by a third of their kind, they met him in a proper stateroom and play commenced. It went on for most of the following two days and evenings. Fortune went back and forth in a way that would have impressed the average person as genuine. Ray kept track, and made occasional bets that ought to have proven disastrous, and when he was alone ran off statistical analyses on his calculator. He was winning entirely too much, and the rate of it was increasing on far too steep a curve. These genial chaps were setting him up for disaster.

When he was a couple of thousand Union credits to the good, he let febrile cupidity glitter from him and said, "Look, boys, you know I'm traveling on the cheap, but I do have money at home and this game is too good for kiddie antes. Suppose I lase my bank to transfer some credit to the purser's office here, and tomorrow we can play for real stakes."

"Sure, Ray, if you want," said the lead shark, delighted to have the suggestion made for him. "You're a sport, you are."

At the appointed hour, he and his companions met again around the table, lit anticipatory cigars, and waited.

And waited.

And waited.

Ray had found the redhead remarkably easy to pry loose from the colonel.

She thought it would be great fun to go slumming and join him in the third-class dining room for the captain's dinner. First class was too stuffy, she said. He escorted her down a corridor, thinking wistfully, and a trifle wearily, that soon the trip would end and he'd disembark in Wotanopolis as broke as ever. She'd made him free of the luxury and spaciousness of her section, but since he avoided the bar—and possible embarrassing confrontations therein—she tacitly assumed that he would pay for refreshments ordered from the staff. Besides, she liked to gamble, and the ship's casino was not rigged.

The sight of Urushkidan distracted him from his generally pleasant recollections. Awkward under Earth weight, the Martian was creeping along toward the saloon reserved for his species; the choice between mealtime segregation and decorum by either standard had been made long ago. He condescended to give the human a greeting: "Well, tere you are. I hope you habe not been found obnoxious."

The trouble actually began with Dyann Korlas, who appeared a moment later in finery of leather boots, fur kilt, gold armbands, necklace of raw gemstones, and polychromatic body paint. Striding up behind Ray, she clapped a hand on his shoulder which almost felled him.

"Vere have you been?" she asked reproachfully. "You vent avay, and you vere so long."

The redhead blushed.

"Oh, hello," Ray said, feeling a touch awkward himself. "What have you been up to?"

Dyann's glance scuttled back and forth. "I think better ve ask vat you have been up to," she laughed. "Ah, you dashin, glamorous Earthmen!"—looking down on him by about fifteen centimeters. She pushed in between him and his date, amiably linking arms with both. "Come, ve go feed together, no?"

They reached the companionway leading to the dining room, and there stood three much too familiar figures. Ray felt a thunderbolt go through his head. He'd not counted on this.

"Hey, Tallantyre!" exclaimed the largest of his poker buddies. Somehow the entire trio seemed bigger than before. "What the hell happened to you? We were going to have another game, remember?"

"I forgot," Ray said around a lump in his gullet.

"Aw, you couldn't've," another man replied. "Look, a sport like you wouldn't quit when he's way ahead, would you?"

"We still got time for a session," added the third.

"But I don't have any more money," Ray protested.

"Now, wait a minute, pal," said the largest. "You want to be a good sport, don't you? Sure you do. You don't want to make any trouble. It wouldn't be good for you, believe me."

The trio crowded close. Backed against the bulkhead, Ray stared past them. Passengers on their way to dinner ignored the unpleasantness, as people generally do. An exception was, of all possible individuals, Colonel Roshevsky-Feldkamp. Though his table was in first class, he must have been getting a drink in the bar—or was his presence more significant than that? Certainly he stood and watched with his iron features tinged by smugness.

Did he put these gullyhanses up to accosting me? Ray wondered wildly. *He could very well be bearing a grudge and—and—would this kind of threat be possible without some kind of* sub rosa *hint that the ship's officers won't interfere?*

"Now why don't you come on back to my cabin and we'll talk about this," proposed the largest. Three tight grins moved in on the engineer. The redhead squeaked and shrank aside.

Dyann scowled and touched the hilt of her sword. "Are these men annoyin you, Ray?" she asked.

"Oh, no, we just want a quiet little private talk with our friend," said the chief card player. He closed a meaty hand on the engineer's arm and tugged. "You come along now, okay, Tallantyre?"

Ray ran a dried-out tongue over unsteady lips. "Dyann," he mumbled, "I think they are starting to annoy me."

"Oh, vell, in that case—" She grinned happily, reached out, and took hold of the nearest man.

Something like a small explosion followed. The man went whirling aloft, struck the overhead, caromed off a bulkhead, hit the deck, and bounced a couple of times more before lying stunned.

Almost by reflex, his companions had attacked the amazon. "Ormun is kind!" she shouted in joy and gave one a mouthful of knuckles. Teeth flew.

The third had gotten behind her. He plucked the dagger from her belt and raised it. Ray seized his wrist. Bigger and stronger, he tore loose with a force that sent the engineer staggering, and followed. Ray lurched against Roshevsky-Feldkamp. Without thought for anything except a weapon to use when the knife confronted him, he yanked the colonel's briefcase free, raised it in both hands, and brought it down on his enemy's head. It made a dull *thwack* and stopped the gambler in his tracks. Ray hit him again. The briefcase burst open and papers snowed through the air. Then Dyann, having put her second opponent out of the game, turned to this third and proceeded with martial arts practice.

Save for the redhead, who had departed screaming, spectators milled about at a respectful distance. Now Roshevsky-Feldkamp advanced from among them, livid. "I'm terribly sorry, sir," gasped

Ray, who didn't think he needed such a personage angry at him. "Here, let me help—"

He went to his knees and began to collect scattered papers and stuff them back into the briefcase. In a dazed fashion he noticed that a number of them bore diagrams of apparatus. A polished boot took him in the rear. He skidded through the mass of documents. "You unutterable idiot!" Roshevsky-Feldkamp yelled.

"You vould hurt my friend?" Dyann said indignantly. "I vill teach you better manners."

The colonel drew his revolver. "Stand where you are," he snapped. "You are both under arrest."

Dyann's broad smooth shoulders sagged. "Oh," she said in a meek voice. "Let me yust carry him"—she pointed at the gambler who was totally unconscious—"for a doctor to see." Bending over, she picked him up.

"March," the Jovian ordered her.

"Yes, sir," she said, and tossed her burden at him. He went over on his backside. She kicked him in the belly and he too lost interest in further combat.

"That vas fun," she chuckled. "Vat shall ve do next?"

"You," said Urushkidan acidly, "are a typical human."

Through the open door of a cabin which had been declared the ship's brig for his benefit, Ray gazed in appeal at his visitor, who had come by request. There was no guard; a chain around his ankle secured the Earthling quite well. "What else could I do?" he pleaded. "Try fighting the entire crew? As it was, it took every bit of persuasion I had in me to get Dyann to surrender."

"I mean tat you fought in te first place," Urushkidan scolded. "I hear it started ober a female. Why don't you lower species habe a regular rutting season as we do on Uttu? Ten you could perhaps act sensibly te rest of te year."

"Well—Please, sir! You're the only hope I've got. They won't even tell me what's become of Dyann."

"Oh, tey questioned her, found she cannot read, and dismissed te charges of mayhem and mutiny. Roshevsky-Feldkamp himself agreed she had acted 'in te heat of te moment,' alto' I beliebe I detected a sour note in his boice. She will be all right."

"I'm glad of that much," Ray said, a trifle surprised to notice his own sincerity. "Of course, no doubt the Jovians figured punishing one of our first interstellar visitors would raise more stink on Earth than it could be worth to them. But what's her illiteracy got to do

80   CAPTIVE OF THE CENTAURIANESS

with it? And how do you know they inquired about that?"

"She mentioned it to me afterward. I ten recalled how carefully I had been interrogated, like ebery witness, to make sure I could not habe seen what was in te colonel's papers from tat briefcase. Obbiously tey are top secret and I suspect tey are information about Eart's military situation, gatered by spies for him to take back in person. You are being held prisoner because you did see tem."

"What? But damn it, I never stopped to read anything!"

"You must habe unconscious memories which a hypnoquiz could bring out. If noting else, tat would alert te Union to te existence of a Jobian espionage network. Dyann lacks te word-gestalts, she could not retain any meaningful images, but you— Well, tat is your bad luck. I suppose ebentually te Terrestrial embassy can negotiate your release, after te Jobians habe had time to cober teir tracks on Eart."

"No, not then," Ray groaned. "They'll never bother. There's a warrant out for me at home. Besides, old Vanbrugh will be only too pleased to see me get the rotary shaft."

"Banbrugh—te Nort American member of te World Council?"

"Uh-huh." Ray slumped where he stood. "And to think I was a plain underpaid engineer till Uncle Hosmer left me a million credits in his will. I hope he's frying in hell."

Urushkidan's eyes bugged till they seemed about to push off his spectacles. "A man left you money and you resent it? Ten why habe you talked about being poor?"

"Because I am. I spent the whole sum."

"Shalmuannasar! On what?"

"Oh, wine, women, song, the usual."

Urushkidan winced as if in physical pain. "A million credits, and not a millo inbested."

"Meanwhile I got into high society," Ray explained. "I made out as if I had more than I actually did, not to defraud anybody, only so as not to be scoffed at. Katrina Vanbrugh—that's the Councillor's daughter—got the idea I'd make a good fifth husband, or would it have been the sixth? I forget. Well, she's not bad-looking, and she has a headlong way about her, and the upshot was that we became engaged. Big social event. Except then a reporter grew nosy, and found out my fortune was practically gone, and Katrina decided I'd only been after her money and now she and her parents were a laughingstock. . . . Vanbrugh had me charged with criminal mis-representation. Quite false—oh, maybe I had shaded the truth a little, but I honestly didn't think it'd make any difference to Katrina when I got around to admitting it, she being as rich as she is—the family just wanted revenge. How could I fight that kind of power? I panicked and skipped. Maybe that was foolish; certainly it's made my case worse. The upshot is that the Jovians can do anything to me they feel like."

He flung out his arms. "Sir, can't you put in a good word for me?" he begged. "You're famous, admired, influential if you choose to be. Couldn't you please help?"

The Martian inflated himself in the equivalent of simper, then deflated and said with mild regret, "No, I cannot entangle myself in te empirical. It is too distracting, and my work too important. My domain is te beauty and purity of matematics. I adbise you to accept your fate wit philosophy. If you wish, I can lend you a copy of Ekbannutil's *Treatise on te Insignificance of Temporal Sorrows.*"

Ray collapsed onto his bunk and buried face in hands. "No, thanks."

Urushkidan waved affably and waddled off.

Presently the spaceship entered orbit around Ganymede. A squad of soldiers arrived to bring Ray down to the moon. Roshevsky-Feldkamp took personal charge of that.

"Where am I going?" the Earthling asked.

"To Camp Muellenhoff, near Wotanopolis," the colonel told him with pleasure. "It is where we keep spies until we have completed their interrogation and are ready to shoot them."

III.

Dyann Korlas needed a couple of Terrestrial days to decide that she didn't like Ganymede.

The Jovians had been entirely courteous to her, offering a stiff apology for the unfortunate incident en route and assigning her a lieutenant in the Security Corps for a guide. Within limits, he indulged her curiosity about armaments, and she found her conducted tours of military facilities more impressive than anything corresponding that she had seen on Earth. However, granted that plasmajet spacecraft, armored gun carriers, and nuclear missiles had capabilities beyond those of swords, bows, and cavalry, still, they took the fun out of combat and left nothing to plunder. She missed the brawling mirth of Kathantuman encampments among these endlessly and expressionlessly marching ranks, these drab uniforms and impersonal machines.

The civilians were still more depressingly clad, and their orderliness, their instant obedience before any official, their voluminous praises to her of the wonders of Symmetrism, the tiny apartments in which they were housed, soon made her nerves crawl. The officer caste did possess a certain dash and glamour which she would have enjoyed, had it not been exclusively male. She had found the Terrestrial concept of sexual equality interesting, even perversely exciting; but the Jovians had not simply changed the natural order of things, they had turned it upside down, and she found herself regarding them as a race of perverts.

The standard sights were often fascinating. Below ground, Wotanopolis was a many-leveled hive of industry; she admired especially the countless engineering accomplishments which made human life here so triumphantly safe and ordinary. The views above ground were often magnificent in their stark fashion: Jupiter like a huge moon, softly lambent, in a twilit heaven; an auroral shimmer in the phantom-thin air, where the force-fields created by enormous generators warded off radiation that would otherwise have been lethal; crags, craters, mountains, glaciers; a crystalline forest, a splendidly leaping animal, the marvel that life had arisen here too, here too.

Yet the impression grew upon her that she was being hurried along, from sight to sight and conversation to conversation, without ever a chance really to talk to anyone, to glimpse whatever soul there dwelt beneath the busy flesh. True, she heard lectures about the superiority of Jovian society and its clear right to leadership of the Solar System, till she lost count. Nonetheless she wondered if the people she met would have been that monomaniacal had her guide not been present. Besides, if they felt they ought to rule, why didn't they just hop into their spaceships and have at the Earthlings?

Everywhere she saw portraits of the Leader, a short and puffy-faced man named Martin Wilder. Once Lieutenant Hamand, the person conducting her, said in awe that, if the Leader was not too occupied with cares of state, she might actually be introduced to him. Hamand looked hurt when she yawned.

Meanwhile, she fretted about Ray Tallantyre. Though she hadn't really seen much of her erstwhile roommate, she had found him uncommonly appealing. In part, she recognized, that was no doubt because, what with one thing and another, she hadn't gotten laid for some time when she boarded the liner, nor had she since. But in part, also, she liked his liveliness and wry humor. They contrasted vividly with the humble men of her homeland. She had confirmed for herself that male Earthlings often deserved the reputation they had won among female Varannians; she suspected that Ray exceeded the average. It was unlikely that he'd adjust well to harem life, but she had no such plans for him. It was impossible that he, belonging to a different species, could father a child of hers. Right now, that was no drawback at all.

She'd been looking forward to developing the acquaintance on Ganymede. Then he got into trouble, and she'd not been able to discover a thing about his present situation. Under pressure, Hamand had put her in touch with an officer of the political police, who said that the case was under consideration and advised her not to get involved. If nothing else, he said, her tour of the Jovian System would end before the matter had been disposed of. He concluded with assurances that Tallantyre would "receive justice," which she did not find very satisfactory.

Her concern sprang from more than attraction. That had caused her to think of Ray as a friend—and in Kathantuma, one did not abandon a friend. They hadn't exchanged blood oaths or anything like that. Nevertheless, the fact that she had enjoyed his company led her warrior conscience toward the illogical conclusion that she owed him her help.

This did not come about overnight, nor in any such clear terms. What she experienced was simply an anxiety which grew and grew. It fed upon her distaste for the civilization which currently surrounded her. If Ray had offended these creatures, well, they needed offending. Could she be less brave?

Ganymede swung once about Jupiter, a period of a week, while Dyann Korlas wrestled ever more with her emotional and ethical dilemma. At last she did the proper thing according to her own beliefs: alone in her quarters, save for a bottle of whiskey, she brought the matter out before herself, considered it explicitly, realized that it was indeed important to her, and resolved that she would no longer stay idle. In the morning she would seek divine guidance.

That decision made, she slept well.

At 0600 hours, as always, lights flashed on throughout Wotanopolis to decree a new day. Dyann bounded out of bed, sang a cheerful song of clattering swords and cloven skulls while she washed and dressed—cuirass, helmet, sword, dagger above tunic and sandals—and sought the kitchenette of her apartment, where she prepared a breakfast that would have sufficed two Terrestrial laborers. Ordinary Jovians knew no such luxuries, but she rated diplomatic housing.

When she entered the main room, she found Hamand present;

crime was alleged to have been stamped out of Symmetrist society, and locks on civilian doors were thought to suggest that those within might be talking sedition. A powerfully built young man, immaculate in gray cloth and shiny boots, he bowed from the waist. "Good day," he greeted. "You will recollect that we are going topside to visit the Devil's Garden. At 1145 we will proceed to Heroville, where we will appreciate the Revolutionary Cenotaph and have lunch. At 1300 hours we have an appointment to fill out the necessary documents for your forthcoming visit to Callisto. Thereafter—"

"Hold," Dyann interrupted. "First I have a reliyious rite."

"I beg your pardon?"

"Vy? You have done no wrong." Dyann gestured to the image of Ormun, standing ferocious on a table. "I must ask for the counsel of this god." She paused, struck by a thought. "You better—vat is the vord?—you better prostrate yourself too."

"What?" cried the lieutenant.

"She does not like atheists," Dyann explained.

Hamand flushed and stiffened. "Madame," he said, "I have been educated in the scientific principles of Symmetrism. They do not include groveling before idols."

Dyann took him by the back of his neck, bore him down to his knees, and rubbed his nose in the carpet. "You will please to grovel," she said amiably. "It is good manners." She spread herself prone, while keeping a grip on him, and recited a magical formula. Thereafter she let him go, rose to a crouch, dredged three Kathantuman dice from the purse at her belt, and tossed them.

"Haa," she murmured after study. "The omen says—vell, I am not a *marya,* a certified vitchvife, but I do tink the omen says I should seek Urushkidan. See, here the Visdom sign lies right next to the Mystery sign, with the Crossed Axes over here. . . . Yes, I am sure Ormun tells me I need to see Urushkidan." She bowed to the image. "Thank you, sveet lady. *Laesti laeskul itorum."* Rising: "Shall ve go?"

Hamand, who had finished swallowing his resentment for the sake of public relations, was taken aback all over again. "Do you mean the Martian scientist?" he yelped. "Impossible! He is doing critically important work—"

Dyann strolled out into the corridor. She had been shown the Academy of Sciences earlier. No matter how alien this warren of passages was to her native forests, she retained a huntress' sense of direction and landmarks. Hamand trailed her, gabbling, barely able to keep her in sight. There were no slideways. Except in the tunnels where authorized vehicles moved, everybody walked. It was a result of the government's concern over preserving public physical fitness in Ganymede's low gravity. Dyann felt feather-light. She proceeded in three- and four-meter bounds. When a clump of people got in the way of that, she sprang over their heads.

The Academy occupied 50 hectares on a high level of town, a pleasant break in an environment where the very parks were functional. Here, grass, trees, and flowerbeds made lanes of life between walls which, admittedly roofless, were at least covered with plastic ivy. Overhead, a teledome gave an awesome vision of Jupiter, stars, Milky Way, the shrunken sun. The air bore faint, flowery perfumes and recorded birdsong. Upon this campus, moving from building to building, were a number of persons, several obviously military personnel but most just as obviously scholars, little different from their colleagues on Earth.

Dyann stopped one of the latter, loomed over him, and asked where Dr. Urushkidan might be. "In Archimedes Hall—over there," he gasped, and tottered off, perhaps in search of a reviving cup of tea.

She might have known, Dyann thought. In front of that door, a soldier on guard clashed with the general atmosphere. She guessed his presence was due to the military significance of Urushkidan's work. Though her appearance startled him, too, rather badly, he slanted his rifle before him and cried, "Halt!"

Dyann obeyed. "I must see the Martian," she told him. "Please to let me by."

"Nobody sees him without a pass," he replied.

Dyann shoved him aside and took hold of the door switch. He yelled and batted at her with his rifle butt. That was his great mistake.

"You should show more respect for ladies," she chided, and removed the weapon from his grasp. Her free hand flung him across the greensward. He collided with Hamand, who had panted onto the scene, hard enough that neither was of much use for some time to come. Dyann admired the rifle—Earthlings on Varann were deplorably stingy about giving such things to her folk—before she slung it across her back by the strap. By now, too many passersby had halted to stare and chatter. Best she keep on the move. She opened the door and passed on through.

For a minute she poised in the hallway beyond, cocking her ears this way and that. They were keen. A faint sound of altercation gave her the clue she hoped for, and she bounded up a flight of stairs. Before another door she stopped to listen. Yes, that was the voice of Urushkidan, bubbling like an infuriated teakettle.

"I will not, sir, do you hear me? I will not. And I demand immediate return passage from tis ridiculous satellite."

"Come now, Dr. Urushkidan, do be reasonable." Was that Roshevsky-Feldkamp? "What is your complaint, actually? Do you not have generous financial compensation, Mars-conditioned lodgings, servants, every imaginable consideration? If you wish something further, inform us and we will try to provide it."

"I came here to lecture and to complete my matematical research. Now I find you habe arranged no lectures and expect me to superbise an—an *engineering* project—as if I were a mere empiricist!"

"But your contract plainly states—"

"Did you tink I would waste my baluable time reading one of your pieces of printed gibberish? Sir, in human law itself, a proper contract requires tat tere habe been a meeting of minds. Te mind of your goberment neber met te mind of myself. It was not capable of it."

The man attempted ingratiation: "You are a leading scientist. As such, you realize that science advances by checking theory against fact. If, with your help, we create a faster-than-light ship, it will be a total confirmation of your ideas."

"My ideas need no confirmation. Tey are a debelopment of certain implications of general relatibity, true. Howeber, tat is incidental. In principle, what I habe produced is a piece of pure matematics, elegant and beautiful. If it agrees or disagrees wit te facts, tat is of no concern to any proper philosopher. And furthermore—" The squeaky tones approached ultrasonic frequencies. "—not only do you want experimental tests, you want to me lend my genius to bulgar military applications! No, no, and again no! Do you understand? I want a ticket on te next ship bound for Mars!"

"I am afraid," said the man slowly, "that that will not be possible."

Dyann opened the door and trod through. "Are they annoyin you?" she asked.

Urushkidan goggled at her from the chair across which he was draped. The room was so thick with the fumes of his pipe that one of the two Jovians present, a bald man in the black tunic of the political police, was holding a handkerchief to his nose. The other was, indeed, Roshevsky-Feldkamp, who sprang to his feet and snatched for his revolver.

Dyann had already unlimbered the expropriated rifle. She aimed it at his midriff. "Better not," she warned him. He froze.

"What . . . you . . . what are you doing here?" stammered the political officer.

"Lookin for Ray Tallantyre," she answered. "Could you tell me vere he is?"

"Guards!" Roshevsky-Feldkamp bellowed fearlessly. "Help!"

Dyann made a leap across the room, seized him by the neck, and hammered his forehead against the desk. With her right hand she kept the second Jovian covered. "I asked you vere is Ray Tallantyre," she reminded him.

"I am glad you came," Urushkidan told her. "Shall we leabe tis uncibilized place?" Two soldiers appeared in the doorway. "Perhaps not."

Dyann swung her rifle around. She was a trifle slow. Both newcomers already had weapons unlimbered, and opened fire. She dropped behind the desk. Twin streams of slugs pierced its mass, seeking her. She took it by the legs and heaved. It arced high over the floor and landed on the soldiers in a burst of drawers, papers, penstyls, and books. They went down beneath it and stayed there, stunned.

The secret police officer had taken advantage of the distraction to snatch forth his sidearm. He trained it on Dyann as she rose. Urushkidan snaked forth a tentacle and pulled him off his feet. Dyann paused to knock Roshevksy-Feldkamp unconscious before she closed fingers around the other man's Adam's apple. "Vere you not listenin?" she growled. "Vere is Ray Tallantyre?"

"Come, no delay, prudence requires we get out of here," urged the Martian.

Perforce, Dyann agreed. She hadn't really intended to get into a brawl. Things had just sort of happened. "Vat's a safe vay to go?" she inquired.

"Tis way. I'be been shown around. Follow me." Urushkidan paused to relieve both officers of their pistols. He carried one in either hand, gingerly, as if he feared they might explode. Dyann frogmarched the political policeman out into the hall after him. Shouts of alarm rang through it, coming nearer; she heard the thud of military boots.

"Hurry," Urushkidan gasped. "Shalmuannasar, we habe te entire Jobian Confederacy after us!" Since he could not move as fast as a human or Centaurian, Dyann expedited matters by picking him up and draping him over her prisoner's head.

They rounded a corner and clattered down several flights of stairs to a steel door marked HANGAR. AUTHORIZED PERSONNEL ONLY. It wasn't locked. Passing through, they found themselves in a cavernous enclosure where several small spacecraft rested on mobile cradles. Mechanics stared at the trio.

"Tese are bessels for scientific use around te surface," Urushkidan explained. "We want one."

A superintendent hurried up, obviously puzzled but afraid to comment. "You heard vat ve vant," Dyann whispered, and squeezed her captive at the shoulder, quite gently, only enough to make bones creak.

"Yes," the officer gasped through the tentacles that curtained his face. "Practice maneuvers. We . . . we have immediate requirement of a fully equipped craft. Mission confidential and—ow-w-w!—urgent."

"Yes, sir," responded a lifetime's training in blind obedience. However, the crew was a little less efficient than usual. They kept stealing looks.

As a teardrop-shaped boat trundled forth, Dyann held most of her attention on the door through which she had entered. Pursuit might reopen it at any instant. Surely by now Roshevsky-Feldkamp and the soldiers had been found. It shouldn't take somebody long to think of the possibility that her group had fled hither.

"I'll start the warmup, sir," the head mechanic said.

"No, don't bother, ve'll take her straight out," Dyann replied.

Aghast, he protested, "Madame, you don't understand. That'll cause carbon deposits in the tubes. You'll risk engine failure, a crash—"

"You find that an acceptable risk," Dyann told the secret policeman.

"Yes, of course I do," he choked. "The . . . the Leader tells us no hazard is too great for the cause."

Dyann propelled him ahead of her through the airlock. In the control cabin, she pushed him into the pilot's recoil chair, which she recognized from her travels around Earth. "I hope you can fly vun of these," she said.

"I hope so too," added Urushkidan. He slithered off the Jovian, secured the airlock, and knitted himself to a passenger seat.

"Ve are goin to find Ray Tallantyre," Dyann instructed the man. Part of her thought that she was beginning to sound obsessive. Yet, given the witch's brew of events in which she had somehow submerged herself, it was as reasonable a plan of action as any. Ray's shrewdness and sophistication might lend her the vital extra help, when Ormun was being left behind. In fact, this appeared to have been Ormun's intention.

"What do you mean?" the officer asked. He seemed a trifle disconcerted and confused.

"Ray Tallantyre, the Earthman that vas arrested off the *Yovian Qveen*," Dyann said with what she congratulated herself was exemplary patience. "You in your service ought to know vere he is kept. Vould some blows refresh your memory?"

"Camp Muellenhoff, you savage!" he got out. "North of the city. You'll never succeed. You'll kill us all."

Dyann smiled. "Then ve vill feast forever vith the gods, in the Hall of Skulls," she comforted him. "Von't that be nice?"

The cradle got into motion, rumbling toward the hangar airlock. Up a long ramp . . . into the chamber . . . darkness outside, as valves closed . . . hollow noise of pumps, withdrawing air. . . . Urushkidan relit his pipe with shaky tendrils. Dyann whistled tunelessly between her teeth.

"I am not so sure we are wise," the Martian said. "Tis bessel cannot carry us away from te Jobian System, or eben to anoter satellite of te planet."

"No, you are not wise," the political officer agreed eagerly.

"Hindsight vill show," Dyann responded. "Meanvile, *you* vould be most unvise not to pilot like I tell you."

The outer valve opened. The cradle rolled out onto the field. Behind that flat expanse, the dome which covered Wotanopolis glowed against sawtoothed mountains, rearing above a near horizon, and starlit sky. The dwarfed pale sun cast luminance from the west. Only one other spacecraft was in sight, a black shape which Dyann could identify as a patrol ship.

"They vill come out after us in force pretty soon," she said. "Vat can ve do about that boat yonder, ha?" She reached a decision. "Ah, yes." Her involuntary pilot received his orders. When he clamored refusal, she reminded him, briefly but painfully, that he was no volunteer but, indeed, an impressed man. The engine thuttered and the little scientific craft rose.

Having reached altitude, she descended again, sufficiently to play her jets across the patrol ship. That was not good for the patrol ship.

Dyann didn't bother to receive whatever they were trying to tell her from the control tower. "Now," she stated as her boat rose anew, "you, my policeman friend, take us to this prison and make them release Tallantyre to us. If this goes okay, ve vill set you free somevere. If not—" she passed the edge of her knife across the back of his hand, neatly shaving off hairs, "you may still be a police, but you might not be a man."

"You unutterable monster," he said.

"It is nicer droppin nuclear missiles on cities?" she asked, genuinely bemused.

"Yes," Urushkidan snickered, "I habe had a digestible pouch full of you Jobians talking about te glories of war and destiny and te will of te Race and historical necessity and suchlike tings. Perhaps in future you will wish to employ more logical rigor."

The flight was short to Camp Muellenhoff. It lay out on the surface, a cluster of pressure huts around a watchtower. There was no

barbed wire; the Ganymedean environment gave ample security. If a spacesuited prisoner did slip away from a work detail, the sole question was whether a local monster would get him before his oxygen or his heatpack was exhausted.

When the boat landed in the area, such a figure was urged toward her airlock by a couple of others. The political officer had radioed ahead the demand he was supposed to, quite convincingly. A voice did rattle out of her receiver: "Sir, I've been ordered to ask if you really want to bring this prisoner back to town. We've lately been alerted to watch out for a party of escaped desperadoes."

"Yes," the secret policeman said between clenched teeth, "I want him back in town. Oh, how I want him back in town!"

The captive stumbled into the cabin. Ice promptly formed over his armor. Dyann gave a command, the boat stood on her tail and screamed off toward parts unknown, the newly rescued person clattered against the after bulkhead and lay asprawl.

Presently, when they were flying on an even keel, he opened his faceplate. Slightly battered, the countenance of Ray Tallantyre emerged. *"Haa-ai,* dear sweetheart!" Dyann cried. She reached for him, touched his suit, and withdrew her hand with a yelp. "How are you?" she asked, not very distinctly since she was sucking frost-bitten fingers.

"Well . . . I . . . well, not too bad," he answered out of his bewilderment. "A rough time but . . . mainly it was truth drugs . . . they told me I'd be shot as a, a precautionary measure—"

"Poor, dear Ray! Poor little Earthlin! Lie easy. I vill soon take care of you."

"Yeah, I'm afraid you will."

"Te immediate question," Urushkidan said, "is, Tallantyre, can you pilot a behicle of tis type?"

"Well, uh, yes, I suppose I can," Ray answered. "Looks like a modified Astrid-Luscombe. . . . Yes, I can."

"Good. Ten we can drop tis creature here. I do not like and/or trust him. He smells of phenylalanine—Dyann! Do you mean we are not simply going to *drop* him?"

"I made my promise," the woman said.

They descended on a rocky plateau, gave the secret policeman a spacesuit, and dismissed him. He should be able to reach the camp, given reasonable luck. Nevertheless he bemoaned his maltreatment.

"And now, vat next?" Dyann asked blithely.

"Lord knows," Ray sighed. "I suppose we find us a place in the wilderness where we aren't likely to be spotted for a while, and take stock. Maybe, in some crazy fashion, we can contact the Union embassy. You and Urushkidan ought to rate diplomatic intervention, and I can ride on your cloaks. Maybe. First we find that hideyhole, and second we prepare to skedaddle if we spy a Jovian flyer."

He strapped into the master seat and tickled the controls. The boat lifted readily, but after a moment began to shake, while ominous noises came through the engine-room radiation wall.

"Could tat be te effects of carbon deposits in te tubes tat we were warned about?" wondered Urushkidan.

Ray grimaced. "You mean you took off without proper warmup? Yes, I'm afraid it is." His fingers danced across the board. The response he got was erratic. "We'll have to land soon. Else we crash. It'll take a week before the radioactivity is low enough that we can go out and clean the jets."

"And meanvile is a satellite-vide hunt after us." Dyann's clear brow wrinkled. "Is Ormun offended because I did not invite her alon? It does seem our luck is runnin low."

"And," said Ray, "how!"

IV.

He used the last sputter of ions to set down in a valley which appeared to be as wild and remote as one could hope for. However, when he got a look through a viewport, he wondered if he hadn't overdone it.

Around the boat was a stretch of seamed and pitted stone, sloping up on every side toward fang-cragged hills. The glow of Jupiter shimmered, weirdly colored, off a distant glacier and a closer pool of liquid methane. The latter had begun boiling; its vapors obscured the tiny sun and streamed ragged across a stand of gaunt, glassy plants. Quite a wind must be blowing out there, though too tenuous for him to hear through the hull. At this time of day, when the hemisphere had warmed, the air—which still didn't amount to much more than a contaminated vacuum—consisted mostly of carbon dioxide, with some methane, ammonia, and nitrogen: not especially breathable. Even Urushkidan couldn't survive those conditions without proper gear. This craft's heating and atmosphere regeneration plants had better be in good working order.

An animal passed across the view in kangaroo-like bounds. While small, it gave him another reason not to want to go outdoors. Ganymedean biochemistry depended on heat-absorbent materials; the thermal radiation of a spacesuited human attracted animals, and carnivores were apt to try eating their way directly to the source.

Ray turned to his companions. "Well," he sighed, "what shall we do now?"

Dyann's eyes lit up. "Hunt monsters?" she suggested.

"Bah!" Urushkidan writhed his way toward the laboratory compartment, where there was a desk. "You do what you like except not to disturb me. I habe an interesting aspect of unified field teory to debelop."

"Look," said Ray, "we've got to take action. If we sit here passive, waiting for the time when we can clean those tubes, we're too bloody likely to be found."

"What do you imagine we can effect?"

"Oh, I don't know. Camouflage, maybe? Damnation, I have to do *something!*"

"I don't, apart from my matematics. Leabe me out of any idiotic schemes you may hatch."

"But if they catch us, we'll be killed!"

"I won't be," said Urushkidan smugly. "I am too baluable."

"You're a, uh, an accessory of ours."

"True, I did get carried away in te excitement. My hope was to aboid habing to waste my genius toiling for a mere engineering project. Tat hope has apparently been disappointed. Well, ten, te logical ting for me to do when te Jobians arribe is to go ahead and complete te dreary ting for tem, so tey will let me go home . . . wit proper payment for my serbices, I trust." The Martian paused. "As for you two, I will try to make it a condition tat your libes be spared. I am, after all, a noble person. I doubt you will eber be set free, but tink how many years you will habe, undistracted, to cultibate philosophical resignation."

Dyann tugged at Ray's sleeve. "Come on," she urged. "Let's hunt monsters."

"Waaah!" Goaded beyond endurance, the Earthman jumped on high—and, in Ganymedean gravity, cracked his pate on the overhead.

"Oh, poor darlin!" Dyann exclaimed, and folded him in an embrace that would have done credit to a bear.

"Let me go!" he raged. "Somebody here better think past the next minute!"

"You really must work on serenity," Urushkidan advised him. "Consider tings from te aspect of eternity. You are only a lower animal. Your fate is of no importance."

"You conceited octopus!"

"Temper, temper." Urushkidan wagged a flexible finger at the man. "Let me remind you why you should heed me. If your reasoning powers are so weak tat you cannot demonstrate *a priori* tat Martians are always right—by definition—ten remember te facts. Martians are beautiful. Martians habe a benerable cibilization. Eben physically, we are superior; I can libe under Eart conditions, but I dare you to try staying alibe under Mars conditions. I double-dog dare you."

"Martians," gritted Ray, "didn't come to Earth. Earthmen came to Mars."

"Of course. We had no reason to bisit you, but you had ebery reason to make pilgrimages to us, hoping tat a little beauty and wisdom would rub off on you. Enough. I am going aft to carry on my research and do not want to be disturbed, except tat when you get te galley going, you may bring me a bite to eat. I can ingest your kind of food, you know. I cannot, howeber, positibely cannot abide te taste of asparagus or truffles. Do not prepare me any dish wit asparagus or truffles." Urushkidan started off along the deck.

"You know, Ray," said Dyann, "I have been thinkin, and you are right. Now is not the time to hunt monsters. Let's make love."

"Oh, God!" the human groaned. "If I could get away from you two lunatics, you'd see me exceed the speed of light doing it."

He stiffened where he stood.

"Yes?" asked Dyann.

"Lord, Lord, Lord," he whispered. "That's the answer."

"Yes, tat's right, talk no louder tan tat while I am tinking," Urushkidan said from the after door.

"The drive, the faster-than-light drive—" Ray broke into a war-dance around the cramped compartment, bounding from chairs to aisle and back. "We've got all kinds of scientific supplies and equipment, we've got the Solar System's top authority on the subject, I'm an engineer, everybody knows that the basic effects have been shown in the laboratory and a real drive is just a matter of development —We'll do it ourselves!"

"Not so loud, I told you," Urushkidan grumbled. He passed by the door and slammed it behind him.

"Dyann, Dyann," Ray warbled, "we're going home."

Her eyes filled with tears. "Do you vant to leave me already?" she asked. "Do you not like me?"

"No, no, no, I want to save our lives, our freedom, that's all. Come on, let's go aft and take inventory. I'll need you to move the heavy stuff around."

Dyann shook her head. "No," she pouted. "If you don't care for me, vy should I help you?"

"Judas priest," Ray groaned. "Look, I love you, I adore you, I worship at your feet. Now will you give me a hand?"

Dyann brightened but insisted, "Prove it."

Ray kissed her. She seized him and responded enthusiastically.

"Yeow!" he screamed. "You're about to break my ribs! Leggo!" As she did: "Uh, we'll discuss this some other time, when we've less urgent business."

"Love," said Dyann, "has gotten to be very urgent business for me. Come here."

After a while Urushkidan opened the door. "If you two don't stop tose noises—" he began indignantly. His gaze went to the aisle. "Oh," he said. "Oh." He closed the door again.

Later, an aroma of coffee drew him back to the forward cabin. A disheveled Ray Tallantyre was busy at the little food preparation unit while Dyann sat polishing her sword and humming to herself.

"Well, hi," said the man with evident relief. "I guess we can get started. First, suppose I ask a few questions, to refresh and expand my knowledge of how this drive of yours works."

"It is not a dribe and it does not work," Urushkidan replied. "What I habe created is a structure of pure matematics. Besides, it is beyond te full comprehension of anybody but myself. Gibe me some coffee."

"You must have followed the experiments, though, and learned a good bit more along those lines from the Jovians who've been trying to build a usable device."

"Oh, yes, no doubt I could design someting if I wanted to. I don't want to. My current interests are too cosmic." Urushkidan accepted a cup and slurped.

"Look," Ray argued, "if the Jovians catch us, they'll force you to do it for them. And afterward they'll overrun Mars along with the other planets. Logistics will no longer be a problem for them, you see, nor will there be any defense against their missiles."

"Tat would be unfortunate, I admit. Neberteless, it would be down-right tragic if my present train of tought were interrupted, as it would be if I gabe your project my full attention, which I would habe to do if it were to habe any chance of success. Te Jobians can afford to employ me on a part-time basis. Let tem conquer te Solar System. In a tousand years tey will be a footnote in te history books. My accomplishments will be remembered while te uniberse endures."

Dyann hefted her sword. "You will do vat he says," she growled.

"You dare not harm me," Urushkidan gibed; "it would leabe you stranded for te Jobians to take rebenge upon."

He finished his coffee. "Where is te tobacco?" he asked. "I habe used my own up."

"Jovians don't smoke," Ray informed him with savage satisfaction. "They consider it a degenerate habit."

"What?" The Martian's howl rattled the pot on the hotplate. "No tobacco aboard?"

"None. And I daresay your supply back in Wotanopolis has been confiscated and destroyed. That puts the nearest cigar store somewhere in the Asteroid Belt."

"Oh, no! How can I tink without my pipe? Te new cosmology ruined by tobacco shortage—" Urushkidan needed bare seconds to reach his decision. "Bery well. Tere is no help for it. If te nearest tobacco is millions of kilometers away, we must build te faster-tan-light engine at once.

"Also," he added thoughtfully, "if te Jobians did conquer te Solar System, tey might well prohibit tobacco on ebery world. Yes, you habe conbinced me, yours is a bital cause."

Ray made no attempt to use the Martian's equations in details or to find elegant solutions of any. He merely wanted to compute the parameters of something that would work, and he proceeded with slashing approximations that brought screams of almost physical anguish from the other being.

He did, however, recognize the basic nature of Urushkidan's achievement, a final correlation of general relativity and wave mechanics whose formulation had certain surprising consequences.

Relativity deals with matter and energy, including potentials, which move at definite velocities that cannot exceed that of light. In contrast, wave mechanics treats the particle as a psi function which is only probably where it is. In the latter theory, point-to-point transitions are not speeds but shifts in the node of a complex wave. Urushkidan had abolished the contradiction by bringing in his own immensely generalized and refined concept of information as a condition of the plenum rather than as a physical quantity subject to physical limitations. It then turned out that the phase velocity of matter waves—which, unlike the group velocity, can move at any speed—could actually carry information, so that the most probable position of a particle went from region to region with no restrictions on the time derivatives.

The trick was to establish such conditions in reality that the theoretical possibility was realized.

"As I understand it," Ray had said, early on, "the proper configuration of quark interchanges will set up a field of space-strain. A spacecraft will react against the entire mass of the universe, won't even need rockets. In fact, we have here the key to a lot of other things as well, like gravity control. Right?"

"Wrong," answered Urushkidan.

"Well, we'll build it anyhow," Ray said.

His ambition was not as crazy as it might seem—not quite. The theory was in existence and considerable laboratory work had been done. Despite his scorn for empirical science, Urushkidan's mind had stored away the data about these and was perfectly capable of seeing what direction research should take next. Moreover, he was in fact the sole person with a complete grasp of his concepts; no physicist had, as yet, comprehended every aspect of them. Given motivation, he flung the full power of his intellect against the problem of practical application. Ray Tallantyre was actually quite a good engineer where it came to producing hardware. That hardware was not really complex, either, any more than a transistor or a tunnel diode is complex; the subtlety lies in the physical principles employed. In the present case, what was required was, basically, power, which the spacecraft had, and circuits with certain resonances, which could be constructed out of available materials. The result would not be neat, but in a slapdash fashion it ought to work.

Just the same, no R & D undertaking ever went smoothly, and this one labored under special difficulties. On a typical occasion—

"We'll want our secondary generator over here, I think, attached to this bench," Ray said. "Tote it for me, will you, Dyann?"

"All ve've done is vork, vork, vork," she sulked. "I want to hunt monsters."

"Bring it, you lummox!"

Dyann glared but stooped above the massive machine and, between Ganymedean weight and Varannian muscles, staggered across the deck with it. Meanwhile Ray was checking electrical properties on an oscilloscope. Urushkidan was solving a differential equation while grumbling about heat and humidity and fanning himself with his ears. Elsewhere lay strewn a chaos of parts and tools.

"Damn!" the man exclaimed. "I hoped—but no, this piece of copper tube isn't right either. I need a resistance with so-and-so many ohms and such-and-such a capacitance, and nothing around seems to be modifiable for it."

"Specify your values," Urushkidan said.

Ray pawed through the litter around him, selected another object, and put it in his test circuit. "No, this won't do." He cast it across the room; it clanged against a bulkhead. "Look, if we can't find something, this project is stopped cold."

Having put down the generator, Dyann went forward. She returned with the boat's one and only frying pan. "Vill this maybe be right?" she asked innocently.

"Huh? Get out of my way!" Ray screamed.

"Okay," she answered, offended. "I go hunt monsters."

You know—passed through the man's head; and: *What's to lose?* He clipped the pan into the circuit. Its properties registered as nearly what he required. *If I cut the handle off*—Excited, he began to do that.

"Are you mad?" protested Urushkidan.

"Well, I don't like the idea of living off cold beans any better than you do," Ray retorted, "but consider the alternative." He rechecked the emasculated frying pan. "Ye-e-s, given a few adjustments elsewhere, this'll serve." Viciously: "Starward the course of human empire."

"Martian empire," Urushkidan corrected, "unless we decide it is beneat our dignity."

"It'll be Jovian empire if we don't escape. Okay, bulgebrain, what comes next?"

"How should I know? I habe not finished here. How do you expect me to tink in tis foul, tick air, wit no tobacco?"

Dyann clumped in from the forward cabin, attired in a spacesuit whose adjustability she strained to the limit. Its faceplate was still open. Her right hand clutched the rifle she had taken, her left her sword. "I saw monsters out there," she announced happily. "I am goin to hunt them."

"Oh, sure, sure," muttered Ray without really hearing. His attention was on a calculator. "Urushkidan, could you hurry it up a bit with that equation of yours? I really do need to know the exact resonant wave form before I can proceed." He glanced up. The Martian was trying to fill his pipe from the shreds and dottle in an ashtray. "Hey! Get busy!"

"Won't," said Urushkidan.

"By Heaven, you animated bagpipe, if you don't give me some decent cooperation for a change, I'll—I'll—"

"Up your rectifier."

The sound of an airlock valve closing snatched Ray out of his preoccupation. "Dyann?" he called. "Dyann. . . . Hey, she really is going outside."

"Apparently tere are monsters indeed," Urushkidan said.

Ray sprang into the forward cabin and peered through the nearest of its viewports. His heart stumbled. "Yes, a pair of gannydragons," he exclaimed. "Must've sensed our heat output—they could crack this hull wide open—"

"I will proceed wit te calculation," Urushkidan said uneasily.

—Dyann leaped from lock to ground. In the weird light and thin shriek of wind, the beasts seemed unreal. An Earthling would have compared them to long-legged crocodiles, ten meters from spiky tailtip to shovel jaws. "Thank you, Ormun," she said in her native language, aimed the rifle, and fired.

A dragon bellowed. In this atmosphere, the sound reached her as a squeak. The beast charged. She stood her ground and kept shooting.

A blow knocked her asprawl and sent the firearm from her grasp. She had forgotten the second dragon. Its tail whacked anew, and Dyann tumbled skyward. As she hit the rocks, both animals rushed her.

"Haa-hai!" she yelled, bounced to her feet, and sprang. She still had her sword, secured to her wrist by a loop of leather. Up she went, over the nearest head, and struck downward. Green ichor spurted forth. It froze immediately.

Dyann landed, got her back against a huge meteorite, and braced herself. The unhurt monster arrived, mouth agape. She hewed with a force that sang through her whole body. The terrible head flew off its neck. She barely jumped free of its still clashing teeth. The decapitated carcass staggered about, blundered against the companion animal, and started fighting.

Dyann circled warily around. The headless dragon collapsed after a while. The other turned about, noticed once more the heat-radiant boat, and lumbered in that direction. It had to be diverted. Dyann scrambled up on top of the meteorite, poised, and sprang. She landed astride the beast's neck.

It hooted and bucked. She tried to cut its head off also, but couldn't get a proper swing to her blade where she was. The injuries she inflicted must have done something to what passed for a nervous system, because the monster started galloping around in a wide circle. The violence of the motion was such that she dared not try to jump off, she could merely hang on.

100   CAPTIVE OF THE CENTAURIANESS

Well-nigh an hour passed before the creature stopped, exhausted. Dyann slid to the ground, whirled her sword on high, and did away with this beast also. "Ho-ha!" she yelled joyously, retrieved her rifle, and skipped back to the boat.

—"Oh, Dyann, Dyann," Ray half sobbed when she was inside and her spacesuit off. "I thought sure you'd be killed—"

"It vas grand fun," she laughed. "Now let's make love."

"Huh?"

She felt of her backside and winced. "Me on top."

Ray retreated nervously. Urushkidan, standing in the entrance to the lab section, snickered and shut the door.

V.

The Ganymedean day drew to a close. Stars brightened in a darkened sky, save where Jupiter stood at half phase low to the south, mighty in its Joseph's coat of belts and zones. Weary, begrimed, and triumphant, Ray stepped back from his last job of adjustment. His gaze traveled fondly over the haywired mess that filled much of the forward cabin, all of the after cabin, and, via electrical conduits through the rad wall, most of the engine room.

"Done, I hope, I hope," he crooned. "My friends, we've opened a way to the universe."

Dyann nuzzled him. "You are too clever, my little darlin," she breathed. That rather spoiled the occasion for him. He'd grown fond of her—if nothing else, she was a magnificent companion, once she'd learned that there were limits to his strength as well as his available time—but she could not simper very successfully.

"I fear," said Urushkidan," "tat tis minor achiebement of mine will eclipse my true significance in te popular mind. Oh, well." He shrugged with his whole panoply of tentacles. "I can always use te money."

"Um-m-m, yeah, I haven't had a chance to think about that angle," Ray realized. "I'm safe enough from Vanbrugh—you don't bring a man to court who's prevented a war and given Earth the galaxy—but by gosh, there's also a fortune in this gadget."

"Yes, I will pay you a reasonable fee for helping me patent it," Urushkidan said.

Ray started. "Huh?"

"I would also like your opinion on wheter to charge an exorbitant royalty or rely on a high bolume of sales at a lower price. You are better fitted to deal wit such crass matters."

"Wait one flinkin' minute," Ray snarled. "I had a share in this development too, you know."

Urushkidan uttered a nasty laugh. "Ah, but can you describe te specifications?"

"Uh—uh—" Ray stared at the jungle of apparatus and gulped. He'd had no time to keep systematic notes, and he lacked the Martian's photographic memory. By Einstein, he'd built the damned thing but he had no proper idea whatsoever of how!

"You couldn't have done it without me," he argued.

"Nor could an ancient farmer on Eart habe done witout his mules. Did he consider paying tem a salary on tat account?"

"But . . . you've already got more money than you know what to do with, you bloated capitalist. I happen to know you invested both your Nobel Prizes in mortgages and then foreclosed."

"And why not? Genius is neber properly rewarded unless it rewards itself. Speaking of tat, I habe had no fresh tobacco for an obscene stretch of days. Take us to te nearest cigar store."

"Yes," Dyann said with unwonted timidity, "it might be a good idea if ve tested vether this enyine vorks, no?"

"All right!" Ray shouted in fury. "Sit down. Secure yourselves." He did likewise in the pilot's chair. His fingers moved across the breadboarded control panel of the star drive. "Here goes nothing."

"Nothin," said Dyann after a silence, "is correct."

"Judas on a stick," Ray groaned. "What's the matter now?" He unharnessed and went to stare at the layout. Meters registered, indicators glowed, electrorotors hummed, exactly as they were supposed to; but the boat sat stolidly where she was.

"I told you not to use tose approximations," Urushkidan said.

Ray began to fiddle with settings. "I might have known this," he muttered bitterly. "I'll bet the first piece of flint that the first apeman chipped didn't work right either."

Urushkidan shredded a piece of paper into the bowl of his pipe, to see if he could smoke it.

"*Iukh-ia-ua!*" Dyann called. "Is that a rocket flare?"

"Oh, no!" Ray hastened forward and stared. Against the night sky arced a long trail of flame. And another, and another—

"They've found us," he choked.

"Well," said Dyann, not uncheerfully, "ve tried hard, and ve vill go down fightin, and that vill get us admission to the Hall of Skulls." She reached out her arms. "Have ve got time first to make love?"

Urushkidan stroked his nose musingly. "Tallantyre," he said, "I habe an idea tat te trouble lies in te square-wabe generator. If we doubled te boltage across it—"

High in dusky heaven, the Jovian craft braked with a fury of jet-fires, swung about, and started their descent. Beneath them, vegetation crumbled to ash and ice exploded into vapor. An earthquake shudder grew and grew.

The boat's comset chimed. She was being signalled. Numbly, Ray switched on the transceiver. The lean hard features of Colonel Roshevsky-Feldkamp sprang into the screen.

"Uh . . . hello," Ray said.

"You will surrender yourselves immediately," the Jovian told him.

"We will? I mean . . . if we do, can we have safe conduct back to Earth?"

"Certainly not. But perhaps you will be allowed to live."

"About tat square-wabe generator—" Urushkidan saw that Ray wasn't listening, sighed, unstrapped himself, and crawled aft.

The first of the newcome craft sizzled to a landing. She was long and dark; guns reached from turrets like serpent heads. In the screen, Roshevsky-Feldkamp's image thrust forward till Ray had an idiotic desire to punch it. "You will surrender without resistance," the colonel said. "If not, you will suffer corporal punishment after your capture. Prolonged corporal punishment."

"Urushkidan vill die before he gives up," Dyann vowed.

"I will do noting of te sort," said the Martian. He had come to the machine he wanted. Experimentally, he twisted a knob.

The boat lifted off the ground.

"Well, well," Urushkidan murmured. "My intuition was correct."

"Stop!" Roshevsky-Feldkamp roared. "You must not do that!"

The boat rose higher. His lips tightened. "Missile them," he ordered.

Ray scrambled back to the pilot's seat, flung himself down, and slammed the main drive switch hard over.

He felt no acceleration. Instead, he drifted weightless while Jupiter whizzed past the viewports.

The engine throbbed, the hull shivered—wasted energy, but what could you expect from an experimental model? Stars blazed in his sight. Struck by a thought, he cast a terrified glance at certain meters. Relief left him weak. Even surface flyers in the Jovian System were, necessarily, equipped with superb magnetohydrodynamic radiation screens. Those of this boat were operating well. Whatever else happened, he wouldn't fry.

The stars began to change color, going blue forward and red aft. Was he traveling so fast already?

"Vat planet is that?" Dyann pointed at a pale gray globe.

"I think—" Ray stared behind him. "I think it was Neptune."

The stars appeared to be changing position. They crawled away from bow and stern till they formed a kind of rainbow around the waist of the boat. Elsewhere was an utter black. *Optical aberration,* he understood. *And I'm seeing by Dopplered radio waves and X-rays. What happens when we pass the speed of light itself? No, we must have already—is this what it feels like, then?* The starbow of science fiction song and story pinched out into invisibility; he flew through total blindness. *If only we'd figured out some kind of speedometer.*

"Glorious, glorious!" chortled Urushkidan, rubbing his tentacles together as if he were foreclosing on yet another mortgage. "My teory is confirmed. Not tat it needs confirmation, but now eben te Eartlings must needs admit tat I am always right. And how tey will habe to pay!"

Dyann's laughter rolled Homeric through the hull. "Ha, ve are free!" she bawled. "All the vorlds are ours to raid. Oh, vat fun it is to ride in a vun-force boat and slay!"

Ray reassembled his wits. They'd better slow down and turn around while they could still identify Sol. He made himself secure in his seat, studied the gauges, calculated what was necessary, set the controls, and pushed the master switch.

Nothing happened. The vessel kept on going.

"Hey!" the man wailed. "Who! . . . Urushkidan, what's wrong? I can't stop accelerating!"

"Of course not," the Martian told him. "You must apply an exact counterfunction. Use te omega-wabe generator."

"Omega wave? What the hell is that?"

"Why, I told you—"

"You did not."

Ray and Urushkidan stared at each other. "It seems," the Martian said at length, "tat tere has been a certain failure of communication between us."

Weightlessness complicated everything. By the time that a braking system had been improvised, nobody knew where the boat had gotten to.

This was after a rather grim week. The travelers floated in the cabin and stared out at skies which, no matter how splendid, seemed totally foreign. Silence pressed inward with a might that would have been more impressive were it not contending against odors of old cooking and unwashed bodies.

"The trouble is my fault," Dyann said contritely. "If I had brought Ormun, she vould have looked after us."

"Let's hope she takes care of the Solar System," Ray said. "The Jovians aren't fools. When we left Ganymede, jetless, it must've been obvious we'd built the drive. They'll want to take action before we can give it to Earth."

"First," Urushkidan pointed out, "we habe to find Eart."

"It should be possible," Ray said. His tone lacked conviction. "We can't have gone completely out of our general part of the galaxy. Could those foggy patches yonder be the Magellanic Clouds? If they are, and if we can relate several bright stars to them—Rigel, for instance—we should be able to estimate roughly where we've come to."

"Bery vell," Urushkidan replied, "which is Rigel?"

Ray held his peace.

"Maybe ve can find somevun who knows," Dyann suggested.

Ray imagined landing on a planet and asking a three-headed citizen, "Pardon me, could you tell me the way to Sol?" Whereupon the alien would answer, "Sorry, I'm a stranger here myself."

Never being intended for proper space trips, the boat carried no navigational or astronomical tables. Since she had passed close to Neptune, or whatever globe that was, she had presumably been more or less in the ecliptic plane. Therefore some of the zodiacal constellations, those from which she had moved away, ought to be recognizable, though doubtless distorted. Ordinarily an untrained eye might have been unable to identify any pattern, so numerous are the stars visible in space. However, after a week without cleaning, the ports here were greasy and grimy enough to dim the light as much as Earth's atmosphere does.

Nevertheless Ray was baffled. "If I'd been a Boy Scout," he lamented, "I might know the skies. As is, all I can pick out are Orion and the Big Dipper, and I've no idea how they lie with respect to the zodiac or anything else." He gave Urushkidan an accusing glance. "You're the great astrophysicist. Can't you tell one star from another?"

"Certainly not," replied the Martian. "No astrophysicist eber looks at te stars if he can help it."

"Oh, you vant to find the con—con—starpictures?" Dyann asked.

"Yes, we have to," Ray explained. "Familiar ones that we can steer by. You're quite a girl in your way, honey, but I do wish you were more of an intellectual."

"Vy, of course I know the heavens," she assured him. "How vould

I ever find my vay around, huntin or raidin, othervise? And they are not very different in the Solar System. I learned your pictures for fun, vile I vas on Earth." She floated around the chamber from port to port, peering and muttering. *"Haa-ai,* yes, yonder are Kunatha the Qveen and Skalk the Consort . . . not much chanyed except—" she chuckled coarsely—"it is even more clear to see here than at home that they are begettin the Heir. You Earthlins take a section right out of the middle betveen those two and make a figure you call . . . m-m-m . . . ah, yes, Virgo."

"And you can tell us how the rest are arranged, and steer us till they have the right configurations?" Ray exclaimed. "Dyann, I love you!"

"Then let's get home fast," she beamed. "I vant to be on a planet." During the outward flight she had been discomfited at discovering the erotic importance of gravity.

"Control your optimism, Tallantyre," Urushkidan said dourly. "Trying to nabigate by eyeball alone, wit only a barbarian's information to go on, we may perhaps find te general galactic region we want, but tereafter we could cast about at random until our food is gone and we starbe to deat."

"Oh, I know the constellations close," Dyann said, "and I know how to take stellar measurements. It vill not be hard to make a few simple instruments, like for measurin angles accurately, that I can use."

"You?" the Martian screeched. "How in Nebukadashtabu can you have learned such tings?"

"Every noble in Kathantuma does, for to practice the—vat do you call it?—astroloyee. It is needful for plannin battles and ven to sow grain and marriage dates and everythin."

"Do you mean to say you are an . . . an . . . an astrologer?"

"Of course. I thought you vere too, but it seems you Solarians are more backvard than I supposed. Vould you like me to cast your horoscope?"

"Well," said Ray helplessly, "I guess it's up to you to pilot us back, Dyann."

"Sure," she laughed. "Anchors aveigh!"

Urushkidan retched. "Brought home by an astrologer. Te ignominy of it all."

Somehow Ray got his shipmates herded into seats, the vessel aimed according to Dyann's instructions, and the drive started. Given the modifications they had made, they could accelerate the whole distance and then stop almost instantly. The passage should not be long.

Except, of course, for the time-consuming nuisance of frequent halts en route to take navigational sights. Ray pondered this in the next couple of days, while he constructed the instruments Dyann required. That task was comparatively simple, demanding precise workmanship but no original thought to speak of. His engineering talent had free play; if nothing else, the problem took his attention from the zero-gee pigpen into which he was crammed.

Starlight was still around. It was merely Dopplered out of visible wavelengths and aberrated out of its proper direction. Both these effects were functions of the boat's speed—if "speed" was a permissible word in this case, which Urushkidan would noisily deny—and that in turn depended in a mathematically simple fashion on drive-pulse frequency and time. The main computer aboard, which controlled most systems, could easily add to its chores a program for reversing optical changes. There were several television pickups and receivers in the hold; normally, explorers on a Jovian moon would use them to observe a locale from a distance, but they could be adapted. . . .

After a pair of days more, Ray had installed in the forward cabin a gadget as uncouth to behold as the star drive itself, but which showed, on a large screen, ambient space undistorted. It was adjustable for any direction. Playing with it, Dyann found a group of stars which made her smile. "See," she said, "now Avalla is takin shape. That is the Victorious Warrior Returnin Vith Captive Man Slung Across Her Saddlebow."

"No," said Ray, "that's Ursa Major. You Kathantumans have a wild imagination."

Seated in the pilot's chair—for she had soon mastered the controls of the star drive, as crude as they were—Dyann continued swinging the scanner around the heavens. Abruptly the screen blazed. Had radiance not been stopped down, the watchers might have been blinded. As was, they saw a vast, incandescent globe from which flames seethed millions of kilometers—"A blue giant sun," Urushkidan whispered. For once he was awed.

Dyann's eyes sparkled. "Let's play tag vith it," she said, and applied a sidewise vector. "Yippee!"

"Hey!" the Earthling yelped. "Stop!"

They whizzed among the flames, dodging, while Dyann roared out a battle chant. Urushkidan huddled in his chair, squinched his eyes shut, and muttered, "I am being serene. I am being serene." Ray tried to recollect his childhood prayers.

The star fell behind. "Okay, ve continue," Dyann said. "Vasn't that fun? Ray, darlin, after this trouble is over, ve vill take a cruise through the galaxy, yust the two of us."

Time passed. The heavens majestically altered their aspect. The conquerors of the light-years floated about, gazed forth at magnificence, and ate cold beans.

"Ve are in the yeneral sector ve seek," Dyann said. "I have been thinkin. First ve go to Varann."

"Your native planet?" asked Urushkidan. "Ridiculous! We are returning directly to Uttu."

"Ve may need help in the Solar System," she argued. "Ve have been gone for two or three weeks. Much can have happened, most of it not good."

"But . . . but what help do you expect to get from a bunch of . . . Centaurians?" Ray spluttered. "It isn't practical."

Dyann grinned. "How vill you stop me, sweetheart?"

He considered the muscles which stirred beneath her tawny skin. "Oh, well," he said, "I always wanted to see Varann anyway."

For a few hours the amazon kept busy with instruments and pilot board. Then, astoundingly to Ray, she found her goal. Waxing in the screen were two yellowish suns very much like Sol. Out of the stellar background, a telescope identified a dim red dwarf at a greater distance. Nowhere else in this part of space did such a trio exist.

"Home, oh, home," Dyann murmured almost tearfully.

"Not quite," Ray reminded her with a certain slight malice. "How are you going to find your planet?"

"Vell . . . vell, uh—" She scratched her ruddy head.

He took pity and thought aloud for her benefit. "Planets are in the plane of the two main stars. They'd have to be. If we put ourselves in that plane, at a point where Varann's sun, Alpha A, appears to be the right size, and swing in a circle of that radius, we should come pretty close. It has a good-sized moon, doesn't it, and its color is greenish-blue? Yes, we ought not to have trouble."

"You are so clever," Dyann sighed. "It is sexy. Yust you vait till ve have landed."

At a modest fraction of the speed of light, a mere few thousand kilometers per second, the boat paced out her path. Before long, Dyann was jubilating, "There ve are! Look ahead! Home! After all these years, home!"

"I would still like to know what we are supposed to do when we get tere," Urushkidan snorted.

"I told Ray vat," Dyann retorted. "You suit yourself."

The man said nothing, being preoccupied. Terminal maneuvers were necessarily his responsibility. They took his entire flying skill and then some. He could use the cosmic drive to shed a velocity which would else have caused his craft to explode on striking atmosphere. However, he could not thereafter use the conventional jets; they were never meant for thick air or strong gravity. Thus he must also come down on the new system, which was incredibly precarious when he didn't have a universeful of room for error around him. He must make a descent which was largely aerodynamic, in a boat hijacked from a moon where aerodynamics was a farce. Probably he would never have succeeded, were it not for experience he'd gained when he spent part of his legacy on rakish sports flyers.

Wind boomed outside. The sky turned from black and starry to blue and cloud-wreathed. Weight dragged at bodies. The hull bucked and shuddered. Far below, landscape emerged. Ray had directed his approach by what he and Dyann remembered of maps—

"Kathantuma!" she shouted. "My own, my native land! See, I know her, yonder mountain, old Hastan herself. Yes, and that town, Mayta. Ve're here!"

VI.

When Ray had thumped the boat down onto the ground and his teeth had stopped rattling, he admitted to himself that this was pretty country. Around him waved rows of white-tasseled grain, wildflowers strewn among them in small brave splashes of color. Beyond the field he glimpsed a thatch-roofed rustic cottage and outbuildings, surrounded by trees whose foliage shone green-gold. In the opposite direction gleamed a river, crossed by a stone bridge which led to Mayta. The town seemed an overgrown village, timber houses snuggled about the granite walls of a castle whose turrets bore lacy spires from which banners flew. Elsewhere thereabouts, the land was devoted to pasture and woodlots, whose verdancy turned blue with distance till it faded into the snow-crowned heights which guarded this valley.

"Home," Dyann exulted. She unharnessed, rose, and stretched sinew by sinew, like a great cat. "And yust feel, darlin, ve got a decent up and down again."

"Uh—yeah." Ray had less pleasure. Fifty percent more pull than on Earth. . . . Urushkidan groaned and collapsed over his own seat like so much molasses.

"Come on out for some fresh air," Dyann said, "and ve vill find us a nice soft patch of turf."

She started to operate the airlock. He prevented her barely in time, and opened the valves the merest crack. Atmospheric pressure outside was considerably in excess of that within. No sense in getting a sinus headache; let the buildup be gradual. "Keep chewing and swallowing," he advised as the inward draught began to shrill.

"Vat? Vell, if you say so." Dyann reached for a hunk of cheese.

When at length they could go forth, it was into a freshness of cool breezes and the manifold scents of growing things, into trillings and chirpings from winged creatures that darted beneath sun-brilliant clouds, into air whose richness made every lungful heady as wine, so that aches and exhaustion vanished. "A-a-ah," Ray breathed. "You were right to make us stop here, sweetheart. What we need most after what we've been through is unspoiled nature, peace and quiet and—"

An arrow hummed past his ear and rang like a gong off the boat.

"Yowp!" Ray dived into the grain. Another arrow zipped where he had been. Dyann stood fast. After a moment, he ventured to raise himself, behind her back, and see what was happening.

From the rustic cottage, half a dozen women ran: a squat and scarred older one, and five tall and youthful who must be her daughters. They hadn't stopped to armor themselves with more than helmets and shields, but they did brandish swords and axes. The archer among them slung bow on shoulder as her companions closed in, and drew a dirk. Several men watched nervously from the farmyard.

"Ho-hai, saa, saa!" whooped Dyann. She herself was in full battle gear, that being the only clothing she had brought along. Her blade hissed free of its sheath. The matriarch charged. Dyann's blow was stopped by her shield, and her ax clanged grazingly off the newcomer's helmet. Dyann staggered. Her weapon fell from her grasp. The rest came to ring her in.

Dyann recovered. A karate-like kick to the elbow disarmed Mother. At once Dyann seized her by the waist, raised her on high, and threw her. Two of the girls went down beneath that mass. While they were trying to disentangle themselves, Dyann got under the guard of the next nearest and grappled.

Centaurian hospitality! flashed through Ray's mind.

A backhanded blow sent him over. Dazed, he looked up to see a daughter looming above. She smacked her lips, picked him up, and laid him across her shoulder. A sister tugged at him—by the hair—and said something which might have meant, "Now don't be greedy, dear; we go shares, remember?" They didn't seem worried about the rest, who were busy with Dyann and would obviously soon overcome her.

A trumpet blare and a thunder of hoofs interrupted. From the castle had come galloping a squad of armored ladies. Their mounts were the size and general shape of Percheron horses, though horned, hairless, and green. They halted at the fight and started to wield clubbed lances with fine impartiality. Combat broke up in a sullen fashion. From his upside-down position, Ray saw that none of the gashed and bruised femininity had suffered grave wounds. Yet that didn't seem to have been for lack of trying.

The guttural, barking language of Kathantuma resounded around. A rider, perhaps the chief, pointed a mailed hand at Ray's captor and snapped an order. The girl protested, was overruled, and tossed him pettishly to the ground.

When he recovered full awareness, his head was on Dyann's knees and she was stroking him. "Poor little man," she murmured. "Ve play too rough for you, ha?"

"What . . . was that . . . all about?"

"Oh, this family say they vas mad because ve landed in their grainfield. That's a lie. They could have demanded compensation. I'm sure they really hoped to seize our boat and claim it as plunder. Luckily, the royal cavalry got here in time to stop them. Since ve are still alive, ve can file charges of assault if ve choose, because this is not a legal duellin ground. I think I vill, to teach a lesson. There must be law and order, you know."

"Yes," whispered Ray, "I know."

Two days later—Varannian days, a bit shorter than Terrestrial —Dyann gave a speech. She and her traveling companions were on a platform by the main gate of the castle, at the edge of the market square. She stood; they sat in leather chairs, along with Queen Hiltagar, the Mistress of Arms, the Keeper of the Stables, and similar dignitaries. Pikes of troopers and lances of mounted ladies hedged the muddy plaza, to maintain a degree of decorum among the two or three hundred who filled it. These were the free yeowomen of the surrounding district, whose approval of any important action was necessary because they would constitute the backbone of the army. In coarse, colorful tunics; body paint; and massive jewelry, they kept flourishing their weapons and beating their shields. To judge by Dyann's gratified expression, that counted as applause. Here and there circulated public entertainers, scantily-clad men with flowers twined into their hair and beards, who strummed harps, sang softly, and watched the proceedings out of liquid, timid eyes.

Ray wasn't sure what went on, nor did he care very much. A combination of heavy weight, heavier meals, reaction to the rigors of his journey, and Dyann's demands kept him chronically sleepy. This evening, a lot of the potent local wine had been added. He could barely focus on the crowd. Beside him, Urushkidan snored, Martian style, which sounds like firecrackers in an echo chamber.

Dyann ended her harangue at last. Both cheers and jeers lifted deafeningly. Long-winded arguments followed, which tended to degenerate into fist fights, until Ray himself dozed off.

He was shaken awake when sunset turned heaven sulfurous above the roofs, and gaped blearily around. The assembly was dispersing, most people headed for the taverns which comprised a large part of Mayta. Stiff and sore, he lurched to his feet. Dyann was more fresh and rosy than he felt he should be asked to tolerate.

"It has been decided," she rejoiced. "Ve have agreement. Now ve must call other meetins throughout the realm, but there is no doubt they vill follow this lead. Already ve can send envoys to Almarro and Kurin, for negotiatin alliance. How soon can a fleet leave, Ray?"

"Leave?" he bleated. "For where?"

"Vy, for Yupiter. To attack the Yovians. Veren't you listenin?"

"Huh?"

"No, I forgot, you don't know our language. Vell, don't trouble your pretty little head about such things. Come on back to the castle, and ve vill make love before dinner."

"But," stammered Ray, "but, but, but."

How do you equip a host of barbarians, still in the early Iron Age, to cross four and a third light-years of space for purposes of waging war on a nation armed to its nuclear-powered teeth?

A preliminary question, perhaps, is: Do you want to?

Ray did not, but found that he had scant choice in the matter. Affectionately but firmly, Dyann made him understand that men kept in their place and behaved as they were bidden.

She did go so far as to explain her reasoning. Centaurians were not stupid, or even crazy. What they were—on this continent of Varann, at least—was warlike. While in the Solar System she had almost automatically, but shrewdly, paid close heed to the military-political situation. Afterward she had plugged the capabilities of the cosmic drive into her assessment. Most of the Jovian naval strength was deployed widely through space. If the escape from Ganymede had, indeed, made the Confederation decide to lean hard on the Union while the balance of power remained in its favor, that ought to leave the giant planet quite thinly guarded, sufficient to intercept conventional attackers but not any who came in faster than light. A raid in force should, if nothing else, result in the capture of Wotanopolis. No matter how austere by Terrestrial standards, that city was incredibly rich in Varannian terms. The raiders could complete their business and get home free, loaded with loot, covered with glory, and well supplied with captives. (As for the latter, there was hope of ransom, or possibly more hope of keeping them permanently as harem inmates. The polyandrous customs of this country worked hardship on many women.) While Earth might disown the action as piracy, it would doubtless not take punitive measures; everybody on the planet would be too relieved when an alarmed Confederation pulled its forces back to the Jovian moons.

Thus the calculation. Numerous ladies, Dyann foremost, recognized that it might prove disastrously wrong and the expedition end up as a cloud of incandescent gas or something like that. The idea didn't worry them much. If they fell audaciously, they would revel forever among the gods; and their names would ring in epic poetry while the world endured.

Failing to convince her otherwise, Ray sought out Urushkidan. The Martian, after an abortive attempt to steal the spaceboat and sneak off by himself, had been given a room high in a tower. Having adjusted a bit to the gravity, he sat amidst trophies of the hunt and covered a sheet of parchment with equations. *This place,* thought Ray, *has squids in the belfry.*

He poured forth his tale of woe. The Martian was indifferent. "What of it?" he said. "Tey may conceibably succeed, in which case we will doubtless be granted a bessel to trabel home in. If tey fail, ten it cannot be a matter of bery much time before te faster-tan-light engine is debeloped independently in te Solar System and somebody arribes here who can take us back."

"You don't understand," Ray informed him. "These buccaneers count on us as experts. They're bringing us along."

"Oh. Oh-oh! Tat is different. We better habe suitable armament." The Martian riffled through his papers. "Let me see. I tink equations 549 tro' 627 indicate—yes, here we are. It is possible to project te same type of dribing field as we use for transport in a beam which

SCHOMBURG

CAPTIVE OF THE CENTAURIANESS 115

imparts a desired pseudobelocity bector to an extraneous object. Also . . . look here. Differentiation of tis equation shows tat it would be equally simple to break intranuclear bonds by trowing a selected type of particle into te state, and none oter. Te nucleus would ten separate, wit a net energy release regardless of where it lies on te binding curbe because of te altered potentials."

Ray regarded him in awe. "You," he breathed, "have just invented the tractor beam, the pressor beam, the disintegrator, and the all-fuel atomic generator."

"I habe? Is tere money in tem?"

The man went to work.

Headquartered hereabouts, the three expeditions from Sol had each left behind a considerable amount of supplies, equipment, and operating manuals. The idea had been to accumulate enough material for the establishment of a permanent scientific base—an idea that faster-than-light travel had now made obsolete. Most of this gear was stored in the local temple, where annual sacrifices were made to the digital computer. It took an involved theological argument to get it released. The point that Ormun must be rescued was conceded to be a good one, but not until the high priestess held an earnest private discussion with Dyann, and was hospitalized for a while thereafter, did the stuff become available.

Meanwhile Ray had been working on design and, with native assistants, some of whom knew a little English or Spanish, getting a team organized. Urushkidan's new principles proved almost dismayingly easy to apply. Everything that wasn't in the depot, native smiths could hammer out, once given the specs. Atomic engines came forth capable of burning anything whatsoever. After consulting the gods, Queen Hiltagar decreed that the fuel be coal. Nobles vied for the honorable job of stokers.

The engines not only drove ships, but powered weapons such as Urushkidan had made possible. It proved necessary for Ray to call on the Martian for more—radiation screens, artificial gravity (after experiment showed that too many Kathantumans got sick in free fall and barfed), faster-than-light communicators, et cetera. These developments might well have taken years, except that the Martian grew sufficiently exasperated at the interruptions that he tossed off a calculus by which the appropriate circuits could be designed in hours.

Given this much, the spacecraft proper could be built to quite low standards. They were mere hulks of hardwood, slapped together by

116   CAPTIVE OF THE CENTAURIANESS

carpenters in a matter of weeks, varnished and greased for air tightness. Since the crossing would be made in a few hours, air renewal systems weren't required; it sufficed to have tanks of compressed gas, with leakage to prevent a buildup of excess carbon dioxide. Ray gave most of his attention to features like locks and viewports. Those had better not blow out! Still more did he concentrate on the drive circuits. They must be reliable during a trip to Sol and back, with an ample safety margin, but soon thereafter, they must fail. Not wishing the Centaurians ill, despite everything, he gave warning that this would happen, and was glad when it was accepted. Everybody knew that wire gave way after prolonged use, and here these ships were festooned with wires. The prospect of an amazon fleet batting about in the galaxy wheresoever it pleased had not been one that he could cheerfully contemplate.

Meanwhile the amazons themselves poured in, ten times as many as the thirty-odd hulls could hold, riding and hiking from the uttermost ends of Kathantuma and its neighbor queendoms to be in on the most gorgeous piece of banditry ever dreamed of. Only Dyann cared much about Ormun, who was just her personal joss, and only Ray gave a damn about Jupiter as a menace to Earth. However, the man was surprised at how quickly the chosen volunteers formed themselves into disciplined crews and how readily the officers of these developed the needful skills. It occurred to him at length that their way of life selected for alertness, adaptability, and—yes, though he hated to admit it—intelligence.

Three hectic months after his arrival on Varann, the fleet departed. After his labors, followed by Dyann's idea of a celebration, he used most of the travel time to catch a nap.

VII.

Enormous in the forward ports, banded with hues of cloud and storm that could have swallowed lesser worlds whole, diademed with stars, Jupiter swelled to vision. Ray's heart bumped, his palms were cold and wet, his tongue dry. Somehow he pushed his way through a throng of armored women. Dyann sat at the controls of the flagship, her gaze intent upon the giant ahead.

"Listen," he pleaded amidst the racket of eager contralto voices, "let me at least call Earth and find out what's been happening. You need to know yourself."

"Okay, okay," she said. "But be qvick."

He settled himself before the comscreen and fiddled with knobs.

Last year, the notion of virtually instantaneous talk across nearly a billion kilometers would have been sheer fantasy. He, though, was using a phase wave with unlimited speed to beam radio photons. It released them at a distance from Earth, which he had figured out on his pocket calculator, such that their front would reach a relay satellite with enough microwattage to be detected, amplified, and bucked on. The phone number attached to the signal was that of the Union's central public relations office. It was the only official one he knew where he could be sure to get a response without running a gantlet of secretaries.

The satellite beamed that reply back in the direction which its instruments had registered—with due allowance for planetary motions, of course. The Urushkidan-Tallantyre standing wave acquired the photons and passed them on. It also happened to acquire a commercial for Chef Quimby's Extra-Oleaginous Oleomargarine; and, when Ray received the information officer, that person resembled something seen through several meters of rippled water. At any rate, her image did. He hadn't had a chance to work the bugs out of his circuits.

"Who is calling, please?" she asked through an obbligato of *"Friends, in these perilous times, how better to keep up your strength for the case of civilization than by a large, nutritious serving—"*

"This is Raymond Tallantyre, calling from the vicinity of Jupiter. I've just returned from Alpha Centauri on a spacecraft traveling faster than light."

"—deliciously vitaminized—"

"Sir," the Union spokesman said, "this is no time to be frivolous."

"—it's yum-yum GOOD—"

"Listen," Ray cried, "I want to give the technology to the Union. Stand by to record."

On the far side of Dyann, Urushkidan slithered to attention. "Hey!" he piped. "I neber said I'd gibe away—"

"Your behavior is in very poor taste," said the official, and switched off.

Presently Ray regained the wit to find a newscast. That wasn't hard; there were a lot of newscasts these days. He gathered that Jupiter had declared war "to assert racial rights long and cruelly denied." Three weeks ago, the Jovians had won a major naval engagement off Mars. They were not yet proceeding against Earth, but threatened to do it unless they got an armistice on terms which amounted to surrender. Without that, they would "regretfully take appropriate measures" against a planet whose defenses had become feeble indeed.

"Oh, gosh," said Ray.

"An armada like tat will stretch capabilities," Urushkidan opined. "Te Union has ships and bases elsewhere. It can cut Jobian supply lines—"

"Not if the Jovian strategy is to make a dash inward, put missile carriers in orbit, and pound poor old Earth into radioactive rubbish," the human mourned. "Meanwhile, those gruntbrains yonder won't believe I've got what's needed to save them."

"Would you beliebe tat, from a phone call?"

"Well . . . I guess not. . . . But damnation, this is different!"

"I see a moon disc ahead," Dyann interrupted, "and it looks like Ganymede. Out of the vay, you two. Ve're clearin for action."

The flagship, which had been a peaceful laboratory boat, came in through atmosphere with a whoop and a holler. After casting about for a while above desolation, she found the dome of Wotanopolis and stopped at hover. The rest of the fleet, still less agile, followed more leisurely.

Lacking spacesuits, the crew could not disembark and break out the battering rams, as had been proposed back on Varann. After studying the situation, Dyann proceeded to the main freight terminal. There she cut loose with her disintegrator beam. The ship-sized airlock disappeared in blue fire and flowing lava. Air streamed forth, ghost-white as water vapor froze. Even a hole so large would take hours to reduce pressure dangerously within a volume as great as that of the city. Dyann sailed on through, into a receiving chamber which was almost deserted now in wartime. She set down near the entrance, unharnessed, and leaped to her feet. "Everybody out!" she yelled in English, and added a Kanthantuman exhortation. Her warriors bawled approval.

With fingers that shook, Ray buckled on helmet and cuirass and drew sword. Meanwhile, the rest of the barbarian fleet came in through the gap and clunked to rest, some on top of others. When all were inside, Urushkidan carried out his part of the mission by delicately melting the entry hole shut, to conserve atmosphere. He would stay behind, also, ready to open a passage for retreat. *How lucky can one being get?* thought Ray, as a swarm of warriors shoved him through the lock.

"Hoo, hah!" Dyann's sword shrieked on high. Her cohort poured after, whooping and bounding. The companion ships disgorged more. The abrupt change of pressure didn't seem to have given an earache to anybody except Ray. The racket of metal and girlish voices made that nearly unendurable. He had no choice but to be swept along in the rush.

Through the resonant reaches of the chamber—up a long staircase, five steps at a time—out over a plaza above, in clangor and clamor—

A machine gun raved. Ray bellywhopped onto the flooring before he had identified the noise. A couple of Varannians tumbled, struck, though they couldn't be too badly wounded to judge from the swiftness with which they rolled out of the line of fire. Across the square, he saw the gun itself, where a corridor debouched. Several men in gray uniform crouched behind it. Whatever garrison the city possessed was reacting efficiently. Ray tried to dig a burrow.

He needn't have bothered. With lightning reflexes, under a weight that to them was gossamer, the invaders had already escaped further bullets, leaping sideways or straight up. Spears, darts, flung axes replied. An instant later, the Centaurians arrived in person. Ray experienced an actual moment of sympathy for the Jovians. None of them happened to get killed either, but they were in poor shape.

An enemy squad emerged from the adjacent corridor. Their rapid-fire rifles could have inflicted fearful damage on the crowded amazons—except that one lady, who knew something about such things, picked up the .50-caliber machine gun and operated it rather like a pistol. The squad scampered back out of sight.

"Hai-ai!" the horde shouted, with additions. Ray, who had acquired a smattering of Kathantuman, might have blushed at these had time allowed. As was, he was again borne off on the tide of assault.

He saw little of what followed. In this warren of hallways and apartments, combat became almost entirely hand-to-hand. That was just what suited the Varannians, and what Dyann had counted on.

He did glimpse her in action when she rounded a corner and found a hostile platoon. She sprang, swung her feet ahead of her while she flew, and knocked the wind out of two men. As she landed on them, her sword howled in an arc which left two or three more disabled. One who stood farther off tossed a grenade at her. She snatched it and threw it back. He managed to catch and return it, but was barely able to duck before she flung it again and it blew in a door behind him. While this game went on, Dyann rendered a foeman unconscious by a swordblow to his helmet, broke the nose of another with the pommel of her weapon, and kneed a third. Then several more Centaurians joined in.

The gang of them went on. They had nothing left to do here. Ray dodged among their victims, past the door which the grenade had obligingly opened, into the apartment beyond. Maybe he could hide under a bed.

A hoarse shout sent him spinning around. Two members of the platoon had recovered enough to stagger in pursuit of him. He would have cried, "Hail, Wilder!" and explained what a peaceful citizen he was. Unfortunately, he too wore barbarian helmet and cuirass.

Before he could raise his hands, a Jovian had lifted rifle and fired. The shot missed. Though the range was close, the man was shaken. Also, in his time on Varann Ray had inevitably developed some strength and quickness. He didn't exactly dodge the bullet, but he flinched fast. His wild sword-swing connected. The Jovian sank to the floor and got busy staunching a bad cut.

His companion charged, with a clubbed rifle that was perhaps empty. Ray turned to meet him and tripped on his own scabbard. He clattered to the floor and the enemy tripped over him. Ray climbed onto the fellow's back, removed his helmet, and beat his head up and down till he lay semiconscious.

I've got to find someplace safe, Ray thought frantically. *Back to the ships, maybe?* He scuttled from the apartment, overleaped the human wreckage outside, and made haste.

Not far beyond, he came to an intersection. A tommy gun blast from the left nearly touched him. "No-o-o," he whimpered, and hit the deck once more.

A boot in his ribs gained his attention. "Get up!" he heard.

He reeled to obey. What he saw was like a physical blow. Elegantly black-clad men, the famous élite guard of the Leader, accompanied Martin Wilder himself. Beside the dictator stood none less than Colonel Roshevsky-Feldkamp—*in charge of local defense?* Ray wondered, and tried to stretch his arms higher.

"Tallantyre!" His old opponent glared at him for a time which took on characteristics of eternity. "So you are responsible."

"No, I'm not, so help me, no," Ray chattered.

"Who else could have brought these savages here?" The officer cuffed the Earthling; head wobbled on neck. "If it weren't for your hostage value, I'd shoot you immediately. But I had better defer that pleasure. March!"

The detachment proceeded wherever it was bound. That chanced to be down a mercantile corridor, on which shops fronted. Smashed glass and gutted displays showed that the Centaurians were already collecting souvenirs.

Wilder condescended to address the prisoner: "Never think that this criminal assault of yours has truly penetrated any part of us. We may have to retire temporarily from our capital, but already help has been summoned and is on its way, the entire navy bound here on a sacred mission of vengeance."

Will the Centaurians stop their looting in time to get clear of that? Ray thought in terror. *Somehow I doubt it.*

"I beg your pardon, glorious sir," interjected Roshevsky-Feldkamp, "but we really must make haste, before the invaders discover the emergency hangar we are bound for."

"No, no, that would never do," agreed the Leader.

"You must get aloft, glorious sir, to take charge of the counterattack."

"Yes, yes. I will strike a new medal. The Defense of the Racial Homeland Medal."

"You remember, of course, glorious sir, that we must not simply destroy the pirate spacecraft," Roshevksy-Feldkamp said. "We must capture them for examination. Afterward, the universe is ours."

"Hoo-hah!" rang between the walls. From a side passage staggered a band of Centaurians, weighted down with armloads of assorted loot. The guardsmen sprang into formation and brought their rifles up.

Something like an atomic bomb hit them from the rear. Ray learned afterward that Dyann Korlas and Queen Hiltagar had, between them, evolved a tactical doctrine that employed scouts to keep track of important hostile units and decoys to distract these.

What he witnessed at the time seemed utter confusion. A kind of maelstrom flung him against a wall and kept him busy dodging edged metal. He did glimpse Dyann herself as she waded into the thick of the fight, hewing, striking, kicking, a veritable incarnation of that Will to Conquer which the Symmetrists preached. Her companions wrought equal havoc. Ray took a minor part in the action. A guardsman reeled near him, tommy gun gripped, seeking a clear shot that wouldn't kill comrades. The Earthling plucked his sidearm from its holster and shot him—in the left buttock, because of recoil, but that sufficed.

Dyann saw. "Oh, how cute!" she caroled while she broke yet another head.

Combat soon ended. Most of the Jovians had simply been knocked galley west, and yielded with dazed meekness. Ray spied Wilder and Roshevsky-Feldkamp being prodded off by a squat, one-eyed, grizzled amazon with a silly smirk on her lips. They were doubtless destined for her harem—their decorations may have struck her fancy—and he couldn't think of two people he'd rather have it happen to.

Only . . . the whole enemy fleet could be arriving any minute—

What Ray did not know until later was that Urushkidan had prudently taken the original spaceboat outside and was using her beams to disintegrate those vessels and their missiles as they descended. Meanwhile he hummed an old Martian work song. There are times when even a philosopher must take measures.

VII.

Official banquets on Earth are notoriously dull. This one was no exception. That the war was over, that the Confederated Satellites would become the Jovian Republic and a respectable member of the World Union, that the stars were attainable: all seemed to call forth more long and dismal platitudes than ever.

Ray Tallantyre admitted to himself that the food and drink had been fine. However, there had been such a lot of both. He would have fallen asleep under the speeches had his shoes not pinched him. Thus he heard with surprise the president of his university describe what a remarkable student he had been. As a matter of fact, he'd damn near gotten expelled.

On his right, Urushkidan, crammed into a tuxedo tailored for his species, puffed a pipe and made calculations on the tablecloth. Left of the man, Dyann Korlas, her bronze braids wound about a plundered tiara, was stunning in a low-cut formal gown. The dagger at her waist was to set a new fashion. True, some confusion had arisen when she placed Ormun the Terrible at her plate and insisted that grace be said to the idol. Nevertheless—

"—unique scientific genius, whom his alma mater is pleased to honor with a doctorate of law—"

Dyann leaned close to whisper in Ray's ear: "Ven vill this end?"

"God knows," he answered as softly, "but I don't believe He's on the program."

"Ve have really had no time together since the campaign, have ve? Too many people, everyvun vantin us to do sometin or other. Vat are your plans for ven you get a chance to be yourself?"

"Well, first I want to try and patent the cosmic drive before Urushkidan does. Afterward . . . I dunno."

"It vas fun vile it lasted, our romp, vasn't it?" Her smile held wistfulness. "Me, I must soon go back to Varann. I vant to do some-thin vorthvile with my life, like find a backvard area and carve me out a throne. You, though—Ray, you are too fine and beautiful for such rough vork. You belon here, in the bright lights and glamour, not amon a bunch of unruly vomen vere you can get hurt."

"Right," he said.

"I vill alvays remember you." Her hand dropped warm across his wrist. "Maybe someday ven ve are old, ve can meet again and bore the young people vith brags about our great days."

She glanced around. "But for now, darlin, if only ve could get avay from here by ourselves. I know a good bar not far off. It has rooms upstairs, too."

"Hm-m-m," he murmured. The prospect attracted. When she wasn't being a warrior, she was very female. "This calls for tactics. If we could sort of slump down in our chairs bit by bit, acting tired—which ought not to surprise anybody that notices—till we've gradually sunk out of sight, then we could crawl under the table and slip out that service door yonder. . . ."

As he did, Ray heard Urushkidan, called upon for a speech, begin a detailed exposition of his latest theory.

LONGSHOT
by Jack C. Haldeman II
art: Jack Gaughan

*The tale told in a bar has a long and
distinguished history in our field,
beginning with Lord Dunsany's stories of Mr. Joseph Jorkens
and the Billiards Club, Arthur C. Clarke's White Hart, Fletcher
Pratt's and L. Sprague de Camp's Gavagan's Bar, and more
currently, Richard Wilson's 5280 Club, Spider Robinson's
Callahan's Crosstime Saloon, and Larry Niven's Draco Tavern.
Here, Mr. Haldeman has taken his series of strange sports
stories to an off-world bar.*

"Hot tip? Humph! A sure thing? I don't want to hear about it." The spacer slammed his drink on the bar and looked the robot bartender right in the electronic eye. "I've been from one side of this universe to the other and if I haven't learned anything else, I've learned that there's no such thing as a sure thing."

The bartender whirred and polished another glass.

"Sure I've played the ponies. I've been around. Nags on Old Earth, Bat Flies on Medi IV, Fuzzies on Niven—I've played them all, money on the nose. Was a time you couldn't keep me away from the tracks. Not anymore. I learned my lesson, but good. How 'bout another? A double."

The robot swallowed the empty glass, produced a full one. He sighed deep in his gearworks, afraid that this was going to be another burned-out spacer with a tale to tell.

It was.

The spacer's name was Terry Freeland, although everybody called him Crash, and his story was bound to be a tale of woe. Judging from the stubble on his face and the condition of his clothes, he hadn't lifted ship in a long time. Besides, if he had any money he wouldn't be drinking in a dump like this.

Except for a run of bad luck, thought the robot, *I wouldn't be pulling beers in a place like this, either*. Still, it beat pumping gas.

"It was on Dimian. You know Dimian? Out in the Rigel sector?" asked Crash, sipping his drink.

The robot nodded. He knew Dimian. A real backwater planet.

"Well, I was landing at the spaceport at Chingo. They got a lot of nerve calling it a spaceport, buncha gravel out in the middle of nowhere. Only two bars in the whole of Chingo, and it's the biggest town on Dimian. Some spaceport. Anyway, I was hauling a load of Venusian lettuce mold hoping to swing a big deal for some dutrinium. Wheeling and dealing, that's my game. Those sentients on Dimian really get off on lettuce mold. So I was coming in for a landing, you know, and . . . hey, I don't know what you've heard about me, but it ain't true I make a habit of bustin' up ships. Just had a few hard landings and a little bad luck, that's all. Like that time. They said I was drunk, but I say their null-field wasn't working right. Sure I'd had a shot or two while I was hanging in orbit, but that don't mean nothing. Do it all the time. Came down a little hard, that's all. Bent a stabilizer. Crunched a couple of scouts, but they were parked where they shouldn't 'a been. Anyway . . ."

It was looking to be a near total loss. They were overstocked on lettuce mold and Crash's profits didn't amount to much more than it took to fix the stabilizer and the two scouts. He hadn't been able to carry insurance since that time on Waycross, so everything was out-of-pocket. Still, he'd managed to pick up a load of dutrinium dirt cheap and if they'd ever finish fixing the stabilizer, maybe he'd be able to unload it on some other planet for big bucks.

He was always looking for big bucks. That's why he went to the track. That's why he listened to Whisky John. It was a mistake. Nobody listened to Whisky John. Nobody with any sense, that is.

Whisky John was born bad news.

"I tell you, it can't miss," said Whisky John. "These yo-yos don't know the first thing about handicapping."

"You mean they actually race these monsters?"

"Sure. That's the whole idea. These Dimians don't know nothing. They work 'em in the field till they get too old to cut the mustard, then they turn 'em loose on the track. These Dimians are crazy wild about betting. Most only thing to do around here."

"So where's the edge?" asked Crash.

"What you do is find one that's been out in the field a long time but hasn't done much work. He may be old, but he'll probably have a few kilometers left in him. I got it straight from B'rrax, a stableboy who sweeps out the stalls, that the sleeper of the year is going to be Heller."

"Heller?"

"That's the one. Eighty-five years old and getting pretty long in the tooth. But he was owned by National and they don't do much dredging, so he's had an easy life. He's the longshot. Two hundred to one. *Two hundred to one!*"

Crash cast a doubtful eye over the field. Monsters they were, too. The natives called them something unpronounceable that was roughly translated as "behemoths." It was an understatement. They looked like three elephants piled one on top of another. Had about as many legs, too. Thirty meters high and Lord knows what they weighed. Crash figured they could dredge pretty good, but he had a hard time imagining them racing around a track.

"Two hundred to one, you say? Eighty-five years old?"

"A sure thing. You can't lose."

"If you're so smart, how come you ain't rich?" asked Crash.

"Bad luck and hard times," said Whisky John wistfully. "I've had more than my share of both. Believe me, if I had any cash I'd put it right on the beast's, er, nose. Had to let you in on this. Figure I owe you one from that time on Farbly." He winked and Crash blushed. It had been close on Farbly, that's for sure. They'd been lucky to get out at all.

"I don't know," said Crash.

"How much you got? Cash."

"Free and clear? Let me see, after the stabilizer, uh . . . about 500 creds."

"Think about it. One hundred thousand creds! Free and clear. No taxes on Dimian. You could get a bigger cruiser, anything. Think about it."

Crash thought about it and the more he thought about it the better it seemed. It was all the cash he had and if he lost it he'd have to eat peanut butter crackers till he dumped the dutrinium. But still—*One Hundred Thousand Creds!*

He placed the bet.

Together they climbed into the stands; tall, rickety old wooden bleachers a good half click from the track. There were a few off-worlders scattered through the crowd, even a couple more humans, but mostly it was wall-to-wall Dimians. Whisky John was right about one thing—Dimians were sure crazy wild about behemoth racing.

Crash didn't know much about the Dimians, except that he thought they were weird. They probably thought Crash was weird, too. They looked like crickets, were about a meter tall, and talked in a high, squeaking rasp that Crash couldn't understand. Whisky John could speak it a little on account of his being marooned on Dimian for a good many years waiting for his ship to come in. Every time he got a few creds ahead, he'd blow it away with some crazy scheme. Whisky John was a mite irresponsible.

Down on the track, several Dimians were herding the behemoths towards the starting line. Crash noted with pleasure that Heller was still listed on the tote board at 200-1.

The Dimians moved the beasts along with huge prods, never getting closer to one than necessary. Crash didn't blame them, they were dwarfed by the massive animals. Looked like mountains being led around by small bugs. Hairy mountains.

"Where are the jockeys?" asked Crash.

"What jockeys? You couldn't pay a Dimian enough to climb on top of one of those monsters," replied Whisky John.

"How do they get around the track?"

"Sometimes they don't. When that starting gun goes off they go where they damn well please. Mostly they head around the track, though, since that's the way they're pointing at the beginning. They

128   LONGSHOT

ain't too smart."

"Which one's Heller? I can't make out the numbers."

"It's easy to tell. He's the one on the left."

"No!"

"Yes."

If behemoths were mountains, Heller was a mountain with rickets. Most of his hair had fallen out. He was a mountain with a bad case of the mange. Half his legs didn't look like they worked right. Where the others had gleaming tusks, Heller had rotten stumps. Where the others had blazing eyes, Heller had sad, dull orbs. He had loser written all over him.

"You mean my money's on *that?*"

"Smart money, too. You can't tell a book by its cover, I always say. He can still hit the fast ball, probably tear the track apart." Whisky John was an incurable optimist, especially with other people's money.

"He's blind as a bat. He can't walk. He looks like he's a hundred years old."

"Eighty-five," corrected Whisky John.

"If he's eighty-five, how old are the others?"

"Average out about thirty, I reckon. That's good for an old behemoth. But remember he's two hundred to one. He's had an easy life."

"Easy life? He looks like a hundred miles of bad road." Crash was trying to figure out if he had time to strangle Whisky John and still run down to get his money back before the race started.

He was too late. The race started.

Crash could tell the race started because the Dimians in the crowd went wild, screaming and jumping up and down. It was harder to tell by looking at the behemoths, though, because they just seemed to be wandering aimlessly around, bumping into each other.

"This is a race?"

"Exciting, isn't it?" said Whisky John.

Three of the behemoths started lurching more or less down the track and the spectators went wild. Some of the others followed the leaders, including, to Crash's surprise, Heller. He wasn't last, either. Not if you counted the two behemoths that had fallen down and the one that was going the wrong way. Crash felt a faint hope rising.

"Come on, Heller," he shouted in desperation, pounding Whisky John on the shoulder.

It soon became apparent why the stands were so far from the track. Once the behemoths started, they went any old which way and didn't stop for anything. Unless, of course, they fell down. They were very good at falling down. They were better at falling down than running. Each time one toppled over, the ground shook. One had crashed through the fence around the track and was wandering out into the desert. Heller was in fourth place and losing ground rapidly.

He had to win or it was peanut butter crackers for Crash. Lots of peanut butter crackers.

The track was a jumble of lurching, tottering behemoths. Half of them had fallen down. The falling down part was easy, but the getting up was hard. Some of them just fell asleep after they flopped, only to be woken up by another one stumbling into them. They were the clumsiest animals Crash had ever seen. The lead behemoth got his legs all tangled up and went down in a heap. The second-place one tripped over him. Suddenly everything had changed. Heller was in second place, straining for the lead.

"Atta boy," shouted Crash, pounding Whisky John's arm some more. "You can do it."

They were lumbering down the home stretch now, neck and, er, neck, their bodies swaying with each ponderous step.

"Don't fall down, Heller. Don't fall down!" Crash's heart was pounding furiously. So was his hand and Whisky John's arm was getting mighty sore.

As they approached the checkered flag, Heller was a tusk behind and giving it all he had. Just before the finish line, however, a gleam came into those eyes that had been dull so many years. Something stirred deep in the beast's massive chest. *Pride! Glory!* He straightened his bent back. He rose up on his crippled legs. He gave a mighty leap forward. *Victory!*

Crash about died.

Two hundred to one. He was already spending his money. Whisky John's arm felt like a chinaberry tree hosting a woodpecker convention.

They went to collect the money. Whisky John did the talking. They handed him a large paper bag full of cred-slips and a huge coil of rope. Whisky John looked pale.

"I swear, Crash, I didn't know." He had sick written all over his face.

"Know what? That's the money, right?"

"Right. One hundred thousand creds. It's all here. But I swear I didn't know, honest."

"We got the money, so what's to worry about? Let's go."

"It's not that easy, Crash."

"What do you mean? We just walk out and it's party time."

"See this rope, Crash?"

"Yeah. Nice rope. Let's go."

"This rope is for your behemoth."

"My what?"

"Your behemoth. Heller. He's yours. It was a claims race—I swear I didn't know—you just won the money *and* the behemoth, every metric ton of him."

"I won't do it. I'll leave him. Let's go." Crash was having none of this. He wanted to start spending his money.

"You can't just abandon him, Crash. He belongs to you now, at least as far as the Dimians see it. They won't stand for it. Behemoth racing is part of their religion and they take it seriously. If you dump Heller they'll kill you."

"Kill me?"

"Tear you limb from limb."

Gulp. Crash could see this was a serious matter. They walked over to the paddock area where several Dimians were washing down the behemoths with large hoses.

"I guess I could race him some more," said Crash doubtfully. "He probably has a few laps left in him. Maybe even make some money out of it."

"That's it, Crash. Hey, I'll be running along."

"You stay right here."

They looked up at Heller. He was panting at a ferocious rate. He looked terrible close up.

"What does he eat?"

"Volmer sprouts. Only the tender ones. About 10 kilos a day."

"Expensive?"

Whisky John nodded.

"Maybe I can sell him."

"That's it. Sell him. Good idea. I guess I'll be—"

Crash froze him with a stare.

"He doesn't look all that bad," lied Crash, trying to make the best out of a rotten situation. He walked towards the towering beast. "Probably lots of people out there would want a winner like him." He stood directly under Heller, looked up at his chin.

"Don't touch him!" cried Whisky John.

Crash patted Heller's massive toe, looked back over his shoulder. "What?" he asked.

Too late.

Heller rolled his eyes and swished his tail. He moaned with the sound of a thousand breaking hearts.

"Oh Lord," said Whisky John. "Now you've done it. A Love Bond."

"A what?" Heller leaned down and licked Crash on the side of the head. It sent him reeling.

"If you touch a behemoth they fall in love with you. Instantly and forever. It's called a Love Bond and there's no getting out of it. It's the peak of the Dimian's religious experience. If you tried to sell him now . . ."

"I know, they'd kill me."

"Limb from limb," added Whisky John with a serious shake of his head. "You are stuck for life."

Crash could see that Heller loved him. Love just oozed from every pore on the poor animal's massive body. He rolled his eyes with love. He waved his trunk with love. He made soul-wrenching groans of love. It was a pitiful sight. Crash felt sorry for the beast.

"He is kinda cute, at that," said Crash. "A fella could get to like him."

They tied the rope around Heller's neck and led him away. The rope was unnecessary; he followed Crash like a giant puppy dog.

Unfortunately, he made a very clumsy puppy dog. He stepped on a grocery wagon, squashed it flat. Crash dug a handful of creds out of the paper bag. He sideswiped an aircar. Crash dug into the bag. He wiped out ten light poles and three traffic lights. Crash dug into his bag and led him out of town.

On the edge of the desert, out of harm's way, Crash sat on a rock and surveyed the problem. He still had a lot of money. Money could simplify any situation. He was beginning to like Heller.

"You know," he said to the behemoth, "you and I could go places together. Do things."

He sat on the rock and talked to Heller for hours, making plans for the future, spinning dream castles that involved lots of Volmer sprouts and won races. Whisky John counted the money out into little piles on the sand. Heller stood and wheezed a lot. The sun fell low on the horizon.

So total was Heller's love for Crash that it must have been contagious. Or maybe it was the wine Crash was drinking. Anyway, the spacer was so overcome by emotion that he climbed a tree and gave Heller a kiss on the nose.

It was too much for poor old Heller. His heart couldn't stand so much happiness. He smiled a huge lovesick grin, moaned, and fell over dead.

132   LONGSHOT

The ground shook. Crash was heartbroken. He had come to love Heller nearly as much as Heller had loved him.

"What am I going to do?" cried Crash.

"Bury him."

"How am I going to go on without him?" wailed Crash.

"You got to bury him," said Whisky John, taking a slosh of the wine bottle. "All very clear."

"What's very clear?" asked Crash, casting a suspicious eye towards the other man.

"It's all Love Bond ritual. Has to be done a certain way. You dig the hole—nobody can help you, got to do it yourself—right where he died. Then you got to get their magical men to come and do their stuff. Then you got to put up a monument, has to be a big one, too. No skimping."

"Sounds expensive."

"A Love Bond is no simple thing."

"How much?"

"See that pile of money there?" He pointed to the rest of the winnings and Crash nodded. "Kiss it goodbye."

"No way out?"

"They'd—"

"I know. Limb from limb. Hole alone'll take me a week to dig."

It took two.

Crash lifted off from Dimian broke as a clam. He ate peanut butter crackers for a long, long time.

"That's how it went," said Crash, setting his empty glass in front of the robot bartender. It was his tenth empty glass. "Learned my lesson." He shook a bent smoke from the crushed pack in his pocket.

The bartender whirred sympathetically. This was one hardluck spacer. He wiped the counter with the bar rag. Crash got shakily to his feet, headed for the exit.

He paused at the door, turned towards the bartender. "That was the fifth race, you said, wasn't it?"

The robot nodded. Good odds, too.

THE JAREN
by Frederick Longbeard
art: Stephen E. Fabian

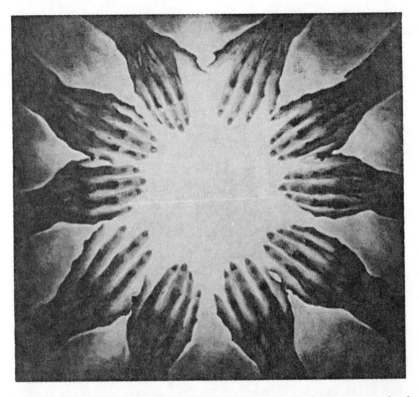

The hunting on Baalphor, as always, was good. My party had bagged its limit of the elusive Haak goats, and we sat around a fire that night—Dr. Velstock, Jamie Fender, the developer Wiggins, and I. The night was warm, yet we stoked the fire for its light—light that prompted memories and loosened tongues almost as well as the Purim that we were drinking in quantities that would have been distressing had we been in more civilized surroundings. But the campfire after the hunt was as ingrained in the race of humans as was the grasp for land, or money, and much older.

We had taken on an old Shikki when we reached Baalphor, to cook, clean up, and haul some of our gear. They are unreliable, to say the least. I don't think anyone has seen one of the dark-skinned humanoids sober—I never have. But they are cheap, and sufficiently obedient when clearheaded enough to understand orders. Our Shikki had gathered wood for the fire, and had retired to the edges of the clearing surrounding our camp, with a bottle of Purim. The old fellow seemed to sock the stuff away in quantities that we found not distressing, but astounding.

The developer Wiggins, his legs stretched out and his back leaning against a log, looked around at the firelight reflecting from the trees, then nodded. "You are right, Hill," he said to me, "this planet has many possibilities." He waved a hand at the night. "Chief among them is no bugs."

I laughed. "I thought you would see it my way, once you visited."

Wiggins nodded. "And you own all this property we have been on?"

"Yes, and quite a bit more. Land here is cheap, but not for long. Other developers have been looking here as well."

The developer smiled, then looked in my direction. "When I like a place, the competition tends to fade away."

"I know. That is why I made an effort to interest you in my proposition. And you like the place?"

Wiggins stared into the fire. "Yes, I think so." He turned toward me and smiled. "I confess that I was worried, never having been on this planet before."

Dr. Velstock leaned forward. "You weren't worried on account of the Mithad, I hope. They have been as docile a bunch as you could ever hope to see, even though they can now vote."

Wiggins shook his head. "My concern was about the Shikkies, but," he held out his hands, "there seems to be nothing to worry about from that quarter."

Jamie Fender laughed. "The Shikkies? You have nothing to worry about from the Shikkies, Wiggins. All they want is a bottle and a dry spot to sleep."

We all chuckled. Wiggins nodded, then turned toward Fender. "I see all this now, but on another planet, it is hard to see things as clearly. Stories about the Shikkies are still used to frighten children where I come from." He cocked his head in the direction of our Shikki beast of burden. "But I see more clearly now."

Dr. Velstock nodded. "Since the Shikkies were conquered, they have been no trouble—"

"No!"

We all looked up. The old Shikki stood at the edge of the clearing, weaving as he held his precious Purim bottle around the neck with a tight grasp. Dr. Velstock laughed. "No offense, old fellow." He turned to Wiggins. "I can't imagine what's got into him."

The Shikki staggered toward us until he stood before the fire. He was tall, and his muscles spoke of a strong youth. His skin was almost black, his hair a shock of white streaked with yellow. His black eyes seemed to study us, but from the level in his Purim bottle I passed it off to drunken behavior.

I stood and pointed my finger at the old Shikki. "Go back to your drinking, Eeola."

The Shikki held the bottle in his left hand. With his right, he pointed at Dr. Velstock. "We are not conquered, human. The Shikazu cannot be conquered."

Velstock shook his head and laughed. "I beg to differ with you, old fellow, but I am as familiar with the war of the four stars as anyone. I was in it."

The Shikki took a pull from his bottle, then squatted down beside the fire. "I too was in the war, human, and I say we were not conquered."

Jamie Fender snickered, then jabbed Dr. Velstock in the arm. "Perhaps our historians have lied, Doctor. I would hear this old fellow's version."

Wiggins laughed and poured himself another cup of Purim. "Let us hear this version. I would like to know why we rule Baalphor and the other Shikki planets, yet the Shikkies are not a conquered race."

He turned toward the old Shikki.

"Tell us your story, and if your throat gets dry, our supply of Purim is handy."

Wiggins laughed roundly, and was soon joined by Fender and Velstock. Normally, I would have joined them, but for once I took a good look at a Shikki. He wore the same kind of leather shirt and black sarong-like underwrapping worn by all the Shikkies, but those eyes—there was a haunted brilliance there that I had never seen before. That dull-eyed, out-of-focus appearance I had come to associate with Shikkies was gone. Eeola stood, observed my companions, then turned away. In a moment, he was gone from the clearing.

Velstock laughed and turned toward Wiggins. "I'm afraid you offended the old fraud."

Wiggins shrugged and took another swallow of his Purim. Lowering the cup, he chuckled. "Shikkies do have a low entertainment value, don't they?" He faced Fender and Velstock. "Enough of that. Are both of you interested in this development proposal?"

136   THE JAREN

I stood. "I should follow the old Shikki."

The developer waved a hand back and forth. "Don't bother. He bores me, anyway."

"I should make sure that the drunken old fool doesn't fall off a ledge and kill himself."

Fender nodded. "It would never do if we had to carry all our own things."

I smiled, then left my companions and turned into the jungle after the Shikki. He was not far. Eeola sat on a rocky outcropping overlooking a steep cliff. The jungle floor spread into the distance, and on the horizon stood the peculiar landmark that marked the center of my property. In the bright light of Adn, Baalphor's only moon, the feature seemed larger than I remembered seeing it during the day. It was a portion of the jungle floor, risen on a huge cake-shaped formation of rock. I turned from it to see the old Shikki finishing his bottle of Purim.

"My friends didn't mean to hurt your feelings. Come back to the fire."

Eeola issued one sharp laugh, then tossed his empty bottle over the cliff. He laughed again, then listened as the bottle smashed on the rocks below. "They do not hurt my feelings." He shook his head. "I should have said nothing, but this place," he held his hands out toward the landmark, "it loosens a drunken tongue."

I lowered myself and sat on a rock facing the Shikki. "This place has special meaning to you?"

Eeola shook his head. "It is of no interest to you."

I held out my hands. "Then why am I sitting here, and why did I ask?"

The Shikki shrugged. "To understand the meaning of this place to me, you must understand me, and for that . . ." he held up an arm and pointed at the sky, "you must understand from where I came." He dropped the arm into his lap and shook his head. "Too much understanding, from a human."

I was not used to Shikkies talking to me in that manner, and my face grew hot. But, for some reason, I held my peace. Eeola sat quietly, and for such a long time, I felt certain the old fellow had passed out. I was about to leave when a pale blue shimmering began in the jungle below. It faded, then began again in a new place. It faded once again and I strained my eyes for it. I turned to Eeola to ask him about it, and the blue light passed between me and the Shikki, then seemed to settle beside him. I could not move; it was as though my buttocks had become rooted to the rock. After a few moments, another such light joined the first, then another, and another, until four separate lights made a circle, with Eeola forming a fifth part of it. Slowly, Eeola turned his head, until he faced me.

"Then, listen, human, while I take words and grant life to those who I am not yet able to grant death."

I would tell you of my Jaren; of Vastar, our warrior *Di*, who took the charge in battle much as he did when we were children; of Gemislor, whose broad back and jokes held us together through flame and privation; of mighty Dob, whose ruthlessness on the field of battle was matched only by his gentleness with a lost or hungry animal; of Timbenevva, whose pipes could make flagging spirits soar, and whose sly tongue could talk the very stars from the sky; and, of myself. I, Eeola, was the youngest member of the Jaren.

The human historians—those who deign to mention it—pass off the Jaren as a military organization; a form of half-squad in human terms; but the Jaren is much more. True, it is the building block of the Shikazu infantry, but it is, as well, family, schoolmates, friends, and yet more even than this. You are the Jaren, and without the Jaren, you are not.

Before entering the military, before adulthood, before instruction at the village *kiruch,* as naked children playing at war with moss forts and water guns, the Jaren is formed. Over forty Earth years ago, in my village on the planet Tenuet, my story begins.

Ahrm was but a tiny village, no more than a wide place in the road on the way to the golden city of Meydal, but its single dusty street crowded with wattle huts was the center of my universe. As a *tikiruch,* a carefree preschooler running naked with my mates, nothing seemed more important to me than joining in Jaren with Vastar. All the children of Ahrm admired Vastar, for even as a callow *tikiruch,* he stood a head or better above the rest of us, could outrun us all, and could wrestle any three of his mates to the ground. In our games, he would choose them, organize them, then win them. When we would take our water guns and deploy through the jungle to ambush phantom armies and shadow monsters, Vastar would always lead us. Even the elders at the evening meeting fire would nod at him, knowing someday Vastar would *Di* a Jaren, and because of that, the Jaren would be great and do heroic deeds. Such would reflect well on Ahrm. I would daydream, but deep in my heart I knew that when Vastar formed his Jaren, I would not find myself one of its five. But toothless old Jevvey, my grandmother, had the faith that I lacked. She once sat before her hut tending her evening meal, stripped *sa* wrapped in yanna leaves, baked in the ground over a bed of turawood coals. She sat as motionless as a smoke-blackened carving, her straggles of thin white hair hanging at the sides of her head.

"The evening finds you sad, little one."

I looked down and nodded. "Yes, Grandmother."

"Must I pull the reason from you as the fishers drag eels from their holes?"

I sighed, then shrugged. "Grandmother, will I *never* be joined in Jaren?"

The old woman snorted. "You are the son of the Ice Flower and the Silver Bird, two respected Jarens. You ask foolish questions."

"But I am small. Even you call me 'little one.' What Jaren would have me?"

Jevvey shook her head. "The ghosts of my Jaren mates weep at your foolishness. Take care, else they shall steal into your hut and rob you of your breath."

I frowned. "I am not a child, Grandmother. You can't frighten me with tales of ghosts."

Jevvey looked at me, her eyes soft and black. "Eeola, I am the last of my Jaren, yet my mates still stand with me. They will always be with me until they call me to the endless sleep." She poked at the steaming ground with a stick. "One day you shall be part of a respected Jaren, and, perhaps years from now, you will see that the Jaren is forever. We are but bone and flesh, but the Light that fills you as an adult never dies." She sniffed and began scooping off the dirt from the cooked *sa*. "It is time for you to go home, little one."

I stood, wished her a good night, then walked the darkening path to my father's hut. Had I not been despondent about my chances of being joined in Jaren, the talk of ghosts would have hurried my steps. Instead, my feet dragged through the dust as I listened to *tikiruch* being called to mealtime by their mothers.

One day a few of us joined Vastar on one of his daring exploits. The *kiruchta,* the older schoolers, were at a clearing deep in the jungle, practicing with shield and wand under the stern instruction of Lodar, the village fencing master. Although the wands were at low energy output, a burst or slash on naked skin would blister it. A stray beam could blind a wide-eyed *tikiruch,* which is why we were forbidden to watch them practice, and which is why we skulked through the jungle to observe our seniors being put through their drills.

Crouching on all fours, peering out from beneath broad yanna leaves, our disrespectful band watched with eager eyes as the *kiruchta*, paired off in twos, traded beams and parries. Each student wore the *be*, the half-dress wrapped around the waist with the tail pulled between the legs and tucked in front. Their skins were already the deep brown of rich soil, with streaks of pink on cheeks, shoulders, and thighs showing where wands in quick hands had found their marks. Each student held the clear wand, each tipped with its burning blue jewel, in the left hand, while right hands clasped the grips of black deflection shields. We giggled watching the students going wall-eyed, with one eye on opponent and the other on Lodar. No student dared let a stray beam fall on the fencing master, for Lodar would take this as a challenge. The student would then have to square off with the master and take his licks.

Lodar strode among the sweating students, pointing here and commenting there. He wore the *nabe*, the forest green full dress of an adult. His shield was slung on his back, but his wand was kept at the ready in his left hand. After a few moments of watching, we noticed one of the students being bested by an opponent obviously his superior at arms. With wand and shield, the hapless *kiruchta* defended himself in a blur of arms, but the coins of chance were against him. As he backed away, the tail of his *be* untucked and fell behind his scrabbling feet, where he stepped upon it, pulling the entire dress from his waist.

As we pained at our stifled giggles, none of us noticed Lodar slip into the jungle and come up behind us. The grizzled old master must have smiled as he saw our row of brown bums sticking out at him from under the yanna plants, but in the flash of an eye, our giggles turned to yelps. Our band jumped to its feet, each one clutching a burning cheek in each hand. Lodar's skilled wand had played across our buttocks, and for the next few days there would be much sleeping on stomachs and eating while standing in the village of Ahrm. The master scolded us and sent us running back toward the village to nurse our dignities.

Each one of us bore a pink stripe as evidence of our infraction, and we were reluctant to bring them to our huts, for when we did our parents would discover our sin. Until the pain of Lodar's wand eased, none of us could bear having the hard hands of our angry fathers popping off of our burned and chubby cheeks. Most of the others fled to hideouts of their own, while Vastar, Gemislor, Dob, Timbenevva and I sulked in the brush behind the village. None of the others were crying, but it was almost more than I could do to swallow my own tears. The Shikazu take humiliation hard, and our striped buttocks would be cause for jokes and laughter for years to come. Our faces burned more fiercely than did our bums.

While we stood sullenly, rubbing our humiliated flesh, I remember with the perspective of youth, thinking that I could not possibly survive that moment. It was then that Vastar laughed. The cream blond of his mane shook, then he threw his head back and howled. Leaping atop a stump, he held out his arms. "Gather 'round me, mates; gather 'round."

The four of us stood before the stump, our humiliation temporarily forgotten in our concern for our friend's sanity. He laughed at the sky, then looked down at us. "Mates, this day we have all been blooded with the same wand, and it is no shame to have Lodar's fire kiss your skin." He smiled, then nodded. "We are one in this, mates, and I would now form my Jaren.

"Gemislor, will you join me?"

Gemislor nodded, his eyes glowing. The elders had commented at many fires at how slow our generation of *tikiruch* was in forming Jarens. Many of them thought it was a sign that the Shikazu spirit was on the wane, but the cause was nothing so profound. We were all waiting for Vastar to form his Jaren in the hopes of being among its number.

"And you, Dob. Will you join me?"

Dob's hulking shoulders pulled back as his spine straightened. "Aye, Vastar. Aye."

"And you, Timbenevva?"

"Aye. Your Jaren I will join."

Vastar turned toward me. I was smaller than the others and the worst runner in Ahrm. My most outrageous dreams did not see me thus. I swear my heart jumped as Vastar spoke.

"And you, Eeola. Will you join me?"

My heart stopped as I felt my mouth ask the question it had to ask. "Why me, Vastar? Why do you choose me?" I waved my hand at the others. "The blind can see why you choose Gem, Dob, and Tim; they are tall, strong, brave."

My lower lip trembled as Vastar stepped down from his stump and placed his hands on my shoulders. "Eeola, a great Jaren must have more than brawn and speed; it must also have brains. This is what my father has taught me, and he speaks the truth. You are the smartest *tikiruch* in Ahrm, except for me. What do you say? Will you join me?"

I nodded as my face exploded into smiles. Vastar smiled back, then turned and mounted his stump. "Our Jaren is formed, and we shall swear so before the meeting fire tonight."

"Vastar," called Timbenevva. "We may wear our paint now that the Jaren is formed. What shall our symbol be?"

Dob admired the blue-painted flying creature he had seen on the left arms of a Jaren from another village. Gem insisted on the bright yellow lightning bolts he had seen on a warrior's hairy chest. Tim and I were both shouting for attention when Vastar held up his hands for silence. "Listen mates. Our sign shall be a single red bar," he turned around and pointed at the pink stripe across his bum, "worn here."

Vastar raised his brow at us, we stood in silence for an instant, then all laughed. We would be spared our fathers' wrath, for the paint would hide the evidence. Laughing so hard he was barely able to stand, Dob ran to the village to secure paint and brushes. In the span of a few seconds I had become locked in life with the finest Jaren Ahrm would ever see and had adopted a curious sign that we would all be sworn to defend with our lives. Of such things are symbols made and destinies forged.

That night the five of us stood across the meeting fire from the hedman of Ahrm and declared our Jaren, our brightly painted backsides facing the people of the village. As I stood with my four tall companions, I could feel the eyes of envy dancing on my back. The pungent smell of turawood came from the fire while the pops and hisses joined the flickering light creating an aura that took us all back to the primitive ages of the first Jarens. The hedman, his deep green *nabe* decked with golden chains, looked up from the village book wherein was entered the signs of all the village Jarens. His voice, though strong, was rough with age. Nevertheless, he fixed us all with an unblinking, black-eyed gaze. "There is no record of a Jaren of the Redbar in Ahrm." He closed the book and held out his arms. "This, then, is the Jaren of the Redbar?"

"Aye." We all responded with our heads bowed.

"Do you swear that your lives, your fortunes, and your futures are now as one, in the name of the Light?"

"We swear it."

"And who shall *Di* the Jaren of the Redbar?"

All but Vastar lifted their heads.

"Vastar of Ahrm is our *Di*."

"And this shall ever be so?"

"Aye."

The hedman nodded, then looked at Vastar. "*Di* of the Jaren of the Redbar."

Vastar looked up. "I am Vastar."

"Do you swear to *Di* this Jaren with fairness, strength, wisdom, and to do your best to bring it before the Light?"

"I so swear."

The hedman looked down, opened the book and held out a single brush dipped in red paint. "Make the mark of the Redbar, then, Vastar, and bring honor to your village." The people of the village cheered as our *Di* walked around the fire, took the brush and made the mark of the Redbar in the book. When he rejoined us, the five of us turned and faced the people, our chests bursting with pride. Our fathers and mothers stood up from the seated people and came to us.

On the dark path leading to my father's hut, my mother kissed me, then swiftly ran ahead to relate the news to my grandmother. My father placed a massive hand on my shoulder. "Eeola, I am pleased for you—and proud. I can tell you now that, because of your size, I feared no Jaren would take you. But this—it is more than I could have hoped for you. Vastar will be a great *Di*, and you all will bring glory to the symbol of the Redbar."

I suppressed a desire to laugh and only nodded. "It is good that I pleased you, Father."

We walked in silence for a time, then my father stopped, pulling me to a halt beside him. He had a curious expression on his face. "Eeola, might I ask you a question?"

"Of course, Father."

"The symbol of the Redbar; you wear it higher up than the others. Why is that?"

I felt my face flush in the dark. "It . . . it's because they are so much taller than I am . . . Father."

My father's right eyebrow went up, while the other curled into a frown. A twinkle grew in his black eyes, then his face relaxed. He nodded and resumed walking down the path. "Come, Eeola. It is time we were getting to our sleeping mats."

I gulped and followed.

In time, the Redbar was presented to the five Jarens of our fathers where we were feasted and given advice. Afterwards, we were presented to the five Jarens of our mothers, again feasted, and inspected as material for future husbands. Until the very last of the Redbar was snared and wed, the Jarens of all of our mothers would scour the village, bragging, begging and negotiating, keeping sharp eyes out for females well placed in respected Jarens of their own.

In the years that followed, the Redbar had little time for such thoughts. Vastar took the duties of the *Di* seriously, and we ran, trained, wrestled and boxed, stopping only to eat and sleep. In time, although they remained taller than I, with the patient help of my brothers, I could run as well and even best them wrestling on rare occasion. However, once we donned our half-dress and began the *kiruch,* it was my turn to help my brothers keep up with me. In between our lessons before the village classmaster, we met in the jungle clearing with Lodar to drill in arms. Lodar would always single out the Redbar for his severest criticisms, and by the look in his eye, I eventually became aware that our painted bums had fooled no one.

After classes and drills, Vastar would take us to the banks of the River Gnawi, where we would take our shield and wand and begin our drills. One on one, two on one, three on one, four on one. Jump, flash, parry, turn, flash—until the five of us ached and our *bes* hung limp between our legs, soaked with sweat. Then, placing our weapons aside, we would plunge into the cool waters of the Gnawi.

One day as we made our way to the riverbank, we heard laughter and splashing. Usurpers had moved into our swimming hole. We came through the trees and entered the clearing and spied a Jaren of village females, also *kiruchta,* using *our* water to cleanse themselves after their drills. Glowers on our faces, Vastar ordered the females from the water. They laughed and made rude suggestions. Our blood boiling, Vastar challenged the female *Di* to a match with wands and shield to decide the question.

The five females came naked from the water, reached to the trees for their half-dress *bes* and covered their lower halves. We hefted our own weapons as they retrieved theirs from the grass, then we squared off. Disaster ensued. Back at the village, nursing our newly roasted hides, Vastar stormed up and down in front of us.

"None of us? None of us won?"

Dob shrugged. "Vastar, I could not keep my mind on my drills. She bounced so. . . ."

"Bah!" Vastar stamped his foot. "We have seen females before! And those females—we grew up with them! We have seen them naked since our first crawls in the dust!"

Timbenevva shrugged. "It is different, somehow."

Vastar snorted. "Different! If that had been war, we would be dead! How can I bring this Jaren before the Light?"

Gemislor rubbed his chin, his eyes cast down. "This is all so true,

Vastar, but explain why you didn't lay your wand on their *Di?*"

Vastar flushed. "Why, my attention was diverted because of the four of you stumbling moonfaces bending all effort to disgrace our Jaren."

Gem's expression did not change as he absorbed the explanation, but his eyes laughed. Vastar blushed, then laughed with us. "Very well, Redbar, but we must keep our minds on our drills. In the years to come, we will be presented with stronger attractions than that. Let us drill."

True to his word, Vastar drilled and drilled us, there in the village street, until the horizon drank the sun. That night, as I lay my aching bones on my sleeping mat, I closed my eyes and dreamt of the lithe, black-haired beauty that had smiled so sweetly just before burning the wand from my hand.

In our years of the *kiruch,* the classmaster beat many things into our heads. Then it seemed to be a blur of facts and items of legend. Only now is it clear that every moment of our instruction was aimed at instilling in us the pride of the Shikazu; the pride of the unconquered warrior race of the planet Tenuet. True, we had merchants, builders, and administrators, but any one of them could push papers, tools, and cash boxes aside, heft wands and shields, and acquit himself respectfully on a field of battle.

The Shikazu cannot be conquered; this was our one eternal truth. And through it, we came to accept that as individuals we could not be beaten, save by another Shikazu. We held nine planets of four solar systems under the wand, races more advanced, more numerous, and physically more impressive; but we held the wand, for we were the Shikazu.

At fencing drill, Lodar taught us nothing of quarter nor of surrender. His one subject: conquer. Press the opponent until he is vanquished, then move on to the next opponent. Those who lost contests at drills were driven by their Jarens to improve, until nothing could stand before their wands. Those who would not, or could not, improve their skills were dropped from drills, and dropped from their Jarens where they would be replaced by the more worthy. No one could bear the shame of a *kazu*—one discarded as being unfit—and a few of these drifted away from the village to live out their lives in the jungle or seek a place amongst the dregs of the large cities. Most *kazu,* however, simply removed the energy guards on their wands and turned them upon themselves. No one wept for them.

This fate, and the constant pressure of my Jaren mates, polished my own skill with wand and shield until the five of us could put our backs together and stand off any ten opponents. Nevertheless, as our skills sharpened, so did Lodar's tongue in his verbal abuse of the Redbar. As time passed we became confident in our prowess with the wand, and ever more ingrained with fierce pride in the Shikazu, our Jaren, and in ourselves as individuals. The day had to come when Vastar was sure enough of himself and his Jaren to no longer accept Lodar's abuse A *Di* with less wit would have seen red and challenged Lodar months before, but Vastar was exceptional, as only befits the *Di* of the Redbar Jaren.

At drills one day, the Redbar was squared off with the Jaren of the White Star. The White Star was senior to us, but we were leaving them in tatters, when Lodar called a halt to the drill. The two Jarens bowed toward each other, and then toward Lodar. The fencing master spat on the clearing's short grass and motioned for the White Star Jaren to retire to the edge of the clearing. Turning to face us, Lodar sneered. "The blood of the Shikazu curdles at the thought of this Jaren calling itself 'Shikazu.' " Lodar's black eyes flashed as he swaggered to stand in front of me. "I cannot understand why this Jaren hasn't dropped this pitiful tree lizard. And you three," he swept his hand at Gem, Dob and Tim, "you should be pulling plows, such hulking, clumsy lumps." He faced Vastar. "How can you bear the shame of keeping this disgraceful Jaren together? Have you no pride?"

Vastar lifted his head, his blond mane held in place by a red band, and smiled at the fencing master. Our *Di* lifted his wand, ejected its energy shield, and held the weapon under Lodar's nose. "Pick your mates, old man. The Redbar is past suffering the senile jabberings of an aging treetoad." Dob, Gem, Tim, and I hefted our wands and ejected the energy shields. The wands would still be at low output, but without the shields, the burns would be deep and possibly deadly. Vastar had challenged Lodar to the *vienda*, the Jaren duel whose winners would be those left standing. There is no first burn and bows with the *vienda*. Instead, the combatant fights until he either wins or can fight no longer.

Lodar tossed back his head and laughed. "Mates? I need no mates to spread this Jaren all over the drill ground. I could throw my wand away, take a switch off a tree and whip the five of you."

Vastar folded his arms, snorted and said in an almost bored voice, "Pick your mates, Lodar, or retire from the field. We have had enough hot air."

146   THE JAREN

The rest of the Redbar laughed. As Lodar narrowed his eyes, nodded, and walked to the edge of the clearing to fill out a combat team of five, I felt the battle blood in my veins for the first time: a clawing, pulsing *need* to join in battle, to fight, to win.

I felt no doubt about our victory; we were the Jaren of the Redbar; we were Shikazu. I looked at my mates and saw the same blood pounding through their veins, narrowed eyes, teeth showing through tightly drawn lips of brown.

With his wand, Lodar picked out four *kiruchta* and motioned them to the center of the clearing. All four were *Di* of their respective Jarens, and known to us all as excellent fighters. Lodar's group squared off with the Redbar, ejected their energy shields and bowed. The Redbar returned the bow and came up at the ready. Lodar spat out the command: "Begin!"

My opponent, the *Di* of the Black Sword Jaren, sidestepped and brought his wand down in a diagonal slash. Without thinking, I instinctively reacted with the trick Vastar had perfected and that we had practiced until the drill was more familiar to us than our names. Squeezing the shaft of my wand, I directed a pulse to the edge of my opponent's deflection shield at the same time I moved from the path of his slash. The force of the beam on his shield caused him to tip off balance the least bit, and as he brought his wand arm up to counter, my wand seared the underside of his arm. In a flash, he brought his shield around, but the damage had been done and he was on the defensive. I laid my wand across his knees, and he began lashing out wildly with his own wand. His eyes were wild as I deflected his attack, then let my wand linger on his left foot. He went down on his left knee, covering himself almost completely with his shield, his ill-directed wand denuding the yanna plants behind me. A flash of brown, and I roasted the edge of his shoulder. His shield went up to cover, and my wand burned into his right foot. As his wand went up, I ran forward and kicked his shield with my foot, sending him sprawling on his back. In less time than it took his shield to sail to the ground, my knee was planted in his chest and my de-energized wand was at his throat. With my shield I came down upon his wand hand, then brought my knee up under his chin. I backed off at the ready, but the *Di* of the Black Sword lay motionless save the heaving of his chest. I turned to aid my mates, but they were waiting for me; Gem and Tim rested with their arms on Dob's shoulders, while Vastar stood above Lodar, our *Di*'s eyes wild with triumph. Lodar pushed himself to a sitting position while the four of us gathered behind Vastar. Our *Di* looked down at the fencing

THE JAREN

THE JAREN

master. "There will be no more abuse, Lodar, and the Redbar will come and go to drills as it chooses." Lodar nodded and we left the field, shouting and punching each other, looking for some way to work off the pressure we still had inside of us. I glanced back to look once more upon our field of victory and saw Lodar standing in its center, hands on his hips, smile wrinkling his face and hot pride burning in his eyes. Since we were the victors, the look confused me. Years later it dawned on me that Lodar's occupation was taking babies and turning them into highly skilled fighters. The Jaren of the Redbar was not the only victor that day.

It was not long after that the Jarens of our parents offered us up for adulthood. My father's Jaren, that of the Ice Flower, and my mother's Jaren, that of the Silver Bird, stood with me before the Light.

When I was but a *tikiruch,* I had feared this test of the Light. But that was when I was a *tikiruch.* As we walked the path to the temple, in my heart I was Shikazu. I feared nothing, and felt confident the Light would serve me, not destroy me. The procession entered the rough stone structure, and inside it was but native rock for a floor. In the center of the structure, an outcropping protruded, and was capped by a carved rock shell. Great chains were attached to the shell and led to the roof, then down again. I stood with my mates around the shell, while the Jarens of our parents hefted the chains and began pulling.

My mates and I joined hands as the chain's slack was taken up. The shell began to rise, and a blinding blue light filled the temple. Higher rose the shell, until it dangled over our heads. I looked toward the light and saw its pulsing shimmer. Throughout the planet Tenuet ran this substance that bound together the Shikazu. Wherever it broke through the surface, the Shikazu covered it with a temple, then brought its best to stand the test of adulthood.

Still holding hands, we knelt before the Light, moved our clasped hands forward, and touched it. Had we been but four, we would have died. Had we been more than five, there would have been nothing. But, we were five, and the Light fused us into one. As its power flowed through us, our Jaren became as the fingers on a single hand, while, in turn, our Jaren became a part of the Shikazu. As we touched the Light, I could *feel* the thoughts of my mates, as they could feel mine. More than that, I could feel us all being filled with the warrior blood, and the mission to defend Tenuet, and the Light, for without the Light, we became nothing.

Apher of the Black Pike Jaren, Vastar's father, called forth from his place at the chains the first stanza of the *Rhanakah*—the service of the Light. "And now you are one in life, as you shall one day be one in death."

The five of us answered. "For we are Shikazu."

Gem's father called forth next, followed by each male parent in turn. "The Light you touch now shall remain with you each, until the last of your Jaren meets the long sleep."

"For we are Shikazu; the Light is ours."

"Witness the power of the Light, and know what you are."

"We are Shikazu; we cannot be conquered."

"You are bound now to the Shikazu, our honor is as your own."

"We are Shikazu and shall serve no other race."

"Stand, then, Shikazu; stand, Jaren of the Redbar."

We stood, let our hands fall to our sides, and watched as our parents' Jarens lowered the rock shell over the Light. The shell in place, there was a moment of quiet, then our parents' Jarens rushed to us, grinning, laughing, cheering, pummeling our backs, then presenting us each with the forest green *nabe*—the robes of adulthood.

All of the Redbar donned the full-dress *nabe* that night, and the next morning we lounged next to our waterhole near the Gnawi discussing our futures. We had long since chased the female Jaren from the area, and in fact we ruled supreme in the village of Ahrm. "We are too big for Ahrm," as Dob observed.

Tim played on his pipes, then fingered the green of his *nabe*. "We have yet to exploit adulthood here in the village. There are females to be learned, councils to attend, and pleasure to experience. Let us at least wrinkle our robes before we seek the road."

Gem sat up, crossed his legs and held out his hands. "Brothers, why do we not place our Jaren at the disposal of the Shikazu Infantry? They would beg to have us in their ranks, and the promise of action is there. A race challenges our territories toward the galactic center side of the four stars." Gem turned the spit on the fourlegged *sa* we'd caught.

Dob nodded. "Aye, the humans."

Tim replaced the pipes in his robe, then scratched his chin. "What are they like?" He sniffed at the cooking *sa*.

"Like us. They come from the same stock, but they are smaller and have many colors."

Tim looked thoughtful. "How do they fight?" Dob only shrugged. "Vastar?"

Our *Di* lay flat on his back, watching through the treetops at the clouds. He closed his eyes, shook his head, then went back to looking at the clouds. "I know nothing of the humans, except that they control many worlds and would have ours as well." We all laughed, since nothing had ever sounded as absurd as this alleged human goal. No race takes from the Shikazu and lives to recount the experience. Vastar rolled his head in my direction. "What about you, Eeola? Are you finding the borders of Ahrm confining?"

I shrugged. "I go with my Jaren."

"What about the female? What's her name?"

I flushed. After we had squared off again at the waterhole with the female Jaren, that of the Golden Dart, I had begun seeing Carrina, the female that had first beaten me, but then had fallen to my wand. Neither my Jaren nor she understood why the scars I had caused her gave me pain. But all the same, she let me kiss and caress them. "Her name is Carrina." I added a stick to the fire.

"Carrina," Vastar repeated. "The Golden Dart is already a respected Jaren. Do you think our mothers' Jarens would approve?"

I looked down and picked at my toenails. "I know not. But it is no matter. The Golden Dart is sworn to enter the army. She must follow her Jaren as I must follow mine." I smiled. "And I doubt that my brothers of the Redbar are agreeable to settling down to wife, home, and brat at this early time—and neither am I."

Dob reached over a thigh-sized hand and clopped me on the shoulder. It was only by the grace of that shoulder having filled out with muscle over the years since the Jaren was formed that I was saved. "Aye, Eeola, we must seek our fortunes—adventure!" He turned to Vastar. "I have heard the humans take mates at will, at any time, and without ceremony; that they act love without love, and without pledges of honor. Is this true?"

Vastar nodded as he sprang to his feet, then crouched before the fire. He ripped a still bloody limb from the *sa*, tore at it with his teeth and wiped the grease from his hands upon his dusty feet. He looked at us all as he spoke around the mouthful of bloody meat. "They are animals."

That day beside the waters of the Gnawi, we decided to strike out on the trail toward Meydal the next morning to see some of the sights. I had never been beyond the limits of Ahrm, and long before the sun chased the shadows from the sky, I was up, waiting impatiently by the dying coals of the meeting fire. I had a small shoulder pack filled with food and things I would need for travel. My shield was slung, and at my waist my wand dangled where it would be handy. As I waited, the smells of the village—the fire, the dust, the life-smell of fat orchids in the jungle—began tugging at my heart. This was my only home. As I knelt on the hard-packed soil of the meeting place, I pulled the short-knife my father had given me the night before from my sash. I forced the blade into the dirt, and as I dug, Dob walked up beside me, knelt and began digging. He smiled at me as we completed our holes. We each took our knives, cut off locks of hair and buried them in the holes. Even if we died, our spirits would come back to Ahrm to reclaim their own. It was a child's fable, and I would have felt foolish had not Dob joined me in my childish ritual.

We heard a snort behind us and we stood to see Vastar, Gem, and Tim, packs on shoulders, shields on backs, standing together looking at us. Vastar held out a hand toward the burying place. "Are we *tikiruch* to be planting hair?" Dob and I were speechless, caught as we were by our brothers. Then Vastar laughed, and the three of them pulled knives, knelt and planted their own. Moments later, my brothers and I left the dim glow of the meeting fire, walked the dusty street of Ahrm and entered the blackness of the jungle trail. In the east, the shadows were beginning to give back the sun.

We walked in single-file with Vastar in the lead. Although we fairly exploded to laugh and rough around at the beginning of our adventure, we maintained silence and kept our eyes on the jungle, for we were not *tikiruch* to be surprised by bandit Jarens or bands of starving *kazu*. Many times we passed Jarens walking in the other direction, and each time we raised our wand hands when they did and placed them across our breasts. As they passed, Vastar would bow his head to the other *Di* who would, in turn, bow his or hers. As the last one in our procession, I would keep watch on the passing Jaren until it went out of sight, while the last one in the passing file kept a watch on the Redbar. There were lone travelers, too, and on these we kept a careful eye. They could be parts of Jarens, but more often than not they would be *kazu* turned to waylaying their betters for food and weapons. When these passed, we would draw our wand arms across our breasts, but Vastar would not bow.

We walked all that morning, keeping a strong pace, and had entered a district where the *nabe* worn by the Jarens were brown, when a lone traveler wearing a leather shirt and black *be* half-dress approached from the other direction. The wand side, his left, was clear, but we kept our eyes on him as he came near. When he came up next to Vastar, a wand came up in the follow's *right* hand. Our wand hands were across our breasts, and there was nothing Vastar could do. But standing behind Dob's hulk, the leather-shirted creature could not see my right hand speed to my sash, take my new knife from it and hurl it past Dob's shoulder at the fellow's head. It was a new knife, and I was not yet familiar with its balance. Instead of the blade sinking into the thief's brain, the hilt struck him on the forehead, splitting the skin. As the thief's lamps went out, he sank to the path. As he hit, we heard scampering feet and rustling leaves in the jungle around us. The fellow's companions appeared to have no desire to tangle with the Redbar.

While I retrieved my blade, Vastar stooped over the bandit and plucked the wand from the fellow's hand. Looking up, he nodded at Tim and Gem. "Keep a watch on the jungle. All of this creature's band may not have taken to the bush." Vastar looked at me as I tucked my knife into my sash. "You spared this bandit, Eeola, and he still lives. What do you suggest we do with him?"

I shrugged. "My mercy was unintentional, Vastar. It was my new knife who spared the scum."

Vastar frowned. "If you intend to keep your hair, Eeola, you must bend your new blade to your will." I nodded. Vastar turned back to the bandit. "Still, what shall we do with him?"

Dob nudged the bandit with his toe. "Why not leave him here, Vastar?"

Our *Di* shook his head. "I would not leave even a *kazu* to the mercy of the jungle and its creatures. Besides, if the creatures don't ·kill him, he will recover and use our mercy to waylay other travelers."

Dob rubbed his chin, then shrugged. "Kill him, then. We have the right."

Vastar stood and backed away from the bandit. "Very well, Dob; have at it."

"Me?" Dob looked at Vastar with wide eyes.

"It was your suggestion."

Dob frowned, grasped his wand and pulled it from his sash. He held the wand for an instant, then lowered it. "It is not as though he could fight, Vastar." Dob replaced his wand and cocked his head toward Vastar. "Our *Di* deserves the honor of our Jaren's first kill."

Vastar snorted, stood and held out the thief's wand in my direction. I took it and watched while our *Di* secured his own wand and aimed it at the thief. He grimaced, looked at Dob, then back at the thief.

I held up my hand. "Vastar, wait."

Vastar heaved a sigh and lowered his wand. "What is it, Eeola? I must be about the work that needs doing."

I held the thief's wand out to him. "Look. It has no power, and the jewel is shattered. If he was out to kill us, it was not with that."

Vastar took the wand, aimed it at an empty spot in the trail and pressed the handle. Nothing. "It is true."

Dob nudged the thief, again with his toe. "Attacking a wanded Jaren with nothing but wit and a lifeless stick bespeaks of no little courage, Vastar."

Vastar shook his head. "The courage of a bandit." He threw up his hands. "Now what do we do with him?"

The thief moaned, opened his eyes and looked at our faces. "I live?"

Vastar threw the dead wand on the bandit's chest. "We will probably live to regret it. What is your name, thief?"

The bandit sat up, holding his head as though it were a sack of shattered glass. "A moment, my benefactors, while I calm the whistles between my ears." After a moment, he lowered his hands to his lap and raised a shaggy grey eyebrow in my direction. "You, small one; is it your skill I should be thankful for or your ineptitude?"

I pulled the knife from my sash, flipped it and caught it by the blade. "Perhaps we can judge this properly if I make another throw."

The bandit grinned through his stubble of grey whiskers and held up a hand. "No offense, lad. I but asked a simple question."

Vastar snapped his fingers. "Old bandit. Your name."

"I am called Krogar by my friends."

"What do the rest of us call you?"

Krogar shrugged. "You hold the wands; you may call me anything you wish." The bandit pushed himself to his feet, stood weaving for a moment, then looked at our faces, stopping on Vastar. "Well?"

"Well, what, thief?"

"Am I to be spared or not? If I am, I'm sure we both have better things to do than standing here. You must be on your way, and I must make my living." Krogar shrugged and looked down. "If I'm not to live, then be done with the task and end this cursed headache that threatens to open the top of my skull."

Despite ourselves, we could but laugh at the old fellow's crust. Vastar looked at us, then waved a hand at the old bandit. "Keep your miserable life and your aching head, Krogar. But beware of this Jaren should we pass this way again." Vastar motioned to us and we fell in line and continued down the trail. I turned once to look back at Krogar, but the trail was empty.

For days we walked the trail, putting up nights in strange villages. At their meeting fires we would relate the news we had come across and the villagers would tell us things they had picked up from other travelers. Often there would be one or more other travelers at the fire, and it was from one of these that we heard of the human conquest of the planet Baalphor. The traveler had come from a town on the edge of the city of Meydal where the terrible news still ran hot through the streets. "The Jarens of Meydal and surrounding towns are entering the army in droves." The fellow scratched beneath his maroon *nabe*, then pointed in the direction we had come from. "I travel to my village of Tdist to gather up my Jaren. We will return to Meydal and enter."

Vastar snapped a stick he had been toying with, then threw the two pieces into the fire. His eyes blazed in the red light of the fire as he turned to the traveler. "I cannot believe Baalphor has fallen—not to *humans*."

The traveler shrugged. "They are numerous, and they have great, powerful weapons, as well as skill in their use."

Vastar made fists with his hands and shook them. "But they are not *Shikazu!* Do you tell me the Shikazu have been *conquered?*"

"No. The Shikazu will remain unconquered until the last of us lays down the wand. The garrison on Baalphor has been destroyed, but even now I suspect the army is preparing to drive the humans off the planet."

Dob snorted and raised his brows in a show of contempt. "Vastar, the army will probably drive the scum from Baalphor long before we can reach the streets of Meydal."

The traveler shook his head. "I fear not, my gross friend. Many new ghosts shall walk before Baalphor falls. The Shikazu controls few planets compared to the humans."

"How many do the humans hold?" I asked.

"Over two hundred. We cannot be beaten, for we are the Shikazu; but there will be a price."

The Shikazu's empire of nine planets had been difficult to imagine; at least, for one who had never been outside of Ahrm. An empire of two hundred planets—it was beyond imagination. I think I felt, at that moment, a touch of fear.

The next morning, we pointed our toes at Meydal to be sworn to the military. Our blood, the blood of the Shikazu, was up and boiling.

In time, the trail widened and we came upon motor carts, as well as more travelers. The closer we came to the city, the wider and more congested the road became. Soon, the road was hard-surfaced and traveled only by sleek, many-colored crafts that would whiz by, blowing the heat and dust from the road over us. The villages we traveled through were constructed of stone, metal, and glass, while the villagers strutted upon upraised paths of stone wearing *nabe* that fought the eye for belief: metal gold, deep crimson stitched with silver, loud pinks, and stripes of every description. Next to the raised walks, merchants shouted of their wares amidst the bustle, and soon the human hordes were forgotten as the five villagers of Ahrm drank in this new world of flash and glitter. In the town of Adelone, we walked one of the upraised paths around a flowered hill upon which stood a grand house of smooth white pillars and arches, then stopped as though stunned as the main street of the town spead before us. The *size* of the buildings! The *crowds!*

Suddenly Vastar's angry face cut off my view. "Look at you! Mouths hanging open, eyes bugged! Get the straw out of your ears! Do you want these villagers to think us unsophisticated?" I looked at the others and realized that our *Di* had not singled me out, but was lashing all of us. He turned and pointed down the street. "There is a station. We need not go on to Meydal."

I followed the direction of his finger and saw the crossed pikes that symbolized the army standing out from the wall of a tall silver and glass building. I tugged at Vastar's *nabe*. "If this is only a town, Vastar, what could Meydal be like?"

Vastar shook his head. "We are here to enter the army; not to see the sights. This is a station, and we can be in service all the sooner."

Dob gained control of his gaping mouth long enough to comment upon Vastar's reasoning. "We will still be sent to the main station in Meydal, will we not? We will be sworn no faster, then, if we travel to Meydal and seek a station."

Vastar raised an eyebrow. "Gem, what say you?"

Gem shrugged. "I would see a little of this city before we are sworn."

There was no need to ask Timbenevva; his drooling tongue almost hung to the walk. Vastar's head gave a curt nod. "Very well, we shall see Meydal, but can we at least inquire at the station here about directions? All of these roads, streets, and side streets are beginning to confuse me."

We stepped off, gawking at the buildings and people, our attention so absorbed that had we been attacked by two crippled, half-witted

158   THE JAREN

THE JAREN

tikiruch, I doubt that victory would have fallen to the Redbar.

Compared to the city of Meydal, the town of Adelone that had stunned us with its grandeur was but a mud wallow. The army officer at the Adelone station had given us transportation passes, and told us we could report to one of the stations in Meydal—this, of course, after signing us up. We had two days to ourselves before reporting. The officer walked us to the pneumo station in the town, and put us on one of the cars. Moments after we lowered ourselves into the plush seats, the car shot along a tube much like a bullet through a blowpipe. Before we had really settled in, a voice from the brightly lit overhead barked at us. We were in Meydal.

As we stepped from the car onto a platform, we simply gawked. Passengers trying to disembark behind us shoved us rudely out of the way, but we hardly noticed. Like a forest of giant sword ferns, Meydal's incredible buildings towered above us. When we walked to the railed edge of the platform to have a better view, we backed away as we realized the platform was suspended high above the ground. We inched back and saw that the buildings extended below the platform just as far as they rose above it. Dob shook his head and laughed so hard he could not stop.

"What amuses you, brother?" I asked.

Dob waved his hand up and down at the magnificent spires of Meydal. "Do you remember how they marveled in Ahrm when my father built a hut with a loft above it, and how afraid I was to be up so high?" He laughed again, and I joined him. It was an overwhelming sight, and I believe we would be gawking there yet had not Larenz come along.

"Seeing the sights before entering the army, jungle cousins?" We turned to see a tall, black-maned fellow decked in crimson *nabe* embroidered along the edges with geometric shapes in gold thread.

Vastar cocked his head at us and spoke to the stranger. "We have already entered. We must report the morning of the day after tomorrow. Who might you be?"

The fellow in red bowed. "Please excuse my thoughtlessness. I am Larenz, *Di* of the Jaren of the Red Claw. Meydal is my city."

Vastar nodded. "We are the Jaren of the Redbar from Ahrm." At Larenz's puzzled expression, Vastar shrugged. "It is a village far to the south." Our *Di* introduced himself and the rest of us to Larenz.

The stranger smiled at us with a display of beautiful straight teeth that contrasted sharply with the dark brown of his face. "Excellent. I am to report at the same time with my Jaren. Do you know

160 THE JAREN

someone in Meydal?"

Vastar frowned. "Why?"

"If you don't, I would be happy to show you the city. If you don't know your way around, you'll miss most of it."

Vastar turned to consult with us, bounced a single gaze off of our eager faces, then turned back to Larenz. "Very well, Larenz. We accept your invitation."

"Excellent. Then, cousins, be kind enough to follow me." Larenz turned and led us off the platform, through a glass door that opened without touching, then into a small box that dropped out from underneath us, disgorging us below at street level. All during our fall to the street, I mulled over the reasons I could think of for this apparent kindness from a stranger, and decided to keep my wand arm limber.

Using our army transportation passes, Larenz of the Red Claw led our Jaren through a maze of tubes and connections, stopping here and there to witness sights he thought would interest us. Of all the sights, the squat sprawl of the government district, with broad, tree-lined streets and gleaming white metal and glass above smooth, well-tended lawns, impressed me the most. But between that and the park, the choice was hard—and the business buildings! The walks choked with bustling adults and children, the streets jammed with sleek, dark vehicles. Meydal was, in truth, a city of wonders.

Even so, as my neck began aching at looking up at the buildings and my feet tired at being slapped upon the hard walks, my interest began flagging. It was at that point I noticed a curious thing: the citizens of Meydal carried neither shields nor wands. Here and there would be an individual properly armed, but his or her *nabe* branded the person as being out of the jungle as was the Redbar. Those decked in the garish finery I had come to associate with Meydalians were unarmed. At one point in our travels, I found Larenz walking beside me, and asked him about this curious fact.

He laughed. "There is no need for arms in Meydal. Do you see slavering beasts crouching on the building ledges, or lurking in doorways?" He laughed again. "The jungle is a long way off, cousin."

I pointed at a few of the people passing in the other direction. "I see the most dangerous beast of all here, and in great numbers."

Larenz halted, stood on his toes and looked over the heads of the crowd on the walk. "You can never find one when you need . . . there! Do you see the fellow in black *nabe* with the red stitching?"

"The one with the club?"

"Aye. It is his job, Eeola, to keep the citizens of Meydal from each other's throats—and purses." We turned and walked quickly to catch up with the others. "He is a member of a Jaren sworn to the police."

I shrugged. "I would not be comfortable leaving my protection to others, Larenz."

"It is our way, Eeola, and it works well enough. There is no need to go armed in Meydal, except, perhaps, in the Human Quarter."

My eyes went wide. "Humans? Here on Tenuet?"

"Why, of course. There are many, many races in Meydal, including humans. Quite a number, too."

"But, Larenz, we are at war . . ."

He waved his hand. "We are at war with a government, Eeola, not a race. Everyone in the Human Quarter is a citizen of Tenuet, as are you and I."

"But . . . they are not Shikazu!"

"No, they are not Shikazu. Would you and your mates like to see the Human Quarter?"

My face felt drained of blood. I nodded and turned to ask the others, but they had been listening. Vastar nodded. "Show the way, Larenz. We would see your housebroken humans."

As filth-covered, gnarled roots are part of a beautiful flower, the Human Quarter was a part of Meydal. In a haze, my mind recalls low, red-black row dwellings, narrow, refuse-strewn streets, strange music and hostile glances. The humans, pink, grey, yellowish, copper, and a few who could almost pass as Shikazu, except for their strange fuzzy hair, moved from the walks as we approached keeping their eyes down, hands shoved into openings in the leg coverings they wore. Females hung from windows in the evil-smelling structures, chattering and shouting among themselves. Many younger humans sat on steps leading to entrances, while others stood along the walk in small groups, laughing and talking. Old ones stared blankly from open windows, seeing nothing.

I turned to Larenz. "Why, Larenz? Why do they live in this manner?"

Larenz only shrugged. "It is their way."

I snickered. "This is the race that rules two hundred worlds?" The others laughed. A group of young male humans turned at the sounds of the laughter and glowered at us.

Larenz waved his hand at the street. "These are not the only humans on Tenuet, Eeola. There are many in rich homes here in

Meydal. But every city of the nine worlds has a human quarter that looks much as this one does. My only explanation is that they are not Shikazu."

The group of male humans spread out across the walk in front of us. My eyes quickly noted that Larenz and my mates were the only Shikazu within sight. Several of the humans pulled knives or wands from garish-looking shirts, while, two and three at a time, other humans joined their ranks, carrying wands, knives, lengths of pipe, and chain. My fingers stole around the handle of my wand.

A tall human, yellow with slanting eyes, stood above the others and in front of them. He threw up his head. "Looks like Baalphor hasn't taught the Shikkies anything."

Larenz waved his hand. "Stand out of the walk and let us pass."

The human spat on the walk. "And if we don't, Shikki?"

Larenz laughed. "Why, we'll burn a path through the middle of you. Now, stand aside."

One of them from the end called, "Ay, shikkishikkishikki!"

A wand came up, and in the flash of an eye, Vastar burned it from the human's hand. The Redbar unslung its shields and stood at the ready. The yellow human held up his hands and shook his head. "Hey, Shikki, we were just having a little fun. Ease off."

Vastar, his eyes bright with blood, dropped his shield a bit and lowered his wand. At that moment, a whirling length of chain sailed through the air at him. Vastar knocked it to the ground with his shield and screamed "Shikazu!" He brought his wand across the chests of the front rank of humans and they dropped to the walk. The rest of us waded in, cutting and burning, the smell of roasted flesh strong in the air. Larenz picked a fallen wand from the walk and joined us, burning the scum with a skill the Redbar had rarely seen outside of its own performances. After only a few moments, the street animals broke and ran. I counted fifteen of the humans left on the walk by the time the police came. The females had stopped their chattering and were looking down upon us, their faces twisted with hate, some with grief. But the old ones still stared through their windows, seeing nothing.

The police were numerous, and upon Larenz's advice, we surrendered our wands and shields to them. Other than those groaning on the walk, few of the humans were gathered up and placed in the holding cell with us. Larenz and Vastar explained that we must report soon to the army, but the police said there was nothing to be done about it. It would take all of five days to process us, get our statements and stand the hearing that would determine if we would have to stand trial. The holding cell was an enormous room, windowless and dark, which reflected our gloomy spirits. We had given our oaths to the army, but there seemed no way to abide by our word. Several times Vastar spoke sharply to Larenz. "A fine guide you are! 'Would you like to see the Human Quarter?' he says!" Vastar swept his arm at the few Shikazu and numerous humans in the cell. "Well, Larenz, we are in the Human Quarter. What now?" He sat on the cell floor with a thump, next to Dob.

Larenz, seated on the floor, leaned back against the cell wall, and stared at the humans seated in the opposite corner of the room. "I had not planned this, Vastar."

Vastar snorted. "I suppose it is nothing to you, but we of Ahrm are honor bound to keep our oaths."

Larenz's eyes flashed at our *Di*. "The oath is no less sacred to a Meydalian, jungle runner!" He started up, but Dob's huge hand found Larenz's shoulder and held him to the floor.

Dob smiled. "Larenz, I would like to know why you singled us out on the platform. Why did we become the object of your generosity?"

Larenz's eyes went from one to the other of us, then he shrugged with his unclamped shoulder. "My Jaren reports soon to the army, as you know."

"As we know."

"My father's Jaren officers the Army of the Fourth Star. I have studied at the *Den-kiruch,* the military school, and after training, my Jaren shall officer an infantry group. Meydalians are good fighters—some say, none better. But my father always speaks well of our jungle cousins. He advised me to put as many jungle Jarens into my group as I could get to join."

Dob nodded. "And, you would have us join your group when it is formed?"

"Yes."

Dob nodded again. "Truly a great honor, Larenz. I have a question—a matter that needs clearing up."

"What is that?"

Dob held his hands up indicating the cell. "The first thing that happened to the Jaren of the Redbar under your skilled leadership is that it was thrown into prison. If we join you, do you then lead us to the penal colony, or perhaps the execution block?"

The rest of us snickered. Larenz grimaced, then shook his head. "I had no reason to expect the humans to attack us here on the streets of Meydal. It has never happened before."

A human on the other side of the cell stood and shouted, "You

164   THE JAREN

Shikkies clammit! Some of us want to sleep."

As the human returned to his place, Vastar began getting to his feet. Dob's other meaty hand clamped our *Di* to the hard floor. "There must be thirty of them, Vastar. If you order it, I will happily join your attack, but it seems to me that we are already in enough trouble."

"They forget their place!"

Dob nodded. "But you forget our place." He nodded again at the cell walls.

Vastar shook his head. "We have given our word to the Army!"

A shadowy figure seated in a corner away from both the humans and our group, stood, scratched itself and shambled across the floor to stand in front of Vastar. It laughed. "Well, well. My ears spoke truly. It is my benefactor from the trail south of Laronan." He turned to me. "We meet again, skullcracker."

I squinted in the poor light. "Krogar? It is you."

Vastar snorted. "What do you want, *kazu?* Another crack on the head?"

Krogar squatted and pointed a finger at Vastar's chest. "I am no *kazu*, young one. Although I am alone and work the trails for a living, I am of a Jaren, that of the Green Dragon of the Village of Sarat."

Vastar aised an eyebrow. "Then where are your mates?"

Krogar looked at the cell floor, then back at Vastar. "They are ashes mixed with those of the defenders of Dashik. We were part of the force that secured the ninth planet for the Shikazu."

"You were in the army?"

"I think I already answered that."

Vastar threw up a hand, then let it fall back into his lap. "If you are Shikazu, and once of the army, why are you a thief? Why do you prey on Shikazu?"

I could not see Krogar's face, but a strange quality came into his voice—an empty, lost sound. "My Jaren was almost twenty years old when my mates walked as ghosts. It works on you in a way I hope you never have an opportunity to understand." Krogar waved his hand, dismissing the subject. "From the conversation I overheard, I detect a desire to quit these walls. Why are you here?"

Vastar pointed at the humans on the other side of the cell. "They attacked us. We will be set free after the hearing, but that means we will miss our reporting time."

Krogar looked over our faces and stopped on Larenz. "You have picked up a new companion."

Larenz returned Krogar's look. "I am Larenz of the Red Claw Jaren, here in Meydal. I too will miss my reporting time."

Krogar rubbed his chin. "Larenz . . . does not your father's Jaren officer the Fourth Army?"

"Yes."

"I suppose your father might look with favor, in a pecuniary fashion, upon one who rescued his son from this disgrace."

Larenz laughed. "It would appear, Krogar, that your position is no more mobile than ours."

Krogar stood, turned toward the humans and shouted: "Jailer, get these foul-smelling creatures out of our cell! Shikazu cannot be forced to share cells with such animals!" The humans began grumbling, and several got to their feet and began approaching Krogar. The thief turned back to us and grinned. "In confusion there is profit." He turned back to the humans, adopted a fighting stance, then rushed headlong into them, knocking four of them to the floor in a tangle of legs and arms.

Larenz and Vastar both stood at the same time and yelled "Shikazu!" We all came to our feet, as did the humans, then closed battle in the center of the floor. A human rushed at me, fists swinging, but I sidestepped his attack and brought up my knee into his stomach. While I grappled with a second, a third planted a fist in my eye. I'm not sure, I didn't take the time to examine him, but I think I broke his neck. In a moment, I was buried under a mountain of cursing bodies. A moment later, I felt the bodies being plucked from me, then saw Dob—a human clutching to his back and one hanging from each leg, picking up my attackers by neck and drawers and flinging them across the cell.

Whistles shrieked, the cell door flew open, and four armed police entered. They carried clubs which they soon brought to bear upon the heads of the humans. In a moment, the full fury of the humans was concentrated upon the police, while Krogar, Larenz and the Redbar separated and went for the open door. Standing in the doorway, another of the police spied Krogar and lifted his club. Krogar shrugged as if to say "I cannot be blamed for trying," then he half-turned away, turned back in a flash and caught the fellow with a foot in the stomach.

The seven of us rushed through the door and over the downed police into the corridor. Krogar waved, turned right and ran. We followed until we saw two more officers rushing in the opposite direction. These two hefted wands, rather than clubs, but Krogar did not hesitate for an instant. I saw him take a burst in the chest just as he leaped into the air to fall against the two police, knocking them to the floor. Gem reached to pick up one of the fallen officers' wands, but Krogar knocked Gem's hand away. "No! If we kill a police, they will never rest until they find us. Leave it." Krogar opened his leather shirt, looked at the ugly burn on his chest, then waved us on. I turned back and saw the corridor choked with police. Most went into the cell we vacated, but eight of them, armed with wands, came our way.

We pounded down the corridor, wand beams flashing about our heads and off the walls. We turned a corner, ran over a guard positioned there, and piled into an elevator. Krogar grabbed the control and the floor dropped out from beneath me. He cocked his head toward the door. "Be prepared to charge when it opens; they will be waiting for us."

Krogar brought the car to a sudden stop, pulled open the door, and joined us in our battle cry as we charged into the lobby of the police building. "Shikazu!" We stumbled into each other as those in front saw first that no one was waiting for us. A receptionist seated behind a counter next to the elevator looked at us with a puzzled expression. Krogar laughed, then began walking toward the door.

The receptionist stood. "One moment . . ."

A clanging sound filled the lobby, and we could see massive shutters slowly closing over the doors to the street. Krogar broke, ran and dived under a shutter, while the rest of us dived under other door shutters. Rolling on the walk outside the police building, I looked around and saw that we had all made it. Still, it would not be safe to linger out on the street for too long. Soon, police cruisers would arrive. Larenz turned to Krogar. "Where now?"

"To your father's house, that I might collect my reward."

Dikahn of the Blue Cloud Jaren, Lord General of the Army of the Fourth Star, and father of Larenz, reclined on his couch as Larenz recounted the history of the past few hours. Krogar stood at his side while the rest of us stood in a row behind them. Aside from the occasion, I was stunned at the grandeur of Dikahn's home. The one room we were in could fit over six of the huts entire families occupied in Ahrm. Dikahn himself was dressed in silver *nabe* and wore a bright red sash encrusted with medals. His black mane was shot with silver, and his black eyes, set in an impassive face as though they were jewels mounted in stone, studied his son. As Larenz finished, Dikahn turned toward Krogar. "You say you were once in the army?"

Krogar bowed. "Yes, Lord General. My Jaren served you in the capture of Dashik more than fifteen years ago."

Dikahn nodded, then turned toward Larenz. "You are an adult, my son, which precludes my warming your backside for today's foolishness. I hope your Jaren will accept your apology." He turned back to Krogar. "Since my son made your acquaintance in a prison, am I hasty in presuming that you were there for some reason?"

Krogar smiled. "My Lord General, it was nothing—a small dispute over property."

"Somebody else's no doubt." The Lord General shrugged. "Still, I owe you for enabling my son to keep his word to his Jaren and to the army. Do you have something in mind for a reward?"

Krogar bowed. "I would not presume to instruct the Lord General in such a matter."

Dikahn nodded, a wry smile tugging at the corners of his mouth. "Tell me, Krogar; under what circumstances did you leave the army?"

The thief pursed his lips, then held out his hands. "It was nothing. A simple dispute over orders that resulted in a minor scuffle."

Dikahn nodded. "And who was the officer you struck?"

Krogar raised his eyebrows in a show of innocence, then he sighed. "A company officer named Vulnar, Lord General. But," he added, "no one served the Shikazu better than I. I was dismissed against my will, and for an unjust reason."

Again, Dikahn nodded. "Krogar, faithful old soldier, I believe your treatment to have been harsh, and I would correct this injustice. Tomorrow you will join my son and his new friends here and report to the barracks in Meydal for army service."

"But, but, Lord General . . ."

Dikahn held up his hand. "No need to thank me, Krogar. This you have earned." The general turned toward Larenz. "You will bring special instructions from me to the station officer. It would not be wise to have you train on Tenuet. Therefore, you and your new comrades will be shipped to the Fourth Army and trained on Dashik. To put you any further away from Tenuet would require going outside the jurisdiction of the Shikazu."

Krogar held out his hands. "Lord General, it has been a long time since I saw service, and I am over forty now, and perhaps the decision to discharge me wasn't as unjust as I thought. . . ."

Dikahn held up a hand. "None of this will stand before my orders, Krogar. Please, let me do this for you for what you did for my son."

Krogar stood straight and cocked his head. "If I don't?"

The Lord General leaned forward on his couch, his eyes deep and cold. "Consider the alternative, my purse-lifting friend."

Krogar studied the general for an instant, then bowed. "Of course, the Lord General's wishes will be observed."

"Of course." Dikahn nodded at Larenz. "Find a servant and arrange quarters for your friends."

"Yes, father." Larenz turned and the rest of us bowed, then turned to follow. Dikahn caught my eye as I was about to go through the door, then motioned for me to remain.

"Close the door."

I did so then walked back and stood before Dikahn's couch. "Yes, Lord General?"

"Larenz said that your village was far south?"

"Yes, Lord General. The Jaren of the Redbar hails from Ahrm."

The general nodded. "Then your fencing master would have been Lodar?"

"Why, yes. Do you know him?"

Dikahn nodded. "He has served with me. He and his Jaren officered a group under me during the last war. A Shikazu is Lodar." Dikahn rubbed his chin, then studied me. "You know that, after training, my son's Jaren will officer a company?"

"Yes. He told us."

Dikahn nodded. "Tell me—what is your name?"

"Eeola."

"Tell me, Eeola. Would the Redbar apply to serve in my son's company?"

"I cannot speak for the Jaren, Lord General, but for myself, I would serve with him." I saw no change on the old general's face, but I had the feeling that I had said just the right thing.

Dikahn waved his hand. "Go and join your mates, Eeola, and thank you."

"Thank you, Lord General." I bowed and left the room.

Dashik is the second planet in the Minuraam system, the Fourth Star of the Shikazu. There is a large Shikazu population on the planet dominating the Borgunz, the squat, powerful, fur-covered creatures that were the planet's original masters. Dashik is lonely, and very, very hot. After our month-long flight from Tenuet and our first look at our new station, and after absorbing the molten wrath of Aragdan, the training instructor assigned to us, we appreciated all the more Lord General Dikahn's peculiar sense of humor.

Training by a field unit is different from group training at a station, such as the centers on Tenuet. Perhaps the station cadres are further removed from the threat of invasion. In any event, the instructors in a field unit know that any moment their charges may be called upon to fight, and fight well. Aragdan, therefore, was a merciless master, and we would have been continually sweat soaked had not the air been so dry.

So much of it was so different from the jungle. Learning the jump racks was the first thing. The jump rack is designed to amplify body movements both in strength and speed. Standing by itself, the machine looks like a skeleton without a head. One backs into it, stands on the foot plates, then beginning with the toe belts, the metal frame is strapped to the body, up the legs, waist, chest, shoulders, arms and wrists. The hands fit into three-fingered metal gloves. At first, our training group spent as much time ramming each other as we did drilling in the racks, but in time we learned the machines, making them parts of us. With them we could run great distances at high speeds carrying heavy weights, or jump to incredible heights, or down from such heights with the rack absorbing the shocks. When the backs of our machines were mounted with the heavy black cubes, we saw why the racks were necessary. To heft one of the cubes took two strong Shikazu, who would, nevertheless, be cursing, staggering, and straining every muscle before they had to put the cube down moments later. Each Shikazu had to carry one, for the cubes powered the wands and shields we carried.

The new wands were connected to the cube by a clear cable, and they could slice metal as a hot dagger slices cheese. The black cube supplied the power. The shields were not the heavy, black deflection squares we were used to, but instead were almost transparent nets, also connected to the power supply. The nets could absorb almost any kind of energy, including sunlight, and convert it in a flash to power that could be used by the wand. For the new weapons, we had to learn new tactics, which meant new drills. The drills seemed unending, but in time the Jaren of the Redbar functioned again as the parts of a well-designed machine. In addition, the Redbar could function in a like manner with any other Jaren in our training group, and the entire group together made a formidable force. Despite his cursing, ridicule and constant haranguing, as we reached the end of our training, we could see the pride—the Shikazu—burning in Aragdan's eyes.

Sprinkled among our hundred and fifty recruits were several who had sworn to the army before, such as Krogar. Most of them were the remaining members of their respective Jarens. They were a curious lot. Some were like Krogar—wanderers, thieves, drunkards—pulled back into the army from outside. Others were more recently divested of their Jarens by the humans during the battle for Baalphor, Dashik's sister planet. These were sullen soldiers indeed. Watching them drill with us, I could not help but think of my own feelings should my mates be lost in battle. When I tried to imagine it, I felt hot rage trying to hold together a life shredded by emptiness and vengeance.

We knew that the old soldiers, as we called them, would officer the groups that were formed from our training group. Five Jarens make up a section, and five sections make up a company. The company is officered by another Jaren, and the odds and ends of old soldiers officered the sections. As was predicted, Larenz and his Jaren of the Red Claw excelled at everything, and a company was formed from our training group officered by the Red Claw. Krogar officered the section in which the Redbar found itself. Despite his light-fingered past, we had witnessed the old thief at drills, and were willing to serve him.

We knew from the first that we were being trained as part of the invasion force that would retake Baalphor. The human destruction of the Baalphor garrison, and the subsequent occupation of the planet by the humans, forged an aura of vengeance and somber purpose about those on Dashik who prepared to right the humiliation to the Shikazu. Army battle cruisers had blockaded the planet and had fought the human space forces to a standstill. The rest was up to us. We were entered into the Fourth Army roster as the Second Company, Fifth Assault Group, Fifth Battle Force, attached to the Baalphor Invasion Armada.

On an evening soon after, I was sent by Larenz to find Krogar and inform him of a meeting of company officers. The black of Dashik's night had almost swallowed the heat of the day, and cool breezes picked at my skin as the desert gave up its warmth. I found Krogar seated on a rock at the bottom of a draw cut into the desert floor by some long-dead stream. As I came up on him, my feet walked on fine sand, and he did not hear me. Then, when I could view the direction the old thief faced, I saw them—four pale apparitions glowing with the Light's color. I gasped, and Krogar turned his head and faced me. "Eeola?"

"Yes." I could hardly hear my own voice.

Krogar held out his hand toward the patches of glowing blue. "Be not afraid, Eeola. Meet my mates of the Jaren of the Green Dragon: Pegda, Yos, Aldaon, and our *Di*, Radier."

I watched the glows. They were unmoving, yet they seemed to flow within themselves as something bearing life. I swallowed. "Krogar, are they . . . ghosts?"

The old soldier placed his elbows on his knees, clasped his hands, and rested his grizzled chin upon them as he studied the representations of his mates. "Ghosts. I wonder. The *Rhanakah* tells us that our brothers stand with us in death as they did in life. Perhaps they are." Krogar remained silent for a long moment, then shook his head. "Perhaps they are nothing more than projections of my mind made visible by what little of the Light that remains in me. This is what some would have you believe."

"And you, Krogar; what do you believe?"

The old soldier shrugged. "I do not concern myself. They are here, and I accept them." He turned and faced me. "Why have you come for me?"

"Larenz . . . he has called a meeting of officers."

Krogar stood. "Then I should be off." He again faced the spots of light. "Be off, my brothers. I am not ready to join you yet. Perhaps soon." The lights rose from the desert floor, faded into the rock wall of the draw, then disappeared. I jumped as Krogar slapped me on the shoulder. "Let us be off."

Our weeks of training concluded, we packed into landing shuttles and were moved to an army attack transport, where we were assigned a compartment. Our jump racks and weapons stood in the shuttles, a silent, motionless, mindless company awaiting only the direction of living bodies to wreak destruction upon the defenders of Baalphor. And how we longed—lusted—for that destruction. As we talked among ourselves during the days it took to reach our staging area around Baalphor, we would often speak of the great heroes that peopled the history of the Shikazu—epics all of us had long since memorized from childhood, but which never grew dull from the telling.

Larenz would bring Krogar with him and go from Jaren to Jaren in our section explaining such of the battle plan as applied to the company. If need be, any member of the company would be able to fill Larenz's place should he fall. Larenz would also recount his favorite Shikazu epics, and did so in a strong, clear voice that seemed louder than it was. Often he would leave the compartment and I would look around at my Jaren, my section, and all of those who made up my company. We were more than twenty-five separate Jarens with a common purpose. We were something of unity, a

172   THE JAREN

single structure of new metal—a Jaren with a hundred and twenty-five mates.

At the staging area, as we stood silently in the landing shuttle, strapped into our racks, I could see the battle blood pounding through my company and could feel it in my own veins. The shuttle lurched downward, gradually pulled forward as it applied power, and swung several times as it maneuvered to make formation with the ship's other shuttles. In the front of the compartment, Larenz listened to the steady chatter of the tactical information channel. We could all hear that the invasion was going according to plan, which meant that our role had not changed. As we came abreast of the human battle lines, the top of the shuttle would open and we would jump out of the compartment into the steaming jungle below. After the area had been cleared of humans, we would strike through the lines and secure a rise in the jungle floor the humans had equipped and manned as a heavy weapons position.

Once we entered the atmosphere, we could feel the shuttle being rocked as the humans threw up their defensive screen of weapons. Inside me, I felt frustration at being unable to strike back during the landing. About us, landing shuttles were being blown from the sky, and perhaps chance would favor us, perhaps not. I looked at my mates and saw none of this in their eyes. In them I read what we had been taught. Some will get through, enough to do what must be done. We train that, if we should be chosen by chance to avenge the Shikazu, we will be ready. If chance chooses us to die, others will be spared by the same chance—others who will assume our burden of revenge.

Larenz held out his hands as the shuttle leveled in its fall. "Stand ready!" At that moment, the shuttle was slammed by a huge fist of energy. Since the racks compensated for the lurch, none of us were knocked down to the deck, but Larenz entered into a heated conversation with the pilot. He turned back to us. "We cannot steer, and we have missed our jump point. Also, the doors will not open. The pilot will attempt to circle around to make our jump point again. At my command, use your wands to cut through the walls of the shuttle. When you land, clear your area, then regroup on the Red Claw. Watch for where we land."

As the shuttle lurched and wallowed, all of us reached to the part of our racks behind our waists and energized our wands and shields. A hum that almost drowned out the pounding of the humans' weapons filled the compartment. Larenz turned to us. "We can't make

THE JAREN

THE JAREN

it! We will be far behind enemy lines when we land. When you land, clear and regroup." He hefted his wand and aimed it at the bulkhead. "Shikazu!"

Those of us against the walls turned our wands against them, unmindful of the splatters of molten metal that clung to our legs. It was soon impossible to see in the spark- and smoke-filled compartment. Then, one plate fell away, then another. The plate I worked on tore away exposing blue skies crossed with red beams and black smoke trails. I jumped, followed by others behind me. The wind tumbled me as an angry swarm of red streaks cut the air around me. Using my arms and legs as counterweights, I gained control of my fall and began playing my wand on the jungle below. A red streak would emerge from the jungle, then I would sizzle that point, catching the return fire with my shield. Before I hit ground, my shield had overloaded and was deflecting, rather than absorbing, energy.

I crashed through the leaf cover and saw that I had landed in the center of a human heavy weapons position. The weapon itself could not be used on me, but the crew quickly pulled hand weapons and fired them in my direction. As though they were stalks of gava cane, my wand swept the humans and cut them down. As I swapped fire with a pocket of the animals entrenched in a protected position, Gem joined me, and together we saw the last of them, then turned our wands upon the weapon to render it useless.

The jungle seemed strangely quiet as Gem, his face flushed with victory, turned toward me. "Ah, it is true! We are the Shikazu! We are unconquerable!"

"Gem, in which direction did the Red Claw land? I could not see."

"That way." Gem pointed into the jungle, gained control of himself, breathed a few times, then nodded. "Yes, this way. The company is strung out all along the enemy line."

We ran from the position into the jungle and were soon joined by one of the members of a Jaren in our section. His gleaming eyes and bared teeth reflected our own. In a few moments we were joined by a few more Shikazu, among them, Krogar and Vastar. Krogar led us through the jungle, picking up more of the company as we went, until we walked into a wall of red light. The humans had brought up a unit to block our attempt to join up with the Red Claw. Entrenched in good defensive positions, their own kinds of weapons and shields deployed, this would be no area-clearing exercise. The main body of our small force, covered by our shields, played our wands over the human positions, while Krogar and the remainder of the force jumped to the right and out of sight. After a few moments, the screams from the human positions evidenced the success of Krogar's flanking maneuver. Krogar stuck his head out of the jungle and motioned us to follow. As I stepped through a row of brush, I saw a human staring at me, the wound in his shoulder and chest still smoking, leaving a sick, sweet smell of cooking flesh. He reached out his right hand toward one of their hand weapons, and without thought, my wand passed across the creature's throat, severing its head from its body. The grisly orb rolled across the jungle floor and came to rest against a tree, eyes still staring.

"Eeola!" I lifted my head and saw Krogar looking at me from beyond a low wall of brush. "Over here! We must move quickly!" He turned and disappeared into the jungle. I hesitated, thinking for some reason that there was something I should do for the remains of this fallen enemy. I could think of nothing. Hefting my wand and shield, I took a last look at those eyes, then followed Krogar's path.

Except for a straggling human or two, the rest of our journey to join up with Larenz was without event. One of the scouts Krogar sent out reported back late in the day to inform him that contact with Larenz had been made. In an hour, we were again a company. Vastar, Gem and I searched the others, and when we found Dob and Tim, we hugged, slapped backs, joked, and roughed around until we were ordered to silence. Other Jarens celebrated as they found their lost mates, but others wept. A third of the company had been lost; either killed or still wandering the jungle.

Larenz conferred with the section officers, then Krogar came back to our section. He gathered us around, then began in a low voice. "The officers have decided to try for our original objective." He pulled a map from his *nabe* and spread it on the jungle floor. He pointed one of his armored fingers at a spot on the map. "We are here. It is a half day's walk to the hill." He stabbed another part of the map. "We will be coming up behind the enemy lines, which could be good or bad. If they do not expect us, we shall surprise them. If they expect us," Krogar looked up at the circle of faces, "if they expect us, there will be that many more of them with which to fertilize the soil." Folding the map, Krogar stood. "Follow me."

Long after the horizon swallowed the sun, we crept through the brush, stopping only to either check or clear the trail ahead. In the night, the humans took to holes, using only remote equipment against us. We easily infiltrated their positions, slid into their holes and blessed them with eternal sleep. The jungle was our home.

In time, a halt was ordered, pickets put out, and orders for rest given. I unstrapped myself from my rack and slid to the ground and was asleep in an instant.

My dreams, if dreams they were, showed Ahrm at the harvest season; the one dusty street piled with jeba cane, gahn roots, and the bright yellow peppers that seared the tongue with a delicious fire. The large blue beln melons stacked in a pyramid, dusty tikiruch creeping in and out of the stands and people, then running into the jungle with their art-acquired fruit. The Redbar with its booty of melons, bursting them against the trees and devouring the ice-green flesh amidst gay laughter and fine belches. . . .

"Up." Vastar tapped my shoulder. I shook the sleep from my eyes and sprang to my feet to begin strapping myself into my jump rack. The sky was yet red as the shadows gave back the sun, and the broad-leafed trees and overhead vines stood out black against the sky. My stomach grumbled to remind me that the company had not eaten since landing. Had we put down as planned, we would be in contact with our forces, and food brought up. Never mind. There would be food once we drove the humans from the hill.

The sky yellowed, and soon those of us at the edge of the clearing that opened before us could see the hill. It was nothing—little more than a bump in the carpet of the jungle. The top, however, bristled with heavy weapons, and on the lower slopes, freshly blasted human defensive positions could be seen. Perhaps, because we had not taken our objective as planned, it remained as a human strongpoint, probably holding up the advance of the Shikazu. In every mind ran the same thought: It is our error; therefore, it is ours to correct.

From where I stood, I could see Larenz nod toward his widely dispersed section leaders, then move out, his mates of the Red Claw close at his back. We halted at the edge of the clearing at the base of the hill, then, upon Larenz's signal, we jumped our racks toward the hill, slashing our wands toward anything that moved or might move. The humans' return fire was delayed only a few seconds, but in that time we were across the clearing and at their throats. The first line fell before us almost without loss, but as we worked our way uphill, the second line of human defenders was reinforced. In addition, several of the heavy weapons on the crest of the hill were turned in our direction. I saw others fall as red beams eluded shields, burning great pulpy holes in Shikazu chests, but I paid them no heed, for the blood was upon me. My wand could not find enough of the humans as it slashed and butchered all those it could find, my shield sucking up their beams to return them through my stick of death.

Still, battle blood or no, we slowed in front of the wall of force placed before us. The defenders—all well-armed—numbered almost a thousand, and as my arm, then my leg, caught human fire, even I cooled in my tracks. Then we saw it: a crossfire of countless red beams swept over Larenz. He fell, his pieces rolling in different directions down the slope.

Time stood still as a primeval roar erupted from the Shikazu. We moved forward as shields of blinding white fury made us gods of wrath, impervious to the feeble weapons of the humans. Our grief shot through our wands and scourged the hill, and the humans melted before us, for they were mere mortals.

Night fell upon the hill, and I thought with amusement of the pockets of humans we had slaughtered—the outraged looks on their faces as we cut them down, their hands stretched over their heads, one or two waving little white flags. The human, says Vastar, has a strange concept of war. The human thinks it to be a game, and when one side bests the other, the losers may throw up their hands, smile and retire to the sidelines to await the next round. The Shikazu expects no quarter, and gives none. If there were such a thing as a human worthy of being spared, what possible reason would the creature have for being on Baalphor?

Hungry as we were, we only picked at our ration blocks. The wine that had been brought up, however, saw more enthusiastic custom. We knew Larenz such a short time, and would that there had been more time, that our grief could have been that much deeper. The top of the hill was almost bare of trees—not by nature's choice, but by ours—and as we sat cross-legged on the ground, downing great draughts of wine and picking at our rations, the stars spread out over our heads. We had no fires, and we did not recognize the stranger as he walked into our midst. "Is this the Second Company of the Fifth Assault?" The voice sounded hollow, but familiar.

I struggled to my feet. "Lord General Dikahn?"

The figure nodded. "Yes."

"It is Eeola . . . of the Redbar—"

The figure nodded again. "Yes, one of my son's companions from the prison." A chuckle worked its way through the old general's grief. Hearing his words, others stood and faced the general. He held up his hands, palms outward. "Please, resume your rest. No one has earned it more." We remained standing until the general nodded and lowered himself to the ground. The remains of Larenz's company in our area gathered around him and sat down. The general looked around at us. "Are you being fed well?"

Several voices muttered an affirmative. We watched as Dikahn bowed his head for a moment, then lifted it. "Who commands this company now?"

Vastar spoke. "The Red Claw still commands this company, Lord General, and will until either it or the company no longer remains."

Dikahn reached out a hand and clamped it on Vastar's shoulder. "Well said, soldier. Well said." He removed his hand, let it fall into his lap, then faced us. "I have no military purpose here, my soldiers, and should be off. There is much for me to do." Dikahn started up, but Tim stood over him.

"Would the Lord General care to hear the song I have made in honor of his son?" Tim held out his pipes.

Dikahn rubbed his eyes and nodded. "I would hear your song, soldier. Play."

Tim began, the haunting strains of the tiny pipes marking well the grief of the company, and, as well, the grief of a Lord General. The simple tune washed over the listeners—sad, yet supported by a will of metal, until all the company had gathered to hear. As Tim ended the first refrain, and began the second, Krogar talked the song of death:

Hear me universe,
This was one of us,
Our comrade Larenz.
His fellows wish him well,
On his journey of endless night,
Wishing only to be at his side,
Slain in battle
As Shikazu.
Give us this, Oh Universe,
That we may be
As our comrade Larenz;
Shikazu.

The notes of the pipes died, and the shadowed scene before my eyes could have been carved from black and dark grey stone. Lord General Dikahn then stood, turned, and was swallowed by the night. One by one we drifted back to our wine and ration blocks.

The next morning, the humans counterattacked with a fury we hardly expected. Those that lived were sent back down the hill, licking their wounds. Afterwards, the Jaren of the Redbar laid Timbenevva to rest. It is hard to explain the feeling of losing a Jaren mate. As an individual, you still live, but losing an arm or leg would cause less grief. No human can understand the desolation, the endless pain of a lost mate. In time, a scab of sorts forms, you go on, but it is missing—that fierce joy that filled us when we whipped Lodar on the drill ground. The feeling of superiority when we defeated the Jaren of the Golden Dart for the rights to the swimming hole. The Shikazu feeling when we took the hill from the humans. Victory still sat well, but it was something less than it was, despite his Light still being with us.

To fill out our military unit, we accepted Zeth, the sole remaining member of the Green Waters Jaren of the village of Kurinaam. He was a jungle brother, but aloof—apart from us. His only two goals left little room for conversation between us: He would kill humans, and he would join his mates of the Green Waters in their endless night. Who could argue with him? He, and his mates, were Shikazu.

But the Redbar was not a unit. When the Company was pulled off the hill, there was still that battle blood—that kill-the-humans feeling—that fired our actions of old. I look back at it now and it seems that, of all things, we wanted victory. Next, we still wanted to live. We had not yet achieved Zeth's single-minded desire to die, and in the process, to take a host of humans with us. It was enough for us to send the humans on the trip.

Our racks were equipped with extra packs, and we carried our rations and shelters with us. Our company was assigned a place in the spearhead that would split the human forces of the Baalphorian Main Continent. In reality, the planet Baalphor has but one continent worthy of the name, but the original inhabitants and subsequent convention had designated several of the larger islands as continents. Neither the humans nor ourselves considered the fight for Baalphor to hinge on anything other than control of the Main. As with all modern armies, the human forces were mobile and widely scattered; however, there were several reinforced positions that commanded wide areas of surrounding ground. Between their defensive screens and well-entrenched fortifications, it was left to our infantry forces to destroy these positions. The most formidable of these positions, and the land headquarters of the human forces, was the Citadel: a batholith thrust from the jungle floor with sides so sheer that not even jungle vines or airborne seeds had found a niche. A single fissure in the west wall allowed access to the top—for those who controlled the heights above and along the fissure. The top of the feature was generally flat, with only trees and other jungle growth to soften its stark appearance. As night defeated day, the pale yellow glows of permanent defensive screens could be seen covering the top, while random bursts of fire cascaded down the fissure. To attack such a thing was madness; to let it remain unharmed, keeping an iron hand on our movement across the surrounding bush, was madness of another kind. We would attack.

Where the shields over the human positions overlapped, neutral slits existed. The nature of these fields was such that beams and high-speed projectiles could not penetrate with effect. Slower-moving landing shuttles, however, might make it through. The strongest evidence supporting this was the deployment of the human forces beneath the screens. Diagrams prepared by orbital survey showed the areas surrounding each of the slits to be heavily defended. There was no trick plan. We would assault at the places and in the manner expected by the humans. We would cast the spirit of the Shikazu against that of the humans. Two waves of shuttles, a total of forty-six, would make the attack. The first wave was to fight through the initial defense ring and secure a position for the second wave. While the first wave held the position, the second would fight through the lines and knock out the screens. As soon as they accomplished their task, the might of the Fourth Army would fall on the position in a massive airborne assault, bringing the Citadel to its knees. Our company was assigned to the second wave.

As we prepared to move into the shuttles, the Jaren of the Redbar pledged the blood of its brother Timbenevva on the heads of the human defenders of the Citadel. Zeth, his mind wrapped in his own thoughts, stood apart from us. I could see that Vastar was bothered by this. A Jaren must work as the fingers of a hand, and clearly, Zeth was not one of us. The racks had already been moved inside our company's shuttle, and while we awaited the command to mount, we squatted outside in the narrow strip of shade cast by the landing craft. As did the others of the company, we discussed the coming battle. After the traditional round of boasts, brags and declarations of bloodletting, our group quieted as each of us played pictures in our minds of skilled wands and screaming Shikazu decimating the humans. My imaginings were interrupted by a strange quality in Vastar's voice. "Zeth?"

Our new member came back from his own mental wanderings and looked at our *Di*. "Yes, Vastar?"

Vastar studied each of us in turn, then turned back to Zeth. "The Redbar has pledged the blood of its fallen mate on the heads of the enemy."

Zeth nodded, his eyes studying the ground. "I was listening."

Vastar nodded. "If you would join us, Zeth, in our pledge, we would join you in pledging the blood of your brothers of the Green Waters."

Zeth brought up his head sharply, his eyes examining Vastar's. His eyes grew bright as he slowly nodded, reached out both hands, clamped one on my shoulder and the other on Dob's. "Their names . . . Perra, our *Di*. Then Vane, Dommis, and Arapen. Your brother's name?"

"Our brother's name is Timbenevva." We each extended our hands and clasped them in the center of our circle. Vastar's eyes studied us as he spoke. "Then, let the Light of our fallen brothers —Timbenevva, Perra, Vane, Dommis, and Arapen—go with the Jaren of the Redbar and Green Waters into battle. Let their strength fill us and their wands join us as the Jaren of the Redbar and Green Waters goes forth to avenge the deaths of its brothers."

We all stood, then hugged and slapped Zeth as we welcomed him to the Jaren, and he welcomed us. We would, again, work as the fingers of a hand; we were a Jaren.

Josahr of the Red Claw, Larenz's Jaren mate, stood in the front of the shuttle's compartment observing the tactical information as we fell toward the Citadel. We knew Josahr to be an excellent leader, and had resworn to him. The shuttle lurched as unseen forces slapped against its hull. Josahr turned to us. "The shuttles going through the slot—those that made it that far—are being burned out of the sky before they can discharge their companies. Only parts of three companies in the first wave have made it to the ground. Our orders have changed. We will turn and go out over the center field of one of the screens and discharge *above* it. Those of us that make it to the ground should be close to the screen's projector battery. Questions?" There were none. Josahr nodded at the pilot, and a moment later the shuttle banked and swung to the left. A moment later, and the overhead of the craft was open. Screaming "Shikazu!" we leaped out over the Citadel.

The familiar wind-blast struck my face as I emerged, then controlled my fall. Below me appeared to be nothing but the jungle-covered Citadel, but in a moment I felt myself slowed as the feeling of a thousand insects crawling on my body began. The landscape below grew wavy and distorted, and all sound ceased. My rack lost all power, freezing me into a spread-legged position, my wand dead and helpless in my hand.

I had little time to think of these things as blinding pains shot through my head, chest, and muscles. Then they were gone and I was falling. As the ground rushed up at me, I braced myself for the impact that would see my end, but power slowly came back to my jump rack and wand. Numerous streaks of red cracked and sizzled the air around us, but the source for most of these was a slight rise in the terrain almost directly below me. I directed my wand below my feet and roasted the site I had picked for landing. Most of the human fire was directed toward the slot where the main body of the second wave was attempting entrance, but I could see from the fire we were drawing that many of us would die. From the stiff, tumbling falls some were taking, I realized that not everyone's racks had gotten back power after falling through the shield.

Even with my rack absorbing most of the shock, striking the ground stunned me and I rolled downhill, coming to rest against a tree. The slashes of my wand had downed several of the humans, but many more remained, and only my unexpected roll saved me. The humans unleashed a red crossfire at my tumbling form, causing themselves much damage as the fire from one side fell into the other's ground. I came up beneath my shield, pulsing my wand at all movements. The red fire slackened as the humans still on their feet sought the safety of trees, rocks, and holes. Soon my shield could absorb no more energy and the red fire splashed off it as I worked my way up the hill. Further to my right, I caught sight of Krogar littering the ground with humans. Beyond him, there were others—all moving up the hill toward the projector. Still more humans broke from above and were cut down by our wands. I would have felt pity for the foolish creatures that stood before us, had not my mind been blinded to all but one thing: destroy the projector.

There was no organized assault, no cover fire and flank. We reached the top of the hill and faced trenches manned by humans determined to make a stand. Behind them stood a tracked vehicle mounted with a dull green dome—the projector. Our wands roasted the trenches while our shields swatted away the enemy fire. Some dropped, but still we moved forward until we stood in the trenches and swept them of human life. The projector crew fell clutching at ripped chests and severed limbs before they could surrender. There was no need to destroy the projector. Krogar climbed the stairs into a side hatch, executed an operator who huddled on the deck whimpering, then reached out a hand and turned off all the controls. I turned from the door and watched as the sky filled with Fourth Army shuttles discharging their companies. The Citadel had been broken.

A quick headcount showed Vastar, Gem, and Zeth to be among

the dead; however, Dob and I could spare them little thought. With the fall of the Citadel, the human lines were rolling up. The revenge for the Baalphor garrison was at hand, and the battle forces of the Baalphor Armada took only a deep breath before locking with the remains of the human forces. A shuttle moved the remains of our company from the Citadel to the jungle below, where we joined other units of the Fifth Assault Group.

A few human units attempted surrender, but their fates removed this course from the list of human options. The battle blood was running hot, and it would not cease until we ran out of humans to kill. We saw only our small part of the advance, but we heard the news from other units. Across the entire Main Continent, the humans were folding and striking north. The Second and Fifth Battle Forces deployed across the humans' lines of retreat, and the rest was a matter of time and blood. Afterwards, Baalphor rocked with our cries: "Shikazu! Shikazu! Shikazu!"

Krogar joined me as I laid my last Jaren mate, Dob, to rest. The pain of losing my mates mixed with the elation of victory confused me. Krogar had brought extra rations of wine, but that only confused me further. As the distance in time from our victory increased, the elation diminished and the pain grew.

Krogar drank deeply from his bottle, lowered it, then studied me for a long time. "At this moment, Eeola, you wonder how you will last out the pain. Perhaps, you wonder, as I once did, if it is worth lasting out the pain." He shrugged. "I can't answer that for you. For myself, something inside of me snapped—you saw me on the trail. It was a death of sorts, living from moment to moment, thinking of nothing, of no one. But this," he lifted his free hand, "this has made me whole again. Our victory reminds us that we are Shikazu. I forgot that once, but never will again. You are Shikazu, Eeola."

I nodded, took a deep breath, and felt a great weight lift from my heart. There would still be pain, but being Shikazu was my shield. In a manner of speaking, all Shikazu belonged to a single great Jaren—a band sworn to our brothers and traditions, founded upon our one truth: the Shikazu cannot be conquered.

As I drank from my flask, Krogar stood and walked into the night. The air was warm, and as the wine relaxed my muscles, I leaned back against a tree and let my mind wander back to Ahrm, where my mates and I planted our hair. Only I had not returned to the village, but I swore to. At the end of my service I would once again walk that dusty path and smell the turawood and jungle orchids. Perhaps, even Carrina of the Golden Dart—if she lived. I would settle into the routine of an elder, wed my woman and raise a hut full of screaming brats that I would see join Jarens and travel the road to adulthood. Perhaps, when Lodar feels his years, I will become the new fencing master, I thought. As these thoughts wandered through my mind, I noticed that on the other side of my skull, there was a difference in the night.

I put down my flask and stood, holding my breath to listen. The tension in the air was wrapped around my heart as though it were some powerful snake. I heard murmurs, a wail, saw the discharge of an energy wand. A weeping figure staggered toward me from beyond the near trees. I could not recognize him. "You!" I shouted. As though the figure had no volition, it stopped and faced me. "What is it? Do you know?" The figure nodded, then hung its head. "What?"

"Tenuet—the Light—has been destroyed!"

Eeola hung his head, then raised it and looked at me. "Now, human, perhaps you can understand." He held out his hands toward the four shimmering lights. "That Light which remains in us—in our Jaren—waits for me." He dropped one hand to his lap, but pointed the other in my direction. "But understand, we are not conquered. Since the war, no Jarens have been formed, no marriages have been made, and no babies conceived. In a few years there will be none of us left. As it came to our brothers and sisters, the endless sleep shall come to us. Is this how a conquered race behaves? The Mithad grows its young to serve you, but the Shikazu will not add to your subjects. Now, we are as the kazu wandering lost in the jungle—awaiting the victory of time. We can be killed, but we can never be conquered. We are Shikazu."

The old Shikki stood, wandered off into the jungle, and was followed by the blue lights. I never saw him again. I looked at that landmark and realized that it was the Citadel. There, and in the jungle surrounding the feature, Eeola of the Redbar Jaren had lost his mates, then the Light that sustained his race.

Was it the old fellow's story that touched me, or was it because of the few schoolmates of my own that lost their lives on Baalphor during the war of the four stars? I don't know. I never signed the agreement with Wiggins—at least, not for that particular piece of property. Baalphor is a big planet, and I don't worry about Wiggins.

Instead, I go to that rocky outcropping every now and then, and watch. It doesn't happen often, but every now and then you can see the lights gathering to welcome one of their own to the endless sleep.

THE

MAGICIAN'S

APPRENTICE

by Barry B. Longyear

*For over two centuries—ever
since it had been settled by survivors from
a circus space-ship—Momus
developed in its own way. But now ...*

Yudo and his two brothers stood looking at their grain field. Green only the day before, it now lay brown and withered. Yudo nodded. "It is the power of Rogor. Your tongue angered him, Arum."

"Bah!" Arum bent over and pulled up a handful of the brown plants, then held them over his head. "Rogor! Since the circus ship brought our ancestors to Momus, we have served no man. . . ."

"Arum!" Yudo held up his hands and looked with horror at his brother Lase.

Lase stood next to Arum and grabbed his arm. "Would you bring down more of this upon us?"

Arum shook off his brother's hand. Throwing the withered plants on the ground, Arum turned to his two brothers. "A fine pair you make. Look at you shaking in your sandals."

Lase wrung his hands, looked to Yudo, then back at Arum. "We are barkers by tradition, Arum. Perhaps we should go to Tarzak and be barkers again."

Arum shook his head. "As I said, a fine pair." He held out his arms, indicating the fields belonging to the three. "After all our work you would have us fetch and carry pitches for others?" Arum put his hands on his hips. "We are men of property. No carnival trickster will change that. . . ."

Lase and Yudo watched as Arum grabbed at his own face and his red and purple striped robe burst into flames. In seconds, Arum lay dead, his body burned beyond recognition. Then it disappeared.

"Arum!" Yudo took a step toward the spot where his brother had been standing, but stopped as a figure clad in black and scarlet appeared on the spot. Its face was hidden by a hood. "Rogor!"

The figure pointed at Lase. "Arum offended me. Do you believe as he believed?"

Lase clasped his hands together and bowed. "No, Great Rogor. Spare me."

"Lase, you would do my bidding?"

"Yes, Great Rogor."

"Then go to all the towns in Emerald Valley and tell them to go to Ris. They are to wait there until I appear."

"Yes, Great Rogor."

"Then, go." Lase looked at Yudo, back at Rogor, then began running across the field toward Ikona. Rogor turned toward Yudo. "For you, barker, I have an important task. Go to the fountain in Ikona. Your instructions are there." Yudo closed his eyes and nodded. When he opened them, Rogor was gone.

Eight days later, far to the south in Tarzak, a young girl looked nervously at a great magician's door. Its black and scarlet curtain hung motionless in the noon sun, while the reflection from the white-washed adobe hurt her eyes. Making her decision, she clenched her fists, held her arms straight at her sides, and marched through the door. Inside, she found herself standing next to a tall, sad-faced barker. He was dusty and smelled of the road. At the back of the small room, a tiny old man in black and scarlet robe sat on a low stool, supporting himself by gripping a heavy, gnarled staff. The old man nodded at the barker.

"A moment, Yudo, while I find out who my hasty visitor is." The old man raised his eyebrows at the girl.

"Fyx, I am Crisal. I—I didn't know you had company."

"I suppose, Crisal, it would have been too much trouble to call to the house. Never mind, little fortune teller. What brings you?"

"Fyx, I would be a magician."

The old magician looked the girl over from the top of her unkempt tangle of red hair to her dusty bare feet. "First, you are a girl; second, you are obviously of the fortune tellers; third, you are rude. Why should I apprentice you to the magician's trade?"

"First, Fyx, women have been magicians before. Myra of Kuumic played the Great Square here in Tarzak only yesterday."

The old man nodded. "Rare, but it has been done. But, Myra is the daughter of a magician. Explain that blue robe you wear—at least, I think it's blue under all that dirt."

"I am of the Tarzak fortune tellers. My mother is Salina. I told her as I tell you, I *choose* to be a magician. I have completed my apprenticeship; no one can force me to be a fortune teller." Crisal folded her arms, her nose in the air.

"Salina, eh?" Fyx scratched his head, then rubbed his chin. "You say you told this to Salina?"

"Aye."

"And what did the Great Salina say to you?"

"She said my life was my own and to do with it what I choose."

The corners of Fyx's mouth went down as his eyebrows went up. "She did? And your father, Eeren?"

Crisal frowned. "He was not understanding."

"I see. Now, about the third thing: your rudeness. Not even my own sons addressed me simply as 'Fyx'."

Crisal cocked her head to one side. "You insist?"

The old man nodded. "Try it once."

The girl bowed, loading her voice with sarcasm scraped from the floor. "*Great* Fyx."

"I see your respect would be more of a burden to both of us than your rudeness. And, now for the important part. Why should I take you on?"

Crisal smiled. "I know how you do your trick of the missing card."

The old man nodded, smiled, and pointed to a cushion next to his table. "Sit there, Crisal, and we will talk later. I don't want to hold up my visitor's business any longer." Walking in front of the barker, Crisal approached the table and sat on the designated cushion.

The barker bowed. "Great Fyx, is this something to say in front of the child?" Yudo pointed at Crisal.

Fyx looked at her, then turned back to the barker. "The little beast is my apprentice, Yudo. She is held under my vow of confidence, which is something she *will* respect!" Fyx turned back to the girl. Crisal nodded, and smiled.

Yudo shrugged. "As you say, Great Fyx. Will you come to Ikona?" Crisal saw fear in the barker's eyes, but it was not fear of Fyx.

"And you say the fee is twenty thousand movills?"

"In advance." Yudo pointed at the stack of bags on the floor.

Fyx nodded. "A handsome sum. We were interrupted before you said what I must do for it."

"Ikona is a farming village, Great Fyx, and our crops die. . . ."

Fyx held up his hand. "Save your coppers, Yudo. I am a magician, not a farmer."

"The crops die, Great Fyx, because of a magician. Rogor the Black One."

"Rogor . . . I have heard of this one, but he calls himself a sorcerer, not a magician."

Yudo bowed his head. "You all call upon the same dark spirits. Ikona has no place else to turn for help." The barker reached into his robe and brought forth an envelope. "The Dark One made this appear at the fountain in Ikona. It is addressed to you."

Fyx opened the envelope and squinted at the sheet of paper inside. Lifting his head, he turned to Crisal. "Fortune tellers do not read, do they?"

"I do."

Fyx held out the letter. The girl stood and walked to the old magician and took the letter. "Read it aloud."

Crisal held the paper to the light and began: "To Fyx, ancient and worthless patriarch of the Tarzak Magicians, Greetings. A fool from Ikona will ask you to come and do battle with me in my Deepland kingdom. He is a fool because he asks you; you are the bigger fool if you accept.

"Stay in the city, carnival trickster, and stay safe. In the Deeplands, I rule without challenge, for I have the power of Momus at my hands." Crisal looked at Fyx. "It is signed 'ROGOR' in a strange way."

"Strange how?"

"In a cross; look."

Fyx looked at the bottom of the sheet and saw the signature in bold letters:

$$
\begin{array}{ccccc}
 & & R & & \\
 & & O & & \\
R & O & G & O & R \\
 & & O & & \\
 & & R & &
\end{array}
$$

"What does it mean, Fyx?"

The magician frowned. "It is a palindrome; a word that reads the same frontwards or backwards. Other than that, it means nothing."

Yudo shook his head. "Great Fyx, it is the Dark One's sign. Show disrespect to it in Ikona, and your crops die. You then must pay Rogor to leave you be."

Fyx looked at a dark spot on the ceiling. ". . . ancient and worthless patriarch . . ." He turned his gaze on the barker. "Yudo, you fool, a bigger fool accepts your offer. Tell that to Rogor."

"I cannot. No one knows where Rogor lives."

Fyx shrugged. "How, then, am I supposed to do battle with the fumble-fingered Dark One?"

Yudo trembled. "Please, Great Fyx. Express your discourtesies after I have left." The barker bowed and backed out through the door. Fyx looked into Crisal's eyes.

"In the barker's eyes, what did you see?"

"Fear. As though Rogor could reach down and pluck him from your house if he chose."

The old magician nodded. Standing, he hobbled over to a chest, opened it and pulled out a black and scarlet robe. He handed it to the girl. "Wash, then put this on. There is a pool in back of the house. We will leave before light tomorrow for the Deeplands."

The next evening at the midway fire to Tieras, Crisal lifted her weary head from the sand and looked over her aching feet at the old magician. Fyx tested the many wads of cobit he had baking around the fire, and finding one done to his satisfaction, he put it into Crisal's sack. "There, that should keep us to Miira when they're all done." The girl let her head fall back to the sand.

"Fyx, aren't you tired? We've been walking all day."

The magician cackled. "So, apprentice, you are ready to end the day, are you?"

"You aren't?"

"I would be a poor master, Crisal, if I failed to give you your lessons."

"Lessons?"

Fyx nodded and dropped the remaining cobit cakes into the sack. "Sit up."

Crisal pushed herself up and sat crosslegged in front of the magician. Before her was a rock, and on the rock was a feather. Fyx sat across the rock from her. "What must I do?"

"Turn the feather over without your fingers. Touch it only with your mind."

Crisal frowned. "I don't understand."

"Look." Fyx pointed at the feather and turned it over as easily as if he had used his fingers. Again, he turned it back. "As a fortune teller's apprentice, you were taught to see as the fortune tellers see, with an extra pair of eyes. Now you must learn to use your extra pair of hands."

Crisal stared at the feather. "This is not a trick?"

"No. It is something you must learn, however, before you can do the better tricks and illusions. Try it."

Crisal fixed her eyes on the white feather, held her breath, grunted, went bug-eyed and began growing blue in the face. It didn't move. Letting her breath out, she shook her head. "It didn't move."

"Pick it up and feel it; rub it against your face. Your mind doesn't know what it's trying to do yet, and you must teach it." Crisal picked up the feather and felt its smoothness with her fingers and with her face. "Place it on the rock and try again."

The girl put down the feather, looked at it through almost closed eyes and imagined tiny hands reaching under and gripping the feather's edge. With her mind she felt resistance as though she were attempting to lift a great rock plate. Heaving against the weight, she strained until she slumped forward letting out her breath. The feather lifted and fluttered to the sand. "Did I . . . ?"

"No, child. You blew it off the rock. But, I saw it rock before it took flight. You have done well for your first try."

Crisal shook her head. "It seemed so heavy."

The old magician placed the feather back on the rock. "If you had never walked before, your body would seem an unbearable weight to your legs. With practice you will gain strength."

She frowned at the feather, then placed her finger on it holding it tight against the rock. Fyx smiled a toothless grin and pointed again at the feather. Crisal jumped as she felt it pulled from beneath her finger. "It *is* no trick then!"

"No trick."

"Fyx, is this one of those dark spirits Yudo said you and Rogor call upon?"

The old man picked up the feather and tucked it in Crisal's robe. "Child, the power you call upon to move the feather is your own. Only you can say if it is dark. Prepare for sleep. I want to make Tieras by nightfall tomorrow."

Fyx turned back to the fire, while Crisal scooped holes in the sand for her hip and shoulder. As she settled in, resting her head against her hand, she saw the magician looking into the fire much as her mother would look for secrets in a glass sphere. The old man's eyes showed fear, but more than that, they showed sadness. As she was about to ask a question of him, he turned and looked into her eyes. Crisal's mind grew cloudy, then blank.

The next evening, as they reached the outskirts of the desert town of Tieras, Crisal watched as the occasional farmer or workman would put his chores aside to stand and bow toward them. Fyx would return the greeting with no more than a curt nod, which was more communication than Crisal had had with him since leaving the fire. During their walk, her fortune teller's eyes revealed little of the future, but much about her master's apprehension. Each step toward Ikona seemed to deepen the creases in the old magician's face.

"Will we stop here, Fyx?"

Fyx looked at her as though realizing for the first time that the girl had been walking beside him all day. "What was that?"

"It is toward night, and we are in Tieras. Where will we stop?"

Fyx looked around, then nodded. "Yes, we have made good time. Have you kin here?"

Crisal nodded. "My aunt, Diamind, lives here with her brother

Lorca. Should we sleep under a roof tonight?"

Fyx pointed at the dark clouds gathering in the west. "One does not need the eyes of a fortune teller to divine the meaning of that."

The girl frowned. "I'm not sure we would be welcome, Fyx. Diamind is my father's sister, and they think much the same."

"About you becoming a magician?"

"Aye. Surely the Great Fyx must have an admiring trickster in Tieras that can be imposed upon."

"Perhaps." As they crossed a small stone bridge spanning a muddy creek, Fyx pointed his stick toward a dark, narrow alley. They turned from the bridge into the alley and could barely walk side by side from the closeness of the walls. Reaching a black and scarlet striped curtain, Fyx stopped and pounded his stick against the wall. "Ho, the house! This is Fyx and an apprentice. Are you there, Vassik?"

The curtain opened exposing an old woman dressed in the scarlet and black cuffs of a magician's assistant. "Fyx, is it you?"

"Aye, Bianice. Is Vassik in? Is he well?"

"Please, enter." Fyx and Crisal followed the old woman into her table room. Seated on a cushion before the table was, what seemed to Crisal, the oldest man alive. "Vassik, it is Fyx and an apprentice."

The ancient's face broke into smiles. "Fyx? Fyx, is it?"

"Aye, Vassik. This is my new apprentice, Crisal." Fyx shoved the girl toward the old man.

"Crisal? Come here, child." Crisal stood next to the old man while he gently passed his hands over her face and body. "Fyx, your eyes are worse than mine. This is a girl!"

"My apprentice, all the same, Vassik. How much would you charge for the use of your roof tonight?"

Vassik shook his head. "For you, Fyx, a special rate. What brings you to Tieras? Sit, sit."

Crisal and Fyx lowered themselves to cushions at Vassik's table. Bianice left the room and returned with hot cake, cheese and wine, then seated herself next to Vassik.

"We go to the Deeplands, Ikona."

"Ah, yes."

"You have heard of their troubles then?"

"I'm blind, not deaf, Fyx. Black Rogor is feared even this far south. What have you to do with him?"

"Ikona has hired me to rid them of the sorcerer."

Vassik nodded. "How do you plan to do this?"

"I have no plan, Vassik. I only have my knowledge that whatever

THE MAGICIAN'S APPRENTICE

powers he has do not come from beyond."

"Well said, but I don't hear as much conviction as there should be. Do you have doubts?"

Fyx shrugged. "Not all is known, and it has been many years since Rogor and I last met."

Vassik waved a hand at Bianice. "Take Fyx's apprentice out to the kitchen to help bring in the food. We would talk alone." The old man dropped two copper movills on the table.

Bianice rose; and Crisal looked at Fyx, who nodded at her. The girl stood and followed the magician's assistant out of the room. When they stood on the other side of the curtain, Bianice grabbed Crisal's arm. "Girl, why do you wear the black and scarlet?"

"To be a magician." The girl tried to free her arm but couldn't. "It's not as if you are paying for this information."

"Fyx uses you for his own ends, child. Do you know what you are getting into?"

"How do you know so much about my master?"

Bianice snorted out a laugh. "Just as you are apprenticed to Fyx, many years ago Vassik was Fyx's master."

Crisal shrugged. "What has that to do with me, or with our mission in the Deeplands?"

Bianice shook her head. "Vassik had three apprentices then: Fyx, Dorstan, and Amanche. Of the three apprentices, Dorstan was the best and soon became the special pride of Vassik. But, Dorstan died and the blame fell on Amanche. He was exiled into the desert from the company of man. You see, Fyx, Amanche and Dorstan were brothers."

"I still don't see . . ."

"Oh, child! Amanche *is* Rogor! You, child, are a film of vapor waiting to be caught between a sledge and anvil."

As the sun broke over the horizon the next morning, its rays stole across the chilly desert, reflected from the river alongside the road to Porse and warmed the brush and trees beginning on the opposite side of the road. The low hills upon which they grew signaled the start of the incline that would become the Snake Mountains soon after Crisal and her master left Miira. Trudging behind Fyx, Crisal noticed neither the scenery nor the scent of the rain-washed air. She watched only the back of the old man and his stick, plodding toward Porse.

"Fyx." The magician continued as though he hadn't heard. Crisal moved up beside him. "Fyx, is Rogor your brother?"

Fyx looked at her, then returned his attention to the road. "It is none of your concern."

"Oh, none of my concern, is it? Then, why am I here?"

"It was your choice."

Crisal fell back and shifted her sack to her other shoulder. After a few more moments of walking, she reached within her robe and withdrew a clear glass marble. Holding it in her left hand in a manner to catch the sun's rays, she stared deep within the tiny sphere. Raw, random patterns in her mind associated, abstracted and drew conclusions, but with little information and Crisal's inexperience, the future was hidden. The past, however, was clear. Fyx had no desire for an apprentice; Fyx wanted Crisal's eyes—the eyes of a fortune teller. Again she moved beside the old man.

"Fyx."

The magician shook his head. "What is it now, pest?"

"What will happen when we reach Ikona?"

"I'm no fortune teller, Crisal. Haven't you consulted your ball?"

Crisal frowned. "Have you eyes in the back of your head, old man?"

Fyx cackled. "No, child, no. But, I can turn my head without moving my hood."

Crisal smiled, then shook her head. "I see nothing past our present footsteps, Fyx. My glass did tell me you wanted me for my eyes, and not as an apprentice. Explain."

Fyx frowned, darted a glance at the girl, then looked ahead. Then, looking down, he cackled. "Your eyes see guilt in me?"

"Aye. That, and fear and sadness."

The magician nodded. "Rogor, the one called black and dark, he is my brother, Amanche. I learned this years ago from the Great Tayla."

"She is my mother's mother, which you knew."

"Aye, that is true. You also know of my brother Dorstan's death?"

"Bianice mentioned it."

Fyx nodded. "Dorstan was better than any of us. The exercise with the feather, the first time, he lifted it from the table and held it for half a minute." Crisal saw Fyx's eyes moisten. "He was quick and all of us knew he would be a master before either I or Amanche perfected our simplest drills. Amanche was jealous with an envy and hatred that knew no bounds. Then one day, Dorstan was found dead."

"How?"

Fyx shrugged. "Amanche told Vassik that Dorstan had challenged him and that his magic was the more powerful of the two. He expected praise, but Vassik threw him before the town of Tieras for judgment. He was exiled to the desert. Tayla the fortune teller heard the story once and concluded that Dorstan had been poisoned."

"There was no magic, then?"

Fyx stopped and faced Crisal. "Child, there is no magic. This one who calls himself Rogor did not use magical powers against my brother Dorstan, because no such powers exist!"

Crisal's face wrinkled in confusion. "But Fyx, I myself have heard you call upon spirits in performance. . . ."

"The act, child. The act. Ever since chance brought our ancestors to Momus on the circus ship *Baraboo*, magicians have had but one trade: to entertain. We do the possible and make it appear to be the impossible. As part of the illusion that we do magic, we burn incense, call upon mythical beings and spirits, mutter nonsense incantations, roll our eyes, wave wands—all to create an aura of mystery. We take the doubt that rests in all of us, that things may not be as they appear, magnify it, and walk home with our purses full of movills."

"But, what about the feather? This is not magic?"

"No more than your fortune teller's eyes. When you see the future, do you use magic?"

"Of course not. Things in motion take certain paths. If you know the path up to the present, it takes no magic to see where a thing will go in the future."

The old man nodded. "But, child, this power of the fortune tellers seems to be magic to those who do not understand it."

Crisal nodded. "Only fortune tellers have this power. But what powers do magicians have?"

Fyx shook his head. "Many have the powers of magicians and fortune tellers, child, but only few train their powers. You are of the fortune tellers, yet you rocked the feather. I can see enough of the future to have sense enough to step out of the path of a falling rock. A trained magician can confuse the minds of others, or even put them to sleep as I did to you our first night on the road."

Crisal frowned. "I can get to sleep under my own power, Fyx. That does not explain the feather."

"With the magician's extra pair of hands, objects can be moved. The best card tricks are aided in that manner. Someday you will be able to put pictures in the minds of others or make time seem to pass very slowly for them. You will be practicing your trade, but others will think it magic."

Crisal nodded and they continued their walk down the road. "A few things are explained, then, Fyx. Are there other powers?"

"You shall learn of them in good time."

Crisal turned her head toward the old man. "The fear I read in your face; is it that Rogor plays upon your own doubts of dark powers?"

Fyx nodded. "I cannot reconcile what I know with what I feel. Rogor is never seen and no one knows the location of his lair. Yet, he destroys entire crops at will and is said to cause illness and death by wishing it. Are there dark powers that serve Rogor? I cannot prove that there aren't."

"But, the guilt, Fyx; why do I see guilt?"

"You are of the Tarzak fortune tellers, Crisal. That I should become an agent to you betraying your tradition . . ."

"That's not it! You think me stupid because I am young."

Fyx cackled and shook his head. "My apologies, little beast." He reached into his robe and dropped a movill into Crisal's hand.

"You think one is enough?"

"Look upon it as the balance of the respect you owe me."

Crisal dropped the copper into her purse and looked sideways at the old magician. "I haven't forgotten my question."

"I suspected as much."

"Well?"

Fyx's face became serious, and his pace slowed, then stopped. "Crisal, I do not know what I am going to meet in Ikona. I have my tricks and illusions, but they don't tell me how Rogor kills by wishing. I need a fortune teller's eyes to see the things I cannot. But . . ."

"But, you fear throwing a child into a battle between you and your brother." Fyx nodded. Crisal walked a few steps, and then turned back to face the old man. "I see something else, Fyx."

"And?"

"I see you arranging this with my mother, Salina. Yes, and Eeren, my loving father, providing the proper amount of disapproval to insure my choice—hah! My choice. Bianice spoke the truth. I am used."

Fyx shrugged. "Eeren and Salina are my friends, and they know of Rogor. You were selected from among all their apprentices as the best. . . ."

"You would try flattery?"

"It is only the truth, Crisal."

Crisal dropped the sack of cakes on the road and kicked it. "I am my own person, Fyx. I dance at the ends of no one's string. Find yourself another pair of eyes." She turned toward Tieras, stomped past the old magician, not looking back.

Around the first bend in the road, Crisal stopped, found a suitable rock, and sat down. Salina must think me still a child, she thought, and Fyx thinks me a fool. And my father! His mock outrage that a fortune teller would want to become a magician. Unheard of! Disgrace! Bah! Crisal stood and kicked the nearest rock, sending it skittering across the road.

She turned to the darkening skies. If the old trickster needed a fortune teller, why did he not hire a master? Why this game about me being a magician's apprentice?

She pulled the feather from her robe and fondled it. This is what I want more than anything else on Momus: to be a magician. I don't want to sit in dark little rooms peering into futures and planning lives. To stand before the crowd, amazing them with my tricks—that is what I want. But is this, too, all sham?

She dropped the feather on the sand, reached her imaginary hands under its edge and heaved with all her might. The feather rocked, rocked again, then turned over. She sat, looking at the feather for a moment, then picked it up and got to her feet. The road was deserted in all directions. She looked to the blackening sky. Did I do that, Fyx? Are you still playing with me? Only wind mixed with a sprinkle of rain answered her.

Crisal looked down the road toward Tieras, and from there, to Tarzak, where she still might be apprenticed to some lesser magician. Perhaps she could follow the fortune teller's trade. Turning to look at the bend in the road toward Porse, she knew that on the other side of the bend, the greatest magician on Momus waited for her to make up her mind. Rounding the bend, she saw Fyx standing where she left him, holding out the sack of provisions.

"We must hurry, Crisal. I fear we are in for a soaking."

Crisal walked up to the magician and took the sack without stopping. As she strode ahead she wondered if she would ever know what she would do before someone else did.

After reaching Porse that evening, they found all curtains closed to them. The uniform excuse was "Rogor would see." The two walked through the deserted-looking town until they came to the square. In the half-light of the stars peering through the parting clouds, they saw an upright figure in the center of the square, head and shoulders slumped over. As they came closer, they could see his feet did not touch the ground.

Fyx held Crisal back. "Stay here, child, while I investigate."

THE MAGICIAN'S APPRENTICE

"What is it?"

"It is not for your eyes, Crisal."

"I thought my fortune teller's eyes were the reason for my company. I cannot see if I do not have information."

Fyx nodded. "Then come, but be prepared. He has been impaled."

Only close to the corpse did the dim light reveal the red and purple stripes of a barker. Crisal froze as Fyx walked around to view the dead man's face.

"Is it the barker who came to your house?"

"Yes, it is Yudo."

Crisal walked slowly around the grisly scarecrow and looked up into a face blessed with death. She heard a noise behind her and started. The old magician was storming around the square swinging his stick around and over his head. "Up, slime!" he called, his voice strong and bitter. "Off of your sleeping cushions, cowards! I, Fyx of the Tarzak magicians, will reduce this town to rubble unless my questions are answered satisfactorily! Up, slime, up!" Crisal watched as the ancient magician went from door to door pounding on the walls, shouting his oaths. No one dared enter the square.

Fyx stood silent for a full minute, then reached within his robe. "Very well, cowards of Porse; let your town be no more!" The magician waved his hand at the nearest house, which immediately burst into flame. Screams from within curdled Crisal's blood. From the next house a man in clown's orange ran to Fyx and fell on his knees.

"Great Fyx, I beg you! Please spare us. We had no choice."

"This?" Fyx pointed at Yudo's motionless body. "You had no choice for this?"

"Great Fyx," the clown blubbered, "the Dark One was here!"

"Rogor? This is his doing?"

"Yes, Great Fyx. Look." The clown pointed to the wall at the far side of the square. In the flickering light of the burning building, Fyx could read:

WELCOME

R
O
R   O   G   O   R
O
R

Fyx walked to the wall, studied it, then returned to the center of the square, next to the corpse. "Clown, come here!"

The clown scurried to the magician's feet, hardly rising from his knees to get there. "Yes, Great Fyx?"

Fyx aimed his stick at the dead barker. "Who did this?"

"Great Fyx must understand, Rogor . . ."

"I must understand nothing!" Fyx delivered the clown a kick in the ribs sending him sprawling in the mud. "Who committed this outrage?"

"Rogor made us do it, Great Fyx. Those who didn't do the work were forced to watch."

" 'Forced?' Did he have an army at your yellow backs?"

"He . . . he has great powers. We were afraid. . . ."

"Afraid? And for this you denied the protection of your town to a traveler? Bah—not only that, you do another's murdering!"

"Great Fyx, the Dark One has fearful powers. . . ."

"Bah! By the grey beard of Momus, I'll show you fearful powers!" Fyx kicked the clown again, waved his hand at the corpse, and suddenly the square was filled with a blinding light. Crisal peeked through her fingers to see Yudo's body at the center of a roaring pyre of white and blue flames that reached up into the night sky. In seconds, the stake supporting the body burned through. "Clown, drive the curs that people this town into the square."

"Great Fyx, what if they will not come?"

Fyx raised his arms and screamed, "If they do not come, I will roast them in their homes!"

The clown scurried off, and one by one, the people of Porse edged into the square, shielding their eyes from the light of the pyre, and from the sight of Fyx. The magician walked around the pyre, looking at the townspeople. By the time the flames had been reduced to glowing embers, Yudo was but ashes, and the people were assembled. Fyx bent over and lifted a handful of embers and held them over his head.

"You will take these ashes and mix them with the mud from this square. Hear me, scum of Porse?"

The people bowed their heads. "Yes, Great Fyx."

"Take the mixture and paint your houses with it. From this day hence, that shall be the color of Porse. Live with your shame and be faithful to it, for if I should ever pass this way again and find as much as a white fence post, Porse shall cease to exist." Fyx searched the crowd until he saw the clown. "You!"

The clown ran from the crowd and kneeled at Fyx's feet. "Yes, Great Fyx."

"Show me the ones who drove the stake into the barker and planted him."

"But, we had no . . ."

"Show me, or in the blink of an eye you shall be nothing but ashes!"

The clown bowed, got to his feet and walked around the square. As he passed by, six men separated from the crowd and approached Fyx with cowed heads. His task completed, the clown stood with the others. "I am one of them."

"Then, stand for your shame!" Fyx marked the forehead of each with his thumb leaving an ugly blue **M**. "Now, into the desert with you, and never let the sight of good men fall upon you." The seven men looked around the square at their neighbors, bowed their heads and walked from the square. As they reached the edge, the crowd parted, not daring even to look. Fyx tossed his handful of embers, now dead, on the remains of Yudo's pyre.

Crisal watched the old magician turn in her direction and walk toward her, his eyes burning with an emotion she could not read. Standing before her, he lifted the hand that had held the embers. It was dirty, but unburned. He placed it on her shoulder. "Come, child. This is no town for anyone to rest in, for they will have none of it from now until their shame is washed away."

Fyx took the street leading to the high road to Miira, the crowd parted, and Crisal followed, trying to decide in her own mind whether what she felt for Fyx was fear or love.

Through the night, Fyx marched toward Miira town as if possessed. Crisal stumbled along behind, marveling at the old man's strength. Twice, rain and wind whipped them, causing the already muddy roads to grow slick as grease with dark, forbidding pools. Unmindful of the mud or the pools, Fyx strode through both as though he were on a hard, dusty street in Tarzak. As the second rain stopped, a dim grey dawn fought against the black clouds. Fyx stopped and turned to the light. "It is dawn."

"You don't miss a thing, Fyx." Crisal dragged herself next to the old man. He turned and looked at the girl, soaked and mud-caked as himself.

"You must be tired, child."

"Ah, Fyx, there is fortune teller's blood in your veins."

The magician raised an eyebrow. "I see you've spent the night honing your tongue. Do you wish to rest or not?"

"Of course." Crisal cocked her head at the drenched landscape.

"But where?"

Fyx reached into his robe and handed Crisal a black wad of raw cobit dough. The lump was crusted hard and weighed heavily in the child's hand. "Pick a spot with neither trees, weeds, nor grass."

Crisal looked around, walked ahead to a sandy place on the east side of the road. "Here?"

Fyx nodded. "Listen carefully. When I tell you, crush the dough ball hard and throw it in the center of the clear spot." Crisal looked at the innocent lump in her hand. "You must be very quick; understand?"

"Yes."

"Then, now!"

Crisal crushed the ball and felt it warm her hand even before she threw it. Before it landed on the sand, it exploded into a blinding column of flame. Crisal turned to Fyx. "Yudo's pyre."

"Yes. With your right hand, feel inside the right sleeve of your robe. Do you feel a pocket?"

Crisal felt about and found an opening. "Yes."

The magician handed her five more of the black dough balls. "Put these in that pocket. You know how they can be used." Fyx nodded at the fire, almost gone out for lack of fuel. "It burns hot, but very fast. The sand will be dry, but only warm."

Crisal put the balls into her sleeve pocket. "Is this to be my first trick, Fyx?"

The magician laughed. "No, child. Your first trick will be learning how to sleep without rolling over on your sleeve!"

Crisal dragged herself onto the warm sand, stretched out, and fell asleep, her right arm straight out from her body.

If Crisal dreamed at all, it was of sleep. The clearing skies and rising sun warmed and dried her robe, and she wriggled happily as she fought back the wakefulness that gnawed at the edges of her sleep. She snuggled her face, cupped by her right hand, against the sand, then remembered the dough balls. Sitting bolt upright, she saw that the loose sleeve of her robe had not been under her.

"Ah, child, you are awake."

Crisal turned to see a woman in singer's white and green sitting next to a tall blond man wearing the black and scarlet. The man nodded at Crisal. "Dorna invited me to warm my backside on your sand, little magician."

Crisal nodded back. The man was young and very strong-looking; the woman, as young, had black flowing hair and dark brown eyes.

Crisal cursed her own freckles and muddy appearance next to the beautiful singer. "Have you seen my master?"

The young magician shrugged. The singer shook her head. "I suppose you should wait here for him." Dorna looked down at the magician's hand around her waist, then nodded her head toward Crisal. Shrugging, he removed his hand, and lay back on the sand, propping himself up with his elbows.

Crisal studied the young magician. "You are not from this planet, are you, magician?"

The man laughed. "No, child. My name is Ashly Allenby. I come from the parent planet."

"Yet, you wear the black and scarlet."

"Even I must eat. What are you called?"

"I am Crisal. I am apprenticed to a great magician."

"His name?" Allenby sat up.

Crisal looked at Dorna and read her eyes. "His name is of no consequence, Allenby." The girl waved her hand around indicating the sand she had dried.

Allenby raised his eyebrows and nodded. "The few movills I have already weep from loneliness. Would you observe a new trick of mine in exchange?"

Crisal shrugged. "If I can determine how you do it, I will still want payment."

Allenby chuckled and withdrew a deck of cards from his robe. As he handed the deck to Crisal, he smoothed the sand before him with his hand. "Pick seven cards you can remember."

"I can remember any seven—or the entire deck, for that matter." Crisal thumbed off the first seven cards and handed them to Allenby.

"No, don't give them to me. Put them in a row, faces up, on the sand." Crisal put out the cards. "Do you have them memorized?"

"Of course."

Allenby spread his fingers above the cards and turned all seven over without touching them. "You're sure you have them memorized?"

"Yes."

"Then, turn over the three of clubs."

Crisal sighted the third card from her left, imagined the tiny hands of her mind under the edge of the card, and heaved. The card turned over, exposing the eight of diamonds. Allenby laughed at the expression on her face. "But the eight is here." She pointed at the card on her far right.

"You are sure?"

Crisal reached for the card and turned it over with her fingers; the six of spades. Dorna the singer nodded in admiration. "An excellent trick, Allenby." The young magician smiled his thanks and gathered up his cards. Crisal frowned.

"Can you tell me how I did that, Crisal?" Allenby tucked his cards away and stood.

Crisal broke her frown long enough to deliver a curt nod. "It is a good enough trick."

Allenby threw the hem of his robe over his shoulder and pointed south with mock drama. "Begads, with such lavish praise at my back, I must hasten to Tarzak and bedazzle the crowds."

Dorna stood. "Must you go, Ashly?"

Allenby bowed and took Dorna's hand, brushing it with his lips. "Aye, beautiful Dorna. I must make Tarzak. A cargo shuttle is said to be there. It is the first since I came to Momus, and I must catch it to send my news back to the Quadrant Secretary of State." He bowed toward Crisal, then hefted his sack and stepped onto the road heading south. Dorna and Crisal both watched until long after he was out of sight.

The girl turned toward the singer. "Dorna?"

"Yes, child?"

"I read something in your eyes, but I cannot fathom what I saw in them. Where is my master?"

The beautiful Dorna smiled, covered her face with her robe, then lowered it. Fyx's toothless smile grinned at the girl.

"Fyx, by Momus' boiled behind—it is you?"

The old man cackled. "Turn your back, child."

"What will you do then; turn yourself into a lizard, or me into a boy?"

"Turn around. I must reverse my robe."

Crisal turned. "All this playacting, Fyx; what did it accomplish?"

"A young magician would guard his tongue more closely with the Great Fyx than with lovely Dorna. You may turn around now."

Crisal turned and saw Fyx before her in his black and scarlet. "Was that not magic, too, Fyx? Where did your wrinkles go?"

"Make a frown, Crisal, and feel your forehead."

Crisal did as she was told. "So?"

"You are young, yet you can make wrinkles; I am old, and can make my skin smooth, although it takes much effort."

"Very well, Fyx, but explain the beautiful Dorna's teeth. You haven't one in your entire head."

"Neither did Dorna."

Crisal folded her arms. "She did too!"

"Think, Crisal. Those wide sensuous lips smiled, but never parted unless a hand or sleeve was before them."

The girl frowned. "I remember . . . no, I feel I remember. You are right; I saw no teeth." Crisal shook her head. "What had the magician to say that was of value?"

"Here, eat." Fyx reached into their sack and produced two soggy cobit cakes. "Allenby comes from as far north as Dirak on the other side of the Snake Mountains. He also passed through Miira on his way to Tarzak. Both towns are black with despair. Rogor is leaving his mark."

Crisal swallowed a piece of cobit, then dropped the remainder into the sack. "Fyx, can we go around Miira?"

"You are thinking of last night in Porse."

Crisal nodded. "These people do not know what faces them; we do not know. I want no more horrors."

Fyx finished his cake and studied the girl. "You think my actions harsh?"

Crisal shrugged. "I understand why they acted as they did."

Fyx nodded. "Imagine this, Crisal: You have a knife in your hand held at Salina, your mother's, throat; I am holding you with a knife at your throat. I tell you that if you do not kill Salina, I will kill you. What would you do?"

Crisal bowed her head, walked to the edge of the dry sand, then walked back. "I would like to think I would die. Is that what you want to hear?"

"That was Porse's choice, Crisal, and they failed."

The girl looked into the old man's eyes. "Will we pass through Miira?"

Fyx nodded. "We must. That is where we pick up our provisions and transportation across the mountains." The old man picked up the sack and handed it to the girl. "We must be off if we are to get there before nightfall."

As they climbed the steepening foothills into Miira, the setting sun picked out with red, orange, and yellow the untended fields, half-cut and-dressed timber logs and deserted streets. The houses, now made of wood, stood empty. Fyx pounded on several doors, but all those he knew in the town were gone. Walking further into the town, they entered the square. Crisal gripped Fyx's arm and pointed at the center of the square.

"Look, Fyx, another murder!"

The old magician followed the direction of Crisal's finger and studied what he saw. In the back of a two-wheeled pull cart, a huge man garbed in the freak's green and yellow was sprawled on a few sacks, his massive arms and legs hanging over the sides and end of the cart. "Come, Crisal. He only sleeps."

As they approached the cart, the huge man opened one eye, then nodded. "You are the Great Fyx."

Fyx nodded. "And you?"

Quick and graceful for his size, the man sat up, then leaped from the cart to the ground. He bowed, aiming his bald pate in Fyx's direction. "Great Fyx, I am Zuma, strongman of the Dirak freaks."

"Dirak?"

"From the other side of the Snake Mountains, Great Fyx."

The old magician nodded, then passed his hand around the square. "Where are they?"

Zuma chuckled, making a rumble that seemed, to Crisal, to vibrate the ground. "The news of your judgment in Porse arrived hours ago. The good citizens of Miira have taken to the hills."

"And you?"

"Me?"

"How do we find you snoozing in the square amidst this rush to return to nature?"

"Hah!" Zuma laughed and slapped Crisal's shoulder, sending her sprawling. "I am Zuma. No more needs to be said."

Crisal picked herself up and scowled at the strongman. "He is here for a reason, Fyx."

Zuma nodded. "That scrap of an apprentice speaks the truth. The town of Dirak sent me to bring you across the mountains."

Fyx rubbed his chin. "Dirak knew, then, that Miira would take this vacation?"

Zuma spat on the ground. "Rogor's arm is felt even on this side of the mountains. Dirak takes no chance that you might be late for lack of transportation."

"You do not fear the Dark One, then?"

"Fear him? Hah!" Zuma flexed his mighty arms, stooped and wrapped them around the wooden cart. Standing, he lifted the cart over his head. "Zuma fears no one." The strongman lowered the cart to the ground as gently as a feather. Turning, he frowned at Fyx. "If I could find the sorcerer, there would be little need for you, magician. But . . ." The huge man shrugged.

Crisal's eyes narrowed as she tried to read the strongman's eyes. "Zuma, my master is hired by the town of Ikona to rid them of Rogor. You are from Dirak."

Zuma nodded. "All four towns in the Emerald Valley, Dirak, Ikona, Ris, and even the fishing village of Anoki, have contributed. Ikona has gotten the worst of it, and they made the contract." Fyx looked at the girl, his eyebrows raised. Crisal only shrugged. "Shall we go then?" He tossed Zuma a purse.

Fyx and Crisal climbed into the cart and settled themselves among the boxes and sacks. Zuma stooped under the pull handle at the front of the cart, stood, and gripped it with his powerful hands. As they clattered through Miira, Crisal studied the back of Zuma's head. Turning to the old magician, she tugged his sleeve. "Fyx . . ."

Fyx touched a finger against her lips and shook his head. "Try and sleep."

"Sleep?" Crisal threw up her hands at the absurdity.

Fyx looked into her eyes. "Sleep." Crisal fought against it, but her mind clouded, then grew dark.

Crisal looked down from a great height and saw a wooden hand-cart being pulled by a powerful man. In the back of the cart were two figures dressed in black and scarlet. The cart left houses behind and made its way up a gentle incline. At times, a turn in the road or an overhanging tree would obscure the travelers, but as the cart pulled onto a high mesa and worked its way around the shore of a small lake, she felt herself drawn to the vehicle. She swooped down, coming up behind and just above the cart. In the cart she saw herself, asleep, her head cradled on Fyx's lap.

Fyx! She called out, but had no voice. *Fyx, what is this?*

See ahead, child, the man pulling the cart?

Fyx, I am frightened.

Do you see him?

Yes, yes, but Fyx . . . Crisal saw the cart turn from the lakeshore to follow a steep road into the mountains.

Crisal, you will enter Zuma's mind and tell me what you see.

Crisal looked at her own sleeping face, then up into Fyx's. *I can't, Fyx. What if he is Rogor?*

You suspected something, then?

I could not read his eyes.

Perhaps what you read was out of your experience. Have you ever read murder?

No.

Then, you would not recognize it.

Fyx, if it is Rogor, will he know I am there?

Crisal saw the old magician look down and stroke the face of the sleeping child, pushing a tangled lock of red hair away from her eyes. *If it is Rogor, he will know, but I will protect you. Do you believe this?*

Yes, Fyx. What must I do?

Look at Zuma's head. Do you see the aura?

Crisal turned and saw a pale glow rippling above the strongman's skin all over his body. *Yes, I see it.*

When I tell you, go to it and blend with it. But, remember, child, whatever happens to you, do not try to speak to me. Do not cry out, and neither fight what you find there nor try to change it. Do you understand?

Yes, Fyx.

Then, go.

Crisal saw the road's incline steepen, and as she touched, then wrapped herself around Zuma's aura, the cart turned, exposing a cliff falling away to the left. The aura was foreign, but she felt herself change a particle at a time until a harmony between herself and the aura was achieved.

Zuma looked over the edge of the cliff and chuckled. No one would ever find the old man and the child down there, he thought. Rogor will line my purse with coppers instead of plague for my crops. The strongman shook off a twinge of guilt. No one can fight Rogor's magic. I must do as I am told.

Seeing the sharp turn in the road ahead with a flat place carved into the wall opposite the cliff, Zuma turned back toward the old magician. "We will stop here and rest." He pulled the cart onto the flat and lowered the handle. Stepping out from under the handle, Zuma began picking up dead twigs and sticks along the road. "I will have hot food for us in a moment."

Fyx nodded and shook the sleeping child's shoulder. Crisal started awake, her eyes wild with fear. Fyx touched her lips and stroked her face. "Come, child. While Zuma prepares our food, there is something I would show you. This part of the Snake Mountain cliff is the highest. It is very beautiful, even in starlight."

Trembling, Crisal stepped down from the cart, followed by Fyx. The old magician took her hand and walked to the very edge of the cliff. "Fyx . . ."

"Hush, child. Just look down and listen."

Crisal looked down, but could not see the bottom of the cliff in the dark. Wind whistled and echoed from the walls, and very far away, she could hear water flowing. Fyx stooped over, picked up a rock and moved so close to the cliff's edge that their toes hung over. Holding Crisal tightly about her shoulders with his right arm, he tossed the rock into the chasm with his left. Crisal listened, but heard nothing but the wind and the water far away. "Fyx, should we stand so close . . ."

"Observe nature's beauty, child, and listen."

Crisal listened and heard the crackle of the fire Zuma had started. She also heard soft footsteps padding up behind them. She tried to pull back from the edge of the cliff, but the old man's grip held her tight. The footsteps came closer, then began running. Crisal turned her head, and three full strides to her right, Zuma ran to the edge of the cliff, arms outstretched, and sailed over, plummeting into the darkness below, followed by a trail of screamed question marks.

Crisal looked up at Fyx. "Why . . . ?"

"That's where he saw us, child. Poor fellow must have an eye problem." Fyx cackled and turned back to the fire. "Come, Crisal. Zuma was kind enough to build a fire."

Crisal looked into the darkness hiding the remains of the strongman, then turned to watch the old magician, a smile on his face, setting up rocks around the fire upon which he would cook their cakes. As she walked slowly to the fire, she thought again about Bianice's comment about a vapor being caught between a sledge and an anvil.

The next morning, having determined that neither Fyx's magic nor their combined strength could move the heavy cart, while Fyx prepared their morning meal, Crisal searched among the sacks and boxes hoping to find enough provisions to support them to Dirak. "There is more than enough, Fyx, if we can carry it all; even blankets for the mountain nights." Crisal continued moving the contents of the cart around, examining the contents of each sack and box.

"Child, if you've found enough food, leave the cart alone so we can eat and be off." Fyx saw that he was being ignored, shrugged, and sat by the dying fire. As he bit into a cobit cake spread with sapjam, Crisal stood in the cart holding a small package in her hands. She climbed down from the cart and walked to the fire.

"See this, Fyx?" She held the package out.

The magician put down his cake, took the package and turned it over. It was white with rounded corners, in two halves held together with a clear, seamless cover. It had no markings. "Do your fortune teller's eyes tell you what it is?"

Crisal shook her head. "I saw in Zuma's thoughts he was bringing something for Rogor. Dare we open it?"

Fyx held the package to his ear, shook it, and shrugged. With his fingernail, he pried up an end of the clear cover, stuck his finger beneath it and made it stretch until the opening was large enough to remove the cover. With the cover removed, Fyx placed the package on his lap and lifted off the top half. Firmly held in place by the moulded bottom half was a mechanism, blue-black with a handle extending from a curved plate. At the top of the plate were numerous black, red, and orange cubes from which hair-thin wires came. Toward the front of the plate, the wires gathered into a cable and terminated at a threaded cylinder that hung loose at the end of the cable. The front of the handle was shaped into five rings, the one closest to the plate larger than the others and containing a metal lever that extended back into the handle. The back edge of the handle had two rings together of the same size. Fyx looked up at Crisal.

"Well?"

"What is it, Fyx?"

The magician lifted the object from the moulded half and turned it over in his hands. Holding the curved plate upright, he clasped his hand around the handle, putting his thumb through the top rear hole and his fingers through the top front four. He cocked his head at Crisal. "Stand out of the way."

Crisal moved aside while Fyx aimed the object at the chasm wall opposite their perch. He pulled the metal lever back with his forefinger; nothing happened. Fyx lowered the thing to his lap and shrugged. "I thought it might be a gun of some design, but it does nothing."

Crisal pointed. "Look, Fyx." The girl's finger tapped the extra ring beneath Fyx's little finger, and again the extra ring beneath his thumb. "If it's a handle, it wasn't meant for hands like ours."

The magician nodded, then handed the object to Crisal. "What do your fortune teller's eyes make of our future now?"

Crisal took the object and sat on the sand next to the fire. She looked at the handle, turned it over, and shook her head. "Fyx, I haven't assembled enough information to make any sense of the present, much less talk about the future." She took the mouldings and cover and reassembled the package, placing it in her sack.

"It doesn't do anything, child; why drag the extra weight?"

Crisal stuffed some cake in her mouth and talked around it. "Allenby, that young magician from Earth, he said he was trying to meet a cargo shuttle. I think Zuma picked this package up there for Rogor. It is something Rogor wants, and now we've got it."

"But, we don't know what it does, nor where it comes from."

Crisal squinted her eyes, looked at her lap, then at Fyx. "Allenby said he had news to send to Earth—no, to the Quadrant Secretary of State. What news?"

Fyx shrugged and reached for another cake. "Some prattle about sending a diplomatic mission to Momus. Also, that his news had attracted the newstellers and that the law they require should be made by the time whoever it is shows up."

Crisal took the remainder of her cobit cake and threw it at the old magician's head. "Old fake!"

Fyx stood, his eyes narrowing in anger. "Brat. Have you lost your mind? I could turn you into ashes in the blink of an eye."

The girl stuck out her tongue and made a rude noise. "I see where you cannot, Fyx. Now, tell me the whole truth. I cannot see the things I have to see without it."

The old magician pursed his lips, nodded and resumed his seat by the fire. "Allenby is an official of the Ninth Quadrant. He has come to Momus to arrange for military protection for our planet."

"Protection? From whom?"

Fyx shrugged. "The Ninth Quadrant suspects an invasion of Momus by the Tenth Quadrant Federation."

Crisal nodded. "And this law; what is that?"

"Momus must ask for the protection, otherwise it would violate laws that govern all the quadrants."

Crisal felt the outline of the package in her sack, then picked up another cobit cake, eating it slowly. "Fyx, what do you know of the Tenth Quadrant worlds?"

"As much as I know about the worlds of the Ninth, child; next to nothing." Fyx stood and hefted his sack. "Can you continue your cogitations while we walk? The morning is aging rapidly."

Crisal nodded, picked up her sack and walked to the cart. "Will your magic keep you warm, or do you want a blanket?"

Fyx snorted, turned his back and began climbing the steep road. Crisal picked up two blankets, tucked them under her arm, threw her sack over her shoulder, and followed.

Three mornings later, Fyx and Crisal stood on the north foothills of the Snake Mountains looking out over the Emerald Valley. Toward the sun, green fields dotted with brown extended to the horizon, leaving space for only a lake, and above the lake, a small village. Fyx pointed his stick at the village. "That is Ikona."

"The two towns before us?"

"The first is Dirak, and the second at the base of the mountain is called Ris."

Crisal looked to her left to see more green fields, dotted with brown, extending until they met a wide expanse of water. She pointed to a small settlement at the edge of the water. "Anoki?"

Fyx nodded. "The brown you see in the fields must be the dying crops."

Crisal studied them, but there seemed to be no pattern, save that the fields closest to the mountain on the other side of the valley had no brown. "What is the mountain opposite us called?"

"Split Mountain. You will see why when we get to Ikona. A great movement in the crust of Momus caused a crooked rent in the mountain that extends deep into its center."

Crisal pointed at the town straddling the road before them. "Dirak, at least, has a welcome planned for us."

Fyx rubbed his chin. "Keep alert; Rogor can plan welcomes, too." He nodded his head toward the three men who stood at the entrance to the town gate.

The old magician hefted his sack and stepped off, working his way down the road to Dirak. Crisal followed a few paces behind, studying the men at the gate. All three wore the black and tan short robes of roustabouts and stood motionless, waiting. When she could see their eyes, Crisal moved up beside Fyx. "I read mayhem in their eyes, Fyx."

The magician nodded. As they approached the three, Crisal saw Fyx's left hand disappear into its sleeve and return again as a fist. The old man put a smile on his face and nodded at the three toughs. "A pleasant morning, friends."

The roustabout in the middle glanced at his companions, then walked toward the two travelers. "You are the Great Fyx?" The man offered nothing for the information.

"Yes. And your name, friend?"

The man looked up the road into the Snake Mountains, then back at the magician. "I am Jagar. Where is Zuma?"

Fyx shrugged. "The strongman took leave of his senses and leaped from a cliff to his death. We could not stop him."

Jagar studied Fyx, then looked at Crisal. "Is this true?"

Crisal looked at Jagar and turned up her nose. "You doubt the word of my master?"

Striking swiftly, Jagar grabbed the front of Fyx's robe. "The cart, old man; what have you . . ." Fyx passed his left hand before Jagar's face, and the roustabout dropped to the ground, twitching.

Fyx arranged his robe and stepped over the body toward the two remaining roustabouts. "Rude fellow." Seeing their companion twitching in the dust, the two turned and fled through the town gate and disappeared down an alley. The magician turned around and knelt next to Jagar. "Crisal, come here." The girl stood across the body and looked into Jagar's face. The man's eyes rolled with terror and spittle dribbled from the corners of his mouth. "I will ask him some questions, child. Tell me what you see."

"Yes, Fyx."

The magician reached into his robe and withdrew a tiny vial filled with a colorless fluid. Opening it, he forced Jagar's teeth open and let three drops of the fluid fall into the man's mouth. In a few seconds, Jagar lay quiet. "Jagar. You hear me?" Fyx waited a moment, then slapped the man's face hard enough to make Crisal wince. "Jagar!"

"Spare me, Great Fyx." The man barely spoke above a whisper.

"Spare you? Jagar, I will ask you questions and you will answer me truthfully. Then, perhaps we may talk of sparing your miserable life."

"I can't . . . talk to you of Rogor, Great Fyx. This is what you would ask?"

"It is. What will Rogor do if you talk?"

"Oh, Great Fyx, he will kill me!"

Fyx cackled. "Hear me, Jagar: you will tell me all I wish to know, or else I shall visit such horrors upon you that you will beg me for that same death."

"Ask, then, Great Fyx."

"The gadget in the cart Zuma was to bring, what is it?"

"I do not know." Fyx looked at Crisal and the girl nodded back.

"Was it for Rogor?"

"Yes. We were told to wait here for it."

"What were you to do with it?"

"It was to be taken to the fountain in Ikona."

"And?"

"That's all, Great Fyx. I swear it."

Crisal knelt next to Jagar. "He does not lie. Ask him if he's ever seen Rogor."

Fyx poked Jagar in the arm. "Well?"

"No. No one has ever seen the Dark One."

Crisal turned Jagar's face toward her with her hand and looked deep into his eyes. "Jagar, where are the people of Dirak?"

"Child, they are in Ris. All of the towns of the Emerald Valley are in Ris."

"Why?"

"The people assemble to form an army and declare Rogor King of Momus."

Fyx looked into the child's face. "Do you see something?"

Crisal nodded. "Yes. I feel I have the parts to an answer. I must still fit them together. We must leave the road and find a quiet place."

As Fyx led the way through the fields toward Ikona, Crisal stopped to examine both green and brown stalks of grain, healthy and rotting melon patches. Reaching some trees near the lake below Ikona, Crisal withdrew her clear glass marble and fell to her knees. Hearing her, Fyx turned and sat next to her. She held the ball in the sun, catching its rays, and used it to focus her mind. Pieces of the puzzle fit together, but something still lay out of her grasp. She dropped the marble to her lap and shook her head. "It is not enough."

"Can you at least see a question?"

Crisal smoothed the sand in front of her knees and drew Rogor's cross with her finger.

```
            R
            O
R   O   G   O   R
            O
            R
```

"Fyx, I must know the meaning of this."

The old magician shook his head. "It is as I told you, Crisal. It means nothing."

"Tell me what you can, Fyx. It is the part I need."

Fyx rubbed his chin. "It could be the hidden cross of a magic square."

"Magic square?"

Fyx shook his head. "There is no magic to them. They were believed to cure illnesses and drive away evil spirits long ago. Some magicians take names that can form such a cross."

"Show me a magic square."

Fyx smoothed the sand next to Rogor's cross. "This is a very old one. It is formed by two words, sator and opera. The words must fit frontwards, backwards and up and down. Like this." The old magician quickly drew the words and word arrangements with his finger.

```
S   A   T   O   R
A   R   E   P   O
T   E       E   T
O   P   E   R   A
R   O   T   A   S
```

"Now, all we do is add an 'N' in the middle, and the word 'tenet' becomes the hidden cross in this magic square." Fyx added the 'N' and smoothed out the rest of the letters.

```
            T
            E
T   E   N   E   T
            E
            T
```

"No magic in it; just a word game."

Crisal studied the word, drew in again the letters Fyx had erased, studied it some more, then erased the entire square. Erasing Rogor's cross, Crisal looked again at her marble.

Fyx raised his eyebrows as Crisal began making marks in the smooth sand. "Let us use the name of Dirak town the same as 'sator' in the tenet square."

```
D   I   R   A   K
I               A
R               R
A               I
K   A   R   I   D
```

"See?"

Fyx shrugged. "What of the rest?"

Crisal's finger flew at the sand. "The towns of Ikona and Anoki we use the same as 'arepo' and 'opera' in the tenet square . . . add a 'G' and there you are."

```
D   I   R   A   K
I   K   O   N   A
R   O   G   O   R
A   N   O   K   I
K   A   R   I   D
```

Fyx nodded. "And there is Rogor's hidden cross. But, what use is this to us?"

"Fyx, if this were a map and Dirak sat on the bottom 'D' of the square," Crisal poked it with her finger, "and if Ikona were here," she stabbed the 'I' above the bottom 'D', "and if the fishing village of Anoki were here," she poked the 'A' in the bottom rank of letters, "where would the extra letter fall?"

Fyx stood and looked at the square, then squatted next to it and drew in a few landmarks. "The 'G' falls at the end of the cleft in the center of Split Mountain." Fyx stood and pointed across Ikona toward the peak. "Now you can see where the cleft begins."

Crisal stood and observed the crooked pass that led deep into the mountain, its walls hanging with bushy vines. The mountain itself was hidden beneath a heavy growth of trees except for its highest point, which grew only scrub trees and brush. "This is your invitation from Rogor." Crisal pointed at the 'G' in Rogor's cross. "We will find his lair at the end of the cleft. It is a trap."

Fyx nodded. "Rogor has gone to great pains to kill me, and yet he points the way for me to destroy him."

"There is more, Fyx. This thing in my sack that I got from Zuma's cart; it is a weapon, or a part of a weapon. It is what killed the farmers' crops. Look." Crisal pulled some half-brown, half-green stalks from her robe. "The part below is healthy, but look at the brown part. It looks as though it had been dipped in boiling water. Can your powders and other tricks protect you against such a thing?

"Fyx, what would happen if Rogor became king of Momus and then asked the Tenth Quadrant Federation for military protection against the Ninth Quadrant?"

Fyx shrugged, then looked down at the square. "As I understand it, the Ninth would have no choice but to let Momus be occupied, such as their laws are." He cackled. "But, child, Momus with a king? Perhaps Rogor can bully this small valley, but how could he become king of Momus? The ruler of Emerald Valley can't speak for the planet."

"Fyx, you saw the fear on the other side of the Snake Mountains, in Miira and Porse."

"And, child, I set them straight in Porse. Have no doubt about it. We can do the same everywhere south of the Snake Mountains. Neither of us will ever see a king in Tarzak."

"But, when you are dead, Fyx, what will there be to stop King Rogor, his terrible weapons and his army of terror-driven thugs?"

"Dead?" The old magician pounded his chest. "I am far from dead, child."

"That is an obstacle Rogor and the Tenth Quadrant would like to remove; that's why Rogor offered the twenty thousand movills."

"Rogor? My contract is with him?" Fyx shook his head and frowned. "My brother was not a clever person, Crisal. Where does this devilish thinking come from? What has he discovered?"

Crisal spread out their blankets and stretched out on one of them. "His thinking comes from the same place that gives him his weapons, Fyx—another world." She patted the blanket next to hers. "Rest. We will need our wits about us tonight."

"We?" Fyx lowered himself to his blanket and put his stick aside. "Child, I promised Salina to turn you back once you had seen the answers to my questions. There is nothing left now but to pit my tricks against Rogor's."

"I told you, Rogor has powerful weapons; not tricks."

"Promise me you will not enter the mountain's cleft."

"But, you will . . ."

"It is my promise to Salina, child! Give me your promise."

"Very well." Crisal rolled over and turned her back to the magician. "I promise to stay clear of the mountain's cleft."

Crisal awakened to a black, starless night. Rolling over, she felt for the magician, but found only his long cold blanket. Even straining her eyes, she could see little more than a dim outline of Split Mountain against the night sky. Fyx was somewhere within that great shadow preparing to do battle—or dead.

Crisal stood and mulled over the stupid promise Fyx had made her give. "What chance have you, old man, against weapons that can roast entire fields?" She stepped off to begin pacing, but stumbled over her sack. Regaining her balance, she pulled back a foot intending to deliver the sack a swift one. Hesitating, she squatted down, opened the sack and took out the white package. The roustabout at the gate to Dirak said he was to deliver it to the fountain in Ikona.

"Yes!" Crisal remembered Yudo, the barker, saying that his letter for Fyx had appeared at the fountain in Ikona. The girl held the package under her arm and stood, her back to the lake, facing the tiny farming village. From there she looked to the peak of Split Mountain. Reaching into her robe, she wrapped her hand around her glass marble. "The brown spots—there are none at the base of the mountain. Up there, on the peak, must be the weapon." Her feet carried her toward the town with its fountain. "And if Rogor's friends have machines that can kill entire fields, moving a letter, a package," she smiled, "or a small child should be no great task."

Crisal stood before the unremarkable fountain in Ikona's tiny square. The streets and houses were deserted, and she examined the structure, unafraid of discovery. The fountain itself was a simple column of mortar and stone with a weak spout of water rising from its center. The water dribbled down into a trough that surrounded the column, then drained off into a hole in the flatstone and mortar walkway that covered the center of the square. Looking behind her, Crisal could see that hers were the only footprints in the square, at least since the last rain. The path she had taken from the lake to the village was well traveled.

"Why do they go to the lake for water, unless there is danger here in the square?" Crisal looked over the top of the fountain to see the peak of Split Mountain. Without stepping on the flatstones, she walked part way around the fountain, examining the walkway. Because of the dark, she could tell no difference, but on the side facing the mountain she could make out a flatstone larger than the others. It seemed to shine, as if it had been scrubbed with sand many times. Picking up a handful of dust from the square, she threw it up, making a cloud between the stone and the mountain. Caught in the air, the cloud passed, and settled to the ground undisturbed.

Crisal looked around the square until she found a rock the size of her fist. Taking it, she walked to the fountain and stepped gingerly on the flatstone walkway. When nothing happened, she let out her breath and slowly approached the large flatstone facing Split Mountain. Squatting next to it, she rolled the fist-sized stone into the center of its shiny surface. The stone sat motionless for a moment, then disappeared, leaving a sharp smell in the air.

Clenching her teeth, Crisal gripped the white package in both hands and jumped into the center of the stone. As she looked at the peak of Split Mountain, she felt tears running down her cheeks. She closed her eyes. "I am *not* afraid!"

"I'm pleased to hear that." Opening her eyes she saw standing before her a grinning figure in black and scarlet. He was old, stooped, and had a blue **M** marked on his wrinkled forehead.

"Rogor!" Crisal dropped the package and reached into her sleeve for Fyx's fireballs. Her movements slowed to less than a crawl as the magician walked up to her and calmly removed the balls from her sleeve.

"You startled me, child. I thought Fyx had shrunk." Rogor took the fireballs and tucked them away in his own sleeve pocket. "Nasty little things."

The magician lifted Crisal and moved her from the platform where she had been standing. Carefully, Rogor examined every pocket in the girl's robe, then tied her hands at her back with a wire pulled from his waist. Having bound her securely, he pushed her to the ground and snapped his fingers. Crisal felt her muscles regain their normal speed, then she sobbed as Rogor went to the platform and picked up the package. He opened it and grinned as he pulled out the blue-black handle. "Ah, child, I should pay you. I have waited a long time for this."

Rogor walked across the platform and stepped down to the smooth hard surface beneath. Crisal noticed for the first time that the entire surface around her was smooth and hard, save for holes from which small trees grew. The magician stopped at a long, slender cylinder mounted on a metal-wheeled cart. He took a small threaded cylinder dangling from an opening on the bottom of the object and connected it to the handle. This completed, Rogor pushed the handle up into the larger cylinder and snapped it into place. "You have brought me the kingdom of Momus." He turned his head in Crisal's direction. "Know what this is?"

"No." She tried to move, but she felt the wire cut her wrists.

Rogor laughed. "Watch!" The magician worked controls at the base of the machine that Crisal couldn't see. The light from the controls cast a greenish glow on Rogor's face. He stepped back from the machine. With a low hum, the wheels turned slightly and the long cylinder tipped down. The hum grew louder for a moment, then ceased.

"That is how you kill the crops, Rogor."

He nodded. "Another unbeliever's crops have died. But, with this new trigger," he walked to the machine and aimed it into the air, "I have the very strength of Momus in my hands." A blinding white beam split the air and parted the clouds above them. Rogor stopped the beam and pushed the machine to the opposite side of the smooth area. "I can even melt mountains if I choose." Crisal pushed herself to her knees and got to her feet. Looking in the direction where Rogor aimed, she saw the great cleft in the mountain.

"No!"

Rogor looked at her. "Eh? Are you so fond of my mountain you could not bear to see me put a hole in it?" He cackled. "Or is there a little old man down in the cleft who might get hurt?" Rogor walked over to Crisal, held her chin with an iron grip and forced her to look

into his face. "Is Fyx down there?"

Crisal tried to spit at Rogor, but her mouth was too dry. Laughing, the magician pushed her to the ground again. "No, child, this cannon would do the trick, but then Fyx would never know." Leaving the cannon, Rogor walked over to some bushes and pushed them aside, exposing another wheeled contraption, this one a black cube. From its top, several large prisms were supported by metal arms. He pushed the machine to the edge of the cleft and began working the controls. "This is what took you from the fountain in Ikona, child. With it I can see anything within a two day's walk, and can bring it to my mountaintop if I choose."

Rogor turned the controls, all the time watching a screen. He frowned as he searched, then smiled. "Much of the path at the bottom of the cleft cannot be seen because of the turns and twists of the walls, but from here I can see the power station at the end of the cleft. Sooner or later . . . yes, that's him. Fyx."

Rogor pushed more controls, then turned to the platform, drawing a pistol from beneath his robe. In the blink of an eye, the back of a black and scarlet robed figure holding a stick appeared on the platform. "Fyx. It is you, isn't it?"

"Rogor?"

"Just so you know, Fyx." Rogor fired the pistol, sending a pencil-thin streak of light through the figure on the platform. The stick fell and the robe collapsed. Rogor took a step toward it, then cursed, seeing the robe flat and empty. Quickly he leveled the pistol on Crisal. "Fyx, I have the little brat in my sights. Come out where I can see you, or I will cut her in two. Come out, and if I even sense your thoughts reaching toward mine, I will kill her!" Rogor looked around to his right, then his left. "Hear me, Fyx!"

"I hear you, Rogor." To Rogor's left, Fyx moved from behind some bushes, naked and looking small and helpless.

Rogor smiled, then laughed, turning the pistol on his brother. "I feel you trying to work my thoughts, Fyx, but I am stronger."

Crisal watched as Rogor straightened his right arm, aiming the pistol dead center. She closed her eyes and tiny hands searched Rogor's sleeve. Finding what they searched for, they wrapped themselves around a blackened dough ball and squeezed. Before she floated into black nothingness, she felt hot flame wash her face.

Crisal opened her eyes and looked up into a face lit with a red light. The face looked over her at the source of the light. "Fyx, it is you." The magician looked down and smiled a toothless grin.

Crisal realized the old man was holding her in his arms. She threw her arms around Fyx's neck and held him tightly. "Fyx, it is you."

"Child," Fyx gasped, "you may succeed where Rogor failed. Let me breathe!"

Crisal relaxed her hold, but kept her head against Fyx's chest. "I killed him, didn't I?"

"You had no choice, Crisal."

"He was your brother."

"I tell you, you had no choice." Crisal looked into the old magician's eyes and read nothing but love. She turned toward the light and saw the sides of the cleft burning. Below, molten rock filled the cleft from side to side. "Let me down, Fyx." Once on her feet, and steady, Crisal looked away from the cleft. The smooth, hard surface was empty. "Where are the machines and the platforms?"

She looked at the magician, and he nodded toward the river of molten rock. "Down there."

"Fyx, they could have made you the greatest magician on Momus!"

The old man raised his eyebrows and turned toward the girl. "Child, I *am* the greatest magician on Momus."

Crisal nodded. "But, what of the Quadrant laws? Rogor didn't build these machines." She pointed at the red, flowing rock. "How did that happen?"

"I turned Rogor's cannon on the power station below. You are right; these are not Rogor's works."

"But, without the machines, how can we prove that Rogor had help from off-planet?"

"We can't. Hence, no act of war can be proven. No one from the Tenth Quadrant will tell of what was attempted here, and neither will we."

"But, if the law . . ."

"Child, what do your fortune teller's eyes show you if the Ninth Quadrant knew about this?"

Crisal frowned. "They would send their own force to counter the forces of the Tenth . . . and they would settle their differences here, on Momus."

The magician nodded. "Great powers usually find someone else's back yard in which to wage their wars. We have spared Momus that."

"What of Rogor's army forming in Ris?"

Fyx turned from the cleft and walked to the mountainside. Crisal followed behind as they began the long climb. Fyx talked over his shoulder as he felt his way down. "They will get tired of waiting for

King Rogor. In a day or two they will drift back to their towns. Some will still talk in fear of Rogor, but next spring the crops will come up again. In a few years, nothing will remain of Rogor except children who will try to scare each other with tales of the ghost of Split Mountain."

Crisal followed until she stumbled, barking her shins on a sharp rock. "Fyx, wait. Let me rest."

The old man turned and stood next to her. "Here is a grassy spot, Crisal. We can rest here until morning."

The girl moved to the place and sat down, rubbing her legs. The magician lowered himself next to her and put his stick on the ground. Lifting up a hip, he plucked a rock from beneath it and tossed it down the mountain. Crisal bit her lip and turned to the old man. "Fyx, I know Salina agreed to let me apprentice to you at your request, but what happens now? Rogor is defeated. Am I needed anymore?"

Fyx let his head fall slowly to the ground and looked at the cloudy sky. "Momus has drawn the interest of powerful forces. I shall return to Tarzak and do what I can. Our troubles do not end here."

"But what of me?"

"You shall rest. Go to sleep."

Crisal felt her mind cloud. "Fyx, I don't like it when you make me sleep. . . ." She saw herself in a black mist, floating free. All around her was black save a wisp of white floating to her left. *Fyx?*

Yes, child.

The black mist parted and Crisal saw stars above and a fluffy blanket of clouds beneath. The wisp of white turned and streaked toward the east. Crisal turned and followed. *Fyx! Fyx, what is this?*

We have done little but work magic, child. Now, I would show you some play!

Where do we fly?

We meet the sun. Hurry, we can go fast—as fast as we wish.

Crisal darted away from the clouds toward the stars, laughed, then dipped into the black mist and up again at Fyx. The magician dodged and cackled. *Fyx, my question. Will I still be your apprentice?* Her companion mist flew a circle around her, then darted toward the yellowing sky ahead. *Well, Fyx?*

Yes, you shall remain my apprentice. She hesitated, then streaked far ahead of the magician. *Someday, Crisal, you shall be the greatest magician of us all.*

The sun burst upon Crisal's sight, and she outshone it.

HOW IT HAPPENED
by Isaac Asimov
art: Frank Borth

There's a perfectly simple explanation—
doing it right would have cost so much!

My brother began to dictate in his best oratorical style, the one which has the tribes hanging on his words.

"In the beginning," he said, "exactly 15.2 billion years ago, there was a big bang and the Universe—"

But I had stopped writing. "Fifteen billion years ago?" I said incredulously.

"Absolutely," he said. "I'm inspired."

"I don't question your inspiration," I said. (I had better not. He's three years younger than I am, but I don't try questioning his inspiration. Neither does anyone else or there's hell to pay.) "But are you going to tell the story of the Creation over a period of fifteen billion years?"

"I have to," said my brother. "That's how long it took. I have it all in here," he tapped his forehead, "and it's on the very highest authority."

HOW IT HAPPENED   227

By now I had put down my reed pen. "Do you know the price of papyrus?" I said.

"What?" (He may be inspired, but I frequently noticed that the inspiration didn't include such sordid matters as the price of papyrus.)

I said, "Suppose you describe one million years of events to each roll of papyrus. That means you'll have to fill fifteen thousand rolls. You'll have to talk long enough to fill them, and you know that you begin to stammer after a while. I'll have to write enough to fill them, and my fingers will fall off. And even if we can afford all that papyrus and you have the voice and I have the strength, who's going to copy it? We've got to have a guarantee of a hundred copies before we can publish, and without that where will we get royalties from?"

My brother thought a while. He said, "You think I ought to cut it down?"

"Way down," I said, "if you expect to reach the public."

"How about a hundred years?" he said.

"How about six days?" I said.

He said, horrified, "You can't squeeze Creation into six days."

I said, "This is all the papyrus I have. What do *you* think?"

"Oh, well," he said, and began to dictate again, "In the beginning—Does it have to be six days, Aaron?"

I said, firmly, "Six days, Moses."

THROUGH TIME AND SPACE WITH FERDINAND FEGHOOT!!
by Grendel Briarton
art: Tim Kirk

In 2147, after conquering the one hundred countries surrounding his capital, the mighty Bwasimba I proclaimed himself Emperor of Africa and announced a grand feast of celebration by the banks of his ancestral Ngusi River.

"One problem remains—" he told Ferdinand Feghoot. "An anthem worthy of me and my fame. But don't worry—our delectable freshwater eels are an unfailing source of omens and oracles."

Tables were set for the Court, and tens of thousands of subjects thronged the high riverside cliffs. Suddenly, excited shouts interrupted their cheering. The Imperial Fishermen had come with their catch, dancing triumphantly—and their ancient chief carried the biggest, most splendid eel ever seen!

Instantly, the crowd went out of control. They swept the old man off his feet. He lost his grip on the huge, squirming eel—which fell off the cliff and was lost again in the river.

Bwasimba, ecstatic a moment before, bellowed in anguish.

"Calm yourself, Serene Highness!" soothed Feghoot. "All is not lost. You now have your anthem—the *Marseillaise!*"

"For that wretched mob?" roared Bwasimba. "It's too good for them! They lost me the finest eel in the world!"

"Exactly," said Ferdinand Feghoot. "That was your oracle. Wasn't it a mob that brought about the fall of the best eel?"

229

GHOSTS
by Keith Minnion
art: Rich Sternbach

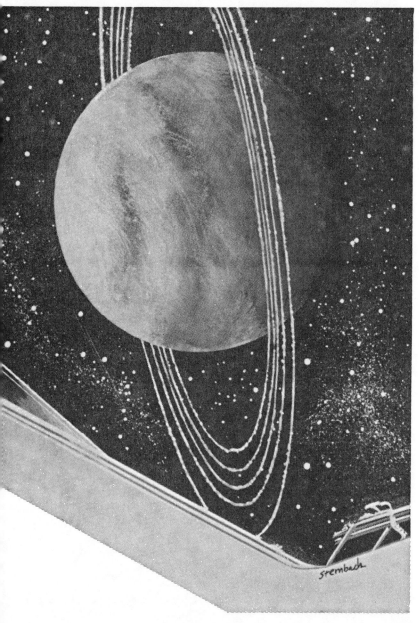

srembach

You know how hard it is, sometimes, to wake up and uncradle, to set up the primary systems and sequences and face the new morning. You know how frustrating it can be, too, to look out upon nothing but clean space, no debris in the cubics you have planned to sweep this day. Or worse, a motherlode of junk, but with a Royal Patrol deployed at its perimeter to guard it. You know the futility of it, then: Uranus is the Lord's Land, north and south, inner ring and outer ring. The Patrols are *everywhere*. How long can you evade them? How long before you are cornered and caught? Will they find you today?

Shooting out to Neptune won't help; it's Royal too. And of course Jupiter/Saturn is Union. No, this is it. *This is it.*

Look at it: Uranus, in the night. The rings are fine lace; this close you can see right through them, like ghosts. And the planet itself: pale porcelain green with hints of ultramarine woven throughout. Beautiful monster; ugly princess. Skim it, sieve it, rake it with field generator sails scarred by the planet wind blowing inbound. And respect the princess, the monster, for though it is your life, now, it can just as easily be your death.

Lonely, solitary work. You like that part of it, anyway. You came here to be alone, and so far you have been. Except for the voices. Like Jonquil told you so long ago (has it been so long?) there are voices here, in the cold Uranus space, so very far from home. No one knows about them, no one hears them but you. Keep it that way. Keep it that way.

No one understood about the voices on Earth. No one wanted to. Chrise! Push those memories away, shove them back to the shadows where they belong. You shudder, remembering.

Yet they are your friends, your only friends. Jonquil, Ben, Jonas and the rest, all of the voices, they have always been your friends, always.

Don't worry about it, Huck. Don't worry about anything. Just sweep what dirty space (dirty *Royal* space, managing a smile) you can find, and for Chrise's sake keep it all to yourself. There must be enough junk left outside of the clouds to live upon. There must be. There has to be. Wake up, Huck. Uncradle, there is one more day to face.

"Huck!" Whispered. "Are you still awake?"

The small boy turned his eyes into the shadows.

"You better get to sleep, Huck. If Mara catches you she's going to beat you again."

232   GHOSTS

It was Jonquil, one of them, the first voice, in fact, who had ever spoken to him.

"I'm afraid, Joni."

"Afraid? Afraid of what? Mara?"

"You're old," the boy muttered, burying his face into his blanket. "You don't have to be afraid."

"I'm not that old, Huck. Why, I was only ten—Earth ten—when I was—"

Light exploded into the room, lancing across the floor, splitting the darkness to aching yellow. Huck was caught in it, eyes wide, tears already forming.

"Were you at it again?" demanded the woman in the doorway. "Who's in here with you?"

There was no one, of course, no one at all. Huck huddled in the corner, pulling his blankets up around him. Mara did not understand about the voices. She just didn't understand.

"I didn't mean it," Huck pleaded.

Mara stared down at him, breathing loudly, barely holding her anger in check.

"I'm sorry, Mara," the five-year-old whined. "Really, I'm—"

"Close your mouth, and your eyes as well, and go to sleep, dammit." The woman whirled around, grabbing the door. "And I don't want to hear any more of this talking to yourself!"

Slam, door.

Silence.

"Huck?"

He shut his eyes tightly.

"Huck . . . ?"

He hesitated at the entrance.

The Royal Court seated at the table in the center of the huge chamber rose as one. "Come," the nearest one said. "Please."

Another indicated a seat, which the young man took, noticeably grateful to have a place to put himself. His nervousness permeated the chamber, causing several of the Court to flash him reassuring smiles and murmur pleasantries.

A very strained-looking woman in full dress rose from the head of the table, cleared her throat, and everyone quieted. The young man glanced at all their faces, looking for answers to—

"My colleagues and I wish to thank you for agreeing to this audience," the woman said. "And of course you must be wondering why you are here."

He spread his hands; he had not "agreed" to anything; he had been *brought.* Should he—?

The woman continued: "My name is Reginald. Chief Secretary to His Majesty Lord Talshire. You have, no doubt, heard the name."

He swallowed dryly. Lord Talshire owned Uranus and Neptune. Plain and simply owned them. Of course he had heard the name. "Why . . . ?" he managed.

"Yes," Reginald said. "We must get swiftly to the point, since there is a definite time factor involved." She activated a table screen and, glancing at it, rattled off: "Your name is Sammael Huck Jastrow, Earth. Twenty-three years old, born and raised same. You are presently engaged in a relatively small-scope illegal scavenging concern in His Majesty's Uranus space—"

Huck found his voice quite suddenly: "Illegal! It's not—!"

Reginald raised her hand impatiently. "Please, that is not our concern at the moment. This next bit of information, however, is: you have been rated the best three-prong proximity pilot outward of Mars, the best, perhaps, in the System." She smiled falsely. "You are valuable, Mr. Jastrow. At any time you are that. But to us now, at this time, you are *priceless.*"

Huck swallowed again. "What's the job?"

Secretary Reginald's smile broadened. "The 'job' involves piloting a proximity shuttle due inward—"

Huck flashed puzzlement. "Sunward?"

"Oh, no." The Secretary—almost unconsciously—pointed to the floor. "Uranus," she said. "You are to fly closer to Uranus than anyone has ever previously attempted. You are to effect the rescue of a skimmer-class craft which at this moment is trapped in a slowly decaying orbit. The ship does not possess power enough to get up to freedom."

"And you picked me?"

The Secretary sighed patiently. "Prior to this morning you were the *fourth*-best proximity pilot, Mr. Jastrow. We picked three others before you, and this morning, before the Royal Police paid you a visit, those three failed in the very mission you are about to engage upon." The secretary paused to note the effect of her words, then continued. "They piloted a four-seater, of course, a *Corsair*-class refitted specifically for proximity flight. You will pilot an equally refitted two-seater shuttle—much more powerful for its mass —making, we hope, for a more successful configuration."

"You seem certain I'm going to agree to this," Huck said, slowly.

"There is nothing to agree to," the Secretary replied. "You will do it." She paused again. "We have approached you in this manner—" spreading her arms to include the rest of the Court "—to assure you of our sincerity, our good will, and of our seriousness. You must certainly realize the political and economic repercussions, not to mention your own monetary compensation . . ."

Huck glanced about the room, then down to his hands, and finally directly at the Secretary. "It has to be someone pretty big, then," he said.

"Surely you must realize?"

"Who?" Raising his voice a little.

"Why, his Majesty Lord Talshire, of course."

The voices had kept a respectful silence up to this point. But then one of them—Jonas—spoke up quite clearly: "Don't trust them past your shadow. But don't worry, they've laid it out fairly clean, and we'll be with you all the way."

Huck opened his mouth, then closed it. Then, to Secretary Reginald: "When?"

"Within the hour, as soon as we ferry you to Miranda and have you tuned up."

One of the Court put out his hand then.

Huck decided not to shake it.

"Spread 'em," the doctor said.

Huck obliged. He shivered when she applied the probes.

"Sorry," she said. "No time to warm them up. My superiors caught me as much by surprise as they did you. Hold it there."

Huck stared at the white light band over the cradle, aware that it wasn't hurting his eyes.

"When was your last tune-up, Mr. Jastrow?"

"One Earth year, sir."

"Ah-hah." She fiddled at an instrument console. "Quarter-year tune-ups are mandatory by law for your type of work, you know," she said. "And call me Sylvia, please."

Huck glanced at her, surprised, then returned his gaze to the light. "Tunes cost too much," he said in answer. "I'm still trying to float."

"Triton?"

"No. Earth, originally."

"Hah. I should have guessed from the accent." She caught his eye, a smile forming. "Try not to feel this," she said then, and something clicked. Huck did, however, in every single nerve of his body. Chrise! he thought in the middle, I hate this!

Then it was over, the probes fell away, and Huck tried (without success) to focus his eyes.

"Congratulations." Sylvia patted his rump. "You'll feel better in a minute. Now for the form-filling." She hit a toggle. "Tape's running. Do you verify the procedure, etcetera, etcetera?"

Huck managed a nod.

"You have to—"

"Verified," he gasped.

The boy saw the other children and paused. "Jonquil?"

She murmured close to his ear: "Stay away from them, Huck. They are waiting for you. The big one there with the ball wants to fight."

The boy sagged against the wall, sinking into the shadows. "But why? What do I do to make them want to beat me up, to hate me like they do?"

Jonquil sighed. "It's not your fault, Huck. If anyone's, it's ours. No one can hear us but you. You're special that way. I haven't been able to find anyone else alive who can hear me as well as you can. I don't think anyone else has either. You're the only one we can talk to. That's why you are so special. That's why we help you whenever we can."

"But what's so important about talking to me? I'm just a kid."

Jonquil laughed sadly. "If only you could know," she said. "If only you could know how important it really is, how important you really are."

Huck peered out of his shadow and saw the children playing a game he wanted more than anything else in the world to join. If only Jonquil and the rest of them were real, he thought. If only . . . but that thought chilled him so much he wanted to cry.

He eased into the cradle; several screens lit up. When he took hold of the grips, more were activated. He felt the ship flow through the grips and cradle and into his body; it felt right; it would be okay.

"Disengage on your signal," the dock chief said.

"Right."

Huck went through the pre-flight check methodically, purposefully, taking his time, then started the sequence. Within moments opposing fields were set up and the shuttle fell away from the dock. It gained speed steadily, falling away from Miranda, the moon, falling into the green-blue gas giant that was Uranus.

Talshire's skimmer was a scant thousand kilometers outside the first substantial methane cloud layer. Totally immersed in the magnetosphere, its field generator shields excited the ion wind to white luminescence. Huck had a visual on it, even from his present height; like a silver comet with an achingly straight tail, below, inward, a few steps from Death's door.

"Tracking you," said the dock chief.

"Thanks."

Falling. Falling into the green-blue disk on the main screen. The planet seemed unnaturally flat—strangely, the rings contributed to this illusion. The shuttle's arching descent was directly toward them. Of course he would pass far inward of the innermost, but the visual threat was staggering.

Huck hated visuals down this far. He looked away, then back again. No longer flat, the more he stared the more the planet began to look concave, distinctly concave, like a bowl, a well, and he was going into it, headlong, eyes wide, a green hole in space . . .

"Trim it up there, Huck. You're drifting."

". . . okay."

Field sails blossomed out like the wings of a beetle. This should be okay, he thought. He just should have known better than to look down the planet's throat. The gas giants were dangerous that way. Their utter immensity was difficult to deal with in so close.

"I'm going blind for a while," he said finally.

"Thought you might." The dock chief chuckled. "That Chrising mother of a planet is a lot to take all at once."

"Yeah." Several screens blanked to grey.

"I was down pretty far a couple of times," the dock chief continued, "droning, of course. Never so low in a shuttle, though." A pause. "Hey, you're doing real fine there, Huck."

Sure. Yeah, I must be out of my mind, doing this, being here. I really must be insane. He rubbed his hands on the cradle cushion. Chrise, I'm scared, he thought suddenly. What am I doing here? Another screen blanked.

"You going to sleep on us, Huck?"

"Sorry." The screen went on again.

He was sweating a little. One of the screens showed him saddled in the cradle, naked, perspiration shining on his belly and thighs. He looked down, wiped himself; and on the screen he looked down and wiped himself.

Jonas whispered in his ear: "My God, even now this frightens me. The only other time I was down this far I . . . never got back up. I didn't have equipment like this, though."

Huck glanced about the cabin futilely. He couldn't reply to him, couldn't do anything but sit and listen.

"How much longer?" he asked, eventually.

"ETA in seven minutes, thirty-six seconds. Check over that docking sequence in the meantime, please. We want it to be your best."

Huck exploded at that. "What the Chrise is that supposed to mean? You give me forty-five minutes to get a fifteen-point procedure down cold? You guys must be crazier than I am! You honestly expect this to work? For Chrising—"

"Hold on . . . news . . . just hold on a moment, Huck, please."

"I'm not going anywhere," he spit out, feeling blood pounding behind his ears.

". . . okay," the dock chief said a few seconds later. "You've got a temporary reprieve. His Majesty has managed to trim his orbit enough to give him an estimate two Earth days—about forty-nine hours—more time until his ship falls too low for effective rescue. If you want to know the truth, he was monitoring your transmission and agreed with you. So you've got a day and a half . . . chalk this one up as a dry run, then. Okay?"

Huck shook his head slowly, cursing every single one of them. Jonas said: "They're recording that heart and blood pressure of yours, you know. Calm down; don't give them the satisfaction."

"Right you are," Huck muttered.

"What's that, Huck?" The dock chief asked.

"Nothing. Just feed me the climb-and-away sequence. My hands are itchy; I need something to do down here."

". . . right."

He found a corner of the Company bar where most of the lights couldn't find him and grabbed it, trying very hard to forget just about everything that was in his head. The two Royal Policemen guarding him retired to a nearby table, trying unsuccessfully to appear inconspicuous.

"When do you make the real run?"

He looked up. She slid into the seat opposite him.

"Little over a day," he said, returning his gaze to the drink on the table. "How's the slash-and-sew business?"

"Ahah. Huck has finally found his voice. At our first meeting—as I recall—I couldn't get you past monosyllables. You prefer 'Huck' to 'Mr. Jastrow', don't you?"

"Yeah. Huck's fine."

"And you can still call me Sylvia." She tapped her fingers on the tabletop, watching him.

He looked up again. "You want a drink?"

She shook her head. "But I would like to have a talk. Moons are small—you can't help but run into people. And Miranda's a small moon. Actually I've been keeping you tightly beamed since your tune." She reached across and touched his arm. He made as though to pull away, but stopped himself. "Then you heard what happened," he said.

"I heard that a young fool named Talshire took out a Royal skimmer in one of his usual drunk/high states and directed its controls due inward. Rumors say he wanted to swim through to the other side. I also heard that a young hotshot proximity pilot was retrieved from some out of the way corner of His Majesty's Uranus space and pressed into immediate service to rescue the foolish Lord from his dire predicament at the very question of life, limb, and . . ." and then she smiled, ". . . money?"

Huck looked at her incredulously. "You think I'm in this for the money?"

"Well, glory, at least . . ."

Huck half-rose from his seat, his expression furious, but when he saw what was in her eyes he collapsed back and muttered a quiet obscenity.

Sylvia patted his hand. "I know how it is," she said. "They got me the same way. There was this certain prince with a certain rare exobiological bug, and there too was I—young and innocent graduate student at Triton S.T. who happened to be doing extensive research on the same said bug—who got whisked away to cure him."

"Did you?"

"Unfortunately, yes; he's piloting that skimmer this very moment. The irony, I know, must be devastating."

"Why didn't you leave, after?"

Sylvia laughed lightly. "If I had, then I wouldn't have met you."

"Cute. I was wondering when you would get around to that. You're my arenar?"

She stiffened slightly; he felt it in the touch of her hand. "I volunteered," she said.

"Oh." He looked down at his drink again. "Sorry."

"I also wanted to spend time with you to ask some questions."

Now it was Huck's turn to smile. "I guess I owe you that, then." He paused to drain half of his glass. "Okay. What's up?"

"I heard the tape of your 'dry run' just before. At two points on it there was a particular type of disturbance which I could not attribute either to the dock chief, to you, or to the mechanisms involved."

"What kind of disturbances?"

"Well, they are difficult to describe with words. I knew what they were, at any rate, though I don't think anyone else who heard the tape did."

Huck felt something touch his spine. Apprehension? "Just what exactly are you talking about?"

"I've been following the work of several University colleagues in the post-mortem life sciences."

"Isn't that a contradiction of—"

"Obviously. It's still relatively new, say, five years since the scientific community accepted the basic premises. Quickly and simply put, these scientists have succeeded in proving that certain kinds of life—specific types of intelligently controlled energies, actually—continue after physical, material life ends."

That hit Huck like walking into a wall. "You mean . . . ghosts?"

"Grossly put, with ridiculous superstitious connotations, but . . . yes. Ghosts."

Huck went cold inside, his face slowly draining of all color. He suddenly did not like the turn of the conversation.

Sylvia continued: "So far they have only been able to gain direct evidence on photographic emulsion films and certain magnetic sound-recording tapes. Deceased individuals are able to effect consistent recognizable changes in these materials."

"And that's what you say you saw in the flight tape?"

"Well, not 'saw' so much as 'heard', but yes. I did."

"Which means?"

"That there was a presence either with you in the shuttle or with the dock chief."

"But . . ."

"But I have a feeling it was you. I checked your records, and came across a statement by one of your mothers, the one named Mara."

Huck abruptly stood, knocking over the remainder of his drink. The two police at the nearby table looked up briefly. "I must say you are thorough," he said, barely managing to keep control of himself. He wiped at the spilled liquor, trying to conceal the emotions flashing across his face.

"Hey," Sylvia said softly, stopping him. "Hey, I understand."

He looked at her, totally exposed, totally vulnerable.

"You've got a couple of hours," she said then. "Would you . . . ?"

§ § §

GHOSTS

Huck was nineteen, and he looked it. He had spent three days at the Newark docks with little food and even less sleep, trying to get off, to go *out*. However, he had found the docks a definite, dismaying anticlimax. The big glamour ships were all in orbit, or on the Moon. The largest ones on the ground were personnel transports, two or three thrusting their prows above the surrounding derricks and odd superstructures; but the most common craft were skimpy four-cradle shuttles. The necessary considerations, air and gravity, made the entire Newark operation excessively complicated. Which all added up to any dock on Earth being essentially outmoded, outdated and fading. But Earth was where he had been born and raised and trained. He had come waving his three-prong pilot rating, which made him—he also found to his dismay—about as desirable as nine thousand nine hundred and ninety-nine of the other three-prongers bumming the docks.

The voices were a help, though.

"He's not looking, Huck. Now!"

And he lifted three oranges from the counter, certain of success.

"I can't go on like this, guys," he whispered to Ben and Jonquil and any of the others who were listening.

"However long it takes, Huck. However long it takes."

"A gentleman crouched by that piling there, Huck," Ben said suddenly. "See him?"

"Yeah. So?"

"So he intends to relieve you of the oranges, most likely with the knife—its vibrating mechanism thankfully in disrepair—which he has hidden in his cloak."

Huck nodded, and as he passed the grease-smeared bum he tossed him one of the fruits. Surprised, the would-be attacker could only grab for it while Huck walked out of reach and out of danger. "Thanks, team," he said.

You are a hard person to understand. You are extremely complex, or utterly, utterly simple. You just can't decide which.

He took off his pants, and then his tunic.

"Oh," she said. "Your *back*."

His expression in the shadows: vacant, tired. "You're the doctor," he said. "What's the diagnosis?"

"Huck, really. . . ."

"No, *really*. What's it look like to you?" And turned to face her, to touch her, the expression still there.

"You . . . someone . . . well, you've been through some terrible beatings a long time ago . . . oh Chrise. . . ."

He hugged her. "Sorry, I'm being cruel. Bitter, actually. Sometimes I spread it around. I bet Mara forgot to include this in the report you read, anyway."

"It was she who—?"

"She was a very frustrated lady . . . no one knew why I was different, and I was the youngest of that Group's children at the time. I spent a lot of time by myself, hiding . . . it was hard to fit in."

"You could have had the scars taken care of, though. Medical facilities on—"

Huck put his fingers lightly on her lips. "It makes for great conversation in bed," he said, grinning. "Besides, like I told you, my scavenging business isn't really floating."

"But after tomorrow you'll be—"

"After tomorrow I'll probably be dead."

"But I thought the extra time—"

"The extra time has allowed me to get the sequencing down fairly well, true. But still, no one has ever done a rescue like this before and succeeded. The odds are definitely not leaning in my direction." He paused, looking at her in the darkness. "Hey, lady, I thought we were here to make love."

"Were we?"

And they fell together, murmuring quietly.

He awoke later, gasping, tangled in sheets. The darkness was absolute. He stared into it, his body shaking uncontrollably for a moment, perspiration down his ribs.

". . . Huck?" Sleepily.

"It's nothing, Sylvia." He took a breath, closed his eyes, then opened them again. ". . . it's nothing."

"Oh, Huck." In the gloom he knew she was looking at him. "Something," she said, almost whispering.

He lay back. "I had a nightmare—drowning in an ammonia sea—the usual. It's—" he stopped himself, breathing heavily.

"Huck, you can get help, you know."

"For what? The nightmares?"

"My colleagues, the ones doing the life-after-death studies . . . if you agree to examinations, I'm sure they—"

He cut her off with a look. Then, shakily: "Please, let's just not talk about that. Really. Okay?"

She nodded, sensing correctly that she had stumbled again on one of Huck's great fears, perhaps his greatest.

But then he surprised her by chuckling.

"What . . . ?"

He turned to her. "Oh, I forgot. You couldn't hear."

"The voices?"

"Yeah. One of them just commented on your technique."

"My *what?*"

"Are you embarrassed?"

"No . . . I just . . . well, it's a little bit of a shock to have to all of a sudden deal with something . . ."

"Unreal?"

"No, of course not . . . it's just . . ."

Huck gathered her close. "How about I ask them to give us a little privacy from now on, okay?"

"Would you?"

"I just did."

They lay in silence for a while, then Sylvia said: "Well?"

"Well what?"

"How was I?"

"How were you what?"

"You said the voice rated my—"

"Oh, yeah. He—his name is Jonas—used an archaic word, but I think you can translate: he said you were 'dynamite.' "

Sylvia lay quietly for a little while longer. Then: "Tell Jonas I said 'thank you', please."

You can see what is happening. Alone with yourself, alone with your thoughts, you can see what is, and what will be. Never before have you had to face this. Never before. Your choices are there, clearly in front of you. Can you do it? Are you strong enough? Either way, *every* way is an easy out, every way but one.

Suddenly—Oh Chrise, it chills you—the thought comes. It has been lurking back there, in the shadows, waiting to leap out and drag you down: *you want to fail,* don't you. Don't you?

"Well, congratulations, Huck," Jonquil said.

"Thanks."

Nothing needed to be explained. Everyone had heard, had seen, had experienced . . . Huck had managed a third-class berth on a Royal light cruiser docked and running out of Tycho. The personnel carrier was already stowing supplies and incidental cargo. Huck squinted through the smog, and picked out its prow from the others, his emotions thrilling to the prospect of his first trip off-planet. Destination was Oberon, a cold Uranus rock, but that didn't matter. It was off, it was away, it was *outside.*

"If you ever come back," Ben said, "we will be here."

That caught Huck off guard. "What do you mean? Aren't you coming with me?"

Silence, for a moment. Then, Jonquil: "We can't leave here, Huck. We died here. The ashes of our bodies are here. We can't go."

"I never knew."

"We never thought you would actually leave, or we would have told you."

"Then there won't be any voices, no one at all, after I lift?"

"Oh, of course. You'll meet others."

"But the law says all people who die get sent inwards to Earth. I remember reading that somewhere."

"And you remember correctly. But not all corpses can be recovered. No, you will meet others, and they will be your friends, just as we were."

"Are," Huck corrected.

"No, dear Huck," Jonquil said gently. "Were."

"Let's go," he said, settling in. "Let's get the show moving."

"You've got it, cowboy. On your signal."

Screens off, now, and he was away. Uranus was down there . . . instruments told him that much . . . but he had no wish to see it. Not this time. He had a headache from the realigning tune Sylvia had given him after breakfast. Plus he hadn't eaten the breakfast, which only made the headache worse.

"How does she feel?"

Meaning the shuttle, not his head. "Fine."

"We were a little concerned about a flutter in your dorsal sail cluster. Would you mind checking it?"

Like a hand traced lightly over the spine of his back . . .

"Nothing. Seems okay."

Gravity tugged at him, gently, gently. He turned on a few of his aft screens.

Miranda was vaguely round. It was as though its sphere had been broken into pieces and then put back together without aid from the original plan. Seen from several thousand kilometers it resembled a green flower on black velvet, irregular in outline, reflecting the color of the planet it orbited.

Huck hung in the velvet between the flower and the green-blue

ringed gas giant, the shuttle enclosing him, helping him maneuver as he fell. He completed a number of operations himself manually to give him something to do before the real work began.

"You're doing fine," the dock chief said. "Five minutes till—"

"Yeah, right."

This is it, kid. This is the one. You have to go through with it. And it all depends on you, now. Just you.

There, the spark, the comet trail of ionized plasma. The Lord Talshire's skimmer had ample shielding—he could afford to waste it thus—whereas Huck's shuttle didn't, and Huck couldn't. He would have to dip, grab, and then climb out as fast as possible, hopefully with sails intact. And though simply described, the maneuver was in reality incredibly difficult. So difficult that—

The comet disappeared, then; like a light turned off: there, then gone. Huck cursed. This had not been anticipated. Not at all.

The dock chief cut in immediately: "Seems His Majesty has gone a bit inward. We've lost all contact up here—plasma interference has scrambled everything. How do you read it?"

"The same. So what do we do? Is he dead?"

"Checking . . ."

From beside him, Jonas whispered: "We know you can't answer, but listen: Lord Talshire is very much alive. He's trimmed his orbit beneath the interference layer. You can still get him."

Huck stared at his instruments, gripping the controls with whitened knuckles.

"Trust us, Huck. We can help you through it."

Then, from above: "We've got nothing here, Huck. If he leveled off in time then he's still alive. You're directed to go through with it, anyway."

"We know what we're saying, Huck," Jonas said. "In my time I would have called this a piece of cake. Agree to it, and quickly. You're running out of time."

Huck looked at his instruments again and discovered this was true. He had no choice, he realized suddenly. He really had no choice at all.

"Is the doctor there?" he asked abruptly.

"No . . . this is a restricted—"

"Well then find her and tell her something for me."

"Huck, the time factor—"

"Just shut up and listen. Tell her it's going to be all right. Tell her I've got help." And pushed the grips forward, plunging into the interference layer before any reply was possible.

You don't want anyone to know about them, about the voices. You've lived with that so long it has become part of you. They must be a secret, they have to be. No one hears voices, no one but people who should be locked up. Locked up. Picked apart. Put back together again. Happy, vacant. Gone.

Why didn't they just leave you alone? It was so good before, it really was, solitary, sweeping the air clean, dodging the Royal patrols, making that tiny amount of profit that let you float at the surface that much longer. Christ, the silences out there were magnificent, the oneness, the universality . . . the *safety* . . .

You are ripped open, now. You are spreadeagled, flayed to the bone. *Someone knows.* She says she understands. Trust her? Trust her? Everyone wants your trust, now. Everyone.

"Listen to me, Huck," Jonas said. "Listen carefully and do what I tell you. I'll work *through* you. It can be done."

Huck stared down at the controls, his mouth slack, his hands clenching the hand grips. "I . . . I can't. . . ."

"You have to! You have to be willing or I can't do a Chrising thing!"

Huck felt Jonas near him, and the others, all the others, all of them with one thought, all of them. . . .

He closed his eyes and swallowed, his pale cheeks flushing red. "How—?"

"Just sit there, let yourself go limp . . . yeah . . . now don't panic on me . . . you and I are about to do some maneuvers with this crackerbox that are bound to scare the living . . ." he paused, ". . . just relax. . . ."

Huck's hands moved by themselves, then. Deftly, to the console, marking out a sequence. Huck watched them. Then all the forward screens snapped on, and he stifled a scream.

"Keep your eyes open, Huck! I can't do this blind!"

Green hell, deep, hot, steaming jungle of liquid emerald blades reaching up to—oh, please. Oh, please. Every past fear was banished instantly in the face of this. Ultimate insanity, demon clouds, death seas . . . got to . . . got to—

"Give me some help, please. I can't keep his eyes open or his head in place."

There, something . . . a speck of black against the chaos, a defect on the screen? . . . Huck focused on it in desperation, trying to orient himself, to place himself within some sane frame of—

A grappling waldo swept across a starboard screen; Huck gasped in relief, recognizing it. Then again, a twin to the first, across a port screen.

"You're doing great. Just great. Concentrate on the skimmer. Any moment now . . ."

A power dive, all sails furled, silver bullet with arms, with hands, reaching. Huck watched, fascinated, as the skimmer grew in size in the forward screen, the Royal crest glittering on its bow. . . . "Help

GHOSTS   247 me, Huck. You've got to help me now. I need all that three-prong expertise. Come on, pal. . . ."

Face it. Face yourself. Face the choice: two ways, two paths, up or down. There, in your hands, the power . . .
You know how it is. You know how hard it is, sometimes. . . .

"Do it, Jonas, just do it."
Contact. The shuttle vibrated with sudden, staccato engine bursts. A horizon appeared on the forward screen, then swung up and away—
"*Help* me, Huck!"
—and appeared again, lowered, and was lost to an incredibly sane, unbelievably perfect starfield.
Sails shot out; the field generators strained toward overload; the vibration was continuous, was everywhere, was everything.
Huck glanced at the appropriate screen and saw the skimmer grappled securely alongside the shuttle. Sudden friend, sudden companion in the madness. "Is it over?" he whispered.
"The worst of it is. Both spacecraft are intact, and the Prince is alive. How about you?"
Huck let out his breath, wiped the sweat from his face and neck. "Alive," he said. "Alive, too."

He opened and closed the door quietly behind him.
In the shadows she turned; he saw a wetness on her cheeks.
"Hey," whispering, standing by the door.
". . . Huck?"
"We did it," he said, a smile forming. "Hey, we did it."

THE TEST TUBE

No ember-eyed debaucher was so fond,
No zealot's fierce allegiance half so true.
How many hours I watched, the boyhood trips
I made to movie houses to adore
Your fragile beauty and your crystal pride,
Your power to kill, or kindle what had died.

You spared the blushes of the naked blonde,
Hiding with veils of vapor her taboo
Attractions, deftly draping breasts and hips
As she lay, gagged, on *Dime Detective*'s floor
And white-smocked Dr. Hooknose grimly tried
To do her harm in ways unspecified.

King's sceptre, bishop's mitre, wizard's wand,
Mad scientists caressed and fondled you
Till smoke poured thick and creamy from your lips
And instantly you both conceived and bore
Out of your teeming steam—defiant Hyde
Or, to placate the Baron's brute, a bride.

—RAY RUSSELL

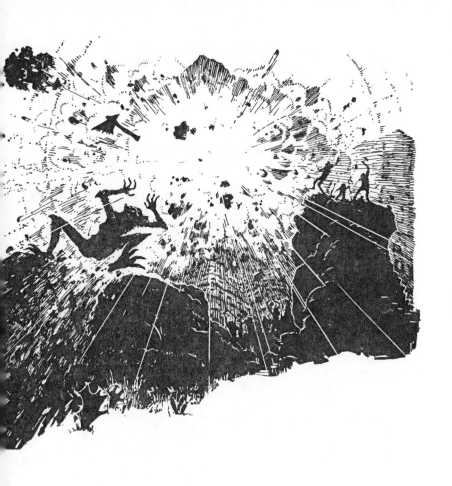

keepersmith

by Randall Garrett & Vicki Ann Heydron
art: Karl Kofoed

Earthbird Class: *Small (96m) destroyers of tremendous power, with hulls having a full 2 mm of endurium plating, and manned primarily with fighting personnel, these ships were designed, not for space warfare, as the larger craft were, but to board and destroy the Snal-things in their hidden deep-space nests wherever they were found.*

Keepersmith stood in the doorway of Keepershome and faced the three people who had come through the chilly morning at his command.

He was a big Man, with wide shoulders and a tough-muscled body that had been hardened by the same heat and pressure that forged raw steel into Smithswords.

"I am leaving," he said quietly.

Only Hollister, eldest of the three, understood.

The aged Macson, whose eyes reflected craftiness but little wisdom, said, "Of course you're leaving! The thaw has begun and your Ironhunt was due several days ago. I was just saying to Yarma—"

"Never mind, Macson," said Yarma. Almost as tall as Keepersmith, Yarma's brawn had slipped and puddled around his waist, but his brain was active and he sensed some little of what Keepersmith meant. "When will you be back, Keepersmith?"

"Before the first snow," Keepersmith answered in his deep voice. "I will return when I can."

And then they all understood.

Keepersmith was clothed as usual for an Ironhunt, in a fur garment which covered his torso but left his arms and legs free, and fur boots thong-wrapped to his knees. At his left side hung his own great sword, the finest ever forged. At his right, in its own holster, was Ironblaster, the legacy of the *Hawk.*

All that was normal: the sword for his own protection, and Ironblaster, which only the Keepersmith could use, which he held in trust for the future when the *Hawk* would return for his people, and which was the only instrument that could draw iron from stone.

But the heavy pack was not normal. Strapped to his back, it was usually empty when he left and full of iron when he returned, but now it was obviously already loaded with supplies.

"Where are you going?" asked Hollister.

"South," said Keepersmith tersely.

Macson blinked. "For how long?"

"For as long as it takes."

"But—you can't do that!" Macson's voice seemed to break, but he cringed back as Keepersmith's dark gaze flashed to his face. "I—I mean, you have duties here!"

"Joom will remain," said Keepersmith evenly. "He is skilled and has iron enough. He will serve you well. And as for duty, it is my duty to go."

After a moment's silence, Hollister said, "Something has happened."

Keepersmith's hard face softened as he looked at the old woman. To Hollister would fall the great burden of leadership once he had gone. Macson and Yarma were useful as leaders only if she led them.

"Perhaps. I cannot say for sure. That is why I must go. To be sure. Joom knows the Reading, and I have left Writing with him which tells why I must go. If I have not returned by snowfall, he will read the Writing in your presence."

"And then?" Hollister looked at him steadily with her wise old eyes.

"Then Joom will be Keepersmith, and another decision must be made."

Yarma looked troubled. "Leave Ironblaster." His voice quavered a bit under Keepersmith's gaze, but he continued. "If there is a chance you won't return, you *must* leave it."

"No. If I leave it, there is less chance I will return. I am Keeper until my death." Without another look, he walked away from the home he had known since he was apprenticed to the last Keepersmith at only ten summers.

Half a day from the village, Keepersmith was still walking steadily through the slowly warming foothills. The air was fresh and slightly chill, and the ground laced with small furious rivulets from the melting snow that came from the mountains behind him, but already there were loudbirds and a touch of budding green in the branches of the hedgelike vecca trees that covered these lower hillsides.

At noon he rested briefly and ate. He drank from one of the icy streams and was on his way again, moving steadily south. The ground grew more level, and the rivulets of water more scarce. When he paused at dusk, he filled a skin with water, and ate sparingly.

The night was clear, and well-lit by Gemni, the double moon, and this was still familiar land, land he had travelled often.

Near midnight he saw a flickering light ahead. He moved quietly to the edge of a stand of tall thran trees and looked out into a small clearing. A last rocky ridge extended here from the mountain range, and under an overhanging cliff some four meters high a small campfire was burning.

Beyond the fire, with his back to the stone wall, sat a scaled creature with four Man-like limbs. He sat motionless, staring with shining eyes which protruded from a delicately boned, chinless face. Firelight reflected from the webwork of scales that was his skin, sending up a sheen that made his skin look wet.

How he likes the fire, Keepersmith thought. *I believe that it was good to teach them about fire. But should we give them the secret of forced fire? Could we trust even Liss with that power?*

Deliberately, he stepped out from the trees, and the eyes of the creature lifted from the fire directly to him. "Sssmith." The soft voice blended with the fire noises.

Keepersmith walked to the fire, squatted down beside it, and put aside his pack.

"Where is it, Liss?" he asked.

The Razoi picked up a bundle from the ground near him and reached into it with a long-fingered hand. The object he handed Keepersmith gleamed in the firelight.

It was a handweapon much like Ironblaster but smaller, and the control knobs along the side were not the same.

The Razoi, unfamiliar with both weapons, could not see the differences. "It *iss* the ssame, Sssmith," said Liss, looking across the fire. "The ssame metal as Ironblasster."

"Yes," agreed Keepersmith, "much the same."

"You ssaid that two dayss ago," Liss reminded him. "Why did you ssend me away sso ssoon?"

"Don't be offended, friend. I could not explain then. I cannot explain yet, but—" Keepersmith turned the thing in his hands so that the firelight highlighted the Writing on the controls:

Kill—Stun.

And across the butt:

I. S. S. Hawk.

"This is not for everyone to see. It is important and I must understand it before I tell anyone else about it."

"Tell *me* about it, Sssmith."

Keepersmith looked up from the shiny thing in his hand and considered the being across the fire. He was a Razoi, one of the oldest of a long-lived race, a member of the tall northern tribe which had for many Man generations lived across the high mountains from the valley where the Men lived.

Keepersmith had met Liss when he was a boy, walking for pleasure in the hills above the Smithy. The Razoi had appeared from behind a group of boulders and had called to him. The boy, frightened because he had heard so much evil of this kind of creature, nonetheless had stood his ground—but the Razoi had only talked to him. In halting Man language he had spoken of friendship, of learning, of sharing.

"You will be leader," Liss had said, and the boy knew then that the Razoi had lain in wait not for *any* Man, but only himself. And it impressed him, as not even learning the Writing had done, that he would one day have to lead the Men on this world.

"You will learn," said Liss. "Teach uss. Teach *me* and I will teach them. We will not fight you."

Then Liss had come down from the hillside to stand in front of him. They had been of a size, the gangly, already muscular thirteen-summer boy and the slim and ageless Razoi. Liss had raised his weapon, a wooden staff with a stone axe at one end and the other sharpened to a point, and had laid it down at the feet of the boy.

"I will khome again. Remember."

Then Liss had walked into the brushy hillside and the boy had stared after him, still speechless.

Liss had come again ten summers later, as the new Keepersmith walked those same hills in wordless grief, struggling to accept not only the loss of a man who had been a father to him, but what that loss meant—the heavy responsibility fallen now to his own shoulders. Keepersmith had accepted the Razoi's friendship then and had not yet regretted it.

The village did not approve when this one Razoi left the guarded trading compound to visit Keepersmith outside—always *outside*—the Smithy. They suspected, but couldn't forbid, that Liss sometimes went along on ironhunts, and had watched while Ironblaster melted into a mountainside. But they did not know that Liss asked only for what Keepersmith could give, and in turn gave him something the lonely boy and the solemn man could never know otherwise—the companionship of an equal.

Another ten summers had passed, and, in all that time, Keepersmith had never spoken to Liss of the *Hawk* or the heritage of Men. He had sensed that it was this knowledge Liss really wanted, but would not ask for fear of offending Keepersmith. The Razoi had been the enemies of Man in the past, and though Keepersmith trusted Liss, they were too different. They would never truly understand one another. And the secrets of the *Hawk* had been guarded by Keepersmiths for generations. Could he be the one to reveal them to a Razoi?

If it weren't for Liss, I'd never have seen this. . . .

Suddenly he lifted Ironblaster from its place at his belt and set both things beside the fire.

Ironblaster was much larger than the other object, but it was obvious that they belonged together. Their shapes were roughly similar and the bright glow of the fire lit up the matching inscriptions: *I. S. S. Hawk.*

"Ssee, Sssmith, it iss sso like Ironblasster. But it is ssilent, while Ironblasster roarss. What doess it mean?"

"It is a message from the *Hawk,*" Keepersmith answered. "A message I do not understand. Liss, what do you know of how Men came to be here?"

"Only that one day they were here. They ran up from the ssouth, purssued by dussteaterss. And they sslew my people, and we fought to live. They drove uss out of our valley and tookh it for themsselvess."

Keepersmith could not conceal his surprise, and Liss smiled grimly. "Ssome things do not need Writing to be remembered."

"Those Men had no choice, Liss. They had a duty—to the *Hawk.*"

"And what iss the *H-hawk?*" asked Liss, hesitating over the unfamiliar word.

"Not all Men agree about that, Liss. Some believe that the *Hawk* is a god, a mighty being who cast us out of the sky to punish us for something we did. Others say that such talk is only superstition, and the *Hawk* does not exist at all."

"And you, Sssmith? What do you ssay?"

"I know the truth, Liss, or as much as the Writing can tell me. This world is only one of many—there are hundreds of others, surrounded by something called space, where there is no air to breathe. The *Hawk* is a ship which could travel between those worlds. It brought my ancestors to this world. . . ."

"And then left them here."

"Why?"

"Not even those who made the Writing knew that. But they were sure of one thing—the *Hawk* would return for them. The first Keepersmith, who spoke for the *Hawk,* said that we must keep all the knowledge we had, so that when the *Hawk* did return we would be ready."

"Ready?" asked Liss.

"To leave," answered Keepersmith, so lost in his own musing that he did not see the spasm which crossed Liss's face. "The *Hawk* will take us all away from your world, Liss. It will be yours once again."

Keepersmith reach over and picked up the small object. "This may be the signal we have been waiting for. Or it may not. I must know for certain; I must go to where it was found."

"*I* found it on the belt of one of the ssouthern—" He used a word in his own language, and the contempt in his voice was unmistakable. "Before he died, he told me where he found it."

"Can you take me there?"

"Yess."

Keepersmith put the small thing in his pack and holstered Ironblaster. Then he stretched out beside the fire.

The Razoi stretched out too, as near the fire as he could get without scorching himself. They lay there in silence for a few moments, and then Keepersmith spoke.

"Are your people bitter, Liss?"

"Ssome of them. But we have akhssepted it. Our livess are better for your potss and your cloth. And now for your fire. My tribe iss ssettled now in *our* valley—we would not wissh to move again."

"Why do the southern tribes raid and kill?"

"There iss only one ssouthern tribe left. They fight and sslay bekhausse—" the closest the Razoi could come to the Man's "k" sound was a throat-clearing noise, "they have always done it. They are sstupid. They are our enemiess too."

"If we must go now, Liss—will you be glad to have us gone?"

The other was quiet for so long that Keepersmith was afraid he had already fallen into the odd open-eyed sleep of his kind. But at last the soft voice came sibilantly across the fire.

"No. You and I, Sssmith, we have made our own beginning. You are teaching me and I will teach my people. We will both be sstronger for it.

"And I would misss you, Sssmith."

That dawn and the many that followed found them moving, Liss in the lead and setting a steady, moderate pace. The passing of time and the changing character of the land made the terrain greener, but less inviting than Keepersmith's mountain valley.

For here, where there was plenty of game and adequate water and little effort needed to grow half-wild crops, there was also continual danger. Pockets of Men had drifted down from the mountains and settled here in a territory that was still claimed by the Razoi as their own.

In places where a single Man village lived in uneasy truce with its nearest Razoi neighbors, both were in constant fear of the south-

ern tribe. Thought to be desert-based and so called "dusteaters" by the Razoi, they were shorter than the northern breed and of slightly different coloring, but they were broad-shouldered, heavily muscled, and ferocious fighters. They struck northward in small bands and then retreated to the safety of the southern desert. They were raiders and bandits, hated by everyone.

Yet the common enemy was not enough to unite the plains peoples into the kind of peace that Keepersmith and Liss shared. The raids only made the Men more suspicious of their neighbors, regardless of their different appearance. A Man travelling with a Razoi was not only unusual—he might be viewed as traitorous.

So Liss and Keepersmith avoided any settlements as they moved southward. They camped one evening beside a clear placid stream lined almost down to the water with broad-leaved fera trees. Keepersmith picked one of its fruits, but the orange hue and crisp skin of the small ellipsoid told him that it was still in its second phase and would be poisonous to a Man. So he rested against the thick trunk of the tree and ate some dried meat while Liss put aside his pack and staffaxe and dived soundlessly into the stream.

Keepersmith watched the shiny green forehead bobbing up every few seconds until it disappeared around an upstream bend. Then he bent over and took the small thing Liss had brought to him out of his pack. He reflected, as he did so, on the importance of the material from which the pack had been made.

The alth was a large carnivore which was hunted for food by the northern Razoi. Its thick skin, virtually indestructible once shaped and properly cured, had been the first basis of trade between Liss's people and the shivering human refugees who had fled northward.

The southward tribes could not stand the cold, but alth skins made the climate livable for Liss's people. They covered cave mouths and the doors of earthern huts, and made warm sleeping nests for the families. They lasted so well that the Razoi had more than they needed, and the Men needed them badly.

But the Men had nothing to trade.

Had it not been summer when the Men reached their valley, they would not have survived. For it took weeks of experimenting and failing before they struck the right mixture and the right process to manufacture a tradable item—a glazed jug which would store water, so necessary to the Razoi through winter and drought.

But trade began in time, and by winter the Men had cured enough alth skins to clothe themselves and make their primitive shelters bearable. And one Man had carefully split squares of the thick hide into supple, thin layers. She had rebound them with a hide thong and begun the Writing.

The Writing was knowledge, and it was the very heart of Keepersmith's life. It contained all the knowledge the *Hawk* had left with them, and all the things they had learned on their own. The pottery formula. All the useless designs and the one successful one for a loom to weave the fibery grainflowers into coarse cloth. The secret of forced fire and the agonizing story of how they tried and failed, that first winter, to forge steel.

And the Writing told of that next summer's hardship, when only Ironblaster saved them from being overrun by wave after wave of southerners returning to fight in the warmer weather. A passage from that section had special meaning for Keepersmith as he held the metal thing:

All the guns are gone now, broken by stone axes or clubs or, bless them, by dying men who would not have them reach the three-fingered hands of our enemies.

The Blaster is all we have left now of the *Hawk*'s equipment, but its explosive effect makes it useless at short range. We have weapons, but they are not much better than the Razoi's, and we are only learning to use them. The Razoi are skilled and strong and savage, and we are all weak and hungry.

Winter will be here soon, and we will have some rest from attack. We have managed to store some food—dried meats and some wild grain. Some of us will survive this second winter, but we will all die next summer if we don't have some kind of short-range weapon more effective than the ones the Razoi carry.

I see only one choice for us. I must take the Blaster with me now, before winter sets in, and hunt out some iron deposits. Then, through the winter, I will try again to forge a workable steel weapon—a sword. That will give us longer reach, and a cutting edge. It may be enough of an advantage.

I am leaving secretly, because I know there are those among us who would see only that I am leaving the settlement undefended. They would not understand, as I do, that if I don't go we have only one bleak winter ahead of us. If I do go, and I am successful, we may live to see the *Hawk* return.

I pray that it may be so.

There was no doubt in Keepersmith's mind that the object he held was one of the "guns" the Writing referred to. It said little about them, except that they operated on the same principle as Ironblaster, and Ironblaster was described and diagrammed in detail.

He heard a splashing sound, and looked up to see Liss climbing out of the water some twenty meters downstream, carrying three large fish. He twisted the head off each one and placed the heads carefully on the bank. Then he squatted down and began to eat the fish in small, delicate bites, thoroughly chewing all the bones except the backbone. He would be a long time at his meal.

Keepersmith looked back at the gun in his hand. Now was the time.

A sharp twist removed half of the butt and revealed a latch which, when pressed, lifted off another section. Keepersmith examined the interior of the gun, comparing it to his knowledge of Ironblaster.

Similar, but far from identical. The Bending Converter was much

KEEPERSMITH

smaller. The Converter used a process which Keepersmith did not entirely understand. He knew that it took common water and converted it into helium and oxygen. But he was not certain why it created the power which, focussed through the barrel of Ironblaster, created enough heat to melt mountains.

He knew what the energy of Ironblaster could do. Fired at a living thing, tree or Razoi or . . . Man, the water in the target turned instantly to high-temperature steam, causing a tremendous explosion. Ironblaster was not a weapon that could be used at close range.

But in the gun which Liss had brought, there was a different sort of apparatus. The power created by the Bending Converter was apparently channelled electrically through a vibrator which changed the tremendous electrical energy into ultra-sonic vibrations and focussed it down the short barrel of the gun.

That much he knew from the Writings.

He frowned in concentration, trying to remember the Writings about Ironblaster.

The reserve energy cell broke water down into hydrogen and oxygen. The oxygen was discharged as a waste product, and the hydrogen converted into helium in the Bending Converter. Ironblaster's reservoir held a good mouthful of water, but there was no reservoir in the smaller weapon. But the Bending Converter was obviously there, and so far as Keepersmith knew, its fuel was—*had to be*—water. Where, then, did the water come from?

Again he searched his memory. The little vents in the rear of the barrel told him they took in air and condensed the water from the air.

And then he suddenly knew what this weapon was. It was something that Ironblaster had never been designed for. It required only the power it could draw from the moisture in the air, and it could kill enemies at close range.

He looked again at the switch on the side.

Kill. Stun.

It was not even necessarily designed to kill. Again his probing eyes looked at the mechanism in the open butt. This weapon should, like Ironblaster, be self-fueling and self-operating. Then why wasn't it? There were stains on the butt which indicated the gun had been used as a club—surely even a southern Razoi would have figured out how to use it properly if it were still working.

Carefully, reverently, he drew Ironblaster from the holster at the right side of his belt and opened it in the way that only he knew how. Yes, they were similar. Not identical, but similar. He traced the thin lines of Ironblaster's circuits and compared them with the smaller, thinner lines of the strange weapon.

It took time, but finally he saw the break. A tiny black scratch across the engraved circuit.

He knew how that could be healed, but would it restore the gun to full efficiency? Without the tools and equipment at hand, there was no way to find out.

His concentration was broken by a scream.

He dropped the gun and sprang away from the tree, looking downstream to where Liss had made his meal. He saw that the Razoi had finished and, according to his habit, had been burying the fish remnants, head and backbone, each at the base of a tree. The scream had come from the creature which had dropped out of the tree above him and clubbed him as the bodies met.

Keepersmith now saw the attacker stand up and whirl to face the unconscious Razoi. It lifted something in both arms above its head, and he could see the gleam of steel. . . .

"No!" he shouted, and ran down the bank, drawing his sword. The figure jerked around, the sword still held high. It was a woman, dressed in a cloth tunic and wearing a sword harness. Her face was an ugly mask of hatred.

"A Man," she said. Her voice was barely a whisper, but it carried infinite menace. "A Man defending this filth. *Defend yourself, then!*"

She was barely ten centimeters shorter than he, and fast, strong and skilled. He saw that the moment her strong right wrist whipped her Smithsword up for a direct slash downward. It was all he could do to parry the blow without killing her.

Her steel rang against his, slid toward his wrist, and he flipped it off the quillions. He had barely time to recover before her slash came in toward his waist.

His parry was almost too late, because she snapped her sword in mid-swing toward his legs. He fended off the slash, but rather than counterattack, he leaped backward.

"Peace!" he called. "We are not enemies!"

But he could tell from the fighting glaze in her dark eyes that she did not even hear him. He had to leap back again as her sword came up in a swoop toward his crotch.

As it passed him he leaped in and swung up his own sword with the flat turned, slapping her hand against the grip. Her weapon spun crazily away and half-buried itself in the soft turf near the river.

She faced him defiantly, shaking her injured hand, ready for the deathblow. When it didn't come at once, she glanced at where her sword lay.

"Don't think of it," Keepersmith said. "Sit down and keep still."

She did, and he saw her clearly for the first time. Her face and limbs were dirty and scratched, her long black hair a filthy, matted mane, her sandals badly worn. But there was still spirit in the eyes that watched him as he moved sideways, his sword still drawn, to where Liss was trying to sit up.

"Are you all right, Liss?"

"Mostly," said the Razoi, rubbing the back of his head and watching the woman.

"Why did you try to kill my friend?" Keepersmith asked the woman.

"Your *friend?* What kind of Man calls a Razoi his *friend?*"

"I do," he answered, quiet power in his voice. "I am called Keepersmith."

All the hatred drained from her face, and amazement took its place. "Keepersmith!" She looked at him, and he could tell that she was comparing the Man before her to everything she had heard about him. He wondered if she would challenge him, but evidently there were few Men on the plains of his stature. There was sullen respect in her voice, as she asked, "What are you doing this far south and—" She glanced at Liss. "—in such company?"

"It is not for me to answer you," he said sternly, and she dropped her eyes. "I ask you again, why did you attack my friend?"

"He is Razoi."

"That is no answer."

She raised her eyes to his face. "It is answer enough for me."

"But *not* for me!"

For a moment more she hesitated. Then she shrugged her shoulders, and seemed to shrink as her defiance faded and weariness washed over her.

"A band of Razoi raided my village," she told them. "I was in the fields, planting. Hilam, my husband, was working on the house—the rains were heavy last winter, and he wanted to build a new roof all made of wood.

"Hilam had insisted that I take the sword to the fields. He said the village was well enough defended, but . . . he was wrong. I heard the alarm and rushed back—but they were already gone. I found Hilam. . . ." Her voice broke, and Keepersmith did not urge her. After a moment she went on.

"I found my husband dead in the doorway of our house. And beside him . . . our son. Six summers only, and Thim had his wooden training sword in his hand. . . ."

She straightened up, and looked at Keepersmith. "I swore vengeance for the death of my family, and for days I have been on their trail. Last night I got this far. They watered here, but I was too tired to go further. I slept in that tree, and when I woke and saw a Razoi here, it seemed he had to be one of them. . . ."

Suddenly Liss spoke up, his voice angrier than Keepersmith had ever heard it. "You thought I was a ssouthern dussteater?" He stood up, but Keepersmith forestalled whatever he had planned to do.

"Liss—be still, please, she does not understand." Then to the woman, "The southern Razoi are his enemies, too. In my mountains there is peace between Men and Razoi. And this is Liss, *my friend.*"

They both looked at Liss, whose usually unreadable face was working heavily as he struggled to conquer his resentment. "I have never killed a Man," he said at last. "And I *would not* kill a child." He turned away, finished burying the fish remnants, and dived into the stream.

The two Men watched him go, then the woman stood up and faced Keepersmith.

"Help me," she said.

"I have my own path to follow."

"But you are Keepersmith, the Voice of the *Hawk,* who watches over us." The reverence in her voice told him what she believed about the *Hawk.* "Give me back my sword and help me destroy the scum who killed my family!"

"No," he said. Her sorrow touched him, but he could not yield to her pleading. He was not, he reminded himself, an ordinary Man. "The *Hawk* has another duty for me.

"But take your sword, in any case." He picked it up off the ground, and held it by the blunted lower third of the blade. As he offered her the hilt, he said, "I do not approve, but if vengeance will be some comfort for your loss, I will not forbid it."

She gripped the handle of the sword, but still he held it. Her eyes questioned him.

"I want your promise that you will not use this against Liss."

She looked startled, as though she wondered if Keepersmith had read her mind. "He is truly your . . . friend?"

"I have said it."

"Then . . . I will not harm him. I swear it."

He released the sword, and she sheathed it with trembling hands. "How long since you have eaten?" he asked.

She shrugged. "A day. Two."

He gestured toward the stream. "Bathe and rest for this day. I can spare you some food."

She hesitated. "The stream—" she began. "The Razoi is there." When he said nothing, she continued heatedly, "*I* swore not to harm *him*—I have heard no answering promise!"

"Liss!" Keepersmith called. The Razoi appeared from the stream almost at the woman's feet. She stepped aside as he came ashore.

"I heard," he said. He faced the woman, standing closer to her than she obviously liked. "You need not fear me. Sssmith is my friend, and your enemiess are mine alsso. If it will easse your mind, I will sstay out of the sstream while you bathe."

Keepersmith and Liss walked back to their camp in silence. Keepersmith was digging in his pack for the food when a sharp cry of pain from the Razoi made him whirl around.

"What did you learn?" Liss asked, holding out the fragments of the small gun. "What did you learn by breakhing it?"

"I did not break it, Liss. It was already broken inside. *That* is what I learned." He took the pieces and snapped them back together, then offered the gun to Liss. He accepted it, balancing it in his hand.

"You give me only what iss worthlesss, ass ussual," he said. The bitterness in his voice surprised Keepersmith.

"Liss . . ."

"I have never ssaid it, Sssmith. Not before thiss. But that one—" He jerked his head downstream. "—to her I am no better than the dussteaters who sslew her people.

"You have ssaid I am your friend. Yet you do not trusst me either. You are the ssame."

"No, Liss!" But the words stung.

"Then why did you give me fire, but none of the ssecret wayss Man can usse it? Why may I watch Ironblasster workh, but never be sshown *how* it workhss?

"Sssmith, do you believe I would usse Ironblasster againsst *you?*"

Keepersmith felt a tightness in his stomach. How would he have felt in Liss's place? He could not speak; he shook his head.

"Then sstop giving me only what we khannot usse. Teach uss how to makhe potss and sswordss. How to kheep that knowledge and give it to our children. Teach uss the Writing!"

Liss was holding the gun out toward Keepersmith, clutching it desperately. His whole body was tense, his voice pleading. "Sssmith, you ssay thiss thing may mean you and your people will leave. We have sshared our world with you—sshare your learning with uss. Sssmith, do *not* leave uss ass you found uss!"

Keepersmith laid down the food and went over to his friend. In all their long acqauintance they had never touched except by accident but now, deliberately, he placed his hands on the Razoi's shoulders. They were cool and still damp from the stream.

"How often have I said that I cannot speak for only myself in these matters? The fate of all Men rests with me.

"But I swear this to you, Liss. If Men are to leave your world at last, I will do everything in my power to see that the Razoi are taught all our knowledge before we leave."

"And if there iss no messsage in thiss metal thing? Will it sstill be as it wass? Dribbless of nothingss for the Rassoi?"

Liss's anguish crystallized the decision Keepersmith had been delaying for twenty summers.

"Then I will try to persuade the others that you can be trusted with more fire knowledge. Please understand, Liss, that is our most important secret; in that I would have to obey their wishes.

"But I *will* teach you Writing. I give you my promise. *Whatever* happens, I *will* teach you Writing."

The scaled face turned up toward Keepersmith.

"You know I have wanted thiss."

"Yes. You have been very patient. And you have been a good friend."

He released Liss, picked up the food, and walked downstream to where the woman was dressed again and sitting on the bank. They sat silently together while she ate. When she had finished, she said, "I will come with you."

"What?" Keepersmith had been staring thoughtfully at the stream, planning how to keep his promise to Liss.

"I said I will come with you."

"Why?"

"They have too long a start. And there is nothing to go back to."

"But you don't know where we are going."

"It doesn't matter. You said it is an errand in the service of the *Hawk*—perhaps this was all . . . arranged by the *Hawk* himself so that I would be willing to help you."

"The *Hawk*," Keepersmith said quietly, "takes no responsibility for the actions of Razoi. You are here by accident,"—but for a brief moment he wondered—"and if you wish to come with me, it is your free choice and no fate decreed by the *Hawk*."

"Then by my free choice," she said, looking directly at him from a face made younger for being clean, "I will go with you."

Keepersmith looked back at the camp, where Liss was stretched out in the last patch of sunlight.

"He travels with us."

She followed his gaze.

"I have sworn not to harm him."

"It is not enough. You must trust him."

She hesitated only a moment before answering, "It is you I trust. But since you speak for him, then I trust him also."

Keepersmith nodded, and stood up to return to the campsite. "We move on at first light."

They travelled faster now, each in a separate silence. Liss led the little column and Marna brought up the rear, and both were glad of the great wall of Keepersmith between them.

Keepersmith's packed food was soon running low, and they had to pause, sometimes for a day at a time, to hunt and to gather the ferafruit that was already ripe in the warmer southern climate. They were never far from a river or stream, so that Liss was well fed. They might have asked him to catch more fish than he needed so that they could share his meal, but they respected his horrified aversion to cooked fish. So the Men snared small game and grazed the edible plants.

It was near dusk of a day so long that Keepersmith knew midsummer was very close when Liss halted abruptly. The tense attitude of his body warned them as no word could do, and Keepersmith and Marna melted into the brush at either side of the rough trail. Liss moved cautiously forward and inspected something on the ground, half-concealed by a bed of fork-leaved creepers. Then he straightened up and waved them forward.

When they stood beside him they saw what he had seen—a brown-ish-green hand covered with dried and flaking scales.

They dragged the body out into the clear. It was a southern Razoi. His angular face had shrunk to fit the skull, and the finely scaled body was totally dehydrated.

"How long has he been dead?" Keepersmith asked Liss.

"It iss hard to tell," answered the Razoi. "One of my people would lookh likhe thiss only a few hourss after death. But thesse ssouthern dussteaterss need lesss water. He hass been dead for many dayss."

"Then they are far enough ahead of us," said Keepersmith.

"For a time," said Liss.

"What does that mean?" demanded Marna. "This is one of the raiders who attacked my village." She touched one of the emaciated legs with her sandalled foot. "I recognize his two-toed track. Are we following them, after all?"

"Not following," said Liss. "But we are going to the ssame plasse they are."

"Why?"

"On the *Hawk's* business," stated Keepersmith, "and I'm impatient to get it done. Liss," he gestured toward the ugly body, "do you want to bury him?"

"A *dussteater?*"

"Then there is no need to linger."

He started off down the partially cleared, winding track they had been following for some days, leaving Liss and Marna to come after him at their own speed.

The demanding march had dulled the edge of Marna's suspicion and Liss's resentment, so that they walked now barely a meter apart in comfortable silence.

"Why don't you want to bury him?" Marna asked suddenly.

"Why sshould I?" came the answer over Liss's shoulder.

"But your people bury their dead, I have seen it. . . ." She stopped abruptly as Liss whirled around to face her.

"He is a *dussteater*," he hissed. "He is *not* one of my people. Do you sstill not see the differensse between uss?"

Startled by the sudden confrontation, Marna held back the sharp words that came so readily to her tongue. Instead she said awkwardly, "I—I am trying to learn, Liss. I have promised Keepersmith to trust you, and I—" to her surprise, she meant it, "I do. But it's hard to trust someone you don't know."

There was a long silence as Liss's bright, wet-looking eyes stared at her steadily. Then he said, "I know what it iss to be denied knowledge. Assk what you will—I will try to ansswer. But let us sstay with Sssmith."

They walked on together, hurrying for a time to make up the few moments lost. When they could see Keepersmith's broad back a few meters ahead of them once again, they slowed their pace.

"About the burying . . ." began Marna.

"Yess. We bury dead things to bring them to life again."

"You mean like the fish, to—uh—"

"Fertilisse the ssoil?" He smiled at her look of surprise, revealing the double ridge of serrated bone that served him as teeth. "It is only the term that I learned from Sssmith. We have alwayss known that buried dead flessh feedss the living thingss near it.

"But we do it for another reasson—to free the sspirit of the dead thing to return again."

Marna frowned in concentration. "How does burying the body of a thing—?"

"It is all one. When the flessh returnss to new growth, the sspirit returnss too. But if the flessh is abandoned, the sspirit is trapped in the dead flessh and it diess."

"But if you believe that—"

"Yess?"

"Leaving that one unburied is a horrible revenge—worse than even I would ask."

The scaled shoulders shrugged. "It iss their own khusstom. It iss one markh of their ssavagery. And it iss why they have dwindled while my people have grown."

"But you did not abandon him out of respect for his custom?"

"No," Liss answered. "I *wanted* hiss sspirit to die. I would desstroy them all if I khould."

"I know *my* reasons, Liss. But why do *you* hate them so?"

"I hate them because they are sskhavengers, and live on the workh of otherss, and never give anything to the earth.

"I hate them bekhause they have been our enemiess ssince before the first Men khame here.

"I hate them," he turned to look at her, "bekhause they made *you* hate *me*."

He increased his pace and moved ahead of her until he was half-way between her and Keepersmith.

She watched the iridescent scales on his back as they moved with his sinuous walk, and said softly, "I don't, Liss. Not now."

A few nights later, they had camped beside a stream, and on Liss's advice had foregone their fire. They had lost the tracks of the southerners, and could not be sure where they were.

Keepersmith sat on a log at the edge of the water, chewing the last of their ferafruit. Something splashed nearby and he looked up to see Marna climbing out of the river. A softer splash upstream drew his attention, and in the bright silver light of the full moons, he saw Liss's shiny head appear and sink again.

"You're not afraid to swim with him now," he said, as the woman pulled her light woven tunic over her head.

"No," she answered, sitting beside him and leaning over to wring the water from her long black hair. "But I don't understand him, either. Or you."

"Me?"

"You are Keepersmith, our leader. And here you are further south than Men have gone for generations. Can't you tell me at least where we are going?"

"I gave you the chance to go your own way," he reminded her.

"And I reject it now as then," she answered hotly. Then more calmly, "But I am walking totally blind. Liss knows more than I do."

"And you resent that?"

She started to speak, paused, and began again. "A season ago I would have given you good and valid reasons why I did *not* resent it."

"And now?"

"Now I am free to admit that I do."

Suddenly Keepersmith laughed. His rich voice rumbled out over the water, bringing Liss to the surface nearby.

"Sssss!" At the quiet sound the laughter stopped instantly. "You are ssometimess a *fool*, Sssmith!"

Keepersmith's voice was choked and hardly above a whisper. "You are right, my friend. But it has been so long since I laughed." He cleared his throat. "Marna has asked me why we are here, Liss."

"Then tell her," came the crisp answer. "Ssoftly." He ducked back under the water and was gone.

A moment later, Keepersmith handed Marna the small gun. She accepted it gingerly, astonished at the lightness and the cool touch of the metal.

"What is it?" she asked.

"Call it—a small Ironblaster. But it doesn't work."

She lifted her eyes to his face with sudden understanding. "The Words say that Ironblaster was the gift of the *Hawk*. This . . .?"

"I don't know," he said grimly. He turned the gun in her hands so that the bright moonlight shone down on the inscription.

"This writing is the mark of the *Hawk*, but—"

She interrupted him, growing more excited as the implications struck her. "Has He . . . Is it time . . . oh, Keepersmith!"

"I have said it. *I don't know what it means!*"

He took the gun from her, gripped it tightly as doubt washed across her face.

"But—you are Keepersmith! The Ironfinder! You taught my village Smith the Words, but you alone knew the Writings! You *speak* for the *Hawk!* If you don't know—"

"Then who does?" he finished for her. "No one does. But I am supposed to. It could mean whatever I say it means. But this time I cannot lie."

"Lie?"

He stood up and walked a few steps along the bank. "I have shocked you. Yes, I lie.

"When a Man asks a question, he needs an answer. Two Men each claim that this varipig is his, or that newborn boychild isn't. Someone must decide for them.

"When is it best to plant—this day or that? Which fields should lie fallow? How many pots should we have for next season's trading?

"An answer. A judgment. I have always offered *my* best judgment, but they—Macson, Yarma, Hollister, the others who have been leaders in the seasons since I became Keepersmith—they believe that the *Hawk* speaks *through me.*"

He turned toward where she sat motionless. The fluid reflections from the river water danced across their faces. Keepersmith's was grim with strain.

"I have never spoken of this before, but I say it now: If the *Hawk* speaks though me, *I cannot tell it.* I have borne this burden *alone.*

"If this," he raised the hand with the gun in it, "is a signal of the *Hawk's* return, the I *welcome it!* For it will mean the end of—"

His head turned sharply at the splashing sound, but not before three-fingered hands had grabbed the ankle and thigh of the leg nearer the river, and unbalanced him. He toppled awkwardly sideways, and slapped loudly into the river.

The water churned furiously, and Keepersmith heaved himself out of the water. He stood on the floor of the river bed and tried to shake off the small yellow-green Razoi clinging to his shoulders and pinning his arms.

At the first sound, Marna had leaped across the small clearing to

where she had left her sword when she went to bathe. Two Razoi rushed out from the forest and blocked her before she could reach it. She spun around and fled into the trees across the clearing.

It was dark under the vine-woven trees. The Razoi who followed her could see better than she, but she was bigger and faster. She swung up to the lowest limb of the nearest tree, waited until they had passed beneath, then dropped to the ground and ran back to the clearing.

Keepersmith was half on the bank. His arms and shoulders were bleeding badly, but his right arm was free and his sword in his hand.

She caught up her sword and whirled to face the two who had followed her. They were shorter than Liss, but wider. Their shoulders bulged with muscles, and they knew how to use their staffaxes. They rushed at her simultaneously, bringing down the axeheads in vicious overhead strokes.

She blocked the one on her right, accepting all the power of the blow on the blunted edge of her sword near the hilt. At the same time she twisted to the right. The second axehead struck harmlessly in the grass, but swept up in a wide horizontal swing aimed at her waist. She turned her wrist to let the first wooden staff slide off the tip of her sword, and jumped backward just in time.

Then she realized she had done exactly what they wanted her to do. Keepersmith's back was unguarded!

The Razoi in the river were struggling to pull him into the water again, where they had at least some advantage. Three yellow-green bodies were floating downstream, already almost totally submerged. But three more still clung to Keepersmith, one of them pinning his left arm in such a way that Keepersmith couldn't strike at him effectively without injuring himself.

The two Razoi Marna had been fighting turned as one and ran for Keepersmith, staffaxes raised and already moving downward.

Marna charged after them, drawing from her body every ounce of speed it held. Too far!

With a last lunge she threw herself under the feet of one of them. He stumbled and went down, and the axe flew away from his hand. He surged to his knees and launched himself bare-handed at her. The weight of his compact body struck her and pinned her to the ground before she could stop rolling and get her sword free.

Through her own desperate struggle, she saw that the second Razoi had reached Keepersmith, and the deathblow was even then on its way down. . . .

A streak of green flashed between Keepersmith and the southern Razoi, and suddenly Liss was there, his staff braced and blocking that powerful blow. The sight brought her new strength as she fought the scaly creature who was trying to fasten his ridged jaws in her throat.

She brought her elbow up under the chinless, snouted face, and pushed. For a straining few seconds he resisted, then his clutching grip was broken and he was propelled off her.

As he staggered backward, her sword came up from the ground in a clean arc and sliced through his neck.

Liss had forced the smaller Razoi toward the trees. She whirled around to see him back into the broad trunk of a fera. In that brief instant of surprise, Liss turned his staff from its cross-brace and jabbed the sharpened point downward. The southerner cried out once and sank dead to the ground.

Keepersmith had killed another of the attackers. The last two knew they were beaten, and as Liss and Marna ran toward Keepersmith, they released him and dived for the deep water in the middle of the river.

Marna halted at the shore and helped an exhausted and bleeding Keepersmith to pull himself all the way out of the water.

Liss dropped his staff and dived after the fleeing Razoi. In a few moments one of them floated to the surface a few meters downstream. Liss returned with the other one and half-dragged him out of the water. He threw the southerner down on the bank with a hissing curse.

"Why did they attack us?" asked Keepersmith.

"You are Men, and we are nearing their sstronghold. That alone would be enough reasson."

"You say that as if it is not the only one," said Marna.

"They know who you are, Sssmith," Liss said. "They know that the Men would be eassier prey without you. And they wanted your sswordss."

KEEPERSMITH 275

"They know me? How?"

"Bekhausse they know me, and there iss only one Man who would be with me." He turned to his prisoner, cutting off their questions. "None of the otherss esskhaped. But this one will lead uss where we musst go."

Keepersmith looked at him in surprise. "You told me *you* knew where it was."

"No," Liss corrected him. "I do know *where* it iss—in a valley in the ssouthern mountainss. But there is only one entransse to the valley, and it iss well hidden. I ssaid that I khould lead you there."

"And if you hadn't captured a dusteater to find the entrance for you? How had you planned to lead us through the hidden entrance?"

"I planned," Liss answered steadily, "to khapture a dussteater to find the entransse."

And now it was Marna who laughed, a clear mellow sound, and Keepersmith joined her.

Soon after that the ground began to rise sharply. They marched faster, stopping only briefly. The southern Razoi maintained a surly silence except when Liss addressed him directly. Then he answered with fear and grudging respect in his ugly scaled face.

Keepersmith and Marna had dressed their wounds with mud and herb poultices, which dried and cracked off within two days, leaving only faint red lines in their skin.

As soon as the land left the level, the ground began to dry out and it wasn't long before they were trudging through a rising, stone-littered desert. Keepersmith had never been this far south, and he asked Liss about the terrain.

"Thesse mountainss are the ssame as ourss. They run from our valleyss far to the wesst, then turn back ssouthward. The wind bringss the rainfall from the ssouth and easst, and the mountainss sstop it here. Beyond the mountainss iss dessert. No Rassoi hass ever khrossed it."

Besides being much drier, these mountains were higher and more forbidding than Keepersmith's. The little party was climbing steadily toward one great sheer cliff which stood out above a group of smaller hills.

At last Liss paused, stopping their prisoner with a sharp word.

"The entransse to their valley iss here ssomewhere," he told them.

"Then let's rest before we go in," suggested Marna. "We have been running on little food, and you need some water, Liss."

The Razoi did indeed look uncomfortable. The dry dusty heat had made the Men sweat profusely, but it was not the heat but the dusty air that affected Liss. His skin was dried out until the tiny scales looked separate and brittle, and he was breathing raspily.

But he said, "No. I thankh you, Marna, but there must be water in the valley if even thiss," he gestured toward their prisoner and used the Razoi word Keepersmith had heard before, "khan survive."

When he heard that word applied to him, the southern Razoi cried out and threw himself at Liss, his clawed hands reaching for the taller one's throat.

Liss was ready for him. He stepped aside and grabbed one of the arms, spinning the southerner off balance. Then he whipped his other arm around the stocky yellowish neck and applied pressure. He grabbed up his staff and flipped it around so that its point was aimed at one of the creature's eyes. He hissed something in his own language, barely loudly enough for his captive to hear it. After a moment the snouted head nodded very slightly.

Liss released him and let him fall to the ground.

"He needed more perssuassion," said Liss. "He will lead uss now."

The southerner stood up, rubbing his throat, and led the way off to the left. For several minutes he wound in and out of the rocks. Then suddenly he darted away.

Liss was right after him, and the two Razoi disappeared into the maze of rocks. The Men could hear clattering stones and the sounds of a struggle, but could not be sure of their direction.

Then they heard a high-pitched cry, and in a few moments Liss appeared, panting heavily. "Thiss way."

They followed him, and paused for a moment beside the dead body of the Razoi prisoner.

"He tried to get through and warn the otherss," Liss said. "I give him honor for that." He looked at Marna. "When it iss over, I will bury thiss one."

Behind them was a narrow crack in what seemed to be an otherwise solid wall of stone. Liss's slim body slipped through it easily, but the two Men had to literally scrape themselves through the rough-edged opening. Beyond it was a space large enough for Keepersmith and Marna to walk upright, a short corridor which ended in sunlight. They looked out into the valley.

It was an awesome place.

It was roughly triangular, and it stretched before them for several hundred meters. At its far end loomed the mountain that had been their landmark. It towered over the valley a kilometer high, and it seemed perfectly smooth along the top half of its face. The valley widened and sloped sharply upward to meet the mountain until it seemed, crazily, that it was the valley which braced up and supported that vast ominous cliff.

Fed by the little rainfall the cliff drained off the passing clouds, and by underground springs which carried the melting snow from the high regions further west, the floor of the valley was green. But the growth was wild, untended.

Keepersmith's practiced eye could see that the valley could support no more than three hundred Razoi, and even that number would require an unusually large stock of fish in the one surface river. It ran the length of the valley and fed into an opening in the mountainside, not twenty meters from where they stood.

They did not expect to find sentries—the concealed entry was protection enough for the valley. Still they moved cautiously toward the river, and Marna and Keepersmith stood watch while Liss dived gratefully into the water. When he climbed out again a few moments later, his skin was already returning to its natural luminous green.

"Now, Liss," asked Keepersmith. "We are here. Where is the metal room?"

Marna started, but did not interrupt. Soon enough she would have answers.

Liss pointed toward the cliff.

"You ssee where the valley rissess and khlimbss the fasse of the mountain?" Keepersmith nodded. "The dussteaters live in holess along that lowesst ridge. Above their holess the way iss ssteeper, but sstill possible. Below the khrest of that nekhsst ridge—" They followed his directing arm, tracking the way with their eyes. "You ssee that darkh sspot? It iss the mouth of a khave. Insside iss where he found the ssmall Ironblasster-like thing."

"In the metal room."

"Yess."

They moved off along the edge of the valley. They had worked their way almost to the foot of the slope when a whistling sound cut through them. Marna made an odd noise and slumped to the ground.

Suddenly twenty southern Razoi came pouring down from the ridge. Above them, protected by the edge of the ridge, others were shouting and swinging strips of hide which cast stones at them.

"Back up the side of the slope!" shouted Keepersmith as he drew his sword . . . and Ironblaster. Liss did not hesitate, but bent down to the ground and with surprising strength lifted Marna in his arms and went scrambling back up the rocky hillside they had just left.

Rocks from the slings rained around them, but his route was fast and erratic, and he made it to the shelter of a group of tall rocks.

There he left Marna. With a word of apology, he took her sword and slid back down to Keepersmith.

The rain of rocks stopped near Keepersmith, for the southerners did not want to disable their own fighters. But he was hard pressed in personal combat, surrounded by waist-high, snarling Razoi and their deadly axes. He needed all his skill merely to defend himself, and even so his living attackers already had to step over dead ones to get at him.

Liss burst into the fray like a whirlwind. Even in that turbulent moment, Keepersmith gained a new understanding. For the sword Liss held was no more strange to him than his own staffaxe. He used it everywhere to its greatest advantage. How long had he been studying it, waiting to own his first sword?

Taken aback by the suddenness and unexpected nature of Liss's attack, the southerners fell back momentarily.

"Break it off, Liss," called Keepersmith. "There are too many of them."

"Then you musst usse Ironblasster!" Liss shouted in return. "Go! I will hold them!"

There was no time for Keepersmith to argue his friend's sacrifice. Keepersmith turned and ran down the center of the valley, luring some of the southern Razoi after him. His long legs easily outdistanced them, and as he ran, he pulled a pair of goggles out of their pocket near Ironblaster's holster, and put them on. The lenses had come with Ironblaster from the *Hawk*.

Wearing them, he turned and raised Ironblaster, and the pursuing Razoi stumbled to a panicked stop.

Even at this range, Keepersmith could not use Ironblaster on the Razoi themselves. The explosion of the water in their bodies, turned instantly into superheated steam by Ironblaster's tremendous power, would consume him.

Through the goggle lenses, Keepersmith saw the valley exactly as it had been. But the sun . . . the sun high overhead was a molten black disc.

He glanced quickly at the mountain towering over him. Along the third and final ridge, the coloring of the rock was different, and all his experience told him that the formation was unstable. If he could disturb it enough to jar loose a landslide . . .

Sick at heart for what he was doing, sorry for the death he would cause but seeing no other way out, and knowing full well that he might be destroying the very answers he sought, Keepersmith aimed Ironblaster at the middle of that third rise of land, some twenty meters below the dark opening which Liss had told him was the entrance to the metal room.

"NOW, Liss!" he warned, and Liss dived away from the southern fighters, who had been startled motionless by the giant voice echoing through the valley. He ran for the shelter of rocks where he had left Marna. He knelt beside her and pressed his face into the rock, covering his head with his arms.

Marna stirred, and moaned. Liss hissed urgently. "Your eyess! Khover your eyess!"

She sat up and looked out into the valley. She saw Keepersmith standing in the clear, aiming Ironblaster upward. . . .

With a cry of terror, she copied Liss.

And Ironblaster roared.

The valley shook with the thunder of it, and Keepersmith could not hear the cries of pain. Every southern Razoi in the valley went instantly blind as Ironblaster's lightning reached up to drag down the mountain.

To Keepersmith it was a clean, straight black line that stretched upward to the face of the mountain. Where it struck, a small black sun bloomed, and moved across the ridge at Keepersmith's command.

To Marna, who raised her head to look in brief, careful glimpses out into the valley, that black line was a searing bolt of light. She did not know, as Keepersmith did, that Ironblaster had been designed primarily for use at great distance in airless space, not to waste a part of its terrible energies heating atmosphere to blinding incandescence. She only knew that the passing filled her mind with fire, and she did not dare to look to where it struck the rock.

The black sun crept along the mountainside, melting a shallow groove in its wake. Then it died.

Keepersmith lowered Ironblaster and removed his goggles.

But the thunder still rang in the valley, rumbled in the stone itself, beneath their feet, all around . . . above . . .

"Liss!" Keepersmith shouted. "Marna! Run this way!"

The two figures scrambled down to the valley floor and ran desperately away from the shaking wall which towered above them. They reached Keepersmith. He turned and ran with them.

For Ironblaster had indeed disturbed the balance of the mountain. Along the narrow groove, vertical cracks were snaking downward, shaking the lower ridge and breaking off great monoliths which toppled outward and skidded down the hillside, dragging loose surface shale with it.

The three ran to the end of the valley, then they turned to watch as the massive weight of the second ridge sagged downward with a thunder not even Ironblaster could match, crushing and collapsing the tiny caves where the southerners had lived.

As the ground slipped away below the gaping, smoking wound, the ridge above it slowly shattered. Great crumbs of rock caromed wildly downward, setting off new landslides until the entire surface of the newly formed, unstable slope was in motion again.

Of this the watchers could only guess from the deafening, ground-shaking noise. For the tortured mountainside had vomited a great cloud of dust to shield its dying.

The sound diminshed slowly, and at last there was utter silence. Taking its own time, a gentle breeze blew the dust clouds away.

And when the dust had cleared, the three of them could only stare for long minutes.

Up there, in the mountainside, above where Keepersmith had made his cut with Ironblaster, the thousands of tons of rock had slid away to reveal a vast metal wall curving outward from the cliff face. Its silver-gray, dusty surface gleamed dully in the sunlight, stretching nearly a hundred meters along the rocky face, and standing over a third as high.

There was one small, doorlike opening in it.

At last Keepersmith turned to Liss. "That is not the metal room the southerner spoke of."

"No," answered Liss. "He ssaid that it wass ssmall, barely ass tall ass you and very sshallow. That—"

There was so much awe in his voice that he could not continue.

"That," echoed Keepersmith, "must be the answer I have been sent here to find."

"Sshall we go with you?" asked Liss, his eagerness so plain that Keepersmith turned a face full of pain to him.

"Not this time, Liss. It is a secret I must understand alone—at least for now."

There were many things he wanted to say to these people who had shared his food and his peril for a long, wild summer. But he merely turned away and began to climb toward the giant shining secret that waited above him.

Liss and Marna watched as his huge figure grew smaller. They suffered helplessly as Keepersmith toiled his way up to the first ridge and then to the second, often falling, always getting up again.

At last the toy Man stood beside the dark opening in the metal wall. He stepped into it, and disappeared. For several minutes they watched anxiously, but when nothing happened, they relaxed their vigil and rested on the ground beside the mud-choked river.

A loud metallic sound rang through the valley, and Marna leaped to her feet, screaming.

"The opening is gone, Liss! I can't even tell where it was! Liss—the thing has swallowed Keepersmith!"

Liss, too, was disturbed. But he had known this Man longer than the woman had. So he calmed her as best he could. "He knowss what he iss doing, your Kheeperssssmith. He will be backh. And he ssaid it—it iss a thing he musst do alone. We khan't help him now. We musst wait."

"Wait?" She realized that it was indeed their only choice. "Of course, we must wait for him, Liss. Wait and watch."

Just after the sun rose on the third day, the door in the small metal wall opened and Keepersmith stepped out. The door closed again behind him.

He walked back to them out of the dawn, carrying a black box and a small gray metal container. His powerful frame had thinned and his face was drawn and weary, but in his eyes there was a new wisdom.

"We are going back," he said.

Liss and Marna stared at him.

"Tell uss," said Liss. "Pleasse tell uss."

Keepersmith opened his mouth, but hesitated. Liss turned bitterly away.

"It iss the ssame," he said. "I am a Rassoi!"

"No, Liss." Marna reached out and touched Liss's arm lightly. "I am a Man, and the secrets of the *Hawk* are not for me either. Only the Keepersmith can know them."

Suddenly Keepersmith spoke in a voice barely above a whisper. "No more." They waited.

"All Men must know what I have learned here. We have lived in the shadow of error for centuries.

"The *Hawk* is not a god, Marna. It is only a machine which carried Men through the space between planets—" His eyes looked through them and they knew he was seeing something in his mind, a memory carried out of the place of secrets.—"between stars.

"The *Hawk* brought our people here; that much is true. But it will never return. Because it never left.

282 KEEPERSMITH

"That—" he said, gesturing toward the great metal wall shimmering in the new sunlight, *"That is the* Hawk!"

"I don't understand," wailed Marna. "Why—?"

"They didn't understand either, Marna. Our ancestors were warriors. Ironblaster found its true destiny here, for it was built for killing! The *Hawk* landed, and some of the Men took Ironblaster and went out into this world searching for their enemies. They came back—and the *Hawk* was gone."

Liss gestured with one three-fingered hand toward the distant metal wall. "But you jusst ssaid . . ."

"That was the error. It didn't leave. It was just that our people could not find it when they returned.

"It must have happened suddenly. One Man was still in the airlock—that was the small metal room, Liss. The door leading into the ship was closed and locked. The outer door was open.

"And then the whole mountainside, disturbed perhaps by the shock of the *Hawk*'s landing, at last gave way and slid down to bury the *Hawk* from the sight of Men. There may have been others outside. If so, they have been buried under that rock for centuries.

"There were only two on the ship itself, the Man in the airlock and one other, sealed helplessly inside. This Man was hurt, and she died soon after—but she has left us this." He held up the metal cylinder. "It is a kind of Writing. A speech Writing. It tells much, and there is even more to learn."

He did not mention the two long racks of Ironblasters that he had seen within the ship; that was knowledge that could be held until later.

"And our ancestors were the fighting Men who had been sent away from the *Hawk?*"

"Yes, and they too left a Writing. The one that we have lived by. They believed that their ship had flown off for some reason, but would return when it could. They wanted us to be ready when it came back. We have been waiting for centuries," his voice tightened, "for a machine that has been buried at our feet!"

Out of the silence that followed came Marna's voice. "What—what will you do?"

"I will tell them the truth. Whatever fate brought me here, I *have* learned the lesson of the *Hawk.*"

"And what iss that, Sssmith?"

"That the waiting is truly at an end. In a sense, the *Hawk has* returned, and now we must save ourselves. We must stop merely surviving and begin to grow." Again he held up the black box and the cylinder. "With these we can start to learn all the lost knowledge of the *Hawk*."

He looked deliberately at Liss.

"We will *all* learn."

"Your people," whispered Liss. "Will they agree?"

"They will," said the big man as he stepped between his friends and led the way out of the Valley of the Hawk.

"I am still Keepersmith."